DANELLE HARMON

The DEFIANT ONE

AVON BOOKS
An Imprint of HarperCollins*Publishers*

This is a work of fiction. Names, characters, places, and incidents are products of the author's imagination or are used fictitiously and are not to be contsrued as real. Any resemblance to actual events, locales, organizations, or persons, living or dead, is entirely coincidental.

AVON BOOKS
An Imprint of HarperCollins*Publishers*
10 East 53rd Street
New York, New York 10022-5299

Copyright © 2000 by Danelle F. Colson
Inside cover author photo by Bryan Eaton
ISBN: 0-380-80908-7
www.avonromance.com

First Avon Books paperback printing: June 2000

Avon Trademark Reg. U.S. Pat. Off. and in Other Countries, Marca Registrada, Hecho en U.S.A.
HarperCollins ® is a trademark of HarperCollins Publishers Inc.

Printed in the U.S.A.

WCD   10 9 8 7 6 5 4 3 2 1

This book is dedicated to Roscoe, Poppy, and Gemma . . . and to every person in this world who treats their own "fur-kids" as all little innocents deserve to be treated . . . with compassion, understanding, a life-long commitment to their welfare, and especially, with love.

After all, animals are kids, too.

Acknowledgments

Any worthwhile project is never a solitary effort, and therefore, I'd like to thank those individuals who were especially generous in contributing their time and attention to *The Defiant One* . . . and to me, whilst I was writing it!

Heartfelt gratitude goes to:

My editor and fellow doggie-mom, Lucia Macro, whose insight, vision and guidance are appreciated more than words can even begin to express; my agent, Nancy Yost, whose patience and encouragement are a godsend; Avon authors Margaret Evans Porter, Julia Quinn, and Kate Smith, whose friendship, inspiration, and fellowship have been a joy to both my personal and professional life; Andrea Coursey, Lauren Bourque, and Antony Stone for their invaluable suggestions both before and after they read the rough draft; my wonderful friends at Newburyport's "Best of British" shop for keeping me laughing and (somewhat) sane; and most of all, to my beloved husband, Chris, who has always been, and continues to be, one of the very best things that has ever happened to me.

Thanks, everyone!

Prologue

November 1777
Blackheath Castle
Berskshire, England

Lord Andrew de Montforte hadn't set out to discover an aphrodisiac.

He was an inventor. He was a man of science. He was an attentive student of the laws of physics, nature, and God. He was *not* a crackbrained amateur, some curious schoolboy mixing random chemicals in the hopes of making a pretty color or getting a violent reaction. However, the discovery of the aphrodisiac was just that, the product of random mixing, and it resulted in a very interesting reaction indeed.

It all started when Andrew and his impossibly interfering, maddeningly Machiavellian eldest brother, Lucien, His Grace the fifth duke of Blackheath, had another furious row concerning Andrew's questionable health. Ever since the fire that had so changed the life of the youngest of the de Montforte brothers, Lucien had been calling in reputed experts in an attempt to "cure" him and return him to the man that he had been.

1

All four of the late duke's sons had been given nicknames by the villagers of Ravenscombe, and Andrew's sobriquet, "the Defiant One," was well deserved. He had been blessed—or perhaps cursed—with a fiery temper, a strong will, and a blatant disregard for his brother's ducal wishes, and his only desire was to be left alone. He wanted to set about getting a patent for his newest invention, a double-compartmented coach designed to carry more passengers than the conventional ones. He wanted to redeem himself in the eyes of both society and the scientific community after his flying machine had plummeted to earth eleven months past, humiliating him in front of not only two hundred onlookers, but the king of England himself. And by God, he wanted Lucien to stop calling in these infernal charlatans—some physicians, some university dons, some men of the cloth—none of whom had been able to tell him what was wrong.

And now the dogs were barking. Andrew, standing in the library and making notes from an ancient book of drawings by Leonardo da Vinci, lifted his head. He shot a glance at Lucien, who relaxed near the fire with a book. His brother never looked up. Narrowing his eyes, Andrew gazed out through the leaded windows that overlooked the meticulously groomed lawns of Blackheath Castle, the copper beeches whose branches were nearly bare, the sparkling moat beyond. A gig was coming up the long drive of crushed stone.

Immediately his expression hardened.

Damn you, Lucien!

Incensed, he slammed the book down on the table, strode past Lucien, and headed for the door.

"Discover something interesting in that old tome of yours, Andrew?" the duke asked, his expression benignly innocent as he finally looked up from his own book.

Andrew whirled, his fists clenched and his eyes full of fire. "What I've *discovered* is another meddling popinjay on his way up the drive, no doubt summoned by you to poke, prick, and prod me, and I'm having none of it."

"Ah, but perhaps Dr. Turner will be able to cure your problem."

"The devil he will. My *problem* is only getting worse, and you know it as well as I do. There is no cure, I am a marked man!"

"Which is exactly why I have asked Dr. Turner to attend you. He is a most respected authority on—"

"Perhaps I don't *want* Dr. Turner to *attend* me. Perhaps I don't *want* any more bacon-brained pillocks examining me as though I were some freak at the village fair. Perhaps I'm sick to death of being treated as if I had no feelings, thoughts, or dignity, and perhaps *you* should damn well start minding your own bloody business for once!"

Andrew stormed out of the room, slamming the door behind him.

His anger, his resentment, and yes, even his fear that one of these "experts" would give him the diagnosis he dreaded burned hotter with every stride he took. Determined not to let this latest fool have so much as a glimpse of him, he stalked down the hall, his height and bad temper making him a formidable presence indeed. Even a trio of comely young chambermaids, who usually giggled and blushed behind their hands when he passed, curtsied

and shrank back against Blackheath's forbidding
stone walls, silently staring after his commanding
figure as it moved down the castle's ancient corridors. . . .

" 'E must've 'ad another row with 'is Grace, I
reckon," said one, sighing as she watched those
broad shoulders round a corner and disappear from
sight.

"No doubt about that. An' I wager I knows what
it's about, too. Lord Andrew's far smarter than all
these doctors and other learned men that 'e's consented to let examine 'im! Ye know 'ow well 'e did
at Oxford! Why, I 'spect 'is patience with the lot of
'em must be pretty well exhausted."

"Can't blame 'im there. 'E's so smart 'e could
probably teach *them* a thing or two!"

Their whispers were lost on Andrew, who didn't
stop until he'd reached his new laboratory on the
second floor of the recently rebuilt west wing. Bar-
ricading himself in the room, he splashed port in a
glass, drained it in one swallow, and finally threw
himself down at his worktable where he wished both
his brother and his manipulations to hell.

It was only as he stretched his long legs out beneath the table, and his toes bumped something soft
and yielding, that he realized he was not alone. He
peered under the table and saw a pair of caramel-
colored eyes, sleek, shining fur that was only slightly
redder than his own tousled queue, and a long tail,
now thumping the floor in greeting.

"Esmerelda. What in blazes are you doing under
there?" Andrew kept a jar of biscuits on his desk;
opening it, he took one out and offered it to the
elegant red and white setter. Always the lady, she

took it from his fingers, chewing it thoroughly before swallowing and pleading with her eyes for more.

She was not alone. Pork, her fat companion, was down there, too. Pork belonged to Andrew's sister Nerissa, and he was as common as Esmerelda was aristocratic. Seeing that Esmerelda had received a treat and feeling left out, the bulldog heaved himself out from beneath the table and waddled up to Andrew. Pork was in no need of a midday snack, but Andrew was a fair-minded man. He took another biscuit, gave it to Pork, and watched as the bulldog bolted the morsel without bothering to chew. Disgusted, Esmerelda turned her head away from Pork with lofty disdain, one lip curling as the bulldog sniffed her muzzle. She was nearly as well bred as the dukes of Blackheath, and would not suffer the attentions of a common cur like Pork.

The dogs might have softened Andrew's surliness if the crunch of gravel outside hadn't reclaimed his attention. Moving to the window and craning his neck, he could just see the doctor's gig, empty now, standing in the drive. His ears burned. He knew they were downstairs discussing him as though he were an object instead of a man, perhaps, even at this moment, on their way up here to invade his private sanctuary. And he could just imagine Lucien walking along with the physician, describing his "condition" in that suave, careless drawl that could be so *bloody* irritating. . . .

"You see, Doctor, my brother was perfectly all right until he was caught in the fire last year. That's when he changed. . . ."

Andrew clenched his jaw. *Why don't you just go ahead and say it, Lucien? Why don't you just go ahead and tell him what we all know is* really *wrong with me!*

His anger, a worthy defense against the fear that always lurked beneath, blazed back into force. *The hell with Lucien. The hell with all of them.*

Mouth hard, pulse starting to hammer, Andrew turned from the window, smashed a space through the papers and notes that cluttered his worktable, and dumped a measure of sodium carbonate into a glass beaker.

"Miserable bastards," he snarled, trying to take his mind off the discussion he knew was occurring downstairs as he absently splashed oil of vitriol into the beaker and watched it fizz to the top. "Miserable, interfering bastards . . ."

He poured himself another glass of port. It had come from Lucien's private stock and was vintage 1754, the year Andrew had been born. He polished off two thirds of the glass in one swallow and then, as if to show his absent brother just what he thought of both him and his port, dumped the rest of it into the beaker. *The devil take it.* He threw in some vinegar and some harmless indigo dye and something left over in a long-forgotten jar, and sat there stewing in his anger as he stared into the solution without really seeing it.

A loud rap at the door jolted him from his sullen reverie. Barking furiously, the dogs shot out from beneath the table, Pork's stout body catching one of the legs. The beaker tipped. Cursing, Andrew grabbed it just in time to save most of the contents, but a stream of purple-garnet liquid spilled onto the floor, where it hissed and bubbled and fizzed like a live thing. The dogs immediately fell on it. Andrew, desperate to haul them off before they could poison themselves, immediately fell on the dogs.

"Andrew, open the door."

"Go to the devil!" he shouted over a fresh outbreak of barking as he pushed the dogs away, grabbed a cloth, and tried to wipe up the spill.

The duke's voice, still mild, had an edge to it now. "Andrew, for the sake of you and you alone, Dr. Turner has left his research and traveled all the way here from Paris. Surely you can spare him a few moments of your time. After all, we only want what is best for you."

"I am tired of people who think they know best for me!"

"Andrew, *must* you behave like such a . . . juvenile?"

Balling the damp cloth and hurling it across the room, Andrew stalked to the door and tore it open.

There stood the duke, looking as impeccably contained as ever, one black brow arching in that unique mixture of reproach and hauteur that he'd probably mastered by the time he was old enough to crawl. He was gazing most intently beyond Andrew's shoulder.

With him stood an erect, white-haired gentleman whose kind, intelligent eyes were widening with shock as he, too, stared at something behind Andrew.

Andrew scowled, turned on his heel—

And froze.

His jaw dropped open. For there was fat, drooling, bug-eyed Pork, struggling quite valiantly to climb up on Esmerelda's aristocratic haunches.

And she was not only letting him, but crouching to make his amorous ascent easier!

"Good God above," Andrew breathed, in astonishment. *"I daresay I've discovered an aphrodisiac!"*

Chapter 1

❧❧❧

Rosebriar Park
Near Windsor, England

"**I** don't care how much he claims to adore me, I am not marrying him, Gerald. He has no chin. He has no teeth. The only thing he does have is a surname that would make me the laughingstock of England were I to accept his offer. I'm telling you right now, I am not accepting it."

"Now really, Celsie, you're being ridic—"

"*I'm* being ridiculous? How would *you* like to be known as Celsiana *Bonkley*? I've told you once, and I will tell you again. I will not marry Sir Harold. Not now, not next week, not ever."

Trying to keep a rein on his patience, trying to ignore the headache that some thirty or forty barking, baying, chaos-causing dogs running loose across the dance floor were bringing on, Gerald, the third and very-much-in-debt Earl Somerfield, stared angrily out over the crowded ballroom of Rosebriar Park, his stepsister's vast Berkshire estate. Here was the cream of the English aristocracy in all its glittering array. Here were decorated generals, French

9

princes, Scottish lairds, famous statesmen. One would think that with such splendid pickings to choose from, she wouldn't have any trouble finding an acceptable mate. But not Celsie. She had standards, and Gerald was beginning to doubt there was a man in the kingdom who could meet them.

"Besides," she added, playfully swatting him with a fan upon which was painted a trio of Russian wolfhounds, "he hasn't yet asked me."

"And what are you going to say to him when he does?"

"Why, the same thing I say to every man who asks to marry me."

"Blazes take it, Celsie, not *that*—"

"Yes, that." She grinned, enjoying his discomfort. "Honestly, Gerald, I cannot understand why you're so upset. I know Bonkley's a friend of yours, but I really don't *want* to get married. You know what happened the last time I tried to become someone's wife."

"Listen, Celsie, just because Lord Hammond died at your betrothal feast doesn't mean that every prospective bridegroom is going to choke to death on a pea!"

"Yes, well, you're forgetting the marquis de Plussons."

"The marquis reneged because that damn dog of yours bit him!"

"Regardless, Gerald, my feet are tired from walking to altars, and I am not inclined to try it again. To be quite honest, I was not inclined to try it the first—let alone the second—time, but Papa, God rest his soul, thought he knew best for me. I am tired of people who think they know best for me. And now here you go again, trying to pass me off on yet a third one, and what will *he* succumb to?"

"Dog germs, probably," said Gerald, acidly.

"Probably not, as none of my dogs would deign to lick the face of one whose breath smells worse than the inside of a chamber pot."

"For God's sake, would you lower your voice?" He shooed off a merry-eyed little turnspit dog that had taken a sudden interest in his shoe. "It's bad enough that tongues are already wagging about you!"

She smiled sweetly. "Are they?"

"Yes, and you know it! Sometimes I swear you delight in making a spectacle of yourself! In making people talk! Only you would dare throw a ball to benefit homeless animals! Only you would stand up in front of all Society and make a ridiculous speech about the plights of cart horses, stray cats, and kitchen dogs! And to ask people to not only donate time and money towards such nonsense, but to invite them to bring their pets along to this   this debacle! *Get off my shoe!* I swear, Celsie, if I step in one more pile of—"

"I do believe I'm thirsty," she said breezily, only the sudden glitter in her eyes belying her anger with Gerald and his endless diatribes. God in heaven, why was he so intent on trying to marry her off? Why did he feel that her business was his own? And plague take it, her speech imploring her guests to consider the sad plight of turnspit dogs had not been ridiculous, it had been . . . impassioned! *Men!* Scooping up the little turnspit, she turned her back on Gerald and moved off through the crush, leaving her stepbrother standing there with his cheeks turning a dark, ugly red.

Whispers followed her across the ballroom, and through the chaotic barking, the laughter of dancers, the strains of the music, Celsie thought she heard every one.

"My God, would you look at her. A damned pity she wasn't born a man. She could teach the lords in Parliament a thing or two about putting some fire in their speeches, ha ha ha!"

"I just can't believe that's the same shy little chit we all wrote off when she was presented for her first Season."

"Well, she *was* ugly, uglier than the arse end of a mule."

"Gawkier than hell, too."

"Remember how you tripped her and made her cry when she was presented at Court, Taunton? My God, that was funny!"

"Well, she had more spots on her face than eyes on a spud."

"And no tits, either."

"And now look at her."

"Still hasn't got any tits."

"No, but she owns half of southern England. To hell with the rest of her!"

Yes, to hell with the rest of me, Celsie thought bitterly, cuddling the little dog and leaning her cheek against its grizzled head as she walked. *And to hell with you, too.*

Cradling the turnspit to her sadly deficient bosom, she continued past the group of swains with head held high. Though she was named for a variety of that most romantic of all flowers, Celsiana knew she was no English rose. She was too tall. She was too skinny. Her face was a collection of angles, with a thin blade of a nose, high cheekbones, and frosty, peridot eyes as cool as a leaf of spearmint. People say you look like your dog. Well, she looked like an emaciated greyhound.

But she was rich, wasn't she?

And that, she thought woefully, made her far more desirable than a full bosom, rosy cheeks, and one of those curvy little bodies that men seemed to so adore.

Yes, to hell with all of you. She reached the refreshment tables, put the turnspit down, and coaxed a frightened whippet out from beneath the cloth with a handful of sugared almonds plucked from a nearby dish. Her own dog, Freckles, a large brown and white Spanish pointer who'd been just a pup when Papa had given him to her for her tenth birthday, lay beneath the table. His dark eyes were now cloudy with age as he watched the other canines crowding around his mistress, the whippet nuzzling her hand for more treats. Celsie swallowed hard and hugged the animals to her, trying to forget the hurtful words she'd just heard. At least Gerald made no secret of the fact that he despised her. Even her own mama, who hopped from bed to bed like fleas on a foxhound, had openly disdained and neglected her once it had become apparent that her infant daughter hadn't inherited her own famous beauty. Hurt, hurt, hurt. Dogs, at least, were loyal, nonjudgmental, and loved you for who you were—not for what you looked like, or how you behaved, or how much money your dear papa left you when he died.

Oh, if only there were such a thing as a *man* who loved as unconditionally as dogs did!

Which was about as likely as a poodle taking on a herd of wild boar.

Straightening, Celsie brushed the sugar from her hands and gazed out over the sea of powdered heads. Dancers whirled and spun in a maelstrom of color, the women laughing gaily, the men—well, a depressing few of them, anyhow—tall, handsome, and elegant in their powdered wigs and rich satins and velvets. She felt detached, excluded, an outcast in her own house. But she would not ruin the evening by thinking about how cruel and shallow people really were. Better that she return her attention to this ball she had given to raise awareness about the plight of the turnspits, those tiny dogs enslaved by cooks to turn the spits that roasted their meats.

She had just pasted a smile back on her face and accepted a glass of punch when she spotted both Gerald and Taunton pushing their way through the crowd from opposite directions and making their way toward her. *Oh, bother!*

"Time for some fresh air," she declared, handing her glass to Gerald, who reached her first. "Here comes Taunton, homing in on me like a beagle on a hare."

"Really, Celsie, must every analogy you use *have* to relate to dogs?"

She was just opening her mouth to deliver a tart reply when the latest arrivals were announced.

"His Grace the duke of Blackheath . . . Lord Andrew de Montforte . . . Lady Nerissa de Montforte."

Instantly all movement in the ballroom seemed to stop, and even the barking dogs quieted as anyone who was Anyone—and anyone who wanted to be an Anyone—converged on the newly arrived trio, bowing, scraping, posturing, smiling. *Sycophants, all of them,* thought Celsie, who had no patience for opportunists and hangers-on. Nevertheless, she was grateful that the duke and his siblings had come, for the presence of the de Montfortes, a family renowned for its generous contributions to society and famed for its extraordinary good looks, would put the seal of approval on her charity ball. Only the presence of the king of England himself would have made it better.

"I say, Lady Celsiana!" Celsie nearly leaped out of her gown. She had forgotten all about Taunton, who had managed to corner her behind the refreshment table. He was dark-haired, with merry blue eyes and a slightly lopsided smile, saved from classic handsomeness by a nose that was too big for his face and a certain lack of chin.

Celsie frowned. What *was* it about these chins tonight?

He was also drunk.

Disgustingly so.

"I say, Lady Celsiana!" he repeated, falling—quite literally—to his knees and clutching her hand for balance. He pressed it to his lips and immediately frowned; it had just been licked by the turnspit and was still faintly slimy. "Would you do me the honor of becoming my wife?"

Taunton's earlier words came back to her. *No, but she owns half of Southern England. To hell with the rest of her!*

Celsie gazed down at him, arched a brow, and said in a high, clear voice, "And would you, Lord Taunton, allow my dogs to sleep in the marriage bed if I were to accept your offer?"

Taunton sobered. Shocked gasps nearly drowned out his stunned reply.

"S-sorry?"

She smiled sweetly. "I said, would you allow them to sleep in the marriage bed? I would be much obliged if you would, for I'm told that her wedding night is a *most* frightening event in a woman's life, and I would like the comfort of their company."

The hinges broke in Taunton's jaw. Then he leaped to his feet, his cheeks turning as pink as the inside of a spaniel's ear. He managed a curt bow, then shot off into the crowd, loud guffaws following him all the way.

Celsie, her dog-painted fan pressed to her smirking lips and her eyes twinkling with mirth, smiled triumphantly after him.

Yes, to hell with the rest of me. And my fortune too, you grasping cad.

"I say, madam, that was the most charming rejection I have heard in some time."

Celsie turned, the smile still dancing on her lips. "Your Grace!" she said, curtsying. "It is good of you to come."

The duke of Blackheath bowed over her hand. "I am glad I did, otherwise I would have missed the delightful setback you just gave that pup Taunton. Really, my dear. You can do better than him. . . . Why, the lad has no chin."

Celsie frowned. Now, how on earth could he have known about her feelings about *chins*?

"Chins aside," she said, raising her own, "he

doesn't like dogs, either. I could never marry a man who doesn't like dogs."

"Ah, yes. Especially one who won't tolerate them in your marriage bed."

Celsie stiffened. The duke had eyes like nightshade, black, unfathomable . . . omniscient in an unnerving sort of way. Was he laughing at her? Mocking her? Flustered, she added, "Never mind that, he would *never* take in a homeless or suffering creature as I would—and do." She gestured toward the open doors on the far side of the room. "Why, I have kennels outside and shelters set up throughout Berkshire just so these poor little animals will have a second chance. I've started a program here in the local village to educate the children. I plan to create more of these programs throughout the county, until *every* animal is saved."

He was listening intently, perhaps *too* intently, his black-ice gaze studying—no, assessing—her in a way that was making Celsie feel vaguely, inexplicably, uneasy. Rattled, she was just about to excuse herself when he gave a slow, spreading smile that might have put her at ease if the cunning gleam hadn't remained in his compelling black stare. "It seems, my dear, that you have quite a soft heart for . . . shall we say, the castoffs of society?"

"As a castoff myself, I suppose my empathy is quite natural."

"Surely that is not how you perceive yourself?"

Her mouth tightened, and suddenly fanning her hot face, she gazed stonily at a group of young bucks gathered around Lady Nerissa de Montforte. "These are the same people who took a savage delight in taunting me when I made my debut. Then, I was just another young chit on the marriage mart. But now that Papa has died and left me everything, they find me irresistible. *Or they pretend to.*" She turned and regarded him with defiant eyes. "Is it no wonder I prefer the kind company of animals? The unconditional love of a dog?"

"My dear girl, you must pay no attention to Taunton and his sort. Why, there are plenty of eligible young men in England, probably right here in this room, who not only could care less about your fortune"—again that slightly unnerving smile—"but would quite happily let your dogs sleep on the bed."

She looked down, finding a sudden interest in her fan. "You flatter me, Your Grace."

"Do I? Well, I purposely sought you out in order to do just that. Flatter you, that is. How much more interesting our world would be if every woman had the sort of courage and creativity you have displayed here tonight."

"I beg your pardon?"

Raising a hand framed in expensive lace, he indicated the swell around them, the dogs dashing between people's legs, the general air of gaiety and carefree abandon. "Why, this grand affair, of course, all on behalf of homeless and abused animals. And what a novel idea, inviting everyone to bring along their favorite canine to support your cause . . . though I must confess I had to leave ours at home." He gave a rueful sigh. "Two of them are not, shall I say, fit to bring out in public at the moment, I am afraid."

"Sorry?"

Blackheath, casually straightening his sleeve, was

gazing out over the crowd from his superior height. "It is all quite tragic, really. . . ."

"What is quite tragic?" demanded Celsie, growing alarmed.

He was still looking out over the room, obviously preoccupied with something else. "Why, what happened to them, of course. They have been most bizarrely affected by a certain solution of chemicals that my brother Andrew forced them to imbibe. They are not . . . themselves."

"A solution of chemicals that your brother forced them to imbibe? What do you mean?"

The duke turned his heavy-lidded stare on her and smiled. "My dear girl. Their particular ailment is not an appropriate topic for a young lady's ears."

"Are you saying that your mad inventor of a brother has been experimenting on animals?!"

"Did I say that? Hmm. Well, yes, I do believe that about sums up the situation. Experimenting on animals . . . Yes. Andrew always did do things that I heartily disapproved of, if only to defy me. . . . Ah, there is Mr. Pitt. If you will excuse me, my dear."

He bowed deeply and, leaving her openmouthed with indignation, moved off through the crowd.

Celsie stared after him for a moment. Then, as her temper flared to life, she drew herself up to her full height.

Preparing for battle, she went in search of Lord Andrew.

Chapter 2

S he saw him from well across the ballroom.

The first thing she noticed was that he had a chin.

The second thing she noticed was that a ring of females surrounded him.

And the third thing she noticed was that Lord Andrew de Montforte had changed since the last—the only—time she'd seen him. That had been back in '72, when she'd come to London for her first Season.

She had been a shy, spot-ridden sixteen-year-old, slouching beneath the awareness of too much height. He had been a tall, rather gangly youth with a sullen, lazy insolence about him that had made him all but unapproachable. Though Lord Andrew was anything but gangly now—with shoulders that filled out his frock coat of dark olive silk and a height to rival his brother the duke's—time did not seem to have improved his disposition in the slightest. Then, as now, a crowd of blushing beauties had surrounded him like dogs all fighting over the same bone. Then, as now, Lord Andrew paid them only the slightest of attention, present in body, perhaps, but little more. With his weight slung lazily on one hip, arms crossed, a glass of champagne dangling from his fingers, and the occasional flicker of a distracted smile—or was it a grimace?—twisting his mouth as he acknowledged each giggling remark, he gazed out and over the heads of his ardent admirers, his sleepy, downturned de Montforte eyes betraying a look that screamed of boredom.

Not just boredom, but defiance.

It was all too obvious that he did not want to be here.

It was all too obvious that in all ways but one, he wasn't.

Probably thinking of his next way to torture those poor dogs, Celsie thought, recovering her anger.

And for some reason, all those brainless ninnies swarming around him like wasps on a September apple, drawn by his broody autumnal looks, his air of ennui, his classic de Montforte handsomeness— or perhaps a seductive combination of all three— only stoked the flames of her temper higher.

Well, *she* was immune to his broody autumnal looks! *She* was immune to his air of ennui! And *she* was immune to classic de Montforte handsomeness, even if he did have a . . . did have a . . . chin!

Smiling acidly, Celsie slid through the crowd and came right up to him.

"Lord Andrew."

He took forever to turn his head and acknowledge her, and when he did, his gaze moved over her in a slow, assessing way that made her wish that someone made fire shields for the human body. "Good evening, Lady Celsiana," he drawled, finally taking his gaze from her bosom and bowing over her hand. Was *he* silently considering her lack of *tits,* too?

Something about his negligent, offhand manner made it seem as though he regarded the gentlemanly courtesy as the greatest of efforts. Or sacrifices. "Interesting party, this."

"Really? You look about as interested as an Irish setter over a plate of boiled mushrooms."

"A strange analogy, perhaps, but nevertheless an honest and accurate observation. No offense, of course. Social events are not my cup of tea."

"Yes, so I gather," she said tartly. "I understand that conducting experiments on helpless animals is?"

Several women gasped. Lord Andrew, ignoring them, raised a brow. "I beg your pardon?"

"Oh, don't try to pretend ignorance. I'm fully aware of what you've done to your dogs!"

"My dear madam, I haven't the faintest idea what you're babbling about."

"Well then, let me refresh your memory. I've heard all about how you force them to drink chemical solutions so you can note the effect on their poor bodies. You ought to be ashamed of yourself."

He stared at her as though she'd just told him she'd discovered a bridge to the moon. Around them, all conversation had ceased. Celsie's fan beat the air a little faster, and dampness filmed her palms. She was getting a crick in her neck from glaring up at that cool, remote face, but she did not back down. Neither did Lord Andrew. Finally his mouth, so sullen and angry before, curved into the barest hint of a smile. A very dangerous, unpleasant smile.

"Ah. *That*."

"Yes, *that*."

"And just where did you come by such information, hmm?"

"Your brother."

"My brother." The thin smile faded. "Of course."

Lord Andrew gazed once more over the heads of the crowd, finally locating the informant, and Celsie swore that if looks could kill, the duke of Blackheath would have to be carried out in a coffin.

Not that the duke appeared to care in the least. He seemed too busy conversing with Pitt and several Members of Parliament to pay any notice to the drama that was dominating Celsie's corner of the ballroom.

She folded her arms. "So, what do you have to say for yourself, my lord?"

"Nothing, madam, that must also be said to you."

"This is a charity ball! The welfare of animals is the whole reason I'm holding it, and if you're abusing them, then I'm going to have to ask you to leave!"

He shrugged and took a negligent sip of his champagne. "Very well, then. Ask me, and I will be more than happy to go."

Celsie stamped her foot. "Are you experimenting on animals?"

"It all depends on what you mean by experimenting."

"You know what I mean by experimenting, you . . . you mad inventor, you!"

Something in his demeanor darkened. It was in the barest tightening of his lips, the chill that suddenly seemed to emanate from his tall, powerful body. Though he remained the very image of unruffled calm, of well-bred élan, there was anger glittering in those lazy, down-tilted eyes now—and it was directed fully at Celsie.

"Very well then, yes, I suppose I have done. Experimented on animals, that is. Do you want the sordid details? Perhaps you wish to hear that I pry open their jaws and pour solutions down their throats so that I can note the effect on their insides. Or that I strap them into flying machines before going up myself. Yes, I suppose that *is* experimenting, wouldn't you say?"

His circle of admirers gasped in horror and, stepping back, began twittering amongst themselves.

Lord Andrew smiled and fixed Celsie with a look of malevolent innocence.

And Celsie was struck speechless.

He saluted her with his glass, looked once more out over the ballroom, and was just lifting the vessel to his lips when he suddenly went still. Frightfully still. His face lost its color, he looked up at the ceiling, and for the span of several seconds, his gaze seemed to turn vacant, as though the man behind those intent, far-too-intelligent eyes had gone away for a moment or two. With an unsteady hand, he put down his glass, shaking his head as though to clear it, and then, giving Celsie a look of confusion and irritation, he swept her a curt bow.

"I beg your pardon. I must go."

"Go where? I'm talking to you!"

He didn't bother to answer, instead turning smartly on his heel and walking away, through his slack-jawed admirers, through the crowd, past the gossipy Lady Brookhampton, and toward the door.

"What's the matter with him?" whispered one fresh-faced girl.

The others clustered close, staring after him. "I don't know! But did you see the way his eyes got all distant? What a pity that one so handsome is also so very *strange.* . . ."

"Perhaps he is ill?"

Celsie, alarmed, thrust past them. "Lord Andrew! I want to talk to you!"

He never slowed, impatiently waving aside the servant who ran forward with his hat, desperate to reach the great doors that led out into the frosty night.

"Lord Andrew!"

He ignored her and pushed through them, so anxious to get outside that he didn't even wait for a footman to open them for him.

Celsie picked up her skirts and ran down the hall after him. She burst outside—and stopped short in dismay, her breath frosting the night air. Over one hundred carriages were lined up out there on the drive, torch light gleaming from their polished paintwork, from the bits and buckles of the horses' bridles, from iron wheels and windows that reflected the clear black night. Somewhere, a horse whinnied. A few giggles came from a nearby coach, where a footman was no doubt dallying with one of her housemaids. From inside she could hear the now distant sounds of the musicians, the laughter of the guests.

Lord Andrew was nowhere to be seen.

Celsie took a deep breath, let it out, and shivering, sat down on the top step of the stairs, her hoops belling out around her. Her frustrated gaze swept the darkened lawn, the distant copse of trees, the low, black horizon filled with stars.

He didn't *really* strap animals into flying machines . . . did he?

She put her head in her hands, blinking, trying to make sense of his strange behavior and wondering what had caused him to suddenly flee the ball. Oh, what a night this was turning out to be, what a—

"Why, Lady Celsie. There you are. I've been looking for you all evening!"

—bloody awful night.

"Good evening, Sir Harold," she murmured, with all the enthusiasm of a hound with heatstroke.

"Celsie, sweetheart, you shouldn't be out here without a cloak," the baronet chided, sitting down beside her and taking her hand. You'll catch your death of a cold!"

"I'll catch my death anyhow, because that breath of yours is enough to fell a horse," she grumbled.

"I'm sorry, my dear. What was that?"

"I said, I'll catch my breath now, because air is a wonderful resource."

He laughed. "What a silly thing to say. Come, my dear. Why don't we go back inside?"

"Because I don't want to go inside. I want some fresh air."

"Shall we walk, then?"

"I prefer to be alone, Sir Harold."

"Yes, but being the gentleman that I am, I am obligated to protect you. To look after you. Especially since I have a very important question that I must ask you, Celsie."

"I'm not answering questions tonight."

"This is a very easy one, my dear. It only requires a simple yes-or-no answer."

"No, then. That is my answer."

He laughed, indulgently. "My dear Celsie. I haven't asked you the question yet."

"No matter, sir, I've still answered it. No." She got up.

He reached up, caught her hand, and quite roughly yanked her back down.

She fixed him with a frosty glare, her anger mounting. "Sir Harold, I *insist* that you release me, now. I have neither the time nor inclination to play games with you."

"I can assure you, Celsie, this is no game. I am in earnest." Still clutching her hand, he went down on one knee, which cracked with the sound of a pistol going off as he bent it.

"My dear Lady Celsiana, would you do me the honor of becoming my wife?"

"No, Sir Harold, as I already told you. Now, if you'll excuse me, I must get back inside. As the hostess, it's ill mannered of me to be out here when I have guests to entertain."

His face hardened. "You would spurn me, just like that?"

"I would spurn anyone, just like that. I have nearly been down the aisle twice, and that's two times too many. I don't want to get married."

"But your brother said . . ." He trailed off.

"My brother said what?"

Sir Harold closed up like an oyster guarding a pearl. "He said nothing. Nothing at all." And then, his face taut with anger, he grabbed both her wrists in one hand, yanking Celsie off balance and against him.

His mouth snaked toward hers—

And was brought up short by the flat blade of a sword, an inch before he would have lost his lips.

"I say, sir, you are obstructing the door."

Both looked up, only to see the lean form of Lord Andrew de Montforte blocking out the stars above.

"I seem to have forgotten my hat," he said, never lowering the sword nor losing eye contact with Sir Harold as his free hand sought Celsie's and lifted her to her feet. "Will you stand and step aside, sir, so that I may go back inside and retrieve it?"

In a strange, scuttling motion, Sir Harold leaped up and backward, away from the deadly blade that never wavered in Lord Andrew's capable hand. "Wh-why, yes, of course, my lord." He grinned and bowed deeply. "Please, be on your way."

"After you, of course."

Sir Harold stopped grinning. "But I——"

Andrew smiled that same dangerous smile Celsie had seen back in the ballroom and, with his sword, gestured toward the door. His grip on her hand made her feel as though it were caught in the jaws of a trap.

"I said, sir, *after you.*"

Sir Harold's face went cold. Then, without another word, he turned and strode angrily back through the doors and inside.

Celsie, her face flaming, was finally able to yank her hand from her unexpected savior's. Oh, the embarrassment of having been caught in an embrace with Sir Harold *Bonkley,* of all people! And the indignation that she'd had to be rescued by the very man who had been so rude to her just minutes before! "Really, Lord Andrew, was that quite necessary?"

He shrugged and slid his sword back into its scabbard. "You looked as though you needed rescuing."

"And *you* looked as though you were leaving!"

"I was. I forgot my hat."

"Well, let me tell you something, my lord. I am no spineless ninny, no birdbrained puff of feathers who needs some *man* around to protect her. I can fight my own battles, thank you very much!"

And with that, she turned on her heel and stormed back inside.

Chapter 3

*S*o *much for gratitude,* thought Andrew, watching her march back toward the ballroom. He noted the stiffness of her back beneath shimmering peach silk, the way her petticoats flirted with her trim ankles, the purposeful manner in which she moved—like a general taking command of his troops. A door slammed and she was gone from sight.

Shrugging, he retrieved his hat, tucked it under his arm, and strode back out into the frosty night.

Prickly witch.

Bloody irritating little bluestocking!

He wished he'd taken his own carriage. Now he was forced to wait out here in the cold for Nerissa and Lucien for God only knew how long. Why the hell had he ever allowed them to talk him into coming to this foolish ball, anyhow?

He should have just stayed home.

He located the ducal coach near the front of the line of vehicles, its paint as black as the sky above. An alert footman ran to let down the steps for him. Andrew vaulted inside and threw himself down on the seat, his breath frosting the cold air. Pulling a blanket around himself, he sat staring into the close darkness.

His anger did not last long. It couldn't, not with the ever-present fear that lurked just below the surface, keeping him aware of the fact that he was flawed, reminding him all too often, as it had done tonight, that there was something very, very wrong with him. Something that was not getting any better with time. Without the anger to sustain him, and surrounded by the darkness of a quiet night while the faraway strains of music and laughter—making him feel excluded, reminding him of the normalcy and safety of other people's lives, making him feel all the more alone—reached him, he felt the fear clawing for a hold on his heart. His nerves. His composure. He thought about the incident in the ballroom, and wiping a hand over his face, found it damp with nervous sweat.

God help me . . . I feel so alone.

He thought about going back inside to try and lose himself in the gaiety of the crowd, but immediately discounted the notion. Someone must surely have noticed his strange behavior.

He thought about getting out of the coach and walking and walking and walking until he was too tired to be afraid, but the idea was not appealing.

Finally he pulled out his notebook and tried to lose himself in his work, trying not to think of what the inside of Bedlam must look like.

He shuddered. Lucien would not commit him, would he?

Would he?

Putting the notebook down, Andrew leaned his cheek against the cold glass of the window and, shivering beneath the blanket, stared miserably out into the night.

As he crossed the foyer, Gerald saw his stepsister storm upstairs, her elderly dog Freckles, hampered by equally elderly joints, trailing in her wake. A moment later he heard a door slam. The noise was so loud that it was clearly audible over the strains of the quadrille that had a hundred people out on the dance floor.

He suspected the worst.

And sure enough, there was Sir Harold Bonkley, his face equally flushed, but with what looked like humiliation, stalking toward him from out of the ballroom.

"Well?" said Gerald, impatiently.

Bonkley snared a drink. "She refused me."

"Damn it, man, I thought you were going to publicly compromise her so that I could come upon you and demand that you marry her!"

"Well, things didn't work out as we planned."

Gerald was furious. "We had an *agreement,* Bonkley. You marry her, get your hands on her wealth, and bail me out of debt. What the blazes is so difficult about that?"

"Getting her to say yes, for one thing. And perhaps I might have succeeded in my quest if that deuced de Montforte fellow hadn't interfered just as things were heating up."

"What do you mean, interfered? The duke has been discussing politics with Pitt for the last fifteen minutes!"

"I'm not talking about the duke, I'm talking about that damned brother of his, Andrew. He came upon us outside on the stairs just as I was about to ravish her. So much for ruining her reputation! I swear, Somerfield, if I'd been armed, he wouldn't have lived to regret it!"

"If you'd been armed, I daresay *you* wouldn't have lived to regret it," muttered Gerald. "He is a master swordsman, Bonkley, and you'd do well to remember it. Now, if you'll excuse me, I must go find my sister and try to talk some sense into her."

Sir Harold fumed at the insult as he watched the younger man go. He had been so sure of success where everyone else had failed that he'd told half the people in the room that he was as good as betrothed to the eccentric heiress. Now she'd made both him and her brother a laughingstock.

His fists clenched with rage.

Draining his glass, he stalked off through the crowd.

Upstairs in her apartments, Celsie waved off her maid, threw herself down on her bed, and still fully clothed, lay on the silken coverlet, trying not to scream with frustration, trying not to hurl something across the room, trying not to think about Bonkley molesting her and how she'd felt when she'd looked up, only to discover that Lord Andrew de Montforte had been her gallant rescuer.

God help her, why did it have to be *him*?

She loathed him! He was surly, arrogant, and ill mannered! He experimented on animals! Why, he'd said himself that he sent them up in flying machines and poured evil solutions down their throats!

The tears came, damn them. She felt them wetting the coverlet beneath her hot face, felt them burning inside her nose and making the back of her throat ache. She did not understand them.

Why am I so upset?

Because Sir Harold Bonkley has ruined my evening, she wanted to shout at herself. But Herself didn't quite believe it, so her grasping mind tried something else. *Because men are constantly trying to order my life to their own wishes, patronizing me, treating me as though I lack a brain and will of my own.* No, that wasn't it either. Toenails clicked on the floor and a moment later the bed sagged as Freckles heaved his big body up beside her. She sat up, wrapped her arms around his neck, and hugged him fiercely. *Because Freckles's face is now completely gray and he can't walk very well anymore and now I've found a strange lump just below his ear and I am scared to death.*

Yes, that was it. *That* was why she was crying. It had nothing to do with the fact that, as usual, nobody had taken her impassioned pleas on behalf of animals seriously. And it had nothing to do with the fact that when Lord Andrew had saved her from Bonkley she'd had a mad inclination to hurl herself into his arms and let *him* kiss her instead.

It had nothing to do with Lord Andrew!

She buried her face in Freckles's neck and sobbed. "Oh, Freck . . . what is *wrong* with me?"

He was too old and too dignified to lick her face. He merely sat there and stoically let her hug him, leaning his body slightly toward hers.

"Nobody wants to hear about the poor little turnspits who run their legs off in hot kitchens so that people's meat might be roasted," she told him brokenly. "Nobody cares about the way cart horses are beaten until they drop, or how hundreds of unwanted, unloved dogs and cats are starving in the streets because there aren't enough homes for them and people keep breeding more and more. No, nobody cares. All they want to do is drink my expensive wine, eat my expensive food, try to win my expensive—and oh-so-wealthy—hand. Oh, how I wish that I'd been born a man instead so that people would take me seriously. How I wish that Papa had had a brother or a son so that I wouldn't have inherited everything." She buried her face in the side of the old dog's neck and hugged him tightly. "And how I wish that there was such a thing as a man capable of loving me as much as you do, Freckles."

With a groan of pain, Freckles lowered his big body down beside her, molding his back to the curve of her body. She stroked his long, floppy ears and wiped her eyes with the back of her hand. Dear old Freckles. That was the thing about dogs, wasn't it? They always understood. They never let you cry all by yourself. They insisted on sleeping with you at night to keep you safe and warm, they were always there whether you wanted them to be or not, and they always knew exactly how you were feeling.

If only *she* knew exactly how she was feeling.

Damn you, Lord Andrew!

That was it. Tomorrow she was just going to have to leave for Blackheath Castle and there, finish the conversation he'd so abruptly ended. Tomorrow she was just going to have to make the journey to see for herself what he was doing to the de Montforte dogs.

Tomorrow she was just going to resolve this mat-

ter, for better or worse, and life would get back to
normal.

She hugged Freckles, and tried not to think of the
lump.

It was not growing bigger, she told herself.

But Herself didn't quite believe that, either.

Outside in the carriage, Andrew must have long
since fallen asleep, for the sound of Lucien's voice
just beyond the door jolted him with a start. He sat
up, blinking, as the sway of the carriage heralded the
duke and Nerissa's entrance.

"Ah, Andrew. There you are. We were wondering
what became of you," murmured Lucien, taking the
seat opposite him and pulling off his gloves. "Too
much excitement for one evening?"

Nerissa bounced into the seat beside Andrew.
"You really should have stayed. Lady Brookhampton's dog jumped onto the refreshments table when
no one was looking and managed to eat the whole
cake. It was hilariously funny!"

"Yes, especially when the poor beast got sick all
over Bonkley's shoe," Lucien observed dryly.
"Rather put an end to things, I daresay." He rapped
once on the roof of the vehicle, signaling the driver
to move on, then turned his enigmatic black stare on
Andrew. "Pray tell, why *did* you leave?"

Andrew set his jaw and stared out the window.
"Because," he bit out.

Silence.

If Andrew weren't gazing out into the night, he
might have seen the quickly veiled look of concern
in his brother's eyes.

He might have seen the ache in Nerissa's suddenly sympathetic gaze.

Instead, all he saw was the tall, pointed, dark tops of the conifers swaying gently against the stars.

"Ah," said the duke, softly. "Another episode, I take it?"

Andrew's silence was affirmation enough.

Nerissa and Lucien exchanged glances. "And here I thought it was Lady Celsiana who might have caused your hasty departure," Lucien mused.

That got Andrew's attention. He turned angrily on his brother. "Yes, speaking of that belligerent little witch, why *did* you set her loose on me like that?"

Lucien raised his brows with feigned innocence. "My dear Andrew, I haven't the faintest idea what you're talking about."

"The devil you don't. You deliberately told her I was experimenting on animals, and the next thing I knew she was tearing me apart, limb from limb!"

"You mean you minded?"

"Of course I minded! It was damned embarrassing."

Lucien sighed heavily, affecting an air of long-suffering patience. "And here I thought I was doing you a favor."

"Doing me a favor?"

"Really, Andrew, how many times have you told me you have no wish to get married? That you are sick to death of pesky females buzzing around you at every social event you deign to attend? That you want nothing more than to get on with your science? The girl seemed to be quite interested in you, you know. Asking me rather personal . . . questions. I merely said what I did to put her off."

"What?"

Lucien crossed his arms and gave a sigh of satisfied boredom. "You ought to be thanking me for my assistance, not condemning it. She *did* leave you alone afterwards, didn't she?"

Andrew met Lucien's blankly innocent stare. Why did he have the feeling his brother was up to something? "I suppose she did," he murmured, frowning.

"So there. I was only acting in your best interest." The duke sighed and closing his eyes, leaned his head back against the seat as the coach left Rosebriar behind. In the darkness of the carriage, nobody could see that he was smiling. "Besides," he added, "I highly doubt that you will see her again."

Chapter 4

Which was wishful thinking, of course.

For Andrew *did* see Lady Celsiana Blake again—a scant thirty-six hours later.

He was still abed when he heard a carriage outside on the drive, and the dogs barking, and a small commotion somewhere beneath his window. His first thought was that Lucien had brought in another charlatan to examine him.

Upon hearing a female voice, he realized it was no charlatan at all, but Lady Celsiana Blake.

A charlatan, he thought irritably, would have been preferable.

Andrew pulled the coverlet back over his head and tried to go back to sleep. Bloody hell, what time was it? Eight? Maybe nine o'clock?

He heard the low murmur of Lucien's voice somewhere downstairs. The duke slept no more than four hours per night. Of course *he'd* be up.

Sure enough, the anticipated knock on his door came moments later.

It was James, his valet. "My lord? His Grace asked me to inform you that you have visitors. Lady Celsiana Blake and her brother, Earl Somerfield, are

39

here. Your presence is requested downstairs."

Andrew flipped onto his side, pulled the coverlet up over his shoulders, and shutting his eyes, burrowed more deeply beneath the blankets. "My presence be damned. Tell His bloody Grace that *he* can deal with her ladyship. I'm of no mind to ruin my day by starting it off in an argument with some irritating female."

"As you wish, my lord."

Andrew waited until he heard the servant retreating down the hall, then, stretching lazily, went back to sleep.

Or tried to.

Moments later, he was jolted rudely awake by a blinding light hitting him in the face. Lucien was at the windows, yanking the heavy drapes back and letting in the ruthless morning sunshine.

"Really, Andrew. It is frightfully ill mannered to keep guests waiting."

"It is also frightfully ill mannered to get a fellow out of bed only to throw him to a damned carnivore," retorted Andrew. The harsh light seemed to drive through his eyeballs and straight through his head into the pillow beneath him. He sat up, knuckling his eyes and squinting against the flooding brightness. "What the deuce is she doing here, anyhow?"

"Why, I invited her, of course."

"You invited her?"

"You seemed rather upset that I . . . shall we say, stretched the truth about your experiments, so I took it upon myself to issue her an invitation to Blackheath just to set the record straight."

"Lucien," gritted Andrew from between clenched

teeth, "I am perfectly capable of handling Lady Celsiana Blake without your assistance."

"Yes, why don't you? Handle her, that is. She and her brother are in the Gold Drawing Room awaiting you."

"Gerald is in the Gold Drawing Room awaiting him," snapped a tart female voice from the doorway. "I am not."

"What are *you* doing here?!" shouted Andrew, bolting straight up in bed, which, given the fact that he slept without a nightshirt, without a cap, without anything, in fact, save for the mat of auburn hair that curled crisply on his chest, was a mistake. Lady Celsiana Blake got an eyeful of bare skin, sinewy arms, and a lean, flat belly laddered with hard muscle.

"A servant brought me up!" she cried, staring at his chest and blushing furiously.

"Here?"

"The duke *said* I was being taken to your laboratory!"

"Damn you, Lucien!" roared Andrew. "What the bloody *hell* is the meaning of this?"

Lucien's casual cross-armed stance, his innocent expression, never changed. "Really, Andrew. I do wish you'd watch your language. There is a lady present."

"Not anymore there's not!" Celsie raged, and jerking her chin up, turned on her heel and marched down the hall in a rustling fury of agitated skirts and petticoats.

"Ought to go after her, I think," mused Lucien. "She's probably heading for your laboratory. . . . Wouldn't want her to find any animal experiments going on, now, would we?"

"You cursed *bastard*!" Leaping out of bed, Andrew swept up a blanket, wrapped it around his hips, and ran barefooted down the hall in pursuit of his visitor.

Celsie was halfway down the hall when she heard him pounding after her. She picked up her pace, turned a corner, and whirled, her face flushed with fury and embarrassment as she confronted the source of her distress. "Don't your servants even know the way around your house?" she howled. "Your brother said the servant would bring me to your laboratory! That was no laboratory, that was your—your—"

"Bedroom!" Andrew shouted, equally furious.

"I have never been so humiliated in my life!"

"Well, don't look at me, *I* wasn't the one who invited you into my blasted apartments!"

"Had I known they were your blasted apartments, I would never have set foot in them!"

"And yet you would have set foot in my laboratory? Without my express invitation?"

"Your *brother* said I could inspect it!"

"My brother be damned! I don't want you or any other nosy, annoying, interfering *female* in my laboratory!"

"What, do you have something to *hide*?" she challenged.

They stood glaring at each other, Celsie quivering with rage, Andrew's fists clenched and his eyes blazing. Celsie tore her gaze from his face. But instead of landing on a place of safety, it fell to his magnificent chest, rising in a perfect inverted triangle of lean muscle and male strength from the blanket wrapped around his hips. Appalled, she jerked her gaze up, and saw instead a clenched jaw cloaked with dark auburn bristle; a set, angry mouth; and rich, sleep-tousled hair that gleamed like burnished chestnuts in the light coming in from the window.

"Oh," she cried, and ripped her gaze from his face.

Instead, it dropped to his feet. His bare feet, with their bare toes and their bare ankles and their bare calves, which were, like that splendid, oh-so-manly chest, sparsely cloaked with auburn hair.

"I'm leaving," she announced, doing an about-face and storming off down the hall.

Andrew marched right after her, his long shadow completely dwarfing her and the path ahead of her so that she could not escape it no matter how fast she walked. "Good."

"I knew I should never have come here in the first place!"

"You are entirely correct, you never *should* have come here in the first place, and at such an ungodly hour, besides."

She spun around so fast that he collided with her chest. She shoved him away. "What do you mean, ungodly hour? It's nearly noon! How was I to know that you sleep the days away? Do you practice your evil experiments by light of the moon, then, so God himself can't see the wickedness that you're up to? *Do you?*"

"I practice my evil experiments at all times of the day, except, of course, when I'm being harassed by meddling females."

"So now I'm a meddling female!"

"You've been a meddling female since the moment I met you."

"And you've been a surly, arrogant recluse who's

nothing short of *strange*! Look at you," she spat, tossing her head and letting her contemptuous gaze rake his body. "Standing there before me, a lady, wearing nothing but a blanket!"

She struck a nerve with the word *strange*, knocking him mentally off balance. Andrew drew back, his eyes narrowing.

"Would you prefer I slip it off, then?" he taunted.

"I'm *leaving*!"

He held himself still as she stormed off down the hall. *Nothing short of strange.* Her remark had shaken him. Infuriated him. Frightened him, for it showed that certain aspects of his behavior had not gone unnoticed. Emotion boiled up inside him as she marched away from him, her little rump swaying beneath yards of shimmering green satin, her shoulders stiff, her nape white and elegant beneath the pinned-up piles of shiny, tawny-brown hair. He felt an insane desire to call out, to let the damned blanket fall and *really* unsettle her. But no. He was unsettling her enough just the way he was, and given her unprecedented attacks on him, he was determined to enjoy what revenge he could take.

She was about to round the corner. In another moment she'd be on her way downstairs. Andrew couldn't let her leave without having the last word. He waited until she was nearly to the stairs before he rashly, recklessly, tossed out a challenge that would change the course of his life.

"I say, Lady Celsiana," he called out, mockingly.

She kept walking, her back as stiff as if someone had poured starch down her spine.

"I say, madam, would you like to see the *evil experiment* I'm working on now?"

That brought her to a stop.

She spun around.

"I thought you didn't want nosy, interfering females in your precious laboratory," she blazed.

"You forgot annoying."

"That's because I don't consider my efforts on behalf of suffering animals *annoying,* though I suppose dog haters like yourself would be inclined to disagree!"

"Oh, I am entirely inclined to disagree. You are by far the most annoying female I've encountered all year."

Celsie bit back an angry retort and turned her head, refusing to look at him. His near-nakedness was having an effect on her that she didn't quite understand, a hot, short-of-breath feeling that partnered her thumping heart. She wished she could stop thinking about his naked chest. Wished she could keep her thoughts off what must be concealed by the blanket. Wished she could think—at all.

"So," he taunted. "D'you want to see my laboratory or not?"

"No, I don't want to see your stupid laboratory after all. It will only upset me. *You* upset me. I was a fool to even come here in the first place."

He crossed his arms, one downbent hand anchoring the blanket low on his hip. "Coward."

Her head whipped around. "I beg your pardon?"

"You profess to be some savior of animals, yet look at you, bolting because you just might see something distressing. Some dog defender *you* make."

Her chin snapped up with renewed pique. She trembled with the urge to fling something at him.

And then she saw the challenge in his far-too-intelligent eyes, and what looked like a teasing smirk dancing about his mouth.

Celsie folded her arms and unflinchingly met his mocking stare, her eyes narrowing.

"Fine then. Since you're so eager to show off your hideous experiments, you can just lead the way!"

Chapter 5

He offered his arm.

Stiffly, Celsie accepted it.

And wished that he would put on some clothes. Any clothes. Lord, even a coat would have done wonders.

Stop thinking about what lies beneath that blanket!

But she couldn't. Any more than she could will away this annoying hot-and-prickly feeling that had so unexpectedly come over her. And as she walked mutely beside him, the air between them stiff with tension, she was disturbingly aware of how tall he was. How refreshing—no, how strange—it felt to find someone whose height surpassed her own, whose very stature made her feel as tiny as she wished she actually were, who made her feel less of a . . .

Well, less of a gawky freak.

Was his—she glanced furtively at the blanket cloaking his hips—anatomy of full stature as well?

She blushed furiously.

"I don't think this is such a good idea after all," she snapped, all too aware of the way her body was responding to her handsome, dog-abusing escort and not liking it one bit.

"It is a brilliant idea."

"What, you clad in nothing but a blanket, me without my maid or suitable escort, and you leading me to God-only-knows-where? I am not sure it is quite so brilliant at *all*."

"It is brilliant because it is obviously not in Lucien's plans."

"What on earth do Lucien's plans have to do with anything?"

He marched her out of the main house and through the doors to another wing. "Really, madam. Do you honestly believe that the servant who brought you to my bedroom didn't do so on purpose?"

"Perhaps he got lost whilst trying to find your laboratory."

"Rubbish. That servant has been working for us for the last twenty years, and his father worked for us before that. He knew perfectly well where he was taking you. I would bet everything I own that he was merely following orders. Lucien's orders. After all, my brother invited you out here, didn't he?"

"No, I took it upon myself to come. I wanted to see for myself what evil cruelty you practice in your laboratory."

His lips thinned in an unamused smile. "I see."

"Well, I'm glad *you* do, because I'm feeling very confused right about now. . . . Why do you say your brother invited me here? And why would he direct the servant to bring me to your apartments when it was obvious you were in no state to receive visitors?"

"Because he's a troublemaking monster who delights in making me miserable, that's why." He shoved open a set of carved oak doors. "Here we are. Watch where you step."

Celsie pulled away from him and came up short. She found herself in a grand chamber, with bookcases built into the walls, a high, plastered ceiling, floor-to-ceiling windows, and a lovely floor of gleaming teak. A huge worktable, crowded with bottles, jars, notebooks, burned-down candles, crumpled-up papers, open books, and a discarded coat, dominated the room. An easel, upon which were scribbled some mathematical or chemical formulas—Celsie had not a clue which—was pulled up beside a high stool. The room smelled predominantly of new paint, new floor, new everything, though Celsie could detect the underlying scents of sulfur, vinegar, and something that had been recently burned.

There was not an animal in sight.

Not a cage, not a leash, not a dead dog anywhere to be found.

"But . . ." She looked up at him in helpless confusion. "Where are the animals you are experimenting on?"

"I do not experiment on animals."

"But you said at the ball that—"

"No, those were my brother's words, and after you attacked me as you did, and in such an embarrassingly public way, I was so angry that I chose to let you believe them. But I never confirmed such codswallop, did I?"

Celsie could only stand there staring at him with

her mouth hanging open. Then she blushed and looked away.

"Oh," she said, in a little voice. "Oh—I am so sorry. . . ."

"I do not get out in public much, madam, but when I do, I would prefer that people do not get any worse an impression of me than they already have."

"I was not aware that people already had a bad impression of you," she mumbled, still unable to meet his gaze.

"You yourself called me *strange,* did you not?"

She suddenly felt very small. "Well . . . yes, I did. I'm sorry, now. It was an unkind thing to say, but you weren't the only one who was angry."

He merely looked at her, turned his back, and walked a few steps away, unwilling, perhaps unable, to accept her apology.

"I said I'm sorry," she said.

Nothing.

She had never felt so embarrassed in her life. Because she had jumped to conclusions and humiliated him in public, he had been forced to leave her ball. And people probably *did* have a bad impression of him now, thanks to the fact that she had been blinded by her concern for his dogs, and thus let her temper get the best of her.

As usual.

Celsie scrunched her hanging, embroidered pocket in one fist. If anyone deserved her anger, it was the duke. *He* was the one who had made her and Andrew the butt of some cruel joke. *He* was the one who had made Andrew positively loathe her. *He* was the one she ought to have been confronting, and by heavens, she was going to have that confrontation right now.

She raised her chin, determined to make as dignified an exit as possible under the circumstances. And then she heard it: toenails, clicking lightly in the hall just outside. It was a welcome sound in the midst of so much awkwardness. A moment later, a tall, rangy red and white setter, tail wagging gently, padded into the room, went up to Lord Andrew, and insinuated herself beneath his hand.

Celsie saw his fingers begin to stroke the dog's head.

"I guess if the dog likes you, I've got nothing to worry about," she said lightly, trying to fill the uncomfortable silence, trying to make amends for her horrible blunder.

He didn't bother looking at her. "This is Esmerelda."

"That's—a pretty name," she said lamely.

"My brother gave her to me as a birthday present three years ago. Thought I'd want to take her bird-hunting, but I don't like to shoot."

"Guns?"

"Birds."

"Oh." She gave a nervous laugh, feeling unsettled by his brusqueness. "I thought all men liked to kill things."

"Yes, well, I'm different. Or, as you said yourself, madam"—he finally turned to look at her—"*strange.*"

His moody, challenging stare burned into hers. Celsie flushed and looked down at Esmerelda, who was bending her body into Andrew's leg, trying to get closer to him, her great dark eyes softening with love as she gazed worshipfully up into his face. Celsie felt awkward. Excluded. Soundly chastised. She began to wish she *had* made her exit. She was starting to grow very hot beneath her chemise, and more than a little uncomfortable by Lord Andrew's brusqueness. Was he incapable of forgiving? Incapable of understanding? For heaven's sake, Taunton, even Bonkley, was easier company than this man. At least she knew how to handle them. . . .

"I think I'd better take my leave," she said.

"Why? I thought you wanted to see my laboratory."

"Yes, well, I wouldn't want to bother you any longer with my nosy, interfering presence," she said, trying for a lighthearted sarcasm that failed miserably.

"You forgot annoying."

Celsie began to take a deep breath, intending to count to ten. Twenty, if she had to. "Lord Andrew—"

"Go, leave, then," he interrupted, making an impatient, shooing motion toward the door. His eyes looked almost savage. "I never wanted you in here in the first place. I never want any *females* in here, because every single one of them is bored within minutes, and I'm sure you'll be, too. So go, before your eyes start glazing over."

"I'm not bored, merely uncomfortable. Your manner does not exactly make a person feel welcome."

He bowed mockingly. "A thousand apologies. My manner is far too honest."

Celsie raised her chin and glared at him. He gazed down at her from his superior height. And she saw then, in his eyes, something he was trying desperately to conceal, something that hid behind his pride, something that was as plain as the hair on his broad, hard-muscled chest, before he glanced away.

He was wrong. Honestly lay not in his manner, but in his eyes. His defiant, surly, and yes, hopeful eyes. They said everything his brusqueness didn't.

He didn't want her to leave.

He would never admit it, but he didn't want her to leave.

"Apologies accepted." She took a deep, steadying breath and let it out on a tentative smile. "Now, let's stop bickering, shall we? I want to see your laboratory. I promise I won't be bored—"

"Women never keep their promises."

"—and besides, I've never met any men of science before," she said, ignoring his gruff words and trying to force geniality from him. "Did you write the formula on that easel over there?"

"Yes," he said, shooting her a glance that said, *Well, who the devil do you* think *wrote it?*

"And did you design and build that great, complicated machine down there on the floor?"

"Yes."

"And look at all those books you have. . . . They appear to be texts on science and math and alchemy. . . . Do you understand them all?"

Again a look of long-suffering impatience. "I *wrote* several of them," he muttered, pulling one down and thrusting it into her hand while he bent over a table and began rifling through a large stack of papers. "That one's my doctoral thesis."

"What is it about?"

"What does it *look* like it's about?"

"It *looks* like it's written entirely in Latin," she

said tightly, but with a cheerful smile so that he would not see how much his rudeness and sarcasm were unsettling her.

"Anyone can see that it's a treatise on the components of air."

"Anyone who's a male and thus privy to an education."

"And what is that supposed to mean?"

"Exactly what it implies. You men think of us as silly, nonsensical creatures when *you're* the ones who get to go off to Eton, to Cambridge, to Oxford; *you're* the ones who get to do Grand Tours of Europe; *you're* the ones talking politics in every London coffeehouse, in every private club, in every private dining room over your brandy after sending us women away because you think such talk would overtax our frivolous little brains. How do you expect us to know Latin and understand the components of air when *our* education consists of learning the proper use of the fan, taking care of babies, and how to sew?"

He stared at her, his expression inscrutable. He had the most intent, focused, single-minded gaze she'd ever seen. It was almost unnerving. And it remained on her for far too long.

"Stop looking at me as though I'm some bug under a microscope," she said, feeling uncomfortable.

He finally turned away, heading across the great room. "I'll grant that men have an advantage," he said levelly, "but most of those who go up to university waste their time drinking, gambling, and whoring instead of studying."

"Did you?"

"No."

"Did you ever want to?"

"No."

"Why not?"

He shot her a quelling look from over his shoulder. "Because I found my studies and lessons far more fascinating than the juvenile pursuits that so intrigued most of the other undergraduates." He moved around a large table, Esmerelda following loyally at his side. "Besides, I am the youngest son, the one who is least likely to inherit the dukedom, the one who must therefore eke out a living by some means other than a fortunate birth. It would not have been wise to waste my education."

Well, thought Celsie, at least she'd got him talking and behaving civilly, instead of snapping out curt replies and shooting her looks of impatience.

"I hope to invent or discover something that will make me famous," he was saying, pausing at the table and one-handedly going through some papers. "Something that will benefit the world, something that will change it as we now know it before my mind"—he flushed—"that is, before I leave this earth. Only a fool would waste his time at university. I may be many things, madam, but I am not a fool."

He knelt down and, bunching the blanket in his fist at one hip, began pawing through more papers on the floor, casting some aside, tossing others recklessly over his shoulder, and treating Celsie to another view of his bare back.

"Ah. Here they are." He extracted several large, slightly crumpled sheets of vellum from the pile and put them on the table, clearing a space through the clutter with his forearm and laying the drawings out for her to see.

She moved up beside him and stared down at one of the drawings. "What is it?"

"An idea I've been working on to improve coach travel."

"I . . . see."

He eyed her narrowly. "Do you?"

"Of course not. Why don't you explain it to me?"

He looked at her as though trying to discern whether she was trying to be sarcastic; then, dismissing her remark, he smoothed the wrinkled paper with the palm of his hand.

"This is my double-compartmented stagecoach," he said, frowning as one of the wrinkles refused to flatten. "I've often worried about the poor people forced to travel atop the roofs of coaches because there's not enough room for everyone inside, haven't you?"

"Yes. Exposed to the elements, bounced around, clinging for dear life to avoid being thrown off, and God help them if they are . . ."

"Precisely." He stood close to her, unnervingly so, his finger tracing the drawing, his bare shoulder just inches from her nose. "This coach, as you see, will have a short set of pull-down stairs leading up to the roof and a second story, if you will, built onto where the rooftop passengers currently sit. Instead of one inside compartment, as there is now, my stagecoach will have two, one atop the other. Not only will it enable more people to travel on a single vehicle, but I predict it will cut down on the number of accidents, injuries, and deaths that are currently seen on the roads now."

Celsie stared at the drawings.

Then she looked up at their creator, this talented,

surly genius, unable to prevent an awed, incredulous little smile from pulling up the corners of her mouth. "You really are very clever."

"No, just determined," he countered, though she saw a faint tinge of color along his cheekbones and a decided warmth coming into his eyes that hadn't been there a few moments ago.

Best not to embarrass him, Celsie thought. She spied the corner of another drawing poking out beneath the ones of the double-compartmented stagecoach, and pointed.

"And what is this?"

He pulled the drawings out, sending the ones for the stagecoach fluttering to the floor. "My idea for a plumbing system that will revolutionize fire prevention in large houses such as this one." He bent his head, his hair flopping over his eyes, and traced some lines with his finger. "This here is a pump, as you can see, which will draw the water from an outside source; the water will be stored in this cask, and fed by gravity into these pipes affixed to the ceiling. At first sign of fire, all one has to do is pull this lever and gravity will release a flood of water, thus dousing the fire and saving the house, and its occupants, from destruction." He shoved the drawings aside. "And this—"

"Lord Andrew."

He came up short, looking down at her with distracted impatience. Celsie had carefully retrieved the stagecoach drawing from the floor and was staring at it in awed pleasure.

"Do you have actual models of your inventions? I'd love to see them."

"Just the stagecoach, out in the stable. I'm afraid

that *building* the confounded things is not as much fun as designing them."

"But you designed a flying machine. I remember the sensation it caused when you launched it from the roof of this very castle last year. All of London was talking about it. The king himself said he had never seen anything so spectacular."

The minute the words left her mouth, Celsie knew she'd made a mistake. His expression altered. Irritation and dismay darkened his face, and he began hunting through more drawings, his movements abrupt. "My flying machine was a failure."

"But according to all accounts, it was responsible for saving your life, and that of your brother Charles."

"It did not perform as it was designed to do."

"So are you going to make another one?"

"No. I have other ideas that are far more useful to society, I think."

"Lord Andrew . . ."

He paused then, reached up to push the unruly lock of hair from his brow, and gave her a look of annoyed impatience. "Yes?"

"Why *did* the duke say you'd been experimenting on animals?"

"I told you, to irritate me."

"But I just don't understand." She looked at Esmerelda, who had lain down at Andrew's feet, her silky shoulders and ribs propped against his bare ankle. "He said something about your dogs being in a state that made them, well, unfit for company."

"Unfit for—" And then his mouth curved in a reluctant grin, and for the first time Celsie saw that he had a very boyish, very attractive, dimple in his chin.

"Oh, *that*."

"That?"

He busied himself collecting the drawings into a pile, as though unwilling to meet her searching gaze. "I had a rather accidental discovery the other day. I was making a solution, and had my mind on something else entirely. I don't quite remember what I mixed together, but moments later, I was rowing with Lucien, Esmerelda and Pork were going insane, and the damned solution spilled onto the floor. Next thing I knew, the dogs were lapping it up—"

"Oh, dear God!"

"Yes, that was my reaction exactly. I tried to pull them off, but the damage was done, they had already ingested some. A few moments later, they were . . ."

"They were what?"

To Celsie's surprise, he actually blushed. "They were . . . uh, trying to make puppies."

"Puppies? Was the bitch even in season?"

His cheeks went even darker at her brazen words. "No. She was not."

"And yet they were . . ." She made a little motion with her hands.

"Yes, they were."

"Good heavens, Lord Andrew, you discovered an aphrodisiac! Have you tried it on anything other than the dogs?"

He stared at her in amazement. "Are you bloody serious? What sort of monster do you think I am?"

"Well, I was just curious. . . . Something like that would be incredibly valuable, you know. Why, just think of all the uses you might have for it!"

"I would rather hope that my carriage or plumbing

would enjoy far greater acclaim," he said, somewhat sullenly.

"I'm sorry. I meant no offense."

"It was an accidental discovery. I could not duplicate it even if I tried, so therefore it is of no value, really, to anyone."

"Can I see it?"

"It is locked in Lucien's safe."

"All of it?"

"Most of it."

"Oh, Lord Andrew, would you consider selling some to me?"

He stared at her incredulously, looking quite shocked. "Whatever for?"

Now it was her turn to blush. "Well, you see, I have a lovely stallion at home who seems to have no interest whatsoever in mares. He is very handsome, with splendid bone, a beautiful, crested neck, and an uncommon amount of intelligence. I would like to breed him so that these qualities might be passed on to his get, but since he will not mount a mare, there's not much I can do, really. I'm thinking that a few drops of your aphrodisiac might just do the trick. . . ."

"And you accuse *me* of experimenting on animals?!" he exclaimed, staring at her in disbelief.

Celsie's face flamed. "I love my horse! I would never give him anything that I thought would hurt him!"

"No?"

"No! And—and just to prove it, I dare you to let me try some of your so-called aphrodisiac myself! Why, I wager that there's nothing in it to cause a . . . a reaction, anyhow! No doubt your dogs were just feeling amorous that day, that's all!"

"You want to try my aphrodisiac on yourself."

"I want to try your aphrodisiac on myself, yes, if only to prove to you that I would never give my animals something I wouldn't put in my own body!"

He just looked at her, one brow raised, weighing the idea in his mind. "No."

"And you accuse *me* of being a coward."

"I dare not think of the consequences if I allow you to sample it."

"What, are you afraid that I might attack you?" She laughed, instantly dismissing such a ludicrous thought. "Really, Lord Andrew, I hardly know you. I am in no danger of falling into your arms, I can assure you."

He looked dubious. She saw his mouth working as he chewed the inside of his cheek, contemplating her challenge, wrestling with himself over whether he should accept it.

"I'll pay you a fortune for those few drops, my lord. And give you one of Sheik's foals just to show my gratitude."

"You're serious, then."

"Dead serious."

He shrugged. "Very well, then," he said, going to a cabinet and inserting a key into its lock. "But don't say I didn't warn you."

Chapter 6

A ndrew knelt, opened the door to the cabinet, and extracted the tiny, precious vial. Aware of his unfortunate tendency to misplace things, he had given most of the solution to Lucien for safe-keeping, but had retained these few ounces, intending them for further study. He really did not want to waste them in a challenge with this woman.

Even if she *was* the only female besides his sister who'd shown an interest in his work.

Even if she *was* the only female who hadn't yawned her way through his laboratory tour after going glassy-eyed with boredom.

Even if she *was* the only female he found he rather *liked* having here.

No, he didn't want to give her the potion. But on second thought, noting the aphrodisiac's effect on a human was further study in itself, was it not? The very idea aroused Andrew's scientific curiosity.

His would-be subject was still standing behind him, right where he'd left her. She did not look worried in the least. Her head was high, her eyes bright with reckless defiance. No doubt she was determined to prove him wrong. No doubt she didn't believe a word he'd said about the aphrodisiac.

No doubt they were both going to regret this.

Andrew suddenly wished he had changed into decent clothing, *any* clothing, and that he didn't stand before her in nothing but a blanket draped loosely around his hips. But then, maybe what had happened with the two dogs had been an accident of chance. Maybe a few days' settling had rendered the solution inert. Maybe Lady Celsiana Blake would drink the stuff and nothing would happen at all.

Maybe.

He poured some water into a glass, tapped several drops of the precious liquid into it, and handed it to her.

Her fingers closed around it. She looked up at him and for the briefest instant he saw a flicker of hesitation, maybe even nervousness, in her eyes before she quickly veiled it with a bravado he was sure she didn't feel. Then, never breaking eye contact with him, she raised the glass to him in mock toast, put it to her lips, and downed it in several quick gulps.

"There," she said, triumphantly handing the empty vessel back to him. "I've consumed it—and I feel just fine."

"I am glad to hear it."

"I feel no urge to tear that blanket from your loins. I feel no urge to ravish you. I feel—"

She paused, blinking, and put a hand to the base of her throat. Her very white, very pretty, very feminine throat. She looked up at him, her eyes widening and registering surprise; and then her hand slid slowly downward, her fingertips drifting over the hollow of her collarbone and out over the rounded swell of one snowy breast.

"—very strange," she finished, obviously unaware of where her hand had gone.

But Andrew was all too aware of where her hand had gone. He was all too aware of where her hand still remained—and what it was currently doing. He looked at her fingers skimming softly out over her breast, touching it through the lime-green silk that covered it, and now circling the nipple, which was, God help him, very aroused and clearly delineated beneath the fabric. Andrew swallowed hard. He could no more take his eyes off the slow, seductive path of her finger than he could have stopped breathing.

Though he did precisely that.

Stopped breathing.

Her lips parted. Her skin took on a rosy flush, and she gazed coyly up at him from beneath heavy lids in a way that made the back of Andrew's throat go suddenly dry. Transfixed, he watched as she licked her lips, a slow, torturous tracing of first the top, then the bottom one, leaving a glistening trail of moisture there that did funny things to his insides as her tongue did a slow circle around the perimeter of her mouth. Her fingers hooked the top of her bodice . . . slowly tugged it, and the filmy chemise she wore just beneath, down.

"Wh-what is in this stuff?" she breathed, faintly.

"I told you, I don't remember."

"Hmmm . . . I suppose it doesn't matter what's in it . . . only how it makes me *feel*."

"And how does it make you feel?" he managed, trying to remember why he'd let her have the solution, trying to keep his mind on track, trying to give his scientific brain the chance to anchor him in reality when it was obvious that his body—carnal thing that it was—had already given up on the idea.

"It makes me feel . . . tingly."

"Tingly?"

"Warm." She blushed, coyly. "I . . . I don't know how to describe it, really. I have the strangest sensation down between my thighs. . . ."

"I—" Andrew swallowed. "I—see."

"It feels—well, rather wet and warm down there." She touched her fingers to her burgeoning nipple. "And warm *here,* too."

Andrew felt a violent erection coming on. His pulse was starting to pound, his will fading irretrievably into the gray fog of his thoughts. "I uh, think I'd better get you back to your brother now—"

"Oh, but I don't *want* to go back to my brother," she said, slipping her other hand into her piled-up hair and, with a single flick of her wrist, freeing it from its pins. She tilted her head back, shook it, and sent the thick, shining mass of hair tumbling down around her shoulders, her bosom, her breast. Then she smiled up at him, her silvery-green eyes dark with invitation. "I want *you.*"

"Lady Celsiana, you are not yourself, you don't know what you're saying . . . what you're doing—"

"Oh yes, I know what I'm saying." She sauntered closer, her tall, slim body no longer stiff, but fluid and silky and feline as she sidled up to him like a cat begging to be stroked. "And I know exactly what I'm doing." She seized his hand and pressed it to the silk of her gown, all that separated his palm, his fingers, from the hard budding nipple just beneath.

"Oh, that feels so much better. Will you make the rest of me feel better too, Andrew?" She gave a shy tinkle of laughter. "Will you touch me in *all* the places that feel so . . . so strange?"

"God help me. . . ."

"God help *you*?" She laughed, a sound that was low and husky and altogether seductive. "Why, *you're* not the one who's hot and cold and tingly and warm and—and—"

It was obvious that she couldn't think of the right word. It was even more obvious that she didn't need to, for now her hand was moving shamelessly, sensually, over the top of her breast and scooping it free of its silken constraints. The nipple was huge. Engorged. Bright, blushing pinky-red like the trim of her gown and hard as the seed of an apple. Andrew stared. Andrew groaned. And now she was rubbing it between thumb and forefinger, looking down at it in fascination, sliding her palm beneath her breast and offering it brazenly to him.

"Would you look at that," she said, with a funny little giggle.

Andrew looked. He couldn't help but look. But oh, if he could only will himself not to *touch* . . .

"Why is the nipple standing up like that, Andrew?"

"Because it . . . it wants—er, it needs—"

"Wants and needs *what*?"

"Nothing."

"Something?"

He stood frozen, the blanket crushed at his hip in one sweating fist, wondering if he ought to make a run for it before it was too late for both of them. In another minute he was going to have to peel her off him; no, in another *second* he was going to have to peel her off him, for now she was pressing herself up against him once more, molding her body to his, tilting her head back to look up at him, rubbing her naked breast against the soft, wiry hair of his equally naked chest.

Esmerelda, with a look of canine amusement, got up from the floor, padded across the room, nosed the door open, and left.

Left it ajar.

Oh, God.

And now Celsiana was kicking off one of her slippers, hooking a leg around Andrew's bare calf, and caressing it with her toes. The sensation of her silk stocking against his hairy leg, the warmth of her flesh against his own, was enough to make his erection feel as though it were going to punch a hole right through the blanket.

Breathing hard, he shot a panicky glance toward the door.

Still ajar.

"Lady Celsiana—"

"Oh, come now, Andrew. Don't you enjoy this?"

"The damned door is open!"

"No one will come. Besides, don't you like to live *dangerously?*"

Her hips were pressing against his, pressing against his already straining erection. And now she was reaching out, dragging her fingers down the cleft of his chest, running her fingernail around his nipple and down over his ribs, following the thin arrow of dark auburn hair toward—

"Madam, please contain yourself!"

"Why? I've been wanting to touch you from the

moment I saw you lying there in that bed. You have such a splendid physique, you know . . . such taut, powerful muscles . . . such a perfectly masculine form. I think I am very glad that you are not wearing any clothes, after all."

"You must stop this, now!"

"Stop what? Let go of the blanket, Andrew. Take it off and let me see if the rest of you is as magnificent as what I can see . . . what I can feel. . . ."

"No, this is *not* a good idea," he said, then let out a choked gasp as her fingers brushed teasingly over the blanket, which he clutched to himself like a shield.

Her fingers settled on the upper edge, her knuckles pressing into the point of one bare hip, her smile coy, teasing, a mixture of virginal innocence and pure, female intuition. "Of course it's a good idea. Surely you don't have something to *hide,* do you?" She tugged persistently at the blanket. Andrew, his hand shaking, clenched it at his hip. And then she grinned and sidled closer to him, rubbing her bare breast, her aroused nipple, against the crisp hair of his chest.

"And you accuse *me* of being a coward," she teased, with a little smile.

Andrew groaned. He was losing control of his will. Of his body. He felt his muscles liquefying as Celsiana began kissing his chest, looking up at him through her lashes, her fingers still tugging at the blanket. He tightened his hold. And now her knuckles were sliding across his bare, taut abdomen, going out to one hip, and then, agonizingly, back to the other, as she traced the blanket's folded rim.

A blanket that Andrew was clutching desperately against himself.

Help, he thought, muddily. Frantically. He backed up, wondering if he could make an escape, knowing, with some carnal part of his no-longer-scientifically-inclined mind, that escape was really the very last thing he wanted.

What he wanted was—

He took another step back. She moved right with him. And then the back of his thighs came up against the worktable. Through the blanket, he felt its hard edge. He felt Cèlsie's fingers tickling, brushing, teasing his belly . . . skimming the bony points of his hips . . . coming back around again and now touching the huge, rigid bulge that he was helpless to hide, helpless to prevent, jutting up through the blanket in proud, unmistakable arousal.

"Oh, my," she said, her eyes widening. "Now, *this* is interesting!"

"Madam, *please,* come to your senses, you will regret this, I tell you, this is—"

Her fingers wrapped around him through the blanket.

"This is . . ."

She squeezed him, and Andrew's knees threatened to buckle.

"This is wonderful," she finished for him, as he reached behind him, and with his free hand, caught the edge of the table. His knuckles felt as though they were going to burst their skin. His grip on the tabletop was the only thing keeping him on his feet. Where his knees had been, there was only water.

"Isn't it, my Lord Andrew?"

"Isn't it . . . isn't it what?" he managed weakly.

"Wonderful."

"Oh God, please help me."

"Let go of the blanket, Andrew."

"No, madam, you will regret this . . . we both will."

For answer, she merely began rubbing his arousal through the blanket, touching him, squeezing him, inciting him, and Andrew thought he was going to explode into a thousand pieces. He wanted her to rip the blanket off. He dreaded what would happen when she did. His eyes began to close. His fingers all but left dents in the tabletop. She bent her head, and he felt her silky hair against his belly, felt her fingers cupping his testicles, and knew he was lost, even as she reached out and pulled the bunched blanket from his slackening fist and slowly dragged it down, off his hips, and off his huge and very hot erection.

Andrew, his senses all at sea, could do nothing to resist.

Absolutely nothing.

Her hand found him. His knees buckled and, letting go of the table, he sank to the floor in defeat, pulling her with him, kissing her desperately.

"The devil take it. . . ."

They fell sprawling into a pile of drawings. Andrew groaned, trying, with the last part of his mind that could still reason, with the last shreds of will that remained to him, to slide backward away from her ruthless seduction, from her maddening touch, but he couldn't hear himself think, couldn't feel himself feel, and knew nothing but the sweetly torturous feel of her hand, her gentle, exploring fingers. It was too much, even for him. His outflung hand managed to snare the leg of a chair; he tried to pull himself to safety, but he was trapped by his own passion. He let go of the chair. He let go of his will. And then, catching Celsiana around the waist, he yanked her up and atop him, rucking up her petticoats as he slid his hand beneath them and up her long, smooth-as-silk thighs.

Oh, God, she was right. Warm and wet . . . oh, so very, very wet . . .

He heard her moan deep in her throat, felt her sigh against his cheek as his fingers sank into her moist cleft and began to stroke her.

"Yes, oh, that feels so much better," she breathed, showering fervent, inexperienced kisses all over his brow, his nose, and finally his mouth. Andrew claimed her lips, quickly showing her how it was done, devouring the innocent sweetness of her mouth. His own breathing grew shallow. Erratic. He felt her palming his abdomen, and now her hand slid down to wrap itself around the base of his manhood, squeezing him oh so gently, oh so firmly. He sucked in his breath on a raw gasp; but when her fingers started to flicker over the engorged tip, he knew it was all over for him. His eyes flying open, he drew his lips back in a silent scream and made a wild grab for the chair leg to anchor himself.

It came over with a crash, hitting the table, then the floor near his ear, with a sound that nearly deafened him. A beaker fell and shattered on the floor, along with several bottles and a half-finished cup of tea. "Bloody hell," gasped Andrew. "Sweet, bloody hell!" And as he shut his eyes and tried, oh dear God, tried to delay his climax, Celsie began making little sobbing gasps that heralded her own coming release. The sound was enough to annihilate Andrew's control. Feverishly he seized her around the waist with both hands, plunked her down atop his rigid manhood as she helped guide him in, and, impaling her all the way to the hilt, began thrusting up into that tight, blessedly wet haven with desperate, frenzied abandon.

"Oh!" she cried. "Oh, I think *that* is what I needed . . . what I *wanted*—oh, please. . . ."

She met his savage thrusts with equal abandon. Her kisses rained down upon his hot forehead, his lips, his face. "Oh, please, Andrew—go faster!"

Her voluminous skirts and petticoats shrouding his body, her hair swinging wildly about his face as she rode him for all she was worth, he felt her inner muscles beginning to contract all around him.

"Faster!"

"Oh, *Godddddddddddd*—" Andrew shouted through clenched teeth as the white-hot explosion finally ripped through his loins. Carried along by her movements, he gave a final upward thrust, his senses splintering as she cried out and hung poised above him, her head thrown back, one breast jutting free, tears of unexpected ecstacy rolling down her cheeks as her climax seized her as well.

Then she fell, panting and exhausted, across his bare chest just as the door crashed fully open.

Shocked silence.

Shocked, stunned, awful silence.

And then a calm and perfectly unfazed voice penetrating it:

"Dear me. This is certainly a most interesting experiment you are conducting, Andrew."

Still weak and dazed, Andrew raised his head.

There was the duke of Blackheath. There was a handful of staring servants.

And there, God help them both, was Celsie's brother, the earl of Somerfield.

"Bloody *hell*," Andrew said, and throwing a hand over his eyes, let his head thump back to the floor.

Chapter 7

"**Y**ou rutting *bastard*!" howled Gerald, drawing his sword and charging forward. "I'll kill you for this, so help me God!"

Lucien calmly reached out and caught the earl's elbow before he could decapitate his youngest brother. "Now, now, Somerfield, if you feel compelled to kill him, please do so outside. Bloodstains are *so* hard to get off a new floor, you know." He gazed down at the hapless pair, his angry sibling flat on his back, stark naked, and covered only by Celsie's petticoats. Not to mention her partially clothed body. "Besides, I am sure that my brother has a perfectly reasonable explanation. . . ." He gave a maddening little smile. "Don't you, Andrew?"

"Damn right I do!" snarled Andrew, hooking a finger around a damp lock of Celsie's hair that webbed his face and glaring up at the intruders from beneath her prone body.

"I, for one, would like to hear it," said Lucien mildly.

"She drank the damned solution!"

"What solution?" thundered Somerfield.

Lucien came forward, retrieved the blanket from

the floor, and tossed it over the couple. "My brother here devised an aphrodisiac," he explained conversationally, as though such discoveries were commonplace amongst English inventors. He crossed his arms and looked down at his brother, a faint smirk playing about his mouth. "Really, Andrew, you disappoint me. I would have thought you had more sense than to test such a . . . *dangerous* composition on a pretty young woman."

"I didn't *test* it, she asked to *try* it!"

Lucien shrugged. "Well then, I would have thought you had more sense than to say yes."

"What do you mean, she asked to try it?" raged Somerfield. "How dare you accuse my innocent young sister of such vulgarity!"

Andrew met the other man's glare with hard eyes. "I daresay your sister is no longer *innocent*, and I must wonder, indeed, whether she ever *was*."

Somerfield's cheeks mottled with outrage, and at that moment, Celsie finally raised her head. Pushing herself up on one hand, she blinked and looked weakly around her, her expression one of confusion and slowly dawning horror. "Good heavens . . . what happened?"

"You ravished me," snapped Andrew.

"I *what*?"

"I said, you bloody well *ravished* me."

"You'll die for that accusation, de Montforte!" howled Somerfield, advancing with drawn sword.

The duke sighed and casually snared the earl's sleeve once again. "Given the circumstances, Somerfield, I do think it wise to retreat to the library so that *you* may calm down, and our young lovers here can recover both their wits and their dignity. Andrew? If you and Lady Celsiana would meet us downstairs in a quarter of an hour, I'm sure that reasonable satisfaction can be had for all parties involved."

"I daresay that *reasonable satisfaction* has already been had by at least one of them!" roared Somerfield, glaring pointedly at Andrew.

"Really? Well, it wasn't me, I can tell you that much."

Somerfield went for his sword yet again, and this time Lucien's eyes lost their amused glint as he seized the earl's arm once more. "Really, Somerfield, you are beginning to annoy me. It would benefit us all if you would demonstrate a little self-restraint. Now, come along. I trust that some cognac will steady you and allow you to address this matter in a mature and rational way."

Steering the hot-tempered earl from the room, he strode toward the door, and it was only as he crossed the threshold and paused to look back over his shoulder, one brow raised and a faint smile on his lips, that Andrew caught the telltale gleam of satisfaction in those fathomless black eyes.

And then he was gone.

"Bastard," Andrew muttered beneath his breath— and in that moment he would have wagered everything he owned that Lucien was—in some way, for some reason—behind this entire debacle.

The "mature and rational" way that Lucien suggested, once Andrew and an upset, embarrassed, and very, very angry Celsie were seated in the library, was an immediate marriage.

Lucien gazed thoughtfully at the pair, sitting as

far apart from each other as the placement of chairs would allow, neither looking at the other, both quietly furious. "Regardless of the circumstances that led to the act, Andrew, there is no denying that you have ruined the girl," he said, pouring another glass of cognac and handing it to his now fully clad brother. Andrew adamantly refused to take the glass and sat staring mutely out the window, his jaw clenched, his eyes blazing as Lucien continued. "You have robbed her of her virginity, her innocence, and any chances of making a successful marriage. Therefore, I think you owe it to her to do the right thing."

Andrew leaped to his feet. "I will *not* marry her!"

"And I will not marry *him*!" cried Celsie, also leaping to her feet.

"Sit down, both of you," said the duke, irritably. "Lord save us, you'd think I just sentenced the two of you to the gallows, the way you're carrying on."

"I said, I am *not* marrying her," Andrew repeated hotly.

"And *I* said, I am not marrying *him*."

"Well, then," said Lucien, smiling and gazing calmly at the earl. "What do *you* suggest we do, Somerfield?"

"He ruined my sister! If he's any sort of a gentleman, he'll do the right thing!"

"*I* wasn't the one who told her to take the damned solution!"

"But you were the one who damn well invented it!"

Celsie could feel herself losing her already frayed control. "Gentlemen—"

"And you were the one who allowed her to take it!" Gerald continued.

"Gentlemen—" Celsie bit out, louder this time.

"And furthermore, *you* were the one who was lying stark naked beneath her," thundered Gerald, advancing on Andrew with fists clenched. "Your brother's right—your judgment is to be questioned, and so, by God, are your motives!"

Celsie slammed her own glass down. "Damn it, listen to you! The two of you go on as though I am invisible, as though I have no brain or will of my own, as though I'm nothing but a—but a—flea on a dog's ear!" She rounded on her brother. "Gerald, I told you before and I shall tell you again, *I* was the one who asked Lord Andrew to give me the solution. *I* was the one who doubted its efficacy. *I* was the one who attacked him, and I am the one who is responsible for this . . . this *mess,* and I will not have you forcing us into some ill-advised union when it is obvious that Andrew has no more wish to marry me than I do to marry him!"

"And what if you're with child?" shouted Gerald.

"If I am with child, that's my responsibility, not Andrew's! He didn't ask for me to . . . to . . ."

"Ravish him," finished the duke urbanely, topping up his glass.

"Damn you, Lucien!" exploded Andrew, as Celsie flushed crimson. "Must you be so damned crude?"

The duke merely smiled and lifted a brow. "My dear brother, I am merely repeating the words *you* used earlier."

"Did I ravish you?" demanded Celsie, her insides clenching.

Now it was Andrew's turn to go red. "Don't tell me you don't remember."

"I don't remember a thing except opening my eyes to find myself—"

"On top of him," finished the duke, smoothly.

"Curse it, Lucien!"

Celsie was trembling with mortification. "Thank you, *Your Grace,* for stating the matter so succinctly," she ground out.

Blackheath merely inclined his head and lifted his glass to her as Celsie turned angry, desperate eyes on Andrew. She saw his own gaze soften, momentarily, before he looked away, his jaw hard. He was as much a victim of this entire debacle as she was. He had warned her not to imbibe the solution, had even tried to talk her out of it. But no. She had taken his warning as a challenge, and now look at what had happened.

"Did I?" she demanded, anger and self-disgust making her voice brittle.

He cleared his throat. "Well, let us say that your manner was nothing short of predatory," he allowed.

"Did you resist?"

"Really, Celsie!" thundered Gerald.

"Did you?"

"Well, I did at first, but to be truthful, madam, you were rather . . . well, persuasive in your designs."

"Oh, dear *God,*" she moaned, momentarily covering her face with her hands. Then, raising her head, she looked Andrew directly in the eye. "Well then, since it was *your* honor that was compromised, *your* body that was—was—"

"Ravished," supplied Lucien, helpfully.

"Ravished," fumed Celsie, eyes flashing, "then I think that *you* ought to decide what should be done."

"This is highly irregular," stormed Gerald, his complexion mottling. "Really, Celsie, I have never heard of anything so preposterous in my life!"

"Be quiet, Gerald. After all, *I* was the one who coerced Lord Andrew into giving me the solution, so therefore, it is up to me to deal with the consequences."

"I thought you said you didn't remember what happened!"

"Well, I remember that much!"

"Regardless, he was the one who deflowered you!"

"Maybe *I* deflowered *him*!"

"Highly unlikely," interrupted the duke, idly studying his cognac. "I daresay Andrew lost his virginity long ago." He smiled and slanted a benignly innocent grin at his brother. "Is that not right, Andrew?"

Celsie saw Andrew turn and glare out the window once more, his eyes like flint.

"So you see, my dear? That settles that."

"That settles nothing," Celsie snapped. "Lord Andrew? What are your wishes in this matter?"

"I have already stated them. With all due respect, madam, I have no need or wish for a wife. Indeed, I would prefer to forget this matter ever happened and simply get on with my life."

"Well then, as I also have no need or wish for a husband, I daresay we are of like mind, and I, too, would prefer to forget it ever happened. Please take me home, Gerald. I find that I am developing quite a headache."

The duke sipped his cognac. "Really, my dear, that's an excuse you should have used an hour ago." He turned to his brother, eyes gleaming. "I beg your pardon. Perhaps *you* should have used it, Andrew."

Celsie thought—hoped—that Andrew was going to kill the duke right then and there. He shot to his feet, his face darkening, his fists clenching at his sides. "The lady has stated her wishes, I have stated mine, and I am leaving."

"So am I," snapped Celsie, also rising.

"But what about my brother's compromised honor?" asked Lucien, raising an innocent brow. "It would be most embarrassing if word got out that he was attacked by a woman and did not enjoy it."

"I never said I didn't enjoy it," Andrew ground out.

"Oh. Well then, that changes things immensely, doesn't it? As you are of superior strength to the lady, and did nothing to defend yourself from her—what did you say?—ah yes, *persuasive designs* upon you, then I daresay we can conclude, after all, that you are as much responsible for this predicament as she is. I really think that *one* of you, at least, should offer marriage."

Celsie had had enough. She strode angrily up to the duke of Blackheath, who remained sprawled negligently in his chair, an amused little smile playing about his mouth as he looked up at her.

"You seem to be rather hard of hearing, Your Grace," she said tersely. "I have already told you that I have no wish to get married."

"And you, my dear, seem to be ignorant of the gravity of this situation. Perhaps if you explain why the idea of marriage to a handsome young man like my brother here is so revolting, I will suddenly find my hearing quite restored."

"Because marriage doesn't suit me, that's why."

The duke was back to examining his cognac. "Ah, yes. I seem to recall that the last two fellows you tried to marry expired under rather extraordinary circumstances, the former, if I remember correctly, by choking on a pea. Hmm. Perhaps marriage doesn't suit your prospective *bridegrooms,* my dear."

"Only *one* of them expired," said Celsie icily. "But even so, we wouldn't want your poor brother here succumbing to the Jinx."

"Rubbish," said Lucien, smiling. "He is a de Montforte. 'Twill take more than a pea to do him in." He looked at Andrew. "Surely you are not afraid of being done in by a pea, are you, Andrew?"

"Why the devil should I be afraid of being done in by a goddamned *pea* when three drops of my solution seem to have done the trick well enough?"

"Ah, but surely it is not as bad as all that. You do not find the lady wanting, do you? She is quite lovely," the duke murmured, lifting his glass to Celsie. "She has spirit, intelligence, and enough money to finance any disastrous little experiments you should choose to . . . *test* in the future. Truly, I cannot see what the problem is."

"The problem is, I do not need some *female* interfering with my time, my work, my schedule, my life. I do not have time for a wife, and I do not want the responsibility of having to look after one."

"Ah, but you should have thought of that before you allowed her to take the solution. Now you may find yourself facing the responsibility of looking after a child. Would you want any son or daughter from this union to be born a bastard, Andrew, simply because you are too stubborn, foolish, and proud to do the right thing?"

Celsie slammed her hand down atop a small table. "Stop harassing him! It is obvious that he has no wish to get married, and I will say once and for all that I don't want to get married, either!"

"Ah. Do you find *him* wanting, then?" asked the duke, smoothly.

"That is not the point! And I have had enough of this absurd conversation. Gerald, I demand that you take me back to the inn. Now."

"Celsie—"

"*Now*. Before I grow even angrier than I already am."

Gerald put down his glass, but his jaw was rigid, his eyes glittering with fury. "Very well then, Celsie. If you will await me in the carriage, I will join you as soon as I have concluded my business here."

She rose to her feet. The gentlemen did as well. Then, with a short curtsy to the duke, Celsie turned and marched from the room, leaving an awkward silence in her wake.

"That settles it, then," said Andrew.

Somerfield put down his glass. "That settles nothing, de Montforte."

Even Lucien, still casually ensconced in his chair, lifted his brows.

"The fact remains that you have dishonored my sister and ruined her beyond repair. If she will not accept restitution, then I demand it."

"I beg your pardon?"

"My second will be calling upon you this afternoon. I will see you tomorrow at dawn, sir—where the two of us will settle this matter like men. Good day."

Chapter 8

"**R**eally, Andrew. I fail to understand why you look so damned gloomy. 'Tis only a sword fight, and I'm sure it will be over well before breakfast. Just long enough to work up a good appetite, I should think."

The two brothers had had a blazing row just moments after Celsie and the earl had departed. Or rather, Andrew had had a blazing row with Lucien, accusing him of deliberately orchestrating the debacle. Lucien had merely sat there in total calm, an infuriating little smile on his face as Andrew raged and howled and tore about like a December gale.

Supper had been a tense, charged affair. Now, the evening meal had long since finished, the table had long since been cleared, the musicians who supplied His Grace and his vast household with the latest and most fashionable music from the Continent had long since retired. Even most of the servants had gone to bed. As well they should; it was ten minutes past midnight.

"I am gloomy for many reasons, but I can assure you, fear of death on the morrow is not one of them," Andrew snapped, not looking up as he pored over the seventeenth-century tome on alchemy that had occupied his attention for the last two hours.

"I am relieved to hear that. You are, after all, a de Montforte."

Scowling, Andrew flipped a page and jotted something in the notebook at his right elbow. "A de Montforte who's been damaged beyond repair."

"Rubbish. You spent hours a day rebuilding your strength once you were able to breathe normally again, and we both know how you accomplished *that*."

Indeed. After the fire had so injured his lungs, Lucien had forced him into a ruthless regimen of hard exercise, challenging him to practice his fencing skills even on those days when Andrew had felt too weak or dispirited to even lift the rapier. As much as Andrew hated to admit it, there wasn't a man in England who could match Lucien's prowess with the blade . . . and as his fencing partner, Lucien had good reason to believe in Andrew's own skill as well.

"Yes, well, if you're looking for gratitude, you're not going to get it," he said curtly. "Not tonight. I'm totally fed up with you and your confounded manipulations. Why don't you just bugger off and leave me alone?"

"Ah, Andrew. You wound me."

"Do I? Well, let me tell you something else. I refuse to go to any more balls, parties, or public gatherings of any sort. I am not normal, and you know it. I will never be normal. One of these days someone outside the family will find out. It's a damned miracle someone didn't find out or at least raise an eyebrow at the ball last night. You may be able to command just about everything except the weather, but even you cannot protect me if people start getting suspicious."

"I have done a commendable job so far."

"Yes, well, I'd rather just stay home. Unlike the rest of you, I hate going out in Society anyhow. Always have. Nothing but a bunch of twittering fops and fools who have nothing better to talk about than politics, scandal, and fashion."

"Well, what *would* you have them talk about? The composition of drinking water? The effect of heat on various gases? The formula to determine the exact distance the earth stands from the sun? Really, Andrew. Your mind dwells in different and far higher places than do ours, indeed, than do those of most people you're likely to meet."

"My point exactly." Andrew flipped a page. "And another thing. I would rather die at Somerfield's hand tomorrow than endure any more of those so-called doctors you keep dragging here to examine me."

"Very well, then. I will drag in no more doctors to examine you."

Andrew rested his brow in the heel of his hand and turned a page, trying to focus his attention on the question of why his random mix of chemicals had produced an aphrodisiac that had come close to ruining his life—if it hadn't already.

But he kept seeing Lady Celsiana Blake, so interested in his work when every other lady he'd ever brought into his laboratory had been bored to tears. He kept seeing her looking seductive and oh-so-desirable in the throes of passion. He kept seeing her bravely trying to retain what dignity she had left while Lucien had baited her and tried to force her into a marriage she didn't want. And he kept seeing her leaping to his defense, taking the blame for the day's disaster instead of allowing him to shoulder it, as any other woman probably would have done.

As any other woman probably would have demanded.

"Well, Andrew," said his brother, pushing back his chair. "Now that we've reached an agreement of sorts, perhaps we can call a truce and be civil to one another? I for one am finding this brotherly strife infinitely wearying."

"Then you should have thought of the consequences before playing games with Celsie's and my lives."

"Games? My dear brother. You're the one who fails to see the gravity of this situation, not me. If you'd only done the gentlemanly thing and offered to marry the girl, you could enjoy a leisurely stay in bed tomorrow morning."

"I'd sooner marry one of her dogs."

"Hmm, yes. I am sure that whoever marries the fair Lady Celsiana *will* be marrying her dogs—that is, if he does not first choke to death on a pea."

"Yes, well, no danger of that with me, as I have no intention of marrying her and I hate peas." Andrew shut the book, poured himself a generous measure of brandy, and fixed Lucien with a hard glare from across the table. "Stay out of my life, Lucien. I'm warning you."

"You're what?" asked Lucien, raising his brows.

Andrew's eyes glittered. "I said, *I'm warning you.*"

"Dear me. That's what I thought you said."

"You manipulated both Gareth and Charles into marriage, but I won't have you doing so to me. Do I make myself clear?"

Lucien gave a dismissive wave of one lace-framed hand. "My dear boy. Charles and Gareth needed to be married. You . . . well, as you have said time and time again, you have contributions to science to make. You have great things to invent. A wife would only get in the way of such lofty ambitions."

Andrew clenched his jaw. Lucien was only echoing words that he had often uttered himself, but for some reason, they sounded mocking when his brother repeated them. He felt his temper starting to ignite.

"Besides," Lucien added, before he could fashion a suitable retort, "I did not tell you to give the girl your potion. I did not tell her to ravish you. And I certainly did not tell her foolish brother to challenge you to a duel. Forgive me for pointing out the obvious, Andrew, but this trouble is of your own making, not mine. The fact that I find it all rather . . . amusing, is neither here nor there."

"I wonder," muttered Andrew, pouring more brandy.

"Well, do wonder over something other than a bottle of spirits. A little is good to steady one's nerves before a duel, but moderation is prudent."

"There is nothing wrong with my nerves. Merely my temper."

"Ah. One hopes your temper will improve by morning, then."

"It will improve the moment you and everyone else in the world stops interfering in my life. I just want to be left alone to do the things I want to do.

That is all I've ever wanted. To be left alone."

"It is not good to be alone."

"*You* should talk."

"I beg your pardon?"

"You heard me," Andrew gritted, his intent russet-green eyes blazing into Lucien's black stare. "You couldn't wait to get Gareth and Charles married off, and I'd bet my last breath you're trying to do the same to me, but what about you? You're the duke. You're the one with an obligation to this family, to your title, to your holdings, to our ancestors. Yet you stubbornly refuse to take a wife and produce an heir. At the rate you're going, the sixth duke of Blackheath will have to come down through Charles."

"Hmm." Lucien was idly stroking his chin. "Perhaps the sixth duke of Blackheath *will* be Charles."

Andrew narrowed his eyes. "And what's that supposed to mean?"

"Why, absolutely nothing." Lucien's tone was far too dismissive, far too blithe, but before Andrew could question such enigmatic words, the duke suppressed a yawn and got to his feet. "I will leave you now, since that is your wish. Only sporting of me to grant it to you." He gave a devilish little smile. "After all, it might be your last."

"I thought it was a second's duty to bolster the courage of his principal, not undermine it."

"No need. As you said yourself, there is nothing wrong with your nerves, merely your temper. Even so, I am off to bed. You ought to be too, I think. Morning comes early."

"Yes. Tomorrow's earlier than usual. Good night."

"Good night."

Lucien, looking down at Andrew's bent, sullen figure, paused to briefly clap a hand to his brother's shoulder as he passed behind his chair. His displays of affection were rare, and it was the closest that he was prepared to come to an apology, but Andrew only flinched irritably, shaking off his hand and never taking his attention off the glass of brandy into which he was brooding.

Silently, Lucien walked from the dining room and out into the hall. Taking a sconce from a wall bracket, he made his way down the long, shadowy corridors. They were deserted, his footsteps echoing eerily against the walls of stone as he made his way toward the tower that housed the ducal apartments.

Past the lonely rooms that had once been Charles's.

Past the empty rooms that had once belonged to Gareth.

Past the rooms—lonely, empty, soon enough if he had any say about it—where Nerissa, even now, slept so innocently.

He paused outside her bedroom for a moment, his palm flat on the door, a poignant little smile softening his severe and unforgiving features. And then he continued on, toward the tower, steeling himself for the climb up the stairs where he had discovered his father lying all those years ago, his neck broken, his eyes glazed and staring, the tears wet upon his still warm cheeks.

It was a memory that still had the power to unnerve him. Even now, twenty years later, it was as vivid as it had been that night he'd flung himself upon his dead father, overcome with fear and anguish at finding himself suddenly and unexpectedly saddled with the weight of adulthood, the responsibility of an ancient dukedom, and, when his grieving mother had succumbed to childbed fever three days later, the care of three brothers and an infant sister.

He had been ten years old. It had been the end of his childhood, and as he had silently watched his parents' coffins interred side by side in the ancient de Montforte vault, his little weeping brothers huddled around him, his baby sister in his arms, he had vowed to his parents that he would take care of his siblings till the day he died. That he would never, never fail in his responsibilities to them.

They came before the dukedom and his obligations to it.

They always would.

He reached the top of the tower that housed the immense ducal apartments, the huge rounded bedroom walled on all sides by tall, leaded windows that commanded a superior view of the downs and valleys for miles around. The November wind whistled mournfully outside. He sent his sleepy valet off to bed and, wrapped in a robe of black silk, went to one of the windows to look out over the night. In the distance, the lights of Ravenscombe twinkled.

It was a long time before he finally retired, sliding wearily beneath the sheets of the great, medieval bed of carved English oak. He blew out the candle and stared up into the darkness above his head, listening to rain beginning to slash against the windows. In this same bed had slept every lord of Ravenscombe and, after the family had been elevated to the next echelon of the aristocracy, every duke of Blackheath. In this bed had also slept every duchess, but Lucien knew, deep in his soul, that this bed would never see *his* duchess.

He held no fear of death, of course. He never had. But he was very concerned that he might not live long enough to see his vow to his dead parents carried out—and each of his beloved siblings happily and safely married off—before dreams became reality.

You will marry her, Andrew.

Upon my life, I will see it done.

Far off in the darkness, a nightingale called. Moonlight parted the clouds and sparkled upon the ancient moat.

And high in his lofty tower, all alone in his vast, cold bed, the mighty duke of Blackheath finally closed his eyes and slept.

Chapter 9

Dawn broke along the eastern horizon in fiery bands of red, orange, and gold. The timeless, high downs glowed with it. Morning mist sparkled upon their grasses like thousands of scattered diamonds, the bare face of chalk rubble here and there marking a road or farmer's path over the majestic hills.

Andrew had not bothered going to bed. He had passed the night in the dining room where Lucien had left him, immersed in books, trying to find something, anything, that might help him understand the potion he had unwittingly created. The ruthless pursuit of answers was the only way he could focus his thoughts. Lady Celsiana Blake had been much on his mind. The impending duel had not been on it at all, and now, at daybreak, surfaced only as a minor irritation that needed to be dealt with.

Despite his toils and an absence of sleep, Andrew looked none the worse for wear. As he emerged from his apartments dressed in a loose white shirt beneath a sleeveless waistcoat, snug leather breeches that all but matched his carelessly waving auburn hair, and tight-fitting riding boots, his entire manner was one of brooding impatience and boredom. Nevertheless, he was a sight that made every maid in Blackheath's employ who was up and about her duties sigh with admiration as he strode briskly past.

Andrew, oblivious as always to the excited commotion he caused amongst members of the fairer sex, found Lucien waiting for him in the Great Hall. He was not in the least bit surprised to see that the duke, freshly shaved and elegantly turned out in black, looked as unruffled and unperturbed as ever. The sight of faint shadows, however, beneath those all-knowing, all-seeing, dark eyes took him slightly aback.

"Sleep poorly?" Andrew couldn't resist taunting, accepting his cocked hat from his valet and tucking it under his arm as the two of them headed toward the door.

"Really, Andrew. And here I was under the hopeful impression that morning would have improved your temper. . . ."

"My temper will not improve until I have ousted all annoyances, interruptions, and interferences from my life, of which this internal woman is one."

"Hmm, yes. And what happens if you are not the victor in this morning's affair? Provided you survive, you are still honor-bound to marry her."

"In which case I hope to God I lose. Anything is preferable over marriage. Even death."

Lucien only gave him a falsely pitying look as they made their way down the steps and climbed into the carriage waiting just outside. There the duke picked up the morning newspaper that lay neatly folded on the seat, opened it, and began to read as the coachman, with two liveried footmen riding behind, cracked his whip over the horses' heads.

Across from him, Andrew gazed mutinously out at the neatly clipped lawns as the coach began to move. The moat into which he and Charles had fallen from the sky in his failed flying machine sparkled in the first weak shafts of sunlight. Then they were through the gatehouse and the coach was picking up speed as it left the crenellated walls of Blackheath Castle behind.

Lucien remained buried in his newspaper.

The duke's nonchalance only irritated Andrew all the more. Leave it to his brother to calmly lose himself in a paper whilst he, Andrew, might soon be lying disemboweled in the field behind Ravenscombe's only public house.

"You have nothing to worry about," Lucien remarked from behind his newspaper. He turned a page. "It is my understanding that Somerfield can handle a sword no better than he can handle a coach and four, so do cheer up, my dear boy."

"Somerfield is the furthest thing from my mind," Andrew bit out.

"Then shall I presume that Lady Celsiana Blake is the closest thing to it?"

Andrew flushed and looked away. There was no way in hell he was going to be drawn into a conversation about *her*. Nor was he about to give his far-too-omniscient brother the satisfaction of knowing his remark was a damn sight too close to the bone. He stared sulkily out the window, not meeting Lucien's eyes, letting his body rock and sway against the leather squabs with the movements of the coach. "My annoyance has nothing to do with Lady Celsiana Blake," he snapped.

"Oh?"

Andrew's angry gaze flashed to Lucien's and met only the back of the newspaper. "It's because I cannot remember what the devil I put into that damned potion," he muttered, which was, at least in part, the truth. "I spent the entire night trying to find answers, trying to discern why the solution behaved as it did. And what did I learn? Nothing. Nil. I should have just given you the whole deuced lot of it for safekeeping instead of holding some out for further testing. Had I done so, I wouldn't be in this damned predicament." He gazed moodily out the window. "Between the fire and now this, I swear, accidental mixes of chemicals are going to be the ruination of my life."

"Perhaps, then, you should stop messing about with them."

"Like hell. I'm a man of science. I can no sooner stop messing about with chemical solutions than I can stop breathing."

Lucien said nothing, but Andrew sensed he was smiling behind his newspaper.

Down through the blunt, noble chalk hills, the coach traveled. Looking out the window as they entered the tiny village of Ravenscombe, Andrew was relieved to see that no one was about. Good. The last thing he needed this morning was a damned audience.

But his relief was short-lived.

As the coach slowed through Ravenscombe's muddy High Street, he saw people moving from behind cottage windows, running out the doors, waving . . . and all hurrying in the same direction in which they themselves were headed.

"Bloody hell," he muttered, sitting up.

Lucien lowered his paper. "Is there something wrong?"

"Yes, there's something wrong. Look outside. This was supposed to be a private affair, not a deuced sporting event."

Lucien followed his gaze. "Hmmm, yes." He went back to his paper and turned a page. "I daresay you'll have to give them a good show, then. You are a de Montforte. They would hate to be disappointed."

"How the *hell* did they find out about any of this?"

"My dear boy. Servants talk. How do you *think* they found out about it?"

Angry amber-green eyes glared into coolly unruffled black ones. Then, with a curse, Andrew sat back in the seat, quietly seething, quietly sulking. All too soon the coach pulled up at the place of rendezvous. Sighing, Lucien lowered and folded his paper, consulted his watch, and waited while the footmen opened the door and lowered the steps.

As the two brothers descended from the coach, a rousing cheer went up from the villagers, most of whom were dressed in their finest clothes, children on their shoulders, dogs barking around their heels. An air of festivity prevailed, and there were even a few vendors selling pastries and pies. The villagers surrounded the rapidly angering Andrew, bowing and scraping and wishing him God's own luck, and it was all the Defiant One could do not to turn on his heel, climb back into the coach, and return to the Castle, where he longed to lock himself away in his laboratory until the Second Coming of Christ.

He would, too. Just as soon as this infernal nonsense was over.

Glaring straight ahead, he walked beside Lucien to the field, glistening with dew, just behind the Speckled Hen Inn. The crowds followed, yelling encouragement and good wishes. There were more people gathered in the field. Too many. They milled about, several rows deep, all of them shouting, cheering, toasting Andrew's impending success.

"This is bloody preposterous!" Andrew snarled, over the noise. He glared at his brother. "Were you behind this as well?"

"My, my, you have been so full of accusations, my dear Andrew, that if Somerfield had not challenged you, I might feel compelled to do so myself. Ah. There is the earl's carriage. And I see that Dr. Highworth's gig is here as well. Shall we get on with things, then?"

"Might as well," grumbled Andrew, wishing he were back in his laboratory or putting the finishing touches on his double-compartmented coach. "I have work to do back home."

He glanced toward Somerfield's coach. His opponent was nowhere to be seen, though an old brown and white dog, its noble head bleached with hoarfrost and lying on its paws, reposed beside one of the rear wheels, blinking sleepily in the thin morning sun.

A rather effeminate young man, his eyes growing round with nervousness as he glanced up and saw not only Andrew, but the infamous duke of Blackheath approaching, stood by the door. *Must be Somerfield's second,* Andrew thought grumpily. No wonder the fellow looked petrified. He would be no match for Lucien, if it came down to it.

And then the door opened and Somerfield descended.

Except it wasn't Somerfield. It was Lady Celsiana Blake, and she was wearing a loose-fitting blouse, tight breeches molded to her long, shapely legs, and what looked like a very confident smile.

Andrew stopped as if hit by a flying wall. He had thought he was over his lung ailment. He had thought he was quite recovered. But now, as his gaze glued itself to those shockingly clad legs, the slim hips and slightly rounded rump, he found he couldn't breathe.

"I say, this is a surprise," murmured Lucien, lifting his brows and speaking for Andrew, who found, suddenly, that he could not.

"Is it?" challenged Celsie, but she was returning Andrew's stunned gaze with haughty contempt. "My brother is indisposed, and so I am fighting in his place."

"What?" cried Andrew, recovering.

She had her long, tawny, golden-brown hair in a ponytail, and this she tossed saucily over one shoulder. Hands on her hips, she met Andrew's stare. "You heard me. He is indisposed. Or, to put it more concisely, locked in his room at the Lambourn Arms with a guard stationed outside his door. On my orders, of course." She smiled sweetly. "There is no need for anyone to be risking his life on my account. After all, Gerald was not the one who was dishonored. I was."

"You can't be serious! I will not, I cannot, fight a *woman*!"

"Why not? I will, and certainly can fight, a man."

"Bugger this, I'm leaving!"

Lucien calmly reached out and caught his arm as Andrew, his temper flaring like a bonfire doused with gunpowder, spun on his heel and tried to storm back to the coach.

"Really, Andrew. It is not like you to back away from a challenge, and one delivered so prettily, as well."

"She's a goddamned *female*!"

"Hmm, yes. I can see that."

"I refuse to take part in something so completely and utterly ridiculous. I have more important things to do back in my laboratory!"

Celsie stood nearby, head held high, though she was starting to feel the same hurt, the same sinking embarrassment, she'd felt at the ball when everything had turned into a disaster. She would not let Andrew see her faltering. She would not let him see how much his rejection hurt. And it *did* hurt to be passed off so lightly. It *did* hurt, not to be taken seriously—yet again. She had thought—hoped—that he would give her all due respect by agreeing to fight her, but he was turning out to be no different from any other man. Condescending. Arrogant. Bloody-minded. She swallowed hard and raised her chin.

"So," she called loudly, making sure everyone around them could hear her brazen challenge. "You would leave, then, and humiliate not only me, but yourself, in front of all these people who have turned out to watch what otherwise promises to be quite the novel sporting match?" She gave a mocking laugh. "My oh my, how their respect for you and your family will suffer, not to mention their liking. Imagine!

A de Montforte, running away from a *woman*!"

Andrew rounded on her, fists clenched, eyes blazing. "So, inviting three hundred people to watch this debacle was your idea?"

"But of course. I wanted added insurance that you would not back out."

Nearby, the duke of Blackheath was idly rubbing his mouth, trying without success to contain a helpless smirk as he regarded Andrew's rapidly escalating plight.

"Of course, she *did* have the smallest bit of help," he allowed.

"I am not doing this," Andrew snarled. "I am *not*."

Again he turned and, bristling with fury, stormed back toward the coach. Celsie's heart fell. Murmurs of disappointment echoed all around.

She would not let him humiliate her a second time.

She waited until he was nearly back to the carriage. And then:

"For all the brains you supposedly possess, you, my lord Andrew, are naught but a coward!"

That stopped him dead in his tracks. For a moment he just stood there, seething, refusing to turn around.

"Had it been a *man* you found here today, you would not be so quick to retreat," she accused, her voice ringing out for all to hear. "But no. Because I am a woman, you deny me the respect you would have given my brother had he been here instead. Because I am a woman, you think I cannot match you over two silly strips of steel. Because I am a woman, you think I am not capable of defending my own honor. Well then, go ahead and take yourself back to your laboratory, my lord Andrew." She tossed her head, letting her contempt, her bitter disappointment, show in her eyes. "Maybe all the rumors about you are correct, after all."

Slowly he turned around. "*What* rumors?"

She smiled. "Rumors that you don't particularly *like* women," she challenged, her eyes hard with anger. "If you know what I mean."

Andrew felt every blood vessel in his head starting to throb. He felt every artery in his body constricting dangerously. And he felt what control he had left on his temper getting ready to explode.

"I should *think*," he ground out in a voice that had gone deadly soft with menace, "that my behavior toward you yesterday would dispute any such *codswallop* you might feel compelled to believe."

"Your behavior toward me yesterday is the sole reason we are both standing here"—she bowed mockingly—"my lord." She turned slightly, flashed a wide, white smile to the grumbling crowd—and came sauntering toward him. Andrew tensed. She had drawn her sword. She was not backing down. She came right up in front of him, stopping so close that he could look down and see the way her breasts pushed against her shirt, taut and firm and high, and the little valley between them. And then she lightly touched the point of her sword to his chin, forcing his gaze away from her bosom, forcing him to slowly raise his head until he looked down at her, his eyes glittering from beneath lowered lashes. "Prove to everyone *here* that the rumors are not true"—she smiled—"and that you care more for a lady's respect than you do for a lifeless jumble of chemicals, compounds, and solutions."

Andrew, the point of her sword still held firmly to his jaw, clenched his fists and shut his eyes, trying to contain his rising fury. Yes, the explosion was coming. He could feel it. God help him, he could.

And then, over by the coach, Lucien cleared his throat.

"I say," he called, black eyes gleaming. "The most *marvelous* idea has just occurred to me."

Celsie and Andrew were still locked eye to eye in glaring combat. Neither one moved.

"And what is this marvelous idea, Your Grace?" Celsie bit out, never taking her gaze from Andrew's, or the point of her sword from his chin.

"I do believe my brother just might be afraid of killing you. Or of being killed *by* you. Therefore, I propose that the two of you go ahead and fight until first blood only, for benefit of both the crowd and your ladyship's own wounded pride."

"The idea has merit," Celsie ground out.

"And furthermore, I suggest that you lend a certain gravity to what might otherwise be considered a rather frivolous matter by playing for stakes. If you win, Lady Celsie, you will never have to hear another word about marriage to this brother of mine you find so odious, ever again."

"And if *I* win?" Andrew bit out.

"Why, if you win, then you earn the right to go back to your laboratory and never be bothered by the outside world, ever again."

"Ever again."

"Ever again."

Andrew's lips curved in a slow, satisfied smile and he was seized by the absurd temptation to throw back his head and laugh like a madman. Oh, this was easy, too easy. These were the best stakes he had ever played for. All he had to do was nick her skin and no one would ever bother him, ever again? One tiny drop of blood and he would be forever left in peace?

Oh, yes. He would be a damned fool to resist such an overwhelmingly tempting offer.

Still holding her challenging stare, he calmly reached up, pushed the sword to one side, and gazed triumphantly down into those sparkling, silver-frost eyes. "Very well, then. I will fight you."

"Good." She backed off, eyes flashing. "And when I beat you, I don't want to hear any more nonsense about marriage. Is that clear?"

"Very clear. And when I beat *you*, *I* want you out of my life for good."

Chapter 10

~~~∽⌒⌒⌒~~~

Gerald, mounted on a fleet chestnut mare, galloped onto the dueling field just as his stepsister, damn her eyes, was preparing to fight.

Incensed, he sent the horse charging through the spectators, not caring whom he hurt or nearly trampled, not caring about anything but a blind need to reach the field in time to redeem himself. Not only had Celsie humiliated him by locking him up, she was stealing his only chance to permanently dispose of Lord Andrew de Montforte and remove the threat he presented to Gerald's financial well-being. Gerald just couldn't let that happen. Thank God he'd been found by his valet, who had released him.

If he could only kill Andrew in the duel, he could keep Sir Harold Bonkley in the picture as a prospective bridegroom. And if Celsie continued to refuse the baron, well, Gerald could think of a score of other desperate suitors who wouldn't mind being married off to an heiress . . . at his price, of course.

He burst through the last of the crowd.

"What are you doing here?" cried Celsie, glaring at him as he yanked the mare to an abrupt halt. "This is *my* affair and I don't need your interference!"

"You are *my* sister and therefore it is *my* duty to defend your honor. So put the sword down, Celsie. Put it down now."

"Get off my dueling field, Gerald. Get off it, and get off it *now*."

He flung himself off his horse, the indignity of having this ridiculous argument in front of not only the de Montfortes, but the entire village of Ravenscombe, sending his temper beyond control. He stormed up to his stepsister, fists clenched, teeth bared. He wanted to throttle her. "*I* was the one who challenged de Montforte. He was the one who accepted. This is *not* your fight, damn it."

"If it concerns me, it *is* my fight."

"It concerns you only insofar as you were the cause of it!"

"And I will be the finish of it!"

"The devil you will!"

Celsie stamped her foot and, with a snarl of fury, turned away, trying to rein in her temper. She might have given in. She might not. She was never to know, for at that moment, Andrew, who was watching her with a mixture of sympathy, disbelief, and—could it actually be an admiring smile, of all things?—stepped forward.

The two men bowed stiffly to each other.

"Somerfield," said Andrew coolly. "No offense, but I daresay your sister is concerned about your welfare. She has just agreed to fight for certain stakes. I propose that you and I take up the duel, but allow these stakes to remain."

"And they are?"

"First blood only," Celsie cut in. "First blood

only, and then we each win the right to be left alone."

Gerald frowned, and looked at her. "Is that all your maidenhood, your innocence, was worth, Celsie? A mere drop of blood?"

She felt herself blush. "I don't want anyone dying over me."

"And what would happen if you were to fight de Montforte here, slipped, and managed to seriously injure if not kill him?"

"Come now, Gerald. Eva herself taught me all I know about swordplay. That is highly unlikely."

Gerald's frown deepened. Around them, the villagers were starting to grow impatient.

"Fight, fight!" someone began chanting.

"Oi! I didn't get up at the crack of dawn just to see a shoutin' match!"

"Get on with it!"

Sensing defeat, Celsie turned and stormed back to the sidelines, where the duke of Blackheath waited. He was smiling, his arms folded loosely over his chest. The sight of him made Celsie all the angrier. How unlike him to stay out of things. And how like him to find amusement in the plights of others!

"Pity," he murmured, watching as Gerald gave his horse into the care of a villager and the two opponents prepared to fight. "I daresay I would have enjoyed watching you give my brother a run for his money."

"I would have won," she said mutinously, unable to forgive him for the way he had treated both her and Andrew in the library. "I would have won, because he would not have taken me seriously enough to give me a *real* fight, would he?"

"I think he takes you very seriously indeed, madam. He would not be here if he did not."

Celsie ground her teeth and looked away.

"You do realize, my dear, that if you had only consented to marry him, we all could have stayed abed this morning?"

"I am *not* marrying him. The subject is closed."

"Hmm. Yes. I suppose it is. . . . And now I must beg your pardon." He bowed and pulled out an elegant silk handkerchief. "It appears the fight is about to get under way. A second has his duties, you know."

"Don't let him hurt him," she ground out, trying not to sound as desperate as she suddenly felt.

"Don't let who hurt whom?"

"Andrew. Don't let him hurt my brother."

He inclined his head and walked away. Celsie's heartbeat began to quicken, and she felt the muscles in her back starting to clench, nausea seizing her stomach.

Of course I'm worried about Gerald. But oh, Lord . . . I could never live with myself if something happened to Andrew. It is my fault that things have come to this. Maybe I'm the one who ought to be fighting Gerald.

Oh, this was getting more and more ridiculous.

And she was feeling more and more sick.

She sat down on the grass and plucked a gone-to-seed dandelion, twirling its stem between thumb and forefinger, taking deep breaths to try and calm herself even as a nervous film of perspiration broke out all down her back. *Don't think about the duel,* she told herself. *Don't think about the fact that someone might get hurt. Instead, think about the animal shel-*

ter you plan to open in Windsor next week. Think about the classes you've scheduled for the village children on proper pet care and management. Think about the turnspits, and how you'd buy up every one in England if only it would save them. . . .

A charged hush had fallen over the crowd. She heard Lucien's smooth, urbane voice reciting the rules of dueling. She heard him calling for first blood only—*thank God*. And as she sat there, bravely watching this horrible affair and beginning to shake with unexplained terror, Freckles ambled up beside her and sat down, leaning his body into hers.

She pulled him close, taking comfort from his presence. "Oh, Freck, I can't believe such foolishness has come to this!"

"En garde!"

The fight began.

Celsie wanted to cover her eyes. She wanted to run back to her carriage and drive until she reached the end of nowhere. Around her, the villagers began shouting, cheering, yelling encouragement.

She didn't want to look.

She couldn't *not* look.

The two men circled each other, each trying to maneuver the other so the sun was in his eyes. Andrew moved with an easy, dangerous grace that caused Celsie's heart to catch in admiration. Gerald was clearly nervous. Neither man was smiling.

Gerald broke first. He charged forward, lunging hard, and in that moment Celsie knew that he was fighting for more than just first blood.

He was fighting to kill.

Horror filled her. She leaped to her feet and would have run forward, but no, that would be foolish, that would be fatal, she could not, would not, dared not break either man's concentration. Again Gerald attacked, and Andrew, grinning, expertly parried his thrust, moving easily and looking as if he was relishing what must be, to him, nothing more than a little early morning exercise. He was toying with Gerald, that much was obvious, though only Celsie's—and surely the duke's—trained eye recognized it. Gerald certainly didn't. So desperate was he to score a fatal hit, he was unaware that his opponent was drawing the fight out, allowing him to salvage his pride and retain his dignity. Celsie's heart swelled with gratitude for Andrew's noble gesture, and though her hands were so tightly gripped they were going numb, she tried to relax.

To simply watch the movements of a master swordsman.

To almost be thankful for the fact that she remained on the sidelines, not needing to concentrate, with nothing else to do but admire what was indeed a very splendid, agile, and breathtaking male body in action . . .

A very splendid, agile, and breathtaking male body that had, only hours ago, made her a woman.

Steel rang against steel. Rapiers flashed in the sunlight, carved arcs in the air. The tip of Andrew's sword caught Gerald's sleeve, slicing it from cuff to elbow, though no blood appeared, and Celsie knew, with mounting awe, that Andrew hadn't intended there to be any. Not yet. *Oh, bless him!* Gerald made a clumsy charge. Again Andrew neatly sidestepped it, his own blade singing in to tear a matching slice in Gerald's other sleeve. He began to maneuver Gerald into the sunlight . . . prepared to deal the coup de grâce . . . and suddenly staggered back, the sword falling from his hand, his staring gaze fixed somewhere in the tree branches overhead.

"Andrew!" Celsie screamed, thinking he'd been hit—

And then all hell broke loose.

"Cheat!" cried Gerald. "You knew I was winning and thought to turn the tables by faking an injury, you cowardly wretch!"

Everything happened at once. Andrew, still staring up into the trees, sank down on one knee. Gerald lunged forward, ready to drive his blade straight through his heart.

And then Lucien was there.

Celsie never knew how the duke moved so fast, or just how he managed to snatch up Andrew's blade from the ground and deflect Gerald's killing blow with a ringing clash that nearly broke her stepbrother's sword in two. Gerald paled and staggered back, his eyes bulging with terror. Never, never, had she seen such murderous fury on anyone's face as she saw on Blackheath's.

And unlike Andrew, Blackheath wasn't toying.

He was going to kill Gerald. And he was going to take a savage enjoyment out of doing it.

"No!" screamed Celsie, running headlong onto the dueling field. "Don't kill him! He's no match for you and you know it!"

The duke ignored her.

Andrew was shaking his head, getting to his feet, his face paling with alarm as he realized what was happening.

And Blackheath—cold, ruthless, vengeful Blackheath—was smiling a thin little smile that made Celsie's blood turn to ice as he circled her brother.

Celsie hurled herself between them, her sleeve catching Gerald's sword and ripping a bloody swath across her arm.

"Stop it!" she screamed. "Stop it, Blackheath! Spare Gerald and I swear to God I'll marry your brother!"

Chapter 11

*H*e had known.

In that heartbeat of an instant, as time seemed to stop and all eyes turned to her, Celsie felt her world sway sickeningly. *God help me, Blackheath knew all along that I would sacrifice myself to save Gerald's worthless hide. He knew it. He was counting on it. Why else did he not slay Gerald immediately?*

He was waiting for me to rush in and save him!

A roaring started in her ears. Some three hundred people were all staring at her. Gerald, pale and shaken, looked like he wanted to murder her. The duke's cold black eyes were triumphant. While Andrew . . .

She couldn't read his expression. And it was so terrible that she didn't even want to try.

The field of spectators began to revolve slowly around her. The clamor in her ears rose, drowning out the hum of voices, becoming as one with the roaring. Celsie, shaking, turned away, her head high. She briefly shut her eyes so she could not see her world spinning, and bravely, determinedly, began the long walk back toward her carriage.

Please, God, don't let me faint in front of every-one—

But God didn't seem to be looking out for her today.

For at that moment, she happened to catch sight of her sleeve, upon which a very red, very bright, very gruesome blotch of her own blood was seeping through the bleached linen. She staggered. Swayed dizzily—

"Celsiana, are you all right?"

And heard Andrew's voice, seeming to come from very far away, though he was only a few steps behind her, running to catch up.

"Celsie?"

"I think I am going to swoon," she managed in a little voice, and the last thing she felt before darkness claimed her was his strong arms catching her before she could hit the ground.

As indeed they did.

For a moment, Andrew stood in surprise, for he hadn't thought that the mettlesome Lady Celsiana Blake was the sort of woman given to fits of the vapors. But then, he really couldn't blame her. Subjected to the near-slaughter of her brother, a sudden and unwanted betrothal, and worst of all, the knowledge that her prospective bridegroom was something of a freak, it was no wonder she had lost her senses.

He felt a flash of sympathy. Of protectiveness. And then he happened to glance up and see Lucien approaching with his sword, and all tenderness exploded into fury.

"An heiress," the duke murmured benignly. He slid Andrew's blade back into its sheath. "Well,

well. I always knew you'd make an advantageous match. Shall we post the banns?"

Andrew's reply caused the blood to drain from the faces of several nearby spectators, for nobody dared speak to His Grace the duke of Blackheath like that. Lucien, however, only raised an amused brow. "Such language," he chided, not blinking an eye as a red-faced Somerfield galloped past, beating as hasty a retreat as his horse could give him. "Really, Andrew, why don't you set the girl down? Not only are you making everyone think you *enjoy* holding her, but I have a feeling she will be none too pleased to find herself in your arms when she awakens."

"And why don't *you* wipe that satisfied smirk off your face before I do it *for* you?" Andrew seethed through clenched teeth.

"Now, now," the duke murmured, letting the smirk remain. "That is no way to speak to the man who just saved your life."

"You're right. Speaking to you is the last thing I feel like doing."

He turned and headed toward the coach, holding Celsiana close to his chest and feeling oddly, disturbingly, protective of her.

"Off to procure a special license, are you? Ah. No wonder you're in such a hurry. . . ."

Andrew was so angry he thought his head might explode. "I am taking her away. From everyone. From *you*. She's going to be upset enough as it is, without waking up to a crowd of strangers gawking at her and offering felicitations on her upcoming nuptials." He glared at Lucien, thinking it was a good thing his arms were occupied, because otherwise Lucien wouldn't be looking quite so smug.

"You're a complete and utter sod. A despicable bastard. A contemptible, soulless monster. I hope you're damned proud of yourself."

"For saving your life? Hmm, yes. I don't think 'proud' is the right word. . . ."

Andrew snarled a curse and kept walking.

Beside him, Lucien reached into the inside pocket of his coat and pulled out a flask. "Very well then, go. But at least take this. I think both of you could use a little sustenance."

"What is it?"

"Brandy. I brought it in the unlikely event you sustained a wound and needed bracing up, but it appears to have found a much better use."

Cradling Celsie in one arm, Andrew snatched the flask from his brother's hand and shoved it into the side pocket of his waistcoat. And then he spun on his heel and strode toward the coach, angry with Lucien, angry with fate, angry that now everyone in Ravenscombe—let alone the woman in his arms—must know there was something more than a little peculiar about him. . . .

Bloody hell. At least her desperate declaration to marry him had distracted people from his own unfortunate plight. He had that to thank her for, at least.

Not that he intended to, of course. The less attention he called to himself, the better.

He put Celsie on the seat and climbed up behind her. Then he took her in his arms, slammed the door, and pounded a fist on the roof. "Drive on!" he ordered harshly.

"But His Grace—"

"His Grace be double damned, *I said drive on!*"

"Where to, my lord?"

"Anywhere. Just get us out of here, and *now*."

The coach jerked and began to move, showing Andrew a sea of faces just outside the window as it wheeled through a wide turn. Irritably he yanked the shade shut. The team broke into a canter and moments later the well-sprung vehicle was hurtling out of Ravenscombe.

On the seat, Andrew held his burden and stared straight ahead, his jaw hard, his heart pounding with a cacophony of emotions, all of them turbulent, none of them pleasant. He would not look down at her. *He would not.* No matter how easy it would be to steal a glance at that splendid bosom without her ever knowing. No matter how much he wanted to run his gaze—and his hands—up and down those long, shapely legs so sinfully wrapped in a man's riding breeches. No matter how much the very thought, let alone the possibility, of either caused his manhood to harden against the taut little bottom that lay so innocently pressed against it.

It was a fight that even the Defiant One could not win. Mutinously he glanced down—and found himself looking into a pair of wide, silvery-green eyes that were staring dazedly up into his.

"Thank you," she murmured.

"For what?"

"Taking me out of there." She closed her eyes, her nape resting on the hard curve of his forearm, her ponytail spilling across his thigh, the seat. "I've never fainted before in my life. How humiliating . . . and to do it in front of several hundred people . . ."

Andrew said nothing. He knew all about how it felt to be humiliated in front of several hundred people.

"Are you all right now?" he asked gruffly.

"Yes. No. Oh, I don't know. . . . Things happened so quickly, my head is still spinning."

"Yes, well, yours isn't the only one."

He was angry, and Celsie knew he had every right to be. Beneath the back of her neck and head, his arm felt like a bar of steel. He was staring out the window, his gaze flinty and hard. His jaw was clenched. She could hear his heart beating beneath her ear. She could feel his chest rising and falling with each breath that he took. And she knew that she ought to get up and move to the other seat. In another minute or so, when she felt a little steadier, she would.

"Andrew—"

He stiffened beneath her. "Yes?" he snapped.

"What happened to you out there?"

"Somerfield nearly killed me, Lucien nearly killed Somerfield, and you threw yourself into the fray as some sort of sacrifice on the altar of our mutual freedom, that's what happened."

"I'm not talking about that."

"Then I don't know what the devil you *are* talking about, except that whatever it is, I *don't* want to talk about it, is that clear?"

"No, it's not." She searched his face, undaunted by his anger. "I just don't understand any of this . . . such as why you fell out there on the field in the first place. One moment you were toying with Gerald, allowing him his pride and dignity, and the next, you were—"

"Nothing happened," he said savagely.

"But—"

"I said, *nothing happened.*"

"It looked like he must have hit you, stunned you, when I wasn't looking. Except I *was* looking—I mean, I couldn't help but look. Is that what happened, Andrew? Did he stun you with the hilt of the sword or something?"

"Yes, that's exactly what happened, so now that we've got that clear, let's talk about something else, all right? Better yet, let's not talk about anything at all. I'm sick of talking. Just leave me alone."

His abrupt and angry dismissal stung. Reality began to press in on Celsie like frozen hands thawing after a snowball fight. Except it wasn't her fingers that were thawing. It was her head. Her heart. *Oh dear God, what have I done?* She had just committed herself to marrying this man, that was what she'd done. She had just ruined both his life and her own. And as the layers of protective shock faded, her emotions surfaced: disbelief, guilt, grief, anger, humiliation, denial; they were all there. She wanted to curl up into a little ball and shut everything out. She wanted to run away and never stop until she reached the ends of the earth. She wanted Freckles. What she *didn't* want was marriage to this man. To any man.

So why did the bitterness in his eyes, his all-too-obvious resentment, hurt so much?

"Andrew," she said tentatively, "I know you're angry, but just because I said I'd marry you doesn't mean you have to marry *me*."

"And how do you think that will make me look in front of three hundred witnesses, eh?"

"I wouldn't have thought you cared."

"Well, I do care. Besides, my brother obviously wants this marriage, and it's quite clear to me now that he's been wanting it from the moment we met at the ball, if not before. Now that he's got what he wanted, don't think he won't blackmail us both if either of us tries to back out."

"He has nothing with which to blackmail me."

"Oh? Do you mean being found on the floor with me in the final throes of passion isn't enough?"

Celsie blushed. "He wouldn't . . ."

"Trust me, madam, he *would*. And as for me, all he has to do is say one word to the right people and my chances of getting into the Royal Society are ruined. I can't risk the scandal, and if you want to continue to move in high circles so that you can beg the plight of your precious dogs, neither can you."

Celsie pressed her lips together in rising anger. He was the most impossible man, equally given to flashes of temper and random gestures of kindness. Just when she was starting to warm up to him, he turned on her like a badly bred cur. She was getting tired of his short, one-word answers, his ill manners, his brusque treatment. She knew he was capable of being nice; she'd seen glimpses of it in his laboratory, when she had taken an interest in his work and he'd shown her the drawings. *That* Andrew was a whole lot easier to handle than this hostile, bad-tempered, bristling one. *That* Andrew was actually quite pleasant and engaging. This one . . . She knew German guard dogs with better temperaments.

"There has got to be a way out of this predicament," she said. "If you're going to sit there and sulk, at least do something. You're the intellectual here. Why don't you put that superior brain of yours to work, sir, and engineer a plan to save us both from a fate that neither of us wants?"

"I can assure you, madam, that I have been putting

my so-called superior brain to work on that very problem since we entered the coach, and so far it has yielded nothing of value."

"Ah. So you can design flying machines and double-compartmented coaches and write complicated mathematical formulas that no one but yourself could ever hope to understand, but you cannot out-maneuver your brother."

"That is because it is far easier to design flying machines and write complicated mathematical formulas than it is to outmaneuver my brother."

"So you think he's somehow behind all this, then."

"Don't you?" he fumed, nailing her with a look of hard fury.

Of course she did. The look on the duke's face right after she had thrown herself between him and Gerald had removed all doubt from her mind that he was behind it. Oh, what a mess this was! If Andrew, with all his intelligence and years of dealing with Lucien, couldn't figure a way out of this dilemma, how on earth was she going to do it?

"Andrew—"

"Look, I said I just want to be left alone, all right?"

"You don't have to be so hateful. And I'm sorry I interfered with the duel, but I had to save Gerald. Had it been *your* brother whose life was in peril, you would have done the same."

"Depends on which brother," he bit out, his eyes hard as he glared out the window.

That did it. Celsie wasn't going to lie there against him a second longer. She started to push herself up on one hand, only to freeze on a hiss of pain. She looked down and saw the bloody sleeve where Gerald's blade had caught her, a sleeve previously hidden beneath the angle of her body against Andrew's own.

Andrew saw it too. "Devil take it," he muttered, pushing her back down onto his lap. "Let me see that."

She snatched her arm away, covering the wound with her hand so she couldn't see it and risk fainting all over again. "No."

"Does it hurt?"

"It does now that I've been reminded of it."

"Here, let me see it."

"Your concern is quite touching, but if you don't mind, I would prefer to have a qualified surgeon look at it, not a mad inventor."

"And *I* would prefer that you leave the 'mad' out of your estimation of me, madam," he snapped, on a fresh wave of unprecedented anger. "I may not have had any formal training in the healing arts, but I can assure you that bandaging your arm is well within my capabilities."

"You're not a doctor."

"I am a doctor. Just not of medicine."

"Of what, then?"

"Philosophy."

"Oh, well, that's helpful, isn't it?"

"Celsiana, let me see your arm. *Now*."

"Oh, very well, then," she muttered, uncovering her arm and looking away so she couldn't see how bad it was. "Though what you intend to use as a bandage is beyond me."

His hands were far more gentle than his tone of

voice as he caught the ripped edge of her sleeve. "Hold still."

With one sharp jerk, he tore the shirt from elbow to cuff. Celsie, who was beginning to wonder if she was squeamish about seeing her own blood, refused to look at the exposed wound. Instead, she gazed up at his face, grave now as he gave his attention to her arm, and tried to take her mind off what he was doing. Looking at his face made it very *easy* to take her mind off what he was doing. Did he have that same intense, focused look when he was inventing something brilliant? Did he give that same single-minded concentration to everything he did? And oh, what would it feel like to have that powerful concentration fully directed on *her*?

In the bedroom?

Now, where on earth had that *thought come from?*

Suddenly flustered, she forced herself to think of her arm instead. He may not be a surgeon, but he went about his task in a confident, no-nonsense sort of way that was wonderfully reassuring. His hands were warm where they steadied her arm, his touch gentle but firm. All too soon he was wrapping the makeshift bandage around the wound, snugging it comfortably, reassuringly, tight. His thumb holding the ends in place, he neatly tied them off, leaving her feeling strangely bereft as he finally relinquished her arm.

"Thank you," she said, sitting up a bit and rubbing her arm through the bandage. "It feels better already."

"Keep it clean and I doubt you'll even see a scar from it."

His gaze met hers, and something warm and undefinable passed between them. Celsie flushed, a jolt of current leaping through her, its heat settling in her very bones even as Andrew stiffened. They both looked away at the same time, and Celsie decided that it was long since time she got up and removed herself to the safety of the other seat.

She slid gingerly off his lap and took the seat across from him. The space around her felt cold. Empty.

The emotions welled up in her heart again. She wrapped her fingers together and squeezed, hard, trying to divert the sudden sting of unshed tears. Out of the corner of her eye she could see Andrew, who had lapsed back into sullen silence, his gaze, like hers, redirected out the window.

Reality was bad enough. But God help her, this punishing silence, this awkwardness, was downright unbearable.

"Where are we going?" she finally asked.

He kept his gaze directed out the window. "Where would you like to go?"

"Anywhere, except back there. What about you?"

"Anywhere, except the altar."

"You really *don't* want to marry me, do you?"

"No, I don't."

"Which proves that you really *don't* want me for my money."

"No offense, madam, but I really don't want you at all."

Though Celsie didn't want to marry him either, no woman wanted to be rejected so bluntly, especially when the one doing the rejecting was without doubt one of the handsomest men in all of England. "Well, I can't blame you there," she said breezily, though there was a hard edge to her voice that she couldn't quite conceal. "I suppose the idea of marrying an heiress must be quite appealing, but even a fortune could never make up for the fact that you'd have a wife with no tits."

His head snapped around. "I *beg* your pardon?"

"You heard me. I know you men all like to compare attributes and acquisitions, and my diminutive chest would be a constant source of embarrassment to you, to be sure."

"Your language, madam, leaves much to be desired."

"So does my chest, if most men's opinions are to be believed."

He flushed angrily. "I could care less about most men's opinions. And for what it's worth, I happen to think you are most prettily endowed."

"And you expect me to believe you?"

"And why the blazes wouldn't you believe me?"

"I know what men say about me."

"Do you, now?"

"I do. And I am utterly convinced that I do not measure up, if you know what I mean."

"No, I do not know what you mean, and I can assure you right now, madam, that the absurd subject which we are currently discussing has no bearing whatsoever on my reluctance to take you to the altar."

"Oh, so you're afraid of choking on a pea, then."

"I am *not* afraid of choking on a pea. I do not even *like* peas. What I *do* like is the complete freedom to live my life as I please, without feminine encumbrances of any sort, be they mistresses, admirers, or, God forbid, wives. I have work to do."

She met his gaze, glare for glare. "Well, *I* have work to do, too. I have a network of shelters throughout Berkshire that need constant upkeep, funding, and attention so they can continue to take in unwanted animals. I'm fighting for the turnspits. I have instituted a program to teach the young people in my village how to properly care for their dogs and cats so they learn that animals are for *life,* just like children, and are *not* expendable objects to be given away, killed, or otherwise disposed of simply because they've had an accident on the floor or are no longer as cute as they were when they were puppies and kittens. Like you, I do not need encumbrances of any sort. So you see, Andrew, *I* have no wish to get married, either."

He stared at her.

"Besides," she continued, "I have yet to find a man who loves dogs as much as I do, who would not only condone but assist me in my efforts to help them, and would also let them sleep on the bed."

He shrugged. "I let Esmerelda sleep on my bed."

"You *do?*"

"Yes," he said impatiently. "What's so extraordinary about that?"

She stared at him, his candid admission defusing some of her anger. "Nothing, except that you are the first man I've ever met to admit to such a thing. Maybe marriage to you will be tolerable, after all."

"You'll be miserable, I can guarantee it. As would any woman with the misfortune to be tied to me."

"What compels you to say such a thing?"

"The fact that I can think of no female who would willingly and uncomplainingly share her husband with his obsessive pursuit of science."

"Well, I can think of no man who would willingly and uncomplainingly share his bed with his wife's dog, so I guess we're even."

He just looked at her, an odd expression in his eye. "Very funny."

"Well, I thought so," she returned, pleased that she'd managed to break the ice a little between them. "Oh, Andrew. What are we going to do?"

"I don't know." He sighed and leaned his brow into his hand, rubbing it as though he was infinitely tired. "We could always quit the country in order to avoid this deuced marriage. France ... America ... no, neither is far enough away from Lucien. By God, the Arctic is beginning to look quite attractive."

"Yes, but you have to admit, it would be an awfully cold place to build a new laboratory."

He lifted his head and looked at her. Again something warm and unexpected leaped between them, but this time he didn't turn away. Didn't chase it off with anger. And as he held her gaze, he began to smile, and Celsie saw, for the first time, that this fiery, bad-tempered man actually had a charm that was quite lethal when he chose to display it.

She looked down at her tightly clenched hands, confused by the sudden jumble of feelings bouncing around in her heart.

"Maybe you'd better take me back now," she said, a little shakily. "I need to get Freckles."

"Celsiana."

Her gaze flashed to his. "Yes?"

"I'm sorry, too. I ... just want you to know that I'm not angry with you, but with fate."

"Thank you."

"And that it's not marriage to *you* that I'm upset

about, but the idea of it in general." He cleared his throat. "You have an uncommon amount of courage. It's hard not to admire it."

She looked up. "For a woman, you mean?"

"For anyone." His eyes were warm. "I want you to know that."

He reached into his pocket then and extracted a small flask. "We'll find a way out of this. Somehow, someway." He uncorked the top of the flask, and the strong fumes of brandy assailed her nose. "In the meantime, I propose a toast."

"To what?"

He smiled, but his eyes were hard and determined. "To outsmarting my Machiavellian brother."

Chapter 12

He offered her the metal flask, still warm from his palm. Celsie took it. She wasn't particularly fond of brandy, so she had only the tiniest of sips. But it was a toast to which she was all too happy to drink. She handed the flask back. He tipped the vessel, draining it.

Their gazes met, coconspirators, allies, on a mutual smile.

And a moment later, it hit her.

Oh, no. Not again!

"Andrew—"

He must have felt it too, because at the same moment he shot to his feet, rapping his head on the roof and cursing loudly. "Hell and damnation! That cursed spawn of the *devil*!"

It was the same thing all over again. The same warm languor spreading through her blood. The same desperate longing to get her hands on this man, under his clothes, on his skin, all *over* his skin. The same prurient, unfulfilled tingling in her breasts and between her thighs . . .

Oh, no.

Oh, yes.

Oh, God!

She flattened herself against the back of the seat, willing herself not to touch him. "For heaven's sake, Andrew, this isn't just brandy, it's—"

"The goddamned potion!" he roared, throwing himself back down in his own seat and twisting his face against the leather squab so he couldn't see her. His eyes were open, glazed, as surely her own must be. She saw his fists clenching and unclenching desperately. She saw the fine sheen of dampness breaking out across his brow, along his jaw and neck, and heard the almost inhuman howl of rage that tore from his anguished throat.

"I'll kill him, so help me God, this time he's gone too far!"

"I don't understand—"

"Lucien was the one who gave me the brandy! *He bloody drugged it!*"

He made a desperate lunge for the door, ready to hurl himself out of the coach at high speed if only to keep his brother from having the last laugh, but his knee caught the edge of Celsie's seat and he fell, heavily. Celsie was never to know whether he grabbed for her shoulders as he went down, or she grabbed for his in an attempt to catch him. It didn't matter. In the next moment, his mouth, hard and angry all over again, was slanting toward hers.

And then he kissed her.

She had never been kissed so thoroughly, so hungrily, so aggressively, in her life. Oh, she'd had the occasional chaste peck from fortune hunters posing as admirers; she'd had cold, sloppy kisses from the pea-plagued Lord Hammond and found puppies' tongues to be drier; and she'd had no cause, based on her own wanting experiences, to think there was anything more to be had from kissing a man than some vastly unpleasant sensations they had all seemed to enjoy far more than she.

But this . . .

She melted under the delicious sensation of his hard, powerful body all but crushing her down against the seat. She felt his hand yanking her shirt free from the waistband of her breeches and sliding up her abdomen beneath the light fabric, his other hand cradling her cheek, holding her head right where he wanted it, his thumb slowly brushing her mouth as his lips drove hungrily against hers. There was nothing cold, wet, or sloppy about the way Lord Andrew kissed; there was nothing chaste about it, either. He knew exactly what he wanted and he knew exactly how to go about getting it, and what he wanted was to put his tongue into her mouth and his hand beneath her shirt and then all over her suddenly sensitive, suddenly on-fire, suddenly very eager and happy-to-be-noticed breast.

Celsie let him.

She moaned deep in her throat as he caught the nipple between thumb and forefinger and gently rolled it. And all the while his tongue thrust against her own, his mouth crushed hers, his harsh, quickening breath glancing off her cheek and a jutting hardness pushing against the top of her thigh.

Celsie, gasping, finally broke the kiss. She stared dazedly up at him.

"My God," he said, breathing hard. "I'm not going to survive this."

"And neither am I, unless you kiss me again."

"This is ridiculous, I hardly know you, I hardly

like you, I want to do all sorts of sinfully wicked
things to you and I can't seem to control myself—"

"I hope you don't even try."

"I don't *want* to try . . . Lord save us, Celsie. I
need to touch you. I need to kiss you."

His lips were against her temple, feathering down
the outside corner of her eye, his breath warm
against her chin. She shuddered, feeling herself go
liquid with answering heat even as her own arms
went around him and her fingers explored the hard
ridge of his shoulders, his nape, the silky queue of
his hair. She didn't know whether to be thankful or
despairing that she'd only had the tiniest sip of the
brandy . . . thankful because she didn't feel drugged
as she had the last time, despairing because she'd
had just enough to take the edge off any inclination
she might otherwise have had to shove him away
from her and straight out of the carriage.

Andrew, on the other hand, had finished off the
entire bottle.

His mouth found hers yet again, needy, desperate.
How warm his lips were against her own . . . how
good he smelled, like some exotic spice from a faraway land . . . and how wonderful his hand felt, driving through her hair, thumbing the velvety skin
behind her ear, tracing the rise of her cheekbone,
while his other hand—

She moaned into his mouth as his hand roved
over, then cupped, her breast.

Her small, insignificant breast, which he would
surely find wanting.

"Andrew . . . you're touching my—my—"

"Breasts? Ah, yes. So I am. I quite like touching

them, you know. They're high and firm and fill my hand quite nicely. Very nice. Very nice indeed . . ."

"You don't find them . . . wanting?"

"I do find them wanting. They want my hands all over them. They want my mouth all over them. They want my tongue and teeth and kisses all over them. God, you're gorgeous. . . ."

He leaned down, his glossy, dark auburn hair filling her field of vision, his breath hot against her bosom and making her heart skip and trip and tumble all over itself as it fought frantically to retain its beat. And then he caught her shirttails in his hands and pulled the garment over her head, leaving her naked from the waist up.

His mouth drove into the faint cleft between her breasts, out over the high, pale rise of the right one. The sensation was enough to make her head dizzy with pleasure.

"A-Andrew, what are you doing?"

"I am kissing your breasts."

"But I thought kisses are for lips!"

"Kisses are for wherever one chooses to put them. And I choose to put mine here . . . and here. . . ."

He was now suckling the fiercely erect nipple, causing Celsie to gasp and squirm and tangle her fingers in his hair in an attempt to find anchorage on a sea of feelings that were totally overwhelming her. *Oh, don't fight it. He's not going to stop. You don't want him to stop. Sit back and enjoy it . . . oh, enjoy it, this is never going to happen again!*

His hand skimmed down her waist, moved out over the soft buckskin of her breeches where they covered her mound, and drove itself between her thighs, forcing them apart.

"And here is another place that quite likes to be kissed," he murmured, rubbing her cleft through the breeches. "Another place where I shall quite enjoy putting my lips. My mouth. My tongue."

"There? H-how can you even think such a thing?"

The coach thundered on, its rocking movement causing her body to scrape against his, his hand to vibrate against her intimate flesh, and heightening the wild, prickly-hot sensations he was creating in her.

"I will do more than just think it." He leaned close, so close she could see the starbursts of green that radiated out from his rust-colored irises, so close that the heat of his gaze drove right through her and impaled her with its intensity. "Let me tell you something, my dear Celsiana. Aphrodisiac or not, I have been wanting to peel these breeches off you from the moment you stepped out of the carriage. I have been wanting to touch those long, silky thighs, to trace the curve of your bottom, to slip my hand between your legs and feel you hot and wet with desire for me for the last agonizing *hour*."

God help her, she was hot and wet with desire already; she could feel the moisture dampening her breeches, knew he felt it against his hand, and knew she ought to be mortified. But how could she be mortified when heat was rising from every pore in her skin, burning every blood vessel in her body, making her head feverish with longing? She gazed, fascinated, up into his intense eyes and felt her leg, bent at the knee, sag back against the squab; her other slid downward, off the seat, the ball of her foot just resting on the floorboards and leaving her wide-open to his questing fingers. . . .

"And I have been wanting to strip you naked and take you on the floor of this coach from the moment we entered it," he said roughly. "There is nothing you can say or do that will curb my desire for you. I want you. I need you. And I will have you."

He bent his head, tasting her nipple once more, drawing it with a taut, ruthless pull into the hot cavern of his mouth even as his hand rubbed her through the breeches, hard, over and over again.

"Oh," Celsie said faintly, sinking back into the seat and closing her eyes as her bones and muscles went liquid. "And here I thought you weren't interested in women . . . that the only thing you cared about was your science. . . ."

"I am interested in you. I just don't want to marry you. Nothing personal, of course," he murmured, the deep reverberations of his voice against her breast, her nipple, both tickling and exciting. "I don't want to marry anyone."

"If marriage means getting to do *this* every day, then maybe it's not such a terrible thing after all," she breathed, watching him through half-lowered lashes as his tongue lazily circled her areola, the nipple in its center as hard as a dog's toenail. "If you married me, Andrew, could we do this every day?"

"Every day and every night."

"But we're not going to get married."

"No. We are going to outsmart Lucien."

"Yes. Outsmart Lucien . . ."

"And make love." She gasped as he deftly unbuttoned her breeches and slid his fingers beneath the warm buckskin to find her silken mound. *"Now."*

"Yes. Now . . ."

His hands caught the waistband of her breeches in

unspoken command. Through the fabric she could feel the warmth of his palms against her hips, the strength of his hands against her thighs. Celsie lifted her bottom from the seat, and slowly, agonizingly, he pulled the soft buckskin down her thighs, pushing them down to her knees and exposing her long white legs—and everything else—to his appraising gaze.

He stared. His eyelids drooped. His breathing changed, and when he looked up at her, she saw that the little striations in his fiery eyes had become very, very green.

"No—keep them open," he said harshly, thrusting his hand between her thighs like a blade when she would have closed them in forgotten modesty. "I want to look at you."

"I swear, I can *feel* your eyes upon me."

"Can you? You'll soon be feeling more than just my eyes upon you."

His gaze burned into hers for another moment, and then he looked back down at her, and stayed looking at her, and every place his gaze touched seemed to burn with a savage, unrequited longing.

Still looking his fill, he dragged his hand higher, his fingertips skirting the soft triangular tuft of hair. Celsie tensed. His hand was big and warm against her belly, and she looked down to see the palm spread out over the alabaster skin, the tip of one finger just nestled within the top edge of her silken curls. He let his hand remain there for a long moment, warming her, tantalizing her, then let it slide downward, his forefinger driving between her cleft and stroking a hidden button of tingling, needle-hot flesh once, twice, three times.

Celsie jumped, then moaned deep in her throat.

"I see that my hypothesis is correct," he murmured, smiling.

"Your . . . hypothesis?"

"Yes. I hypothesized that you would be hot and wet and ready for me. You are."

"It's embarrassing."

He was still stroking her with the tip of his forefinger. "It's flattering."

"It's beyond my control."

"It's making me hard. So hard that I ache."

She flushed and, as he continued that slow, maddening stroke, heard strange little whimperings coming from her throat, bringing his intense gaze back to her face. His hand paused, becoming rigid against her. "What is wrong, Celsiana? Yesterday you were a tigress. Today you are a kitten. Am I the only one who is going out of my mind with need?"

"No . . . but you're the one who drank the whole damned bottle of laced brandy. I only had a sip. Just enough to keep me from saying no . . ."

"If you want me to stop, I'm afraid you'll have to bodily throw me out of this carriage."

"I don't want you to stop," she managed, opening her eyes to stare fixedly up into his face.

"Then if you have any fears, qualms, or misgivings, you have only to voice them and I will soothe them to the best of my abilities."

"I have no fears. After all"—she faltered, feeling a sudden pain in her heart—"I am no longer a maiden, am I?"

He sobered. His gaze softened, and for a moment, he was the Andrew she had only glimpsed, the one who had gently stroked his dog's head, the one who had respected her on the dueling field, the one who had warily joked with her a few moments ago, the one who was usually gaoled behind the bars of anger and rudeness. "As I expect you do not remember much, if anything, of what occurred between us yesterday, I'll have you know, Celsie, that I still consider you a maiden in all senses of the word except one."

Celsie. He had called her Celsie. Something hitched inside her heart.

"And I shall contrive to treat you as gently as a maiden deserves to be treated."

So he said. And all the while, she could feel the hard, flat blade of his hand thrust against her dampening cleft, the thumb lazily caressing the silky hair there and igniting the whole area into something hot and twitchy and wanting. She wanted his hand to touch her even more intimately, though she could not think how that would be possible. She wanted his thumb to move slightly more toward the very center of these oh-so-strange, oh-so-delightful feelings. And she wanted—

The coach hit a bumpy section of road, and Celsie, still gazing up into Andrew's smoldering eyes, gasped as the jerky movement of the coach caused his hand, which he himself hadn't moved, to begin agitating her exposed, already aroused flesh.

"Oh!" she cried, her mouth falling open, her blood frying in her veins as she saw the wicked gleam in his eyes.

"A rather singular sensation, is it not?"

"You—how could you know?"

"I know a lot of things about your body, madam, that you have yet to learn. And I also know that in a few moments, this road is going to change to chalk rubble for a good mile or two, and then your senses are *really* going to explode when these iron-clad wheels go vibrating over it."

"Will it feel . . . good?"

"Oh, yes," he said, chuckling darkly. "It will feel *very* good."

God help her, she felt good *now*. She felt good as her lover knelt down on the floor of the coach, stretched her out on the seat, and began kissing the still warm spot on her belly where his broad palm had so recently rested. And she felt very good as his tongue, drawing little circles on the taut, electrified skin there, began moving closer and closer toward where his hand, shuddering rapidly with the movement of the coach, still lay, his fingers stroking her, his thumb pushing hard against that hot button of sensation.

Celsie whimpered and moaned, her head twisting on the seat, a strange, wonderful sensation building inside her like a horse gathering itself for a titanic hurdle. . . .

"You may not remember all that happened between us yesterday, madam," he breathed, his lips now seeking the outermost curls of her femininity, "but I guarantee you shall never forget what's about to happen between us now."

One hand on her breast, the other holding her legs apart, his hot mouth dragged through her curls and planted itself with hard, unrelenting firmness *there*.

Celsie cried out—and at that moment the coach hit the chalk rubble that he had heralded, making the vehicle, making her body, making Andrew's tongue as it plunged and dipped within her moist folds, shudder with a rapid, unceasing crescendo of agitation.

"Oh, God!" cried Celsie, gasping.

He raised his head the merest of inches. *"Faster,"* he shouted to the driver above.

"Oh—oh, you fiend!" wailed Celsie, as the coach picked up speed, and so did the maddening agitation that was repeated in every cell in her body, in Andrew's mouth as he opened it wide against her shamelessly wet cleft once more, in his stiffened tongue as it pressed against that hidden button of flesh there, licking, stroking, the rumble of the chalk beneath the wheels rapidly agitating it beyond anything Celsie was physically capable of enduring.

"Oh, please—oh please, oh please," she sobbed, her fingernails clawing at the seat.

"Faster!"

The escalating rumble of the wheels, rapidly shaking everything inside the coach like the onset of an earthquake, was too much. Celsie came against him with a harsh, rending cry, her body arching straight off the seat, his tongue never retreating but only pressing harder, deeper—

"Oh, oh God and the devil *help* me!" she screamed, flailing in the seat, writhing against his tongue, her hair whipping wildly back and forth as she climaxed once more. And then, just when she thought she would die, he drew back, thrust his fingers, vibrating with the shudder of wheels over rubble, deep inside her, and watched her senses explode yet a third time.

She was still convulsing when he climbed on top of her, opened his breeches, and drove himself into her, hard, thrusting over and over again until he finally reached his own satisfaction.

And on the box above, the driver never heard a thing.

Chapter 13

B y the time Gerald reached his room at the Lambourn Arms, his terror had abated and self-disgust sat in his gut like an undigested bone. He galloped up to the stables, handed his winded horse to an ostler, and stalked into the taproom.

A glass of hard whiskey calmed him. A second fortified him. A third managed to restore some of the courage that His Grace the duke of Blackheath had so easily stripped him of, and halfway through his fourth, Gerald was on his way back out to the stables.

He would deal with the duke. He would make him see reason, make him see how unsuitable his brother was for Celsie.

He would make sure this marriage would *not* go through.

Moments later, he was in the saddle once again, wheeling his already exhausted mare and sending her thundering toward Blackheath Castle. Gerald had his doubts that the duke would even receive him. The duke did—but arrogantly kept him waiting in the Great Hall for a full forty minutes, which was enough to infuriate Gerald all over again.

Presently a footman came for him.

"His Grace will see your lordship in the library now," said the servant, bowing. "If you will just follow me."

Gerald found his nemesis standing before a wall of bookcases, idly perusing an old leather tome. The duke had changed his clothes, but was still dressed in black, or rather a deep, inky-blue velvet that, on his lean and dangerous frame, was somehow even more sinister. His back was turned, his manner unhurried. He took his time replacing the book, then turned, a cold, terrible smile just touching his mouth, and his eyes as warm as a cobra's.

"Ah, Somerfield. I have been expecting you. Do sit down. I would offer you some refreshment, but I am not feeling particularly well disposed toward you this morning." Again that chilling, unpleasant smile. "I trust that you understand why, under the circumstances."

He reached for the decanter to pour a drink for himself, but Gerald, who wanted to get this business over with, wasted no time in pleasantries. He glared at the duke's handsome profile, severe, aristocratic, a nearly unbroken line from nose to backswept brow, and said rudely, "I cannot permit Celsiana to marry your brother."

Blackheath never faltered. Never allowed even the faintest suggestion of a reaction to mar his expression. Nonchalantly watching the sherry splash into the crystal goblet, he said, "Well, that is indeed unfortunate, as I am in favor of the union."

"In favor of it? Are you mad, man?"

"Mad?" Black ice glittered in the duke's eyes as he calmly raised his glass to his lips. "I can assure you, I am quite sane. In fact, I find myself wondering if you, Somerfield, are the mad one."

Gerald, fortified with liquor, bristled. "I don't know what you mean."

"Don't you? Yesterday you challenged my brother to a duel because he refused to offer for the lady's hand. This morning your cowardly and pathetic attempt on his life nearly cost you your own. And now here you are again, protesting the impending nuptials. My patience with you, Somerfield, is dangerously short. I should think you'd have had more sense than to come here spouting nonsense that will do nothing but strain it all the more."

Gerald's hand shook; he wished he had another drink.

"I am willing to pretend that this morning's little *incident* was the product of your overwrought passions, Somerfield. I am even willing to pretend a certain civility toward you for the sake of my soon-to-be sister-in-law. But what I cannot pretend is to even try to understand why you suddenly find Andrew unsuitable, when yesterday you wanted him to do right by Celsiana. Quite a sudden change of mind, no?"

"It wasn't a change of mind, I was simply caught off guard yesterday by what even *you* will admit were shocking circumstances. Celsie is supposed to wed Sir Harold Bonkley, and if she marries your brother instead, it will make both Bonkley and me the laughingstocks of polite Society."

"I fail to understand why a marriage between the two will be so detrimental to what"—again that deadly smile—"*dignity* you and Bonkley possess."

"At the ball the other night—we told everyone

who matters that Bonkley and Celsie were as good
as betrothed!"

"Then you are foolish as well as cowardly."

"I demand that you do everything within your
power to put an end to this lunacy!"

The duke lifted one black brow and put down his
glass. "You *demand*?"

Gerald sputtered and flushed crimson.

"My dear Somerfield," Lucien continued
smoothly. "I can assure you that I have no intention
of putting an end to it whatsoever, as I happen to
think our siblings are very well suited." He brushed
a speck of lint off his sleeve and turned his stare,
which had gone very black, and very wintry, on his
guest. "Surely you don't find my brother wanting,
do you?"

Gerald felt his guts seize up. He did not know
Lucien well, but something on an animal level of
instinct warned him that he was treading on dangerous, if not deadly, ground. Too much whiskey, however, made him reckless.

"Damn right I do! He's aloof. He's arrogant. He's
obsessed with crackbrained inventions and love po-
tions, which proves that he's not only strange, but a
pervert. In short, Blackheath, he will make my sister
miserable. He has no prospects for an admirable ca-
reer or future, and he has nothing whatsoever to offer
Celsie. Absolutely nothing."

The duke regarded him for a long, uncomfortable,
unblinking moment. Gerald felt dread tingling up his
spine. His palms began to sweat.

"And do you think that this Bonkley, whose name
I can hardly utter without pitying his poor bride, will
make your sister any happier than my brother

might?" murmured Blackheath in a dangerously soft tone.

"He, at least, has—has prospects!"

"Does he, now? Pray, enlighten me."

Gerald opened his mouth, and then shut it. Sir Harold Bonkley had nothing over Lord Andrew de Montforte, and both of them knew it.

Blackheath gazed at him for a moment longer, and then, with a long-suffering sigh, returned his attention to his sherry. "D'you know, Somerfield, I am beginning to suspect that your real complaint with my brother has nothing to do with the fact he compromised your sister, but that he is not, shall we say"—he held up his glass, examining the golden depths—"malleable."

"What?"

The duke turned his head and flatly met Gerald's gaze. "Not malleable to your wishes, that is. I'm afraid my brother has always done, and will always do, exactly as he pleases. You will not bend him to your will."

"I don't know what the devil you're talking about."

"Don't you? Ah, but I think you do. It does not escape my notice that you would quite like to see your sister married to Sir Harold so you can control him, and thus your sister's fortune."

"I *beg* your pardon?" cried Gerald, outraged.

The duke's smile was studied politeness, but the black eyes were dangerously cold, flat, and deadly. "It is no great secret, my dear Somerfield, that your sister allows you to live at Rosebriar because you have nowhere else to go. And it is no great secret that you have amassed a rather considerable number of gaming debts and now find yourself without the means to make good on them. Of course, a union between Sir Harold and your sister offers the perfect solution to your little dilemma, does it not?"

Gerald spluttered. "How dare you, sir!"

"I dare quite a lot. It is a particular defect in my character—or so I'm told." Smiling faintly, the duke went back to nonchalantly studying his sherry. "Really, Somerfield, if you are so desperate to get your hands on a fortune, maybe you should consider marrying an heiress yourself and have done with the matter."

"You insult me, sir!"

"A thousand apologies," Blackheath murmured. "Perhaps the fact that your sister usurped you on the dueling field this morning has left you feeling a bit deprived? We can rectify that, you know. I can assure you that I wouldn't mind getting up at dawn tomorrow at all"—he turned his head, smiling blandly as he met Gerald's gaze—"if you understand my meaning."

Gerald felt the blood drain from his face. Involuntarily he took a step backward, sliding a finger beneath his stock and preferring to let the challenge go unanswered. "So you will do nothing to stop this unseemly union, then."

"On the contrary, my good man, I will do all in my power to ensure that it is made."

"Then I have nothing more to say to you," Gerald said, and turning on his heel, stalked from the library.

Lady Nerissa de Montforte was in her apartments, tending to her morning correspondence over a leisurely cup of chocolate, when a brief knock on the door signaled the presence of her eldest brother.

"Ah, Nerissa," said Lucien, wearing that self-satisfied smile she had long since come to know and dread. "I am delighted to find you at your letters. You may wish to write both Charles and Gareth, I think, notifying our dear brothers of the impending wedding."

"What wedding?" asked Nerissa, confused.

"Why, Andrew's, of course."

"Andrew's?"

"Surely you didn't think I would allow him to remain a bachelor until his hair goes gray, did you?"

"Andrew's getting married?"

Lucien stroked his chin contemplatively. "Yes, and imminently, I should think."

Nerissa surged to her feet, her correspondence forgotten. "Lucien, what have you done?"

"My dear sister, *I* didn't do anything. While dueling with Somerfield, Andrew had one of his . . . episodes. Somerfield was about to kill him, so I stepped in, and the fair Lady Celsiana Blake threw herself between us, begging me to spare her brother's worthless life."

"And did you?"

"Yes, but only for a price."

Nerissa's blue eyes narrowed. *"What* price?"

"Why, marriage to Andrew, of course. Oh, don't look at me like that, my dear. It is all for his own good, as well as the girl's. Lady Celsiana Blake is going to make him very happy indeed. Though, of course, he doesn't quite realize that yet . . ."

"I cannot believe I'm hearing this. Andrew is the last person on earth who should be married, who wants to be married, who will benefit by being married."

"On the contrary, Nerissa, marriage will do him good."

"Lucien, how *could* you do this to him?"

"My dear Nerissa, I have already told you. He did it himself."

"Oh, and I suppose that *you* didn't have something up your sleeve at the ball the other night when you set Lady Celsiana on him by telling her he was experimenting on animals and then making Andrew believe your action was anything but innocent?"

Lucien merely smiled.

"And I suppose your having the servant bring poor Celsiana to Andrew's apartments while he was not only still abed, but in a state of shocking undress, was also *innocent*? You go too far, Lucien!"

"It will be a superb match. Andrew will thank me for it someday, and so will the lady who is destined to be his wife. He is quite smitten with her already, though I daresay he'll never admit it. She is quite smitten with *him* already, though I daresay she'll never admit it, either. But ah, the eyes tell all. . . . 'Twas a good thing there was steel between the two of them this morning, otherwise I fear our two lovers might have caused quite an embarrassing scene, and in front of the entire village of Ravenscombe, too."

"Steel between *them* this morning? Entire village of Ravenscombe? I thought dueling was a private affair! I thought Andrew was to fight a duel with that odious man Somerfield, not his sister!"

"Well, that was the plan, but the situation went a bit . . . awry."

"How?"

"Why, the lady locked up her own brother and arrived in his place. It would have been injurious to both her and Andrew's honor had he not agreed to fight her. Oh, don't look so appalled, my dear. Somerfield managed to free himself and arrived just in time to take his rightful place on the dueling field. It was only when he attempted to murder Andrew that I thought it timely to intervene." He smiled, obviously pleased with himself. "Celsiana herself declared that she would marry our brother if only I would spare hers."

"Oh, dear God . . ."

"It all happened rather quickly. . . . I daresay the lady is as unconventional in her behavior as our brother is in his. But ah, the look on Andrew's face when she, instead of Somerfield, stepped down from the carriage . . . it was beyond priceless. Our poor brother didn't even have time to recover from his shock before she was insisting that he fight her."

"She didn't!"

"She most certainly did."

"And did he?"

"He most certainly did."

"Oh, Lucien!"

"Have no fear, Nerissa. She may very well be an accomplished swordswoman, though she could not, of course, have hoped to match Andrew in skill or strength. Still, I thought it prudent to suggest that the two of them fight till first blood only . . . though Somerfield was determined to fight for far more than that when he reclaimed his place on the dueling field."

"Oh, dear God . . ."

Nerissa, recovering, took a deep, bracing sigh and

faced her brother. Everything was falling into place. "So you would have killed Somerfield knowing his sister would do anything to save him."

"But of course."

"And *you* were doubtless the one who arranged for the whole village to turn out, so that you'd have plenty of witnesses for whatever manipulation you had planned."

"And why not? They see so little in the way of entertainment. . . ."

Nerissa, tight-lipped and angry, pushed back from her desk. "Lucien, what you have done is not only upsetting, but totally incomprehensible. Why? *Why?* Though I do not condone your actions, I can understand your tricking Gareth into marrying Juliet so that her baby could have its proper name; I can understand your giving Charles the push he needed to offer for Amy when his confidence was at an all-time low; but this—this is heinous! It is cruel sport indeed! Andrew is a dreamer, a loner . . . *different*! He doesn't need a wife! He doesn't want to get married! He simply wants to be left alone!"

"So he has informed me. But what's done is done, I'm afraid," said Lucien, looking anything but contrite.

"And I suppose the next life you're planning to *manage* is mine?"

"Only if you don't do a good job of managing it yourself."

Nerissa swept up her letters and slammed her chair back against her desk. "Do you know something? I hope that someday, after you've schemed and manipulated all of our lives to your liking, you'll get a taste of your own medicine. That some woman will bring you to your knees. Because when that happens, I'm going to be the first one in line to celebrate your long-overdue downfall!"

Real amusement shone in Lucien's black eyes. "I can assure you, my dear, that it will never happen."

"Ohhhhhh! You are insufferable!" Nerissa snapped, and turning on her heel, marched from the rooms.

Lucien remained where he was, waiting for her angry footsteps to diminish before he allowed his smile to fade. From far away a door slammed, and he let out a sigh of infinite weariness as he picked up her discarded pen and replaced it in its holder.

Contrary to Nerissa's hopes, no woman would ever bring the duke of Blackheath to his knees.

His time, as he well knew, was running out.

Chapter 14

The carriage was halfway to London.

The effects of the aphrodisiac had long since worn off, leaving only an awkward and very uncomfortable silence in its wake—and no small degree of mutual resentment toward he who had given it to them. Andrew brooded in his seat, one arm outstretched across its back, refusing to look at Celsiana as he chewed his bottom lip in private, sullen contemplation.

Opposite him, Celsie, mortified by her recent wanton behavior, sat with the rigidity of a setter on point, her legs clamped together, her arms tightly crossed, her gaze directed out the window.

The silence continued.

Seemed to stretch into forever.

Presently Andrew decided he'd had enough. If she didn't want to speak to him, fine. He didn't particularly want to speak to her, either. Thinking to shut out both the awkwardness and this woman who was proving to be the ruination of his life, he reached into the pocket of his waistcoat, extracted a notebook and pencil, and, balancing the latter on one drawn-up knee, began to sketch out plans for an idea that had been tormenting him ever since it had taken root in his mind an hour earlier.

He should have known, though, that problems could not be shut out. Especially one whose name was Woman. And typical of her kind, she chose the exact moment he tried to involve himself in something else to break the unbearable silence between them.

"I'm sorry," she stammered, leaving unspoken the subject of her apology. "I—I was not myself. . . ."

"Yes, well, I'm sorry too."

He kept on sketching, not wanting to discuss the particulars of their recent behavior, trying to find escape and normalcy in the familiarity of his work.

But that wasn't going to happen.

"What is that?"

"A notebook," he replied, without looking up.

"I can see that. What are you doing?"

"Sketching."

"Sketching what?"

"I don't know yet. I haven't given it a name."

"May I see?"

Andrew tightened his lips. Was she just feigning interest in his work in order to ease the tension, to make conversation when neither knew what to say to the other? Probably.

He ignored her and tried to focus on his drawing.

"Andrew, may I see the sketch?"

He sighed. Any pleasure he might have taken in her curiosity was outweighed by his impatience with her constant interruptions when he was trying to think. Not that he *could* think, with her sitting just opposite him. Not that he *could* think with the memory of possessing her lovely, long-legged body still burning a hole in his concentration. God help him, all he really wanted to do was take her back in his arms and make love to her all over again, this time slowly, sweetly, and without a chemical catalyst.

What the devil was wrong with him? Had he been holed up in his laboratory for so long that he was willing to bed even this woman who irritated him like a thorn between stocking and skin? He sure as hell didn't want to marry her. Marry her! Bloody hell. Union with *her* would be anything but peaceful. Anything but conducive to his dreams and designs. Stony-faced, he turned the notebook face-out so that she could see his crude sketch.

"Well—that's . . . interesting." Her brows drew together in confusion. "What is it?"

"An improved spring system to make carriages more comfortable. I intend for it to absorb some of the bumps"—his gaze bored flatly into hers—"and *vibrations* from the road."

Her chin snapped up and bright stains of color appeared in her cheeks. "It was the aphrodisiac, you know," she said, as Andrew bent his head and continued sketching. "I would never have behaved like that under normal circumstances."

"A pity, that."

"A pity?"

He kept on sketching. "If I'm going to be saddled with you for a wife, I should hate it if the only way into your bed is by way of a potion."

"And if I'm going to be saddled with you for a husband, my bed is off limits to you anyhow, so you might as well stop thinking about it."

"Ah, yes. I had forgotten. You prefer the company of dogs, don't you?"

"That remark was uncalled-for and you know it."

He kept on sketching, feeling the angry weight of her gaze upon him, feeling a great churning emotion boiling up inside him. He had never felt so trapped in his life. So hopelessly outmaneuvered, so bitterly manipulated. He was going to kill Lucien with his bare hands. He was.

"Besides," she added, "there is no way I'd allow you into my bed unless my feelings change, and the way you're treating me, that is *not* going to happen unless you invent another brilliant potion, this one to create artificial love."

"Ah, so artificial lust is not enough, eh? You must have love as well? Hmm. Artificial love. Perhaps that will be my next project."

"The only project you ought to be working on is finding a way out of what looks to be an inevitable marriage destined straight for the pits of hell. And furthermore, I do wish you would stop sketching for a moment. I'm talking to you."

"And I'm talking to you."

"It would be nice to have your attention while we're carrying on this conversation."

"You have my attention."

"I don't have all of it."

He lifted his gaze, quite nonchalantly, and let it settle on her. "There. You have my complete attention."

"It *was* the aphrodisiac," she repeated, lifting her chin.

"Madam, I suggest you forget the damned aphrodisiac and its consequences. What's done is done. If we can't find a way out of this damnable marriage, we can at least work on making our lives tolerable within it. You'll go your way, I'll go mine, and we can count ourselves fortunate if we don't run into each other more than once a month."

"That doesn't sound like a tolerable marriage to me."

"No?"

She bent her head and found a sudden interest in the button that held her cuff closed. "It sounds like a lonely one. It sounds like you're going to hole yourself up in your laboratory and shut both me and the world out and never go anywhere with me, never do anything." She shrugged, a little, fluttering, embarrassed gesture that showed an odd and unexpected vulnerability. Her voice dropped, and her interest in the button seemed to intensify. "If we're to be married, I'd at least like to see you once in a while."

"Why?"

"Why?" she repeated, looking up at him as though he possessed the intellect of a five-year-old. "Because husbands and wives are supposed to spend time together. Because even though we shall have a marriage of convenience—"

"You mean a marriage of contrivance."

"Convenience, contrivance, no matter what you choose to call it, the fact remains that we could come to at least *like* each other, given half a chance, and people who like each other usually enjoy being together."

"I see. So you think we could end up liking each other."

"Well, we can certainly try to at least be nice to each other," she said sullenly, bending her head and fiddling with the button once more. "I know you're angry with the duke, and you know I'm angry with him as well. Putting the aphrodisiac in the brandy was nothing short of diabolical. Thanks to him, you and I got off to a bad start. Thanks to him, we've been nothing more than puppets in his hand. Of course we're angry—we have every right to be"— she looked up at him then, her eyes almost pleading—"but do we have to take it out on each other?"

Andrew swallowed and looked away, out the window.

"The least we could do is try to get along," she continued plaintively. "Neither one of us wants this marriage, but if we put our heads together and try to find a way of preventing it, we'll accomplish far more than sniping at each other. And if we're nice to each other, I should think it a natural course of events that liking comes next."

"And then this absurd thing called *love*?" he drawled.

She met his flat stare with equal resolve. "Not if you continue to behave like a bear with a toothache."

"Sorry," he muttered, his eyes hard as he looked out the window once more. "I might manage *liking*, but love is beyond my comprehension."

"It is beyond mine as well, but it can happen, even in a marriage of convenience."

"Contrivance."

"Whatever."

He leaned back, pulled his sword from his scabbard just enough to sharpen his pencil on it, and resumed sketching. His emotions were unstable. He didn't want to like her. He didn't want her to like him. He just wanted her to stay away from him— nothing more.

And yet why, when she lowered her defenses as she was doing now, and got all nice to him even though he was doing his damnedest to push her away, did he feel a softening toward her that terrified him?

A . . . liking?

"I just want to make one thing clear," he muttered, his attention on the sketchbook. As he watched, the pencil, seemingly of its own accord, sketched a crude rendering of Lucien. "I don't want to be married, and I don't want to share my life with anyone." The pencil was drawing a sword now—a sword swinging in an arc toward Lucien's neck. "I don't want you coming into my laboratory when I'm working. I don't want you asking me questions when I'm trying to think, bothering me when I'm trying to design. I just want to be left alone. It's bad enough that I'm going to be saddled with a wife I don't want, but one who fully intends to make demands on my time will be nothing short of unbearable. I have work to do, so don't expect that I'm going to escort you to balls, parties, dances, the opera, and all that other rot that I have no use for."

She blinked and stared at him, obviously taken aback. He saw the stains of angry color in her cheeks. Saw the way her face seemed to go taut, and sure enough, her eyes were more silver than green, a clear indication that he was pushing her past her level of patience.

But she smiled.

It was an icy, strained gesture, but damn her, she smiled.

"Do we have an understanding?" he asked mildly.

"No. We do not. Because I have some demands of my own."

"Do you, now? Let me guess. Dog in the bed, dog at the table—"

"This isn't about dogs, it's about *us*. It would be nice if we could make appearances in Society as a married couple, instead of you holing yourself up in your laboratory all the time, which is what I suspect you intend to do."

"You are very intuitive, as that is exactly what I intend to do."

"You know, you're *proof* of why dogs are so much better than men! They, at least, don't mock the idea of love, and they give it freely, uncomplainingly, and unconditionally. They have nothing more important in their lives than their humans. They love you till the day they die. And they, at least, *want* to spend time with you!"

"I can assure you, madam, that I am quite happy to spend time with you—preferably in your bed, where I can assure you that I will make you far happier than even your precious Freckles could ever dream of doing."

There was no green left in her eyes. "You're sick."

"Undoubtedly."

"And you'd better understand right now that I'm not kicking Freckles out of my bed for *you*. If you won't leave your laboratory to make room in your life for me, then I'm not making Freckles leave my bed to make room in it for you."

"Then in that case, I hope your bed is a large one so that it can accommodate the two most important males in your life."

"And I hope *you* can accommodate my wishes that we go out in Society once in a while!"

"Sorry, I don't care for social events. They're boring."

"They don't have to be. Why, we can dance. We can socialize. We can try to get people to take kindness to animals seriously."

Andrew was sketching again. A decapitated Lucien was lying on the ground now, another sword sticking through his heart. "I would prefer to stay home," he murmured, scribbling. "However, you are quite free to attend as many of these excruciatingly thrilling events as you wish."

"Fine, then. I will."

"Good."

The awkward silence was back, this time worse than it had been before. Andrew went back to his sketch—but the fire behind his original idea was gone, his savage delight in making an effigy of Lucien had vanished, and now only lifeless, empty lines looked back at him. *Sod this,* he thought, tossing the sketchbook aside. Now, on top of everything else, he felt guilty for deliberately hurting her feelings. His guilt fed his anger, and his anger, the ever-present fear about his condition and the eventuality that it would be discovered.

He stole a glance at his companion, who was back to staring out the window once more. She had a lovely profile. A nose that made him want to kiss it. Lips that—Bloody hell, what the deuce did she want out of him, anyhow? She knew he didn't want a wife. He had thought she had wanted to go her own way as much as he did his. And now she wanted to spend time with him, to foster a friendship, to drag him out into Society, where it was all too likely that he would have another *episode* and people would finally know the truth about him. He wiped a hand over his face. If that happened, his science would never be taken seriously by his peers. If that happened, he would be laughed right out of the Royal Society before he even managed to get into it.

"I can see this isn't going to be easy," she muttered, still gazing out the window with a hopeless, sad expression on her face.

That expression was fatal to Andrew's anger. It was so much easier to shove her away when they were arguing. But this bald expression of hurt . . .

He just couldn't stand it.

"I'm sorry," he said gruffly. "I am an unpleasant creature. Not very good company for you or anyone else."

"I'm sorry, too. You deliberately baited me and I snapped it up like a beagle would a bone."

She turned her head then. Their gazes met. Her mouth curved in a fleeting, apologetic smile—and then her gaze dropped, only to land on the sketchbook on the seat.

She frowned. Andrew tensed. And then she reached out, picked it up, and studied Andrew's rendering of his decapitated brother, the headless corpse with a sword through the heart, the drops of blood running from the ragged neck.

Andrew bit his lip, not knowing what her reaction was going to be. Disgust? Anger? Horror?

It wasn't what he expected.

Laughter.

A burst of it escaped her mouth, only to be quickly muffled by her hand. She kept her hand there and looked up at him, her eyes dancing with mirth.

Andrew felt the corners of his own eyes crinkling.

She took her hand away then, and began to giggle. Andrew grinned and reclaimed the sketchbook. And this time, when their gazes met, neither looked away.

Chapter 15

~~~~⟶⟨⟩⟵~~~~

A ndrew and Celsie weren't the only ones who felt like killing the duke of Blackheath.

Gerald, along with his valet and Celsie's dog, reached Rosebriar late that evening. Gerald's temper had cooled somewhat, though anger still simmered just beneath the surface. He could think now, instead of just react. And think, he did.

Blackheath, damn his eyes, had hit upon the truth: Gerald had nothing against Lord Andrew de Montforte personally, as a bridegroom for Celsie, save for the fact that he couldn't control the Defiant One the way he knew he could control Bonkley and a score of other men he could think of.

So as far as Gerald's bailing himself out of debt was concerned, that was a problem.

He didn't know whom he despised more: the arrogant duke of Blackheath, whose wishes were only one rung down the ladder from God's; the duke's bat-brained brother for creating the love potion that had stolen Celsie right from out of his grasp; or Celsie herself for refusing to lend Gerald any more money than she'd already done. She was a selfish, ungrateful bitch, no better than her whoring mama.

And now he could hear barking coming from the kennels outside, could see Freckles standing next to his water bowl, empty and dry, and looking up at Gerald in quiet expectation. Gerald ignored the old dog. He hated its sorrowful eyes. Hated the claim it had on Celsie's life. Bloody hell, his sister cared more for these stupid beasts than she did her own brother. She was willing to pour all her time, energy, and money into them, but she wouldn't lift a finger to pay off his debts.

He despised the de Montfortes, Celsie, even his own father, who'd promptly lost all interest in his only son the moment he'd met and married Celsie's beautiful mama, worshipping her until the discovery of her in bed with another man had broken his heart and hastened an untimely end. 'Sdeath, he felt as though the entire world were against him.

Just as he knew every creditor on earth was banging on his door back in London. Good thing he could hide here for a while, though after he'd tried to kill Andrew this morning, it was a certainty that Celsie would throw him out when she returned.

He couldn't escape debtor's prison forever. He needed blunt, and plenty of it, and if he couldn't get it from Celsie one way or another, he was going to have to find it from somewhere else.

He left the hall and went outside, needing fresh air, needing to think. Freckles, abandoning his dry water bowl, followed painfully, but sore and tired and unable to keep up with Gerald's long stride, soon fell behind. The earl didn't bother to wait for the old dog. He was sick of dogs. Sick of everything.

It was as he strode out past Celsie's neglected rose gardens that a snippet of the conversation he'd had with His Arrogance the duke of Blackheath came filtering back to him. . . .

Really, Somerfield, if you are desperate to get your hands on a fortune, perhaps you should consider marrying an heiress yourself and have done with the matter.

Gerald stopped in midstride.

By God, that was it. That was the answer.

Marry an heiress himself!

Of course, he had to find one first. And far more challenging, he had to make her fall in love with him enough to want to marry a penniless earl with a less-than-sterling reputation and a penchant for the gaming tables.

But how?

He stared down at one of the garden's last roses, blooming bravely in the moonlight despite the fact that any time now, it might wither beneath the season's first hard frost. *That aphrodisiac. I have* got *to get my hands on that aphrodisiac.*

An impossibility, of course.

And then he thought of Eva.

By mutual consent, Andrew and Celsie had decided to go to London, to give themselves time to think—away from their families and the troubles they'd left behind. By the time the coach finally pulled up before the elegant wrought-iron gates of de Montforte House, the moon was a soaring beacon that lit up the night sky.

Andrew, shivering in his sleeveless waistcoat, had spent most of the trip in silence. He had wanted to be alone with his thoughts, alone with his problems. The slight softening he felt toward Celsiana was both

welcome and somewhat worrying. He was determined to keep her at arm's length—but she had
found a chink in his armor. Truth be told, he was
much happier being friendly with her than antago-
nistic. Even now, looking at her on the opposite seat,
dozing peacefully beneath the lap rug he'd put over
her after she'd fallen asleep, he felt a sharp pang of
tenderness in his heart. He didn't like being so rude
and abrupt to her—but it was necessary. He couldn't
let her get close to him.

He had too much to lose.

And now the coach had stopped. It was time to
get out.

"Celsie."

She didn't move.

Andrew leaned forward and touched her shoulder.
"Celsie, wake up. We're here."

She made a faint, unintelligible sound, pulled the
short blanket up around her shoulders, and didn't
move any further.

The door opened and a footman let down the
stairs. Andrew didn't quite know what to do—so he
did the only thing he could do.

He stood as best he could, slid his arms beneath
Celsie's sleeping body, and lifting her from the seat,
stepped down from the coach.

She was tall for a woman, but she was all legs,
her bones light, her weight insignificant. She fit easily in his arms. He liked the feel of her there. He
liked the way that, in her half sleep, she nestled her
cheek against his chest, one palm placed trustingly
against his heart. Again he felt that curious stab of
tenderness. Aware that the footman was standing

there trying to remain inconspicuous, Andrew turned and carried her into the house.

Issuing commands to the servants for food, hot baths, and rooms to be made ready, he bore his sleepy burden up the stairs. He would not, of course, remain with her. He had no intention of sleeping with her. He would stay as far away from her as possible.

Reaching the top of the stairs, he turned and carried her into his rooms, thinking that would be the best place for her until morning when they could sort this sordid mess out.

She opened sleepy eyes as he shut the door behind her and laid her on the bed. Immediately wariness came into them when she saw where he had put her.

"Relax, I'm not going to touch you," he said gruffly.

"Where are we?"

"London. De Montforte House. You're in my bed, but have no fear, I have no intention of staying." He drew back, away from her, giving her privacy and space. "A maid will be up shortly with some supper, and they're already preparing water for a hot bath. Good night."

She sat up. "Where are you going?"

"I, madam, am exhausted. I'm going elsewhere, and there, after supper and a bath, I'm going to bed."

"Oh."

He turned, irritably, and looked at her. She was still on the bed, though obviously uncomfortable about being seen in such an intimate place. She still had the lap rug, clutching it rather tightly around her shoulders. She looked unhappy. Confused. And heartrendingly vulnerable. The tender feeling she aroused in him irritated him.

"Now what?" he asked impatiently.

She sighed and ignored his curtness. "This isn't right. I have a town house here in London, too. I think I'd better go there instead. . . ."

For some reason, his peevishness increased. "Fine, then. Go."

"Yes. I think that would be for the best." She flashed him a look he couldn't quite decipher and started to get off the bed. He noticed that she kept her eyes down, away from him, as though the experiences of the past two days had sent her beyond mortification. Her cheeks were pink. He would not feel sorry for her. He would not. She kept the lap rug tightly shut around her.

"You can take our coach," Andrew said.

"Thank you."

"Maybe we can meet in the morning over breakfast." He turned away from her, feeling oddly bereft, oddly betrayed, oddly confused over why he was feeling suddenly angry with her all over again. "We, uh, need to discuss how we can get out of this devilish predicament."

"Yes. What time should I call?"

"Whenever."

She raised her gaze then, and met his. "I'll make it around noontime, then. I know you're a late sleeper."

"Trust me, madam, I don't expect to be getting much sleep tonight."

She nodded in understanding. He bowed to her, and she turned and walked out of the room, leaving him standing there alone. Andrew's palms went damp. His heart turned into a racehorse. He hailed her, almost desperately. "Wait."

She turned, the look in her eyes almost hopeful, but no, he was imagining it.

"You can take one of my greatcoats if you want," he offered. "You wouldn't want anyone to see you wearing"—he jerked his chin to indicate her breeches and stockings, just visible beneath the short blanket—"that."

"Thank you," she said, slipping off the woolen throw and putting it across the back of a chair. He went to the wardrobe, retrieved a heavy woolen coat, and gently settled it around her shoulders, letting his fingers linger longer than they should as he adjusted it.

"There." He swallowed and drew back, rather reluctantly. "Until tomorrow, Lady Celsiana."

"Until tomorrow, Lord Andrew."

There was an expression in her eyes that he couldn't quite read. Something like sadness. Or hurt. He couldn't quite discern which. He didn't *want* to discern which. He had to get this woman out of the house, out of his life, before his anger broke down even more.

He turned away so he wouldn't have to see her disappear, when something outside the tall window that looked down on the street caught his eye. His curiosity aroused, he took a few steps toward it and froze.

"Dear God . . ."

The street was glowing with an eerie amber light, but where the cobbles should have been, there was only a broad, flat ribbon of gray bracketed by lines of bright yellow and white. Strange, frightening noises filled his head. Strange, frightening lights dazzled his eyes. Andrew stared, the hair on the back of his neck rising. Holding his breath, too afraid to move, he slowly raised his gaze, trying to locate the source of the eerie light . . . and saw that the full moon, riding so high above the city, was repeated over and over and over again the length of the street, in a perfect, unbroken line of amber moons all glowing down on the scene beneath him.

He shut his eyes and gripped the sill of the window, his knees shaking, and when he opened them a heartbeat later, everything was as it should be.

Only one bright moon, riding high in the night sky above. Cobbles, over which the iron wheels of carriages, gigs, and coaches were rumbling and rattling. Smart-stepping horses, pedestrians on foot, a dog sniffing around in a gutter.

And Celsiana, who had come up behind him and put a concerned hand on his arm.

"Andrew?"

He gave his head a good shake, as though he could shake away the madness, as though he could forget all those amber moons that had been lined up above the street just a moment ago. "Did you see it?" he asked harshly.

"See what?" She went to the window, frowned, and turned concerned eyes on him. "Andrew, are you all right?"

"Yes, yes, I'm fine," he snapped, turning on his heel. He was trembling. He ground the heels of his hands into his eyes, wanting only to flee before he ended up telling her of the strange moons and lights he'd just seen outside that very same window.

Before he ended up telling her that he was going mad.

But she was there, her hands gripping his rigid forearms. She pulled them down, dragging his fists away from his face, seeing the panic in his eyes. Her gaze was dark with concern. He shut his eyes as she palmed his forehead. "You're ill. You're sweating. You're as white as the tip of a beagle's tail."

"Celsie, leave me alone. Go away. Go away, *now*."

"I will, after I make sure you're all right."

"For God's sake, woman—"

Her grip around his wrist was fierce as she dragged him away from the window and back toward the bed. "Stop acting like a foolish *man* and sit down for a moment. You were ill this morning, too, weren't you? That's why you fell during the duel. Oh, don't think you can deceive me, Andrew. Gerald didn't stun you with his sword; you're ill. And you need to rest."

"I'm fine, I just . . . need some food, that's all."

"Andrew, *sit*."

"I beg your pardon?"

"You heard me. Sit!"

He had no chance to recover from his amazement at being the first human on earth, surely, to be given an obedience command, before she shoved him down and backward. Andrew sat. Somewhat stunned, he allowed Celsie to tug off his boots, to remove his stock, to sit on the bed beside him and lift a concerned hand to his brow to check for fever.

The devil, but he had never had anyone fuss over him before. Maybe his mother had, but he'd been young when she'd died, and he sure as hell couldn't remember it. His life had been spent in self-imposed solitude. He'd never craved affection of any sort. But now, here she was touching him. Worrying over him. What a novel feeling. What a *nice* feeling.

Embarrassed, he smiled a little weakly. "I suppose you're going to tell me *down* next."

"Actually, that's exactly what I was going to tell you." She completely missed his feeble joke and stood back, studying him narrowly. "Well, you're cooler now, but you still don't look well at all. I'm going down to the kitchens to find something for you to eat so you won't have to wait for a meal to be prepared. Some food, hot tea, and a nightshirt ought to be just the thing. Now, get under those covers and don't move until I return, is that clear?"

"What?"

"You may be ill, my lord, but I know for certain that your hearing is quite unimpaired."

Andrew was staring at her. "I'm not sure whether I should be grateful, amused, offended, or amazed by such . . . treatment. . . ."

"You can be all of them except offended," she said, giving him a fleeting smile that brought out the sparkle in her eye. "After all, I'm treating you no differently than I would a dog."

"Coming from anyone else, that would be an insult. Coming from *you,* I suppose I should consider it the highest of compliments."

She grinned. "Yes, well, just so that you don't get too high an opinion of yourself, you've got a long way to go before I choose you over Freckles." She turned and headed for the door, but Andrew was still sitting up, watching the sway of her bottom and her mile-long legs in the shockingly snug breeches.

He was still looking when she, reaching the door, turned and gave him a glare of mock severity.

He understood. Sliding down beneath the covers, he pulled them up to his chin and gave a long-suffering sigh.

It was then, and only then, that she left him.

Chapter 16

When Celsie tiptoed back upstairs with a tray in her hands twenty minutes later, she half expected to find Andrew sound asleep in bed. Instead, he was sitting up, his back against the headboard and his notebook balanced against one blanket-clad knee. His pencil scratched rapidly across the page.

She stood in the doorway for a moment, just watching him. He was so focused on what he was doing that he hadn't seen her. The light from a bedside candle flickered over his intent face, gilding a complexion that still looked more wan than it should. He had untied his queue, and rich waves of dark chestnut hair gleamed in the light and hung in his eyes and about his shoulders. He kept pushing the hair back off his brow. It kept flopping forward. He looked incredibly boyish, unconsciously distracted. Handsome. She stilled, just watching him. There was something eminently fascinating about observing a genius at work, creating wondrous new inventions that would someday change the world. Celsie couldn't prevent the swell of admiration, and for a moment—a brief, insane moment—she had an urge to go to him, to slide beneath the covers with him, and kiss the mouth that looked so grim and unhappy until it was smiling once again.

What are *you thinking?!*

It must be a lingering aftereffect of the aphrodisiac. It had to be. Just like her absurd hope, when she had been about to leave, that he would ask her to stay—

And her crushing disappointment when he had not.

She cleared her throat to announce her return. His head jerked up in startled surprise.

"Hello," he said. To her amazement, he immediately stopped writing, shut the notebook, and putting it dutifully on a bedside table, gave her his complete attention. Celsie raised her brows. Well now, this was a change. Had her little sermon in the coach got through to him, after all?

"Feeling better?" she asked, smiling in acknowledgment of his improved manners as he took the tray from her hands.

"Much."

"Good. Here's a fresh pot of tea, and I found some leftover pork pie in the kitchen, peas, and potatoes boiled in their jackets."

She'd made up two plates. He took one for himself, along with flatware, and handed the tray back to her so that she would have something on which to eat her own food.

"No, you take it," she said, trying to wave away his kind gesture. "You're the one who's in bed. You'll have nothing to balance your plate on."

"I've got my lap."

"You'll spill something. Here, wait." Holding the

tray in one hand, she pulled up the night table and put her own plate on it, as well as the teapot and cups. She handed the empty tray back to Andrew.

He eyed her wryly, but finally relented and accepted it.

"I trust you're a very good dog trainer," he mused, setting his plate back down on the tray, straightening up a bit in bed, and tucking in to the pork pie.

"Why do you say that?"

"You don't take no for an answer. Dogs will walk all over you if you let them. I bet no one walks all over you—dogs and people included."

"Is that a compliment?"

"Do you want it to be?"

She shrugged. "Compliments are always easier to take than insults, so yes, I think I do want it to be a compliment."

He smiled. "It was intended as one."

She poured him a cup, wondering why her hand felt suddenly shaky. She could feel his gaze upon her. Her blood warmed in response, and her heart was doing strange things beneath her pitifully inadequate bosom. It was almost easier to function around this man when he was being surly and brusque. When he chose to be charming, it was flustering. Unnerving. And this whole act of pouring tea for him while he was lying abed felt intimate. *Too* intimate. Was this what wives did for their husbands when they woke up in the morning?

"Milk and sugar?"

"Please."

She stirred both into the cup and handed it to him. He went to take it, but the cup was hot, and there was nowhere to put his hand, for she was the one holding the handle. Their fingers touched; he drew his back.

"Sorry," she said, and hastily set the cup down, feeling foolish and awkward and more than a little silly for her sudden nervousness.

Conversation. I've got to make conversation. But what on earth does one say to a reclusive man of science? What do we have to talk about? And why do I suddenly feel so nervous?

She watched him sip the steaming brew. "You still look rather pale," she said, noticing how dark his hair looked against his skin.

He shrugged. "I don't get out much, you know. Comes from spending too much time in my laboratory instead of out of doors."

That wasn't quite the truth, of course. Andrew spent a fair amount of time out of doors; he liked to ride. He liked to study nature. He just didn't like to wander far from the privacy—and safety—of Blackheath Castle. He sipped his tea, keeping his gaze downcast. Good thing she hadn't wanted to see his notebook. He'd been recording what he'd seen outside the window in the hopes that it might yield something of benefit to science or medicine or those who wanted to remember him long after he became a chained, drooling idiot in Bedlam. He shuddered uncontrollably, nearly upsetting his tea. The fear was there. It was always there.

"Shall I find you another blanket?" she asked, noting his shudder.

"I'm fine."

"You're cold. You don't look well." She set down her own plate. "I think I will send for the doctor."

"No. Don't."

"Lord Andrew—"

"I feel better already. Truly." He turned his most persuasive smile on her. "I'm just tired, Celsiana. I didn't get any sleep last night. I have a lot on my mind. A little food and a good night's rest are all I need."

"Why didn't you sleep last night? Surely you weren't worried about the duel, were you?"

"The duel? That was the last thing on my mind. No, madam, I spent the night with my nose buried in a book, trying to discover what I could about my accidental aphrodisiac. I'm exhausted. Nothing more."

She just narrowed her eyes and looked at him.

"Really," he added, trying to be convincing as he held her gaze. But there was something in her eyes that was nearly his undoing. Concern. Kindness. She was worried about him.

His grin faded. As much as he was enjoying this very novel experience of being fussed over by a woman, as seductive as he found her touching concern for him, he felt like a cheat.

He had to tell her. After all, unless he could think of a way to escape the matrimonial noose, she was going to end up marrying him. She deserved to know the truth about what she was getting herself into. And she deserved to know that Lucien had dragged in every researcher, every specialist, every authority on dementia and madness and other mind disorders from every corner of Europe, and that none of them—not one—had been able to come up with a diagnosis, let alone a prognosis for his condition.

His gut clenched. Yes, he had to tell her. But could he risk her reaction? Could he stand her pity, her certain shudder of fear and revulsion? There was no way in hell she'd want to marry him once she learned the truth about him. So why didn't he tell her? What was stopping him? Didn't he *want* to call off this marriage?

Then again, maybe she wouldn't want to call it off—in which case, he'd have to point out the possible benefits of his illness to her. Ha, ha, ha. Laughter was the way to get through the worst that life had to offer, wasn't it?

Just think, Celsie. If your money ever runs out, you can just exhibit me at Bedlam and start charging a fee for people to see me. I can hear them now. Ah, look! There's the famous Lord Andrew de Montforte, inventor of failed flying machines and successful aphrodisiacs and mad inventor in the truest sense of the word! And look, he wears a collar and lives in a cage and drools just like one of his wife's dogs!

Anger seized him, and the bite of pork pie he'd just taken went to sawdust in his mouth. He pushed his plate to the edge of the tray, his appetite gone.

Her hand was on his brow. "You *are* ill, aren't you?"

"I'm fine."

"Then it must be the peas."

"Sorry?"

She gave a pained laugh. "Don't tell me you haven't heard all about the Jinx. How the man I was originally supposed to marry choked to death on a pea. And here I am, serving you peas, and you're probably thinking you're going to choke and die on one as well."

"Madam, I can assure you that since I detest peas as a rule, the only way I could possibly choke on one is if you were to force it bodily down my throat."

"I wouldn't force anything down the throat of a man who was feeling ill. Especially a food he happened to detest." She took the tray away, her mood brusque and businesslike once more, in keeping with his own. "I think I'd better leave. You need to sleep, and I . . . I need to think."

"Yes—I daresay you'd better."

Please stay. I don't want to be alone with my thoughts, with the fear, right now. I need you. Please stay.

But he didn't voice such thoughts, of course. Instead he said nothing, merely gazing sulkily at the opposite wall, fighting a battle with himself that seemed to have no victor, his fingers clenching and unclenching a corner of the blanket.

Celsie looked at him in confusion. His was staring broodily past her and toward the window where he'd first taken ill. He looked impossibly virile. Impossibly attractive.

Impossibly alone with whatever was tormenting him.

Once again, she could feel the banked anger radiating from him. She could see that he was fighting with something inside. And she could sense that he needed her, and needed her badly, though she knew that loners were the last people on earth who could ever recognize such a need, let alone give in to it.

She ought to know, of course. She'd spent most of her childhood alone.

As though sensing her thoughts, he looked up, his eyes stormy, his mouth set. He regarded her for a long moment, then turned his head and gazed morosely into the empty hearth.

"I thought you were leaving," he muttered.

She reached out and started to touch his arm, then caught herself. He looked pointedly down at the hand that would have touched him. Feeling a bit sheepish, she drew it back.

"Go," he said again, jerking his head to indicate the door. "Go, take the tray with you, and enjoy your meal elsewhere so you don't have to contend with my insufferable moodiness."

"Andrew, do you want to . . . talk?"

"No, I don't want to talk. I want you to leave. Now."

"What have I done?"

"Nothing. I just have a lot on my mind, all right?" He threw back the coverlet. "In fact, why don't you sleep in here, and I'll go somewhere else."

Her hand darted out, stopping him. "No—you stay." She restrained him with a hand on his chest. Beneath his fine lawn shirt, she could feel the mat of crisp hair, the rocky hardness of muscle, and yes, the beat of his heart. His gaze dropped pointedly to her hand, but she did not remove it, though heat crept into her cheeks and made her remember all that they'd already shared. She looked up and unflinchingly met his hard, sullen stare. "You're the one who's not feeling well. You stay here, and I'll go sleep in another room."

His gaze remained locked on hers for a long moment. Then he looked away. "Fine."

She reluctantly drew her hand back, curling her fingers upon themselves. "Shall I leave you with your tea, then?"

"No. Don't leave me with anything—except my bad mood."

"Maybe your bad mood will go away if you talk about it. You might feel better for having shared your troubles."

He gave a bitter laugh. "I might, but you most certainly would not. Therefore, let us not speak of it further. Good night, Celsiana. Sleep well."

The abrupt dismissal stung. Celsie looked at him, quietly suffering, his head turned away and his gaze directed toward the dark window. What was he hiding? Why was he so reluctant to confide in her? She longed to comfort him, but she didn't know how.

Sighing, she gathered up the remains of their dinner. He just lay there staring out the window, clenching and unclenching the blanket. The silence was awful. The tension in the room was even worse. Celsie picked up the tray. *Fine, then.* If he wanted to enjoy his bad mood in solitude, she'd leave him to it. She wasn't about to make things worse by reacting to it or, God forbid, insisting on staying when it was obvious that he wanted nothing more than to be left alone.

Men! Were they all this impossible?

"Good night, then, Andrew. I hope that morning improves both your appetite and your mood."

Chin high, she turned and headed for the door, hoping he'd call her back, that he'd relent and share his troubles with her, for it was not good to go to sleep angry, and she knew, even if he did not, that he needed her in a way that he might never admit.

But he did not call her back.

He just let her walk out of the room.

Celsie, deflated, shut the door behind her and

wandered off to another bedroom. Hours later, she was still tossing, turning, and staring up at the ceiling. And as she lay there in a strange bed, in a strange room, in a strange house, she began to wonder if marriage to the brilliant, temperamental man who slept just down the hall was going to be the biggest disaster of her life.

Desperately wishing that Freckles were there to keep her company, she stared miserably out the window across the square to the lights of another town house.

Dogs were better than men, after all.

Chapter 17

❦

At about the time that Celsie left her brooding companion and unhappily sought out another place to sleep, Lucien returned to Blackheath Castle.

It was late and he was travel-weary. Still, he was not surprised, upon entering the Great Hall, to hear that his brothers had arrived and were waiting up for him in the library. Handing his coat and hat to a footman, he went to join them.

There was Charles, sitting beside the hearth, the firelight gilding his fair hair as he stared glumly into the flames. He was in civilian clothes. Gareth sat a few feet away, his face troubled. Both glanced up as Lucien entered the room, their expressions changing immediately to ones of relief.

"By God, where the hell have you been?" Charles demanded with uncharacteristic anger.

Lucien raised his brows. "Dear me. And here I thought I left the nursery years ago." Smiling, he extended his hand to his brother in greeting. "Really, Charles, I know that fatherhood is a role you're quite enjoying, but if you think that I, of all people, am going to fall under your parental blanket, you are sadly mistaken."

Charles flushed. "We were worried about you. And Andrew."

"Yes, where *is* Andrew?" Gareth asked, coming forward to greet his brother.

"In London, from all accounts," replied the duke, accepting a glass of brandy from Charles. "Which is precisely where I have been, obtaining a special license so that he can marry without delay. The bishop owed me a favor or two."

"So it's true, then," Charles muttered. "Nerissa said you'd been interfering in Andrew's life just as you did in ours."

"It was necessary to interfere."

Charles merely leaned against the door molding and regarded Lucien with flat dismay. "I suppose that Andrew is completely unaware of your *generosity*."

"Oh, I think he is very much aware. Perhaps he will even thank me one of these days, which is more than the two of you have ever done."

Charles raked a hand through his hair. He looked tired. Confused. Frustrated. He turned on his brother. "Damn it, Luce, I just don't understand this. None of us do. What on earth has possessed you?"

"The devil, probably," returned Lucien, downing his drink.

Charles tightened his mouth and turned his pale blue eyes on Lucien, giving him a direct stare that demanded honesty, that demanded an answer, that demanded an end to all pretenses of carefree insouciance. Nothing could have more seriously weakened Lucien's resolve to guard the truth from his brothers. Nothing could have undone him faster. He turned his back on them so he wouldn't have to face them.

"Lucien?" Gareth prompted. Charles didn't say a word; he just stood there, waiting, every inch the cool army officer, even out of uniform.

Lucien moved to stand before the fire. He thrust his hands under his coattails and, hands on his hips, gazed silently into the crackling flames. "Charles," he said at length. "From the time you entered this world, you have been groomed to become the duke should I die without issue."

From behind him, he sensed the sudden tension, but neither brother spoke for a moment. Finally, Charles said, "Are you trying to tell us something?"

"Of course I am trying to tell you something. I just don't know how."

"Are you dying?" Charles asked baldly.

Lucien hesitated. "No. Nothing like that." He turned, walked to the window—anything to avoid meeting Charles's direct blue stare, and Gareth's concerned one—and gazed out over the downs, sleeping under their blanket of starlight. He didn't want to tell them the truth. He vowed that he would not.

"Do you remember the day we buried Mama and Papa?" he asked, still gazing out the window.

"Yes," said Charles, Gareth echoing him.

"Well, on that day I made a silent vow to them that I would take care of you. All of you." He turned and faced them. "What I am doing for Andrew is part of that promise."

"Oh, for God's sake, Luce, we're all adults," Gareth muttered, annoyed. "We don't need you to take care of us."

"A promise is a promise," Lucien said tightly, meaning it. "And I consider your individual happiness as part of the vow I made. Therefore I will see Andrew married."

Charles stared at him. "And you think that will make him *happy*?"

"Andrew doesn't want to get married," added Gareth.

Lucien poured himself another brandy. "Andrew needs to be married."

"Good God, man!" exclaimed Gareth. "And you accuse *Charles* of taking his parental duties seriously?"

"I am the head of this family, and as such, I have a responsibility toward it."

"What about respecting others' wishes?" Gareth flared. "What about allowing people to live their own lives without your interference, to make their own mistakes, to seek their own paths? Why must you always act as though you know best?"

"I *do* know best." Lucien smiled. "At least, in this case."

Charles, always more serious than Gareth, merely stood leaning against the doorjamb, his head turned toward the fire. He was quietly angry. He would not look at Lucien.

"This discussion is pointless," he said finally, straightening. "I'm going to bed."

"Charles—"

"We will leave for London before dawn," he said, giving Lucien a sharp look. "Whatever you broke, Lucien, I'm sure the rest of us can mend. Good night."

He bowed crisply and left. Gareth watched him

go. Then he turned on Lucien, who still stood quietly before the fire.

"Well?" said Gareth.

"I think you'd best go to bed too," Lucien said affably. He pretended that Gareth's anger meant nothing to him. He pretended that Charles's words hadn't hurt. His brothers thought him a monster. He was used to it.

Gareth merely glared at him for a moment; then he, too, spun on his heel and left the room.

Unlike Charles, he didn't even bother to say good night.

Celsie awoke to the gentle patter of rain outside.

It was not yet dawn. She lay there in the gloom, listening to the peaceful sound of water running down the windows, trickling down the eaves. Automatically she stretched her feet out, seeking Freckles, but the bottom of the bed was empty. Celsie came fully awake, feeling oddly lost, ill at ease. For as long as she could remember, she had slept with a dog or cat or both. But of course, there were no dogs or cats here. She was at de Montforte House. In a room that smelled, lingeringly, of roses.

Probably Lady Nerissa's.

She pulled the covers up over her shoulders, snuggling down beneath them and thinking that she really ought to get up now, and find her way to her own London town house before the duke's servants woke. She didn't need any more stains upon her reputation than she already had. But oh, it was so warm and delicious under the blankets. . . . She'd sleep for another ten or fifteen minutes. No more. Then she would leave.

But something besides the rain had woken her. She opened her eyes and gazed about the slowly lightening room. At the tall rectangles of the windows, aglow with gray light. At the furniture just taking shape from out of the darkness.

At the tall figure of a man leaning negligently against the doorframe.

She stifled a scream.

"Sorry," said Andrew, straightening. "It's only me."

"Damn it, you're enough to scare the courage out of a Great Dane!" she sputtered. "How long have you been standing there?"

"I don't know. Twenty minutes. Two hours. A long time."

She sat up in bed, pulling the covers with her. "What do you want?"

"Company."

"I thought you wanted to be left alone. You made that perfectly clear, earlier."

He stepped into the room, clad in nothing but a long white shirt which covered him down to midthigh. His hair was loose about his shoulders, dark and wavy in the half-light. His feet were bare, his calves long and powerful. The sight of him, tall, slightly disheveled, and nearly naked, was enough to make Celsie's throat go dry. He looked better than breakfast.

Better than another few hours of sleep.

Better, even, than the thought of leaving.

"I want to apologize for my bad behavior last night," he said.

"Now? Couldn't this wait till morning?"

"No."

"Very well, then. Now that you've apologized, why don't you go back to bed." ˉ

He shrugged. "What's the sense? I've got too much on my mind to sleep."

"Well, why don't you go design another flying machine, then. Or something to help the turnspit dogs so they don't live such horrible lives. Or better yet, a potion to render yourself invisible. I find it most disconcerting to awaken only to find a man staring at me."

"I can't help staring at you. You . . . you're beautiful."

The quiet, matter-of-fact way he said it sent a lightning bolt of feeling straight into Celsie's heart. *You're beautiful.* No one had ever told her that before. No one. She didn't know how to react to it. Feeling suddenly confused, vulnerable, and more than a little flustered, she pulled the coverlet higher. "And now I'm embarrassed."

"You shouldn't be. Besides, I'm just making an observation. Nothing more."

"I think I'd prefer that you contain your observations to science, not women dressed in their nightclothes and trying to get some sleep."

"Do you realize, Celsiana, that if we don't find a way out of this marriage, the first thing we'll see when we wake up every morning will be each other?" He bent his head and rubbed his toe against the doorjamb. His hair fell over his brow, one eye, obscuring his expression. "It's baffling, but for some strange reason, I don't find that a particularly repulsive thought." He lifted his head, looking as vulnerable as Celsie felt. "Do you?"

"No. I suppose you *are* a little better-looking than Freckles."

"Listen, Celsiana—"

She tensed, holding the sheets tightly around her.

"I'm sorry I was such an ogre last night. I'm sorry that I allowed you to go away thinking that I was angry with you, when indeed, I was not angry with you, but with the fates that have made me what I am." He took a deep breath. "And I'm sorry that if you end up having to marry me, I'm going to make the most abominable of husbands."

She fixed him with a direct glare. "Are you trying to get into my bed, Lord Andrew?"

He looked up, surprised. "Do you *want* me in your bed, Celsiana?"

"Of course not. It would be unseemly."

"Yes. Yes, I suppose it would be."

She curled and uncurled her toes. "On the other hand—"

He raised his brows.

"On the other hand, I must confess that this is the first time since I can remember that I've slept alone. I guess I miss Freckles."

"And I'd probably make a poor substitute."

"Yes. I daresay you would."

Silence. An expectant, waiting, hopeful silence.

"I suppose I'll go back to my room, then," said Andrew, with a faint smile. "Unless you decide you want me to be Freckles for the rest of the night, in which case I'll gladly crawl under the covers with you."

"Why should I let you do that?"

"Well, first there is the fact that I'm having trouble sleeping, knowing that you're—well, here. Secondly, there is the fact that if we're going to end up being married, it doesn't really make much difference what our current sleeping arrangements are. And thirdly . . ."

"Thirdly?"

He grinned a little sheepishly. "I'm cold."

She sighed and leveled a flat look at him that belied the way her heart was suddenly beginning to pound. "Do you *have* to be so damned charming?"

"Sorry. I am not trying to be charming."

"That's precisely why you *are* so charming." She flipped back the coverlet. "Very well, then. Join me if you like. But . . . no touching. Just sleeping."

"You cannot mean that."

"I do mean it."

"Do you honestly think that I can come over there, join you in that bed, and *not* touch you?"

"I think you can try."

"This might be beyond my capabilities."

"Then maybe you ought to go back to your own bed," she said, wondering why she suddenly hoped with all her heart that he would not. "Really, I can't understand why it should be so very difficult. If you can design flying machines and incredible inventions, surely you can lie in this bed without touching me."

He padded across the floor toward the bed, smiling faintly. "Why is it that I'm perceiving this as some sort of a challenge?"

"Is that how you perceive it?" she asked, sliding over to make room for him.

"Well, how else would I perceive it? You invite me into your bed but won't let me touch you—and this after we've already made love not once, but twice. Why deny our desires now?"

"Because it's not even light out and I would like to go back to sleep. You can either stand there and sulk, or get into bed. Now *I'm* getting cold."

He joined her, of course. She never had any reason to think that he wouldn't. Oh, if he could be like this *all* the time—charming, witty, at ease with himself and with her—instead of turning into a bad-tempered dragon whenever the fancy struck him!

The mattress sagged a little as he climbed up. Celsie, moving as far to the edge of the bed as she could without falling off, tensed, her skin from ear to toe prickling in anticipation of an accidental touch. He pulled the coverlet up and scooted down beneath the weight of it and the blankets. The pillow sighed as it took the weight of his head, and the blankets gapped around her knees and shoulders, letting in a faint draft where his body lifted the covers from her own.

They lay there for a few moments, each stiff and expectant and feeling slightly awkward. Celsie was keenly aware of his size, his virility, his very *maleness* in this rose-scented, femininely appointed room. Now she was *really* wishing that Freckles were there. Having the big dog's body between herself and Andrew would go far toward ensuring there were no . . . accidental touches.

Maybe a pillow would work—

"So tell me about these turnspits," he said, his deep voice only a foot from her ear.

She lay as stiff as a dog's hackles, arms down at her sides, barely daring to breathe. "What's there to tell?"

"I want to know why their plight is so important to you. What you intend to do to help them."

Now, *this* was a safe topic, and one that she could thoroughly exhaust—probably enough to send him off to sleep, if she was lucky. After all, it seemed to bore most people; why not Lord Andrew, whose interests seemed to revolve around science and extraordinary inventions and being in a bad mood?

Somewhat despairingly, knowing she'd soon lose her audience, she said, "Have you ever been in the kitchens of Blackheath, Andrew? Or any kitchen, for that matter?"

"Hmm, no." He crossed his arms beneath his head, one elbow accidentally touching Celsie's ear. "I can't say I have."

Celsie determined not to move, though she was keenly aware of that elbow. "Well, if you would bother to go down into the kitchens of most great houses, you'll see an iron wheel, somewhere near the hearth where your meats are roasted. The wheel is called a turnspit, and the little dogs that are enslaved to turn these wheels, and thus your meat so that it roasts evenly, are called the same."

"Dogs are used to turn the wheels?" he asked, the pillow shifting a little as he turned his head to look at her.

"You know, you really need to get out of your laboratory once in a while and see what goes on in the real world. Of course they are! Aren't all innocent beasts exploited in one way or another by the human species?"

He merely looked at her, his features barely discernible in the gloom. But she could see his dark eyes only inches away, his lips so close she could feel his breath upon her cheek.

"I'll tell you something else, too," she said, staring up at the dark ceiling so she wouldn't have to look into that handsome, searching face. "Not only are these poor little dogs confined within these wheels, but many cooks put hot coals on the iron tracks so that they run their legs off in a futile attempt to keep their paws from being burned."

"You're bloody joking!"

"I'm not."

"How dreadful . . . Good God, I never knew."

"It *is* dreadful, isn't it?" She began to relax, warming to her subject as she realized she had not only his attention, but his sympathy for her cause. "Now you know why I'm trying so hard to make people find an alternate way of cooking their roasts. Animals have feelings, just like we do. They're not meant to be hurt, or abused, or exploited for our sakes. They're innocent, and helpless, and they're meant to be loved—just as we love our children."

"There are those who don't even love their children, Celsie."

"I know."

"And there are those who would say that since animals lack souls, they don't deserve to be treated any better than they are. That it's perfectly all right to treat them as expendable objects. Not, of course, that I adhere to such an opinion . . . just playing devil's advocate."

"I know you are. But who's to say that animals don't have souls? I believe, with all my heart, that they do. I believe they go to heaven, each and every one of them, because they are innocent, and therefore sinless. And I believe that God, who created animals just as he created humans, and made them of the same exact flesh and bone and blood, loves them as much as he does us."

She felt the customary pang of frustration gripping her and swallowed hard, for she wanted to change the world, change people's attitudes, and she knew that she never could, because there would always be cruel, insensitive people as long as the earth turned.

"But oh, if I say such things, people laugh at me," she continued dejectedly. "They smile politely, and pretend to care, but only in order to indulge me. Funny what having money does, isn't it? Fools. I know what they really think. It's a good thing I didn't live a century or so ago, or I would have been burned as a heretic. But you know something? Let them all laugh. Let them all whisper behind my back. People have enough champions; animals do not. If something suits a purpose, exploit it. If something gets in the way, destroy it. It doesn't matter if it's a living, breathing creature, with a heart and feelings and ability to feel pain, loneliness, and grief just like we do. Man's wishes are the only ones that matter, aren't they? Man's wishes cause everything else to be stamped down, to be stamped out. God, how I hate it!"

Her tone had become impassioned, plaintive, angry. She turned her head on the pillow and regarded Andrew. In the faint gloom she could see that he was watching her, his eyes thoughtful. There was a little smile on his face. Was that mockery she saw there? Amusement?

"You think I'm ridiculous, don't you?"

"No. I don't think you're ridiculous at all, Celsie."

"What do you think, then?"

Something in his gaze softened. "I think you are a woman ahead of your time."

"You're not laughing at me, then?"

"Do I look as if I'm laughing?"

"No," she said, exhaling, the fight going out of her. "No, you don't."

"I admire you for your courage in standing up for something you believe in so strongly. For your courage in confessing to me something that is obviously very close to your heart."

"Yes, well, it has made me even more of an outsider than I already was. Not, mind you, that I care one way or another."

"I know the feeling. . . ."

"What feeling?"

"Of being an outsider."

"But you don't care, either."

He smiled. "No. I do not."

His confession, along with the deeply intense, quiet way he was regarding her, was starting to do things to Celsie's insides. It was starting to do things to her resolve not to like him, her resolve not to touch him. She turned away and stared up at the ceiling. "I've always loved animals more than people . . . maybe because people are cruel and animals are not . . . maybe because I just never really fit in with people."

"I know that feeling, too."

She turned her head and met his intent gaze. "Do you?"

"Of course. I'm a 'mad' inventor. Most people I meet couldn't be bothered to show an interest in the things that I do, in the dreams that I have; and since they don't understand my work, or my visions, they write me off as 'peculiar' and choose not to bother with me. I am like a horse with six legs. They don't know what to make of me, they can find no common ground with me, and so I am best left alone—which suits me just fine, of course."

"I think your work is incredibly fascinating," she said heatedly.

"Then you are the exception, rather than the rule."

"And I think your dreams are going to change the world."

He smiled. "Well, I don't know about that, but trust me, Celsiana, I do know what it's like to be ridiculed for my beliefs, for my passions, for my dreams of improving life as we know it—just as you know what it's like." He unfolded his arms from behind his head, putting them beneath the blankets to escape the chill. "Even now, I shudder when I remember what my peers in the scientific community said after my flying machine failed and dumped Charles and me in the moat—and this in front of the king himself. I shudder to think what they will say when they find out I've created an aphrodisiac and can't even remember what went into it. Talk about mortification. . . . Here I am, an inventor and man of science, and I didn't even record the substances that went into making what could very well end up being the most incredible discovery of this decade, if not this century."

There was pain in his voice. Tentatively Celsie reached out and found his hand beneath the covers.

His fingers curled around her own.

They remained that way for several moments, just

holding hands, looking up at the ceiling, neither saying a word.

"Know what's rather funny?" she said, at last.

"What's that?"

"Here we are, two misfits who think we can change the world. . . . Perhaps we're better suited to each other than either of us had thought."

"I suppose we would be very well suited indeed, if either of us had any inclination to get married."

"Yes. I think it's better that we remain friends rather than spouses. Marriage would probably ruin our burgeoning friendship."

"We're working on that, aren't we? Being friends?"

She heard the smile—and what sounded like hope—in his voice. She turned her head and saw that he was watching her, his expression inscrutable.

"Yes—yes, I suppose we are." She smiled slowly. "Though I don't think friends usually lie together in the same bed."

"No one will know. I'll be out of here by the time the servants are up."

"You'd better be. The last thing we need is for anyone to catch you here. There'll be no escaping the matrimonial noose then!"

"I promise to leave at first sounds of stirring downstairs."

"And I'll go back to my own town house shortly thereafter."

"No one will be the wiser."

"No one."

She squeezed his hand. He squeezed hers back. Celsie shut her eyes, listening to the rain, taking pleasure in the heavy warmth of the coverlet, the drowsy heat radiating from Andrew's body. Eventually the sound of the rain began to grow distant. She sighed, turned over, and instinctively curled closer to him.

Just as instinctively, his arm went around her, heavy, warm, protective.

Celsie's last thought was one of gratitude. It was nice not to have to sleep alone, after all.

Chapter 18

～⌒◯◯⌒～

"**O**h, *bother*," muttered Nerissa as the mud-splattered coach drew up outside de Montforte House just as it was growing dark. "There's Perry's mother, heading straight toward us. You'd think she was just waiting for us to get here, the way she's hurrying out of her house. That malicious gossip is the last person I feel like seeing."

Nerissa was tired and irritable. Charles and Gareth had arrived late the night before, and, having left so early this morning none of them had got much sleep. Now her brothers rode just outside the carriage, Lucien some distance ahead and mounted on his hellish black stallion, Armageddon. Charles, astride his steadfast military mount, Contender, flanked the coach, every so often conversing with Gareth, who was aboard his fleet Thoroughbred, Crusader.

Their wives, Juliet and Amy, shared the coach with Nerissa.

"You will excuse me if I don't feel like being sociable where *she* is concerned," Juliet muttered in her soft American accent, watching the plump harridan rushing across the square toward them. She'd

203

had experiences—none of them pleasant—with Lady Brookhampton before, and Nerissa didn't blame her for disliking the woman who had so maligned Gareth, her husband.

"She's hailing Lucien," Amy remarked, looking out the window when Juliet would not. "She's curtsying to him. I can see her mouth going."

"I can imagine," said Juliet, acidly.

The coach came to a stop. Lucien guided his prancing, frothing stallion up to the window. "Good evening, ladies. Sorry to inconvenience you, but our neighbor has just invited herself in for tea." He gave one of his maddening smiles. "Shall we refuse her?"

"Yes," said Juliet, tightly.

"Yes," said Amy, noting Juliet's set face.

But Nerissa looked away. She didn't like Lady Brookhampton either, but hoping that Perry would soon ask her to marry him, knew it wouldn't be wise to make an enemy of his mother. Sullenly she asked, "What is she so excited about, anyhow?"

"What do you think she's so excited about? Andrew arrived late last night. She thinks he's running from some sort of trouble and wanted to be the first to let us know."

Nerissa let out her breath on an irritated sigh. "Oh, how I wish that woman would mind her own business for once. I don't suppose she mentioned whether or not he was alone, did she?"

Lucien's expression gave away nothing. "She did not say."

"Then it seems we have no choice but to invite her in," Nerissa muttered. "Not that I want to, but—"

"But if you want to marry her son, you'd better stay in her good graces," finished Lucien.

Moments later, the men were giving their horses into the care of waiting grooms and handing the ladies down from the coach. As a group, they walked through the tall, spiky iron gates, Juliet coldly ignoring Lady Brookhampton, Amy distantly polite, and Nerissa feeling as though this was going to be a very long morning indeed.

The butler, Harris, met them in the house's marbled entrance foyer, bowing deeply to the duke, and then to the others. He looked vastly uncomfortable. Worried.

"Your Grace," he said in a low voice, "If I might have a private word with you?"

"By all means, Harris. Let us go into the library, shall we?"

The two moved off. Footmen appeared, all silent and tight-lipped, to take the ladies' cloaks and Charles and Gareth's hats and greatcoats. The two brothers exchanged glances. The three women frowned. Only Lady Brookhampton, chattering away like a magpie, seemed oblivious to the charged tension that filled the house.

"I say, Lady Nerissa, you really *must* come over for tea tomorrow afternoon," she was saying, pointedly excluding Juliet and Amy, both of whom she despised—one for stealing Gareth right out from under her enterprising daughter Katharine's nose, the other for stealing Charles. "There's so much I need to catch you up on! Everyone's talking about France, of course—terrible how we might soon find ourselves in another war with them, thanks to those horrible colonists in America. Why, I hear that they've sent their emissary, a Mr. Franklin, to Paris, seeking French aid! Oh, Lord save us if the Frogs decide to start another war because of those vile, treasonous rebels—"

"Excuse us," said Gareth, taking Juliet's arm before she could respond to the obvious taunt. Charles did the same with Amy, and the two moved off with their American wives, leaving Nerissa alone with Lady Brookhampton.

"I say, what *is* the matter with them?" Lady Brookhampton asked, feigning innocence.

Nerissa opened her mouth to deliver her own tart response—and saw Lucien returning. Unlike the butler, he did not look vastly uncomfortable, or terribly worried, in the least. He looked . . .

The way he always did when he was up to something unspeakable.

God help them.

"What are you two doing standing out here in the foyer?" he asked smoothly. "Come, come inside. Tea will be served shortly in the parlor." He removed his gloves and handed them to a footman. "Oh, by the way, Nerissa. Harris tells me that a package arrived for you last night." He winked. "I suspect it's from some lovesick young swain. He put it on your bed."

Nerissa flushed, feeling a moment of excitement—and panic. Whoever had sent the package must have known she was coming to London. And the only one who might have known was Perry. Oooh! She was dying to run upstairs . . . but what if Perry hadn't been the sender? What if it had been some other man? She'd have a fine time explaining *that* to the woman who would probably end up being her mother-in-law. . . .

"Aren't you going to fetch it down?" Lucien asked, grinning. "I am sure we're all dying to know who it's from. In fact, why don't you take Lady Brookhampton up with you?"

He gave her a look that clearly said, *And keep her away from Juliet and Amy for as long as possible.*

Some things never ceased to amaze, Nerissa thought. She could almost—*almost*—forgive her brother for all his scheming and manipulation of other people's lives in the face of his consideration for not only the situation at hand, but the feelings of his two American sisters-in-law.

"Of course," she said, trying to hide her dismay at having Perry's mother with her when she unwrapped the package. "Will you come upstairs with me, Lady Brookhampton?"

She did not expect the older woman to refuse.

And of course, she didn't.

Nerissa headed for the stairs.

Something had woken her.

Celsie dragged open her eyes. She was surrounded by a wonderful, drowsy warmth, and it came as something of a shock to find that the warmth came not from a dog, but from the very long, very hard, very male body against which she was curled. Actually, she was more than just curled against that long, hard, male body. Andrew lay on his back, and her head was nestled within the cup of his shoulder, a fold of his shirt tickled her nose, and she could hear his heart beating quietly beneath her ear. He was still asleep and breathing deeply, his arm slung heavily, possessively, across her back.

She opened her eyes further, looking above the fold of Andrew's shirt and across the room toward the window. It was still raining outside, and the sullen gray light coming through the parted drapes made it impossible to tell whether it was an hour past dawn or an hour before sunset. One thing for sure: The room was chilly. Almost too chilly to rise from this bed and make her escape before anyone was aware of her presence.

She had to leave. Now. Yet she didn't want to crawl from the warm cocoon of covers, to move away from the broad, solid chest upon which she'd been dozing. How very surprising. She ought to be bolting from this bed like a hare from a greyhound. Instead, she found herself thinking that she could not remember the last time she'd woken up to such pleasant coziness. Why, if someone had told her yesterday that sleeping with a man was far nicer than sleeping with a dog, she would never have believed it. But it was true. Sleeping with a man *was* nicer.

And you didn't wake up to find paws stabbing into your back.

Downstairs, she could hear the servants moving about, and from somewhere came a tantalizing waft of toast. Celsie tensed even as her stomach gave a responsive growl. The rumbling didn't abate but continued on, gathering both loudness and intensity until it sounded like an angry mastiff confronting a poacher. Celsie winced, hoping it wouldn't wake her bedmate, but he didn't stir, his long lashes lying against pale cheeks shadowed with reddish-brown bristle, his head turned slightly on the pillow, his chest rising and falling slowly in time with his deep, steady breathing.

She repositioned herself within the heavy curve of his arm, resting her chin on the rise of his chest muscles so that she could gaze at his face. He was easy to look at. Too easy. She liked the way his nose angled back and met his forehead so that both made a nearly straight line, with barely an indentation to mark the bridge; it gave him a noble, intelligent profile. She liked the way his hair, so thick and glossy, fell in rich waves around his face, its warm, dark chestnut hue set off by the deep brown color of his long, straight lashes. She liked the way his mouth looked firm and sculpted, even in sleep, the lips sensual without being too wide, now slightly parted and putting thoughts in her head about how nice it would be to lean down and kiss them.

God help her, she liked everything about him—

Well, almost everything. His unpredictable moods left a lot to be desired.

But with him lying asleep on the pillow, it was easy to forget his surliness. It was easy to imagine him how she wished he were all the time: the way he'd been earlier, when they had lain side by side, hand in hand, and talked about their respective dreams just like two old friends. Celsie had met a lot of men in her life. Some were handsome, but empty between the ears. Others were witty and intelligent, but hopelessly unattractive. Yet Lord Andrew . . . He seemed to combine the best of both worlds. He was an attractive blend of sharp intelligence and splendid good looks, of creativity and imagination, of kindness and wit, of courage and vulnerability.

Vulnerability.

Yes, she knew he had felt vulnerable last night, when he had all but driven her from the room. Yet why? Lots of people took ill. Just because he was getting a cold or wasn't feeling well was no reason to feel ashamed. . . .

He was frowning in his sleep now, his breathing changing, his eyelids moving slightly as he dreamed. Celsie couldn't help herself. She reached up and tenderly smoothed the frown lines from his brow. His lashes fluttered, and sleepily, he opened his eyes.

Oh, God help me—I want to kiss him!

"Good morning," she whispered, smiling.

He blinked once, twice, before lifting a fist and knuckling his eyes. He looked warm and groggy and positively delicious. "Mmmmm . . . a good morning indeed," he mumbled, yawning. "To stay inside, that is."

"Isn't it? My stomach's been growling for the past half hour, but I was too comfortable to move."

"And here I feared I took up too much room in the bed. . . ."

"Well, yes, you do take up a lot of room, but at least you don't snore—which is more than I can say for Freckles."

"Ah yes, that paragon of comparison again," he said dryly. "I'm delighted to find that I've emerged the victor in at least one contest with that matchless mutt."

"He's not a mutt, he's a Spanish pointer," she said, returning his own smile. And then: "Do *I* snore?"

"No, but you do steal all the covers. I awoke a while ago and I was bloody freezing." Reaching out, he caught the long, golden-brown fall of her hair, dragging his fingers through the silky tresses and admiring them in the faint gray light. The sensation of his fingers combing through her hair was wonderful; it was all Celsie could do not to purr, especially when they left her hair, skimmed the outside of her shoulder, and trailed down the curve of her upper arm and around toward her breast.

She tensed and caught his hand.

"You feel awfully damned good," he said. "Told you I wouldn't be able to just sleep, with you beside me all night."

"You did a good job, so far."

"I must have been too exhausted to do anything *but* sleep. But I'm not exhausted now, Celsie. I'm wide-awake. *All* of me is wide-awake. I think it's best if I beat a hasty retreat back to my own rooms before I start something we'll both regret."

She smiled sadly, knowing he was right but wishing he weren't.

"Yes. And I'd better sneak out and return to my own town house before anyone recognizes me." She gazed into his eyes, loving the way they sloped down at the outer corners, giving him a lazy, sleepy look that, combined with the dimple that appeared on those infrequent occasions when he chose to smile, was enough to make her heart melt all the way down into her toes.

Heaven help her, her heart was melting *now*.

And so was her resolve to leave.

Still comfortably lying against and on his chest, she began to lean down, toward his now-smiling lips, a farewell kiss, nothing more—

When the door opened.

Celsie's head jerked up. There, standing in the doorway, was Lady Brookhampton, whom she remembered from her charity ball. With her was a beautiful young woman with bright gold hair and blue, blue eyes that were widening in shocked surprise.

"Nerissa!" howled Andrew, yanking the covers over Celsie's head to protect both her modesty and his sister's eyes from the implications of what they'd been up to. "What the thundering blazes are you doing here?!"

Nerissa's chin snapped up. She put her hands on her hips and, equally flustered, glared at him. "Well, this *is,* after all, my bedroom! I might ask what the blazes *you're* doing here!"

"I daresay the answer is obvious, my dear," drawled Lucien, coming up behind them and regarding Andrew with a victorious, maddening little smile. "Lady Brookhampton? Why don't you wait for us in the parlor. We'll join you shortly."

"Of course," murmured the older woman, narrowing her eyes with gleeful malice as she cast a last, lingering look at the bed. She gave a little *hmph,* turned on her heel, and left.

The duke shook his head slowly back and forth in a faintly chastising way. "Really, Andrew. The damage you're doing to the family name . . . Abducting a lady without concern for her reputation, ravishing her without benefit of wedlock, taking over your sister's bed . . . Dear me. What *will* people think? What, I wonder, did Lady Brookhampton think?"

Andrew felt as though he was going to burst an artery. *"Why the devil was Lady Brookhampton even up here?!"* he roared.

"Because Lucien said that a package arrived last night for me!" interrupted Nerissa, turning furiously on her urbane, unruffled brother. "But there was no package, was there? You just used that as an excuse to get Lady Brookhampton up here, didn't you? You know she has the biggest mouth in all London! You *wanted* her to catch Andrew and Celsie together!"

"Dear me," murmured Lucien, grinning faintly and pulling at his chin. "Do you really think me capable of such a diabolical plan?"

"He's been engaged in diabolical plans since the ball!" shouted Celsie, flinging back the coverlet at last.

"Ah, there you are, my dear. I knew you were under there somewhere."

Andrew, still in bed, could feel his blood pressure rising. He could feel his muscles beginning to constrict with an emotion that went beyond fury. He shut his eyes, balled his fists, and began counting to ten. "Nerissa, please leave us," he said through clenched teeth.

"Why?"

"Because what I am about to say to our brother is not fit for your ears. And what I am about to *do* to him is going to mean years of cleaning in order to remove the bloodstains from the carpet. It will not be a pretty sight, I can assure you."

"Then in that case, I'm staying. After all Lucien has done to ruin your life, and after all I'm sure he'll do in an attempt to ruin mine, I should dearly *love* to see you do something that will make such a satisfying mess. Would you like your sword? I'd be happy to get it for you."

"There's a pistol on the highboy that would do equally nicely," snapped Celsie, glaring at the duke.

"My bare hands will suffice," Andrew gritted, swinging from the bed.

"Now, now, children, enough is enough," said the

duke with infuriating mildness. "You will have to think of creative ways to murder me later on, because right now there are far more pressing matters that demand your attention. Nerissa, you may leave us now."

"I will not!"

"Don't argue with me, my dear."

Nerissa took one look at Lucien's face, tossed her head, and turning on her heel, stormed off.

Andrew sat there, his hard stare burning into Lucien's. "I know what this looks like, but I can assure you that nothing happened between Celsie and me. We only *slept* together, not *slept*."

"Yes, that's *all* we did!" added Celsie, her face quite an incriminating shade of pink.

"Yes, well, do try telling that to Lady Brookhampton," murmured Lucien with infuriating suaveness. "And everyone else who will soon know about your ruination, my dear." He moved into the room, arms crossed, looking like a king who had just won the last country he had yet to conquer. "Really, Andrew, I do hope you're going to do right by the girl. She did, after all, say that she would marry you. But things have happened so quickly, have they not? Hardly enough time to prepare for such a momentous event . . . Ah, well. I am"—he grinned—"as usual, here to help."

Still wearing that infuriating smile, he reached into his coat pocket, extracted a sheet of vellum, and with a casual flick of his wrist, snapped it open.

"What the hell is that?" snapped Andrew.

"Why, the special license that I've already procured for you, of course. I took the liberty of calling on an acquaintance of mine, whose bishopric he owes, most directly, to my influence. One good turn deserves another, don't you think?"

Andrew clenched his fists to keep them from swinging. He took deep breaths in a herculean effort to remain calm. "And I suppose you also took the liberty of having someone follow us from Lambourn to London, which is why, I suppose, you knew that Celsie and I were here?"

Lucien smiled thinly. "Ah, Andrew. You know me too well, I fear." He bowed. "I shall leave you now, so that you can make yourselves presentable. The rest of the family are downstairs, and they are all anxious to meet their sister-in-law-to-be."

Andrew exploded. He grabbed the nearest thing he could reach—the candlestick beside the bed—and flung it at his brother's smiling face.

Without even flinching, his expression never wavering, Lucien calmly reached out and caught it. With deliberate care, he put the candlestick down on the highboy that stood near the door, and turned his maddening smile on Celsie.

"I should warn you about your prospective husband, my dear," he murmured. "Temper goes with red hair."

And then, bowing once more, he turned and left them.

Chapter 19

Leaving the bed, Andrew stalked to the door and slammed it. There he stood, leaning his side against it, his brow bent to one hand. His shirt covered him down to midthigh. Celsie could see his mouth moving, could hear his soft tirade of profanity.

"I am sorry," she said.

"Yes, so am I. Plague take it, there's no way out of this now. Not with the bitch of Brookhampton armed with enough gossip to destroy your reputation forever. Bloody hell. Damn and thunderation. I am going to kill him, I swear it."

Celsie rose from the bed. She, too, still wore her linen shirt, though the hem covered her down to the knees. She walked slowly up to Andrew and tentatively laid a hand on his shoulder. He didn't shake her off but merely stood there, still leaning against the door, head bent and his hard, sullen eyes staring emptily at the floor. Her heart ached for him. What a horrible existence he must have had, with a monster like Lucien for a brother.

"I won't hold you to it," she murmured. "I could

never force you or anyone else to do something you have no wish to do."

"And I could never face myself or anyone else if I were not to do right by you," he said, swallowing hard. "I should never have brought you here, should never have come into this room last night, should never have let you try that blasted potion—"

"Shhhh," she murmured, and then, knowing she was taking a huge chance, knowing she was going beyond the boundaries of friendship, she put her arms around him.

She expected him to violently recoil. She thought he might shove her away in disgust. Instead he did neither, just standing there stiffly, allowing her to hold him. He filled her arms, big and strong and hard beneath the softness of his shirt. She rested her cheek against the cup of his shoulder and held him.

Just held him.

"I guess I've got to ask you to marry me, then," he said a little shakily.

She stared at a nearby chair without really seeing it. "I guess I've got to accept."

He raised a hand to shove the hair out of his face—and suddenly he was returning her embrace, clinging to her as though she were the last anchor holding him against a storm-tossed sea. His head dipped toward hers and he claimed her lips, his tongue plunging into her mouth, his hand sliding behind her waist, splaying up her lower back and pulling her hard against him.

It was a kiss of desperation. Of comfort sought and comfort given. But both knew they could not put off the inevitable. After a few moments they reluctantly broke it, and just stood there in each other's embrace, her cheek against his chest, her arms around his waist.

"I guess that now that we've got some news to share, I'd better present you to the rest of the family," he said quietly. "But if you're too embarrassed by recent events, if you wish to plead indisposition and remain up here, I will quite understand."

She took his hand and gazed deeply into his suffering eyes. "What, and leave you to the dragons all by yourself? No, Andrew. If we're going to be married, I will carry my own weight. And when need be, even yours."

He looked at her with a mixture of sorrow and despair and maybe even hope.

"Now, come, let us at least get dressed," she said. "We might as well get this over with."

They sat on the bed, discussing necessary arrangements. Then Andrew, seeing that Celsie had nothing to wear but the shocking breeches and shirt in which she'd arrived, sent for his sister. Nerissa came up, looking faintly uncomfortable but making a heroic effort to act as though nothing untoward had happened. Andrew noticed that Celsie kept her chin high, her eyes averted. His heart went out to her. How awkward she must feel, facing the woman who would soon be her sister-in-law. How mortified she must be, having been discovered in Nerissa's own bed. But Andrew knew that Nerissa was more than familiar with Lucien's cruel manipulations herself, and sure enough, his sister instantly took pity on Celsie, breaking the ice by making a disparaging remark about the brother they all wanted to strangle. He saw relief and gratitude flood Celsie's tight features. Then, satisfied that the two were warming to each other and trusting Nerissa to find some suitable clothes for Celsie, Andrew went downstairs to face his family.

Lady Brookhampton, thank God, had gone—no doubt bursting at her strained seams to spread what promised to be the year's juiciest gossip. Juliet and Amy were in the parlor, relaxing after their long journey. Only his brothers were in the library when Andrew entered, and with the exception of Lucien, they rose to greet him.

"I'm getting married," he said sullenly.

Charles and Gareth were full of surprise, confusion, and wary congratulations. And of course, questions. Too many questions. Andrew answered them as best he could, trying not to sound as resentful and volatile as he felt. He did not look at Lucien. He was afraid that if he did, one glance at that smug face would land him in gaol for murder. And now Charles was asking him another question. Andrew forced his mind back to the present. The wedding arrangements? Yes, the nuptials would take place immediately. No, her father, may he rest in peace, could not give her away, her mother was off in Italy with some new lover, and her brother, for whom she bore no love and even less respect, would not, if she had anything to say about it, give her away either.

"She wants Freckles," he explained, helping himself to a cup of tea.

"Who the hell is Freckles?" asked Charles and Gareth in unison.

"Her best friend," said Andrew, with protective evasiveness.

Gareth raised a brow. "Odd name, that. Freckles. Hmmm."

"Is it his given one or a nickname?" asked Charles.

"Why assume Freckles is a he?" mused Gareth. "Sounds more like a woman's name than a bloke's."

Lucien, reposing in a chair near the fire, crossed one ankle over the other and casually reached for the evening paper. "Freckles is the lady's dog."

"Her *dog*?" exclaimed Charles and Gareth in unison.

"You two ought to go onstage singing harmony," snapped Andrew, sensitive to any possible or perceived criticism of Celsie and ready to defend her if the situation called for it. Scowling, he looked down as he lifted his teacup, thus missing the surprised— and amused—look his brothers exchanged.

"Sorry," said Gareth, hiding a grin beneath the pretense of rubbing his chin. "No offense, man."

"Yes, no offense," Charles added, with a warm smile meant to defuse the bristling defensiveness he perceived in his youngest brother. "Where does she live, Andrew? If it would make either of you any less morose, I'd be happy to go fetch the dog and bring it back here to London."

Andrew gave a sulky shrug. "No need. Besides, we're not getting married here in London, but at Blackheath."

"I see," said Charles, glancing at Lucien as the duke calmly opened his paper. "And where will you live?"

Andrew, too, glanced at Lucien's severe profile. "As far away from certain interfering *monsters* as possible."

"The lady owns substantial property in Berkshire," drawled the duke from his chair. "I'm sure she can support Andrew in as much style as he desires."

"Sod off," Andrew snapped.

Charles, ever the gentleman, pretended to ignore the flare-up of animosity between the two. "Berkshire, eh?" He sipped his tea and set the cup down in its saucer. "Nice that you'll be so close. I say, Andrew, I can't wait to meet her. Nerissa said she's gorgeous."

"She is." Andrew turned away to hide the sudden flush of pride that touched his cheeks. Then, realizing that Charles was only trying to ease the tension in the room, he allowed a pained but fleeting grin. "Hell, I probably would have got her into trouble even without benefit of the aphrodisiac."

"She must be more than just gorgeous," Gareth remarked, from his own chair. "You've had stunning women throwing themselves at you for years, but I've never seen you pay any notice to any of them. Now *I'm* curious to meet her, as well!"

Andrew was starting to find this conversation stifling—especially knowing that Lucien was probably sitting there gloating over his more-than-significant part in things. He reached inside the pocket of his frock coat, withdrew his notebook, and suddenly wanting to retreat from his family, his predicament, and any gentle teasing his brothers might feel compelled to hand out, moved to the far side of the room. There he perched on the edge of a chair and began sketching, blocking out the light conversation between Charles and Gareth, and the sound of Lucien every so often turning a page of his paper.

Maybe if he lost himself in an idea, he could temporarily forget the catastrophe his life had become, the calamity his future promised, the casualty that had been his freedom. He focused on the blank page before him, put pencil to paper, and proceeded to lose himself in his latest project.

A project that, when finished, would be his wedding present to Celsie.

Ah, relief. Ah, blessed forgetfulness of immediate problems as the pencil flew as fast as his mind allowed it. The execution of the idea came naturally to him, as easily as molding a loaf of bread might have come to a baker, and as he sketched, and made calculations, and allowed for various gear measurements, tension, and resistance to heat, his mood eased and he began to relax a bit, lulled by the familiar comfort of putting his mind to work. And yet his mind kept returning to Celsie herself. To how she had held his hand last night, her defenses down, just being a friend. To how she had hugged him after all escape routes had been blocked, sympathetic to his despair when she must have been feeling just as devastated herself. Something caught in his throat. She was really quite remarkable. And brave, too.

And as Charles had guessed, gorgeous.

Again that flush of pride. God help him, he was actually looking forward to introducing her to the rest of the family. To showing her off a little. He wondered how she would get on with Juliet and Amy, and hoped she wouldn't feel like an outsider because she was English aristocracy and they were from the American colonies.

He calculated a measurement and jotted it down. Hell, maybe it was a good thing he was marrying a woman who, unlike most of her gender, was obsessed with dogs instead of babies. He didn't think he'd be very good around a baby. All that spit-up and screaming and vile-smelling diapers and mess and stuff.

He shuddered.

"Cold feet, Andrew?" asked Charles, who had risen, crossed the room, and was now standing at a nearby window, idly watching the rain pound the cobbles and swell the gutters outside.

"Not yet."

His brother put his hands on his hips, rucking up his coattails, and kept his gaze on the view outside the window. He was a thoughtful man, kind and considerate of others, and his own sobriquet, the Beloved One, was most appropriate. Without turning from the window, he lowered his voice for Andrew's ears alone.

"Have you told her yet, Andrew?"

Andrew's pencil came to a sudden halt. Charles's quiet inquiry flung a dose of reality over him, waking him from his temporary dreamworld as if someone had just roused him with a bucket of ice water. "No," he murmured uneasily, casting an eye at Lucien in the chair across the room. "I, uh, don't seem to have found the right opportunity."

Charles said nothing, merely standing there with his hands beneath his coattails, his pale blue eyes gazing out the window and candlelight gilding his hair. The house servants had spread a layer of straw atop the cobbles of the street just outside so that the clatter of passing carriages wouldn't reach the duke's ears, and Charles was idly watching a chattering flock of sparrows who were picking amongst it for food in the fast-fading light.

"I've often wondered why you were so affected and I was not," he murmured at length. "After all, we both breathed the stuff."

"Yes, well, I breathed it longer."

Charles was still gazing out the window, pretending nonchalance when Andrew knew him well enough to know he was troubled. "Have you had any more episodes lately?"

"A few."

"I suppose those damned doctors haven't been able to help any. . . ."

"Of course not. I refuse to see any more of them."

"Have the episodes got any worse?"

"Define 'worse.' "

"More frequent? More intense? Different from what they always were?"

Andrew went back to sketching. "No. Same as they've always been, though I never see the same things twice. I'm keeping a notebook. Maybe someday when I'm a drooling, chained idiot in Bedlam, someone will benefit from them."

Charles flinched as though he'd been struck.

"Sorry," Andrew said, wishing he hadn't made such a flippant remark, for now he'd upset his brother, and Charles was only showing the compassion that came as naturally to him as crazy ideas for even crazier inventions came to Andrew. He got up and tucked the notebook back into his coat pocket. "I say, I think I hear the ladies coming," he said, giving Charles a good-natured clap across the shoulder and turning toward the door. "Ah look, here they are now."

Lucien and Gareth rose from their chairs, and all four de Montforte men bowed as Celsie, accompanied by Nerissa, Juliet, and Amy, entered the room, her head high as she tried to hide her sudden nervousness. Her stomach was in knots. She was trembling like a whippet. *"Oh, what are his brothers all thinking? That I'm ugly? Flat-chested? Oh please, God, don't let me be an embarrassment to Andrew, don't let them pity him his stark and ugly bride, please don't let this be a repeat of the past, of all the times I've been teased and ridiculed for being such a skinny, stork-legged crow. . . .*

But nobody was thinking anything of the sort. Though all four women were lovely, Andrew had eyes only for Celsie. *His* Celsie. For a moment, his heart forgot how to beat. For a moment, his lungs forgot to take in air.

He could only stare. Her thick, tawny tresses had been left unpowdered and were piled high on her head, a few loose curls escaping to frame her face. A simple choker of pale pink pearls encircled her neck. Her gown was a glowing green silk the color of spring leaves, the skirts embroidered in vibrant salmon and gold threads, the stomacher the color of ripe peaches. The fitted silk clung to her tiny waist, her slender arms, showing her figure off to perfection and complementing the clear, bisquelike tone of her skin. Despite the nervousness in her eyes, she looked as regal as any princess. And then those eyes sought out his own, and leaving Charles at the window, Andrew hurried forward to take her hand, bowing over it and kissing it lightly between the knuckles.

"You are a vision," he said hoarsely, and then,

unable to keep the pride from his voice, unable to keep from touching her, he slid a possessive arm around her waist and turned her so that they both faced his brothers. "Charles, Gareth, I would like to present Lady Celsiana Blake—my betrothed."

Gareth was grinning widely, and even Charles wore a relieved smile as they came forward to take Celsie's hand and make the appropriate—and well-deserved—exclamations over her beauty. And as Andrew, standing beside her with his chest pushing so hard against his waistcoat that he thought the buttons were going to pop right off, watched her respond with modesty, grace, and dignity to the shower of compliments, he knew that everything was going to be all right.

He found himself grinning.

Freckles, beware. I'm going to make this woman happier than you could ever dream of doing!

Chapter 20

❧

The wedding was held a fortnight later.

It was a private ceremony, with the vicar of Ravenscombe performing the honors in the ancient Norman church that had served the earls, and later the dukes, of Blackheath for the last five hundred years. If the cleric thought it a strange thing that the Defiant One was finally getting married, he kept it to himself. If he thought it a strange thing that apparently none of the bride's family had come to see her pledge herself to him, he made no comment. But when the bride, heartbreakingly lovely in a gown of pale green tissue shot through with silver, walked up the aisle clutching the leash of an old, limping dog instead of the arm of a male relative, well, even the Reverend Williams, who had seen quite a bit in his day, raised a brow.

One sharp, speaking look from the commanding black eyes of His Grace the duke of Blackheath, however, brought that eyebrow straight back down to its proper place. The Reverend Williams cleared his throat and guided the bride, whose knuckles, he noted, were clenched white around the dog's leash, to the left of the groom, and proceeded to set about his business. But when he got to the part where he asked who was to give her away, he found himself at something of a loss, for there seemed to be no one with her at all, save for that sad-looking old dog with the big, pendant ears and soulful eyes gazing out of its gone-to-gray face.

"Freckles," she announced, in a voice that challenged him, that challenged anyone, to mock her wishes. She swallowed hard and reached down to stroke the dog's brown and white neck in a rapid, nervous way. "Freckles is giving me away. But not really, because he's still going to sleep on the bed with us."

"I, er . . . see," said the vicar, looking quite helpless.

The bride, still standing all alone, flushed and turned a tremulous, slightly embarrassed smile on her bridegroom, who didn't seem surprised, or uncomfortable, by her proclamation at all.

"Is that not right, Andrew? That Freckles will sleep on the bed with us?"

His reply was equally earnest. "Yes, Celsie. Freckles will sleep on the bed with us."

Williams drew out his handkerchief and mopped his brow. He was going to need a drink after this one. Maybe even two. He shot a confused look at the duke, but His Grace was his usual enigmatic self. Lord Gareth was grinning, and Lord Charles was trying, and failing, to maintain a suitably militaristic expression in keeping with his splendid scarlet and white army uniform.

As for Lord Andrew, he had a look in his eye that promised dire harm if Williams or anyone else so much as questioned his lady's wishes. Very well, then, thought Williams. If she wanted the dog to give her away, and if Lord Andrew condoned its sleeping on the bed, that was their life. He was only here to marry them, God help him.

I will never understand the aristocracy, not if I live to be a hundred.

"Witnesses, then?" he asked, with a dubious look at the old dog. *If it's Freckles, I'm having three drinks. And then I'm retiring and moving back to Cornwall.*

Lord Andrew glanced at his brother Charles. "Major de Montforte will witness our vows," he said tightly.

"Er . . . you do not wish His Grace to witness them, my lord?"

"I damned well don't," snapped Lord Andrew, glowering.

Williams flinched. He glanced nervously at the duke, but His Grace was gazing at the altar, his expression inscrutable, his entire manner unaffected.

The bride added, "My brother Gerald will also witness them."

Her ladyship has a brother? Why isn't he, and not the dog, giving her away?

"And where *is* this brother?" asked Williams, gazing rather helplessly about him.

Lord Andrew, looking more dashing than the vicar had ever seen him in an exquisitely cut suit of striped olive silk, russet smallclothes, and snowy white lace at throat and wrists, impatiently jerked his head toward the back of the church. There, in the cool, gloomy shadows, a young man sat, his expression cold, his eyes smoldering with anger. *Hmm, well, yes,* thought Williams. *I don't blame you,*

*young fellow, for being in such an ill temper. It's
not every day that a dog takes your rightful place at
your sister's side.*

"Please proceed, Williams," said the duke tightly.

Clearing his throat, the vicar picked up the *Book
of Common Prayer* and recited the age-old words.
"Dearly beloved. We are gathered together here in
the sight of God, and in the face of this congrega-
tion, to join together this man and this woman in
holy matrimony. . . ."

He saw the bride swallowing hard, wrapping and
unwrapping the leash around her hand, her head bent
as she stared, blinking, down at the elderly dog. He
saw the concerned way Lord Andrew was watching
her. She happened to look up and catch her bridegroom's gaze upon her; she offered a brave and
tremulous smile, and his own flashed, briefly, wanly,
in return. Seeing it, Williams let his voice fill the
church, trying to drown out the reservations he had
about tying these two together, trying to drown out
the otherwise charged silence, trying to drown out
the tension among the family members that made the
very air around them seem to crackle. He was doing
the right thing. Wasn't he?

He thought of all the clergymen over the centuries
who'd stood in this very spot and married countless
de Montfortes before him, of the dead sleeping in
their tombs all around, of the last duke and duchess,
their elaborate tomb a stone's toss away. Had any of
theirs been . . . hasty marriages? He was aware of the
way Lady Gareth and Lady Charles exchanged soft
glances with their husbands as he recited the binding
words of love, honor, and commitment. He was
aware of the duke gazing at his parents' tomb, his

expression still. He was aware of the excited murmur of some three hundred villagers outside, all looking forward to spending the rest of the day feasting and drinking at the tables His Grace had set up so that all could share in the celebration. Williams must have faltered, for now the duke was turning that inscrutable black stare, which would allow no mistakes, which would tolerate no question of the soon-to-be Lady Andrew's wishes, on him, silently commanding him to continue.

He had suspected that this was no love match, but when Lord Andrew raised his deep, aristocratically accented voice for everyone—even the now-dozing dog—to hear, Williams began to wonder if maybe there was more here than met the eye. . . .

"I, Andrew Mark de Montforte, take thee Celsiana Blake to my wedded wife, to have and to hold from this day forward, for better, for worse, for richer, for poorer, in sickness and in health, to love and to cherish, till death do us part, according to God's holy ordinance; and thereto I plight thee my troth."

He noted the way Lord Andrew's gaze held hers, and the silent look—was it friendship? resolution? relief?—she returned. And then she, too, spoke the timeless words, her voice clear, high, and determined.

So maybe it *was* a love match, then. That pleased him.

"The ring, please."

Heavy silence filled the church and all eyes were on Lord Andrew as he removed his signet ring and, gently taking his bride's hand, slid it partway over her finger. Lady Nerissa, standing beside the duke, sniffled loudly. Lord Charles and Lord Gareth were silent and still. His Grace the duke of Blackheath had a look on his face that Williams didn't even try to interpret.

And at the bride's feet, the old dog began to snore, so loudly that Lord Andrew had to raise his voice to be heard over it:

"With this ring I thee wed, with my body I thee worship, and with all my worldly goods I thee endow: in the name of the Father and of the Son and of the Holy Ghost. Amen."

The bridegroom slid the ring the rest of the way down his lady's finger. And as Williams bade the young couple to kneel, and began reciting the final words of the ceremony that would bind them together forever, he saw what could only be triumph—and weary relief—in the duke's harsh face.

Ah, yes, now he understood. God hadn't been the one to "join these two together in holy matrimony" . . . it had been Blackheath himself.

He pronounced them man and wife and watched in satisfaction as Lord Andrew kissed his bride, and Lady Nerissa wiped at her eyes with her handkerchief, and the family—all except the duke, who remained standing where he was, spurned and alone—swarmed around the newlyweds to hug and congratulate them.

"Well, now that the formalities are over, let's eat, drink, and be merry!" said Lord Andrew, looking relieved that the hard part was over.

And then, reaching down, he impulsively scooped up the big, sleepy old dog in his arms and carried him from the church, his wife gazing up at him in sudden adoration, the rest of the family following in their wake.

Four drinks, thought Williams, shaking his head and shutting the *Book of Common Prayer* as he waited for Lord Charles and the bride's angry brother to come up and sign the register. *Four drinks. And I've earned every one.*

The woman had slipped into the church toward the end of the ceremony and silently taken the seat beside Earl Somerfield.

She wore the latest fashions from Paris. Her dragon-green gown was made of the most expensive silk that China could produce. A fabulous choker of emeralds encircled the long, slim column of her neck, emphasizing its graceful white beauty, the flawless allure of the shoulders and bosom into which it flowed. The emeralds were a gift from the king of France in gratitude for services its wearer had performed for his country, though she was no courtesan, no royal mistress, but something far more dangerous and cunning indeed. Beneath fashionably powdered hair topped by a saucy-angled hat that threw the upper half of her face into shadow, slanting green eyes—as watchful, as predatory, as a cat's—studied the inventor of the aphrodisiac as he pledged himself to Lady Celsiana Blake.

"Took you long enough to get here, *cousin*," muttered Somerfield from out of the corner of his mouth, reminding her, much to her enduring disgust, of the distant connection she shared with this odious cretin. "The newlyweds are off to Rosebriar Park this evening, taking the contents of his laboratory—and most likely, the aphrodisiac—with them. If you'd arrived any later, we wouldn't have had a prayer of getting our hands on it!"

The newcomer never took her smiling, watchful gaze off the scene being played out near the altar. "You really shouldn't underestimate my abilities, Gerald."

Somerfield merely shot her an irate look, irritated all the more by her soft American accent, which had long since picked up the cadences of the English, not to mention French, upper classes amongst whom she dwelled.

She smiled her dazzling, malevolent little smile. "You may or may not be aware of it, Gerald, but we have France within a hairsbreadth of helping us win this tedious war with Britain." Her voice was a low, husky purr that was right in keeping with her wicked green eyes and silky feline smile. She flipped open her fan and, from above it, proceeded to study each of the people surrounding the altar. "I was most necessarily detained."

"Let me guess. You're up to your eyeballs in political intrigue, acting as Marie Antoinette's unofficial adviser and dining with that wizened old Franklin fellow. You won't rest until you get France involved in this stupid war, will you?"

"No." She smiled. "I won't. I can't. It's the only way to win it."

Somerfield, pulling at his stock, leaned closer and, through the side of his mouth, bit out, "I *want* that potion, Eva!"

She rolled her eyes with long-suffering patience. "Now, Gerald, we both know that you shall have your potion—or at least, enough of it to procure yourself a worthy heiress. The rest of it, of course, I will retain as payment for the trouble I shall put myself through in obtaining it."

"What do *you* need it for? You've been married, widowed, and have condemned all men to hell as it is."

"So I have. But in the deadly games of politics, intrigue, and war, a woman would be a fool not to make use of any available *persuasion* that might come to hand. The potion is not for me, of course. I've had my fill of men and their base lusts, cruelties, and weaknesses. Oh, no. I want that potion for America. You see, I am on a very special mission from the queen, and the fate of nations depends on my getting that potion and delivering it into her hands."

"The fate of America, you mean."

She smiled. "But of course."

"And how are you going to obtain it?"

Her mouth, hard one moment, fatally beautiful the next, curved in an amused smile. She rapped him lightly with her fan. "Really, Gerald. If you think I'm about to tell you, you're as stupid as the rest of your gender."

Gerald pursed his lips and went back to sulking. His pride smarted. So he was stupid now, was he? It was no consolation to know that Eva disliked and distrusted men in general. And it annoyed him that she wouldn't take him into her confidence. Why, *he'd* been the one to write to her about the aphrodisiac! It was *his* discovery, not hers!

And yet he was just going to have to swallow his pride and let her do what she'd come here to do. She could pick a lock in less time than it might take to open it using a proper key. She could charm the celibacy out of a priest. She had more charisma than the most decorated general, more courage than the fiercest lion—and more wiles than the cleverest fox. As the beautiful young widow of an elderly French diplomat, she consorted with princes, dined with kings and queens, and had connections in the very highest of places.

Gerald could never hope to steal the aphrodisiac on his own.

But Eva . . .

Wicked, wily, wonderful Eva . . . A small vial of potent liquid and a crazy young inventor would be child's play to her.

Eva, of course, didn't give two figs about Gerald and his silly heroine worship. The ceremony was ending, the family now gathering around the newlyweds to embrace and congratulate them. As Celsie turned around, Eva got her first good look at her face and was struck by how much her stepcousin—once a gangly, pimply-faced young girl who had cried her way through her first Season, now a stunning young woman who would surely be the toast of one—had grown. And she looked happy, bless her, beaming as her handsome husband bent down to gather up a large, doddering old dog in his arms. That pleased Eva somehow. If any woman could find happiness with a man, Eva didn't begrudge her, though experience had taught her not to try and do the same. She watched as Celsie's young lord turned and, the dog in his arms, led the procession back up the aisle, frowning as he spotted Gerald—and his uninvited companion—in the shadows.

Eva quelled any softness she'd been feeling and countered with her silky smile. Time to get back to the business at hand. Beneath the wide, jaunty brim of her hat, her eyes narrowed to thoughtful green slits as she sized up each of her would-be adversaries.

The bridegroom was obviously obsessed with his bride, though he was trying his best to hide it. He was likely obsessed even more, Eva suspected, with thoughts of his impending wedding night.

Her smile remained as she inclined her head in greeting. He would be no trouble.

And there, walking just behind him with an exotic beauty on his arm, the tall, charismatic army major, fair-haired and resplendent in his regimentals, his white crossbelt glowing in the dimly lit church, his pale blue eyes coolly competent . . . a possible problem, but Eva knew a dyed-in-the-wool gentleman when she saw one. His morals would be too high, his naïveté too great, to recognize the danger that she would soon present.

She gave a bored little sigh. No, he would be no trouble, either.

And there, yet a third brother, tawny-haired and laughing, his arm wrapped casually around the waist of his dark-haired wife. Ah yes, he was a Member of Parliament, wasn't he? She thought he looked familiar. Possibly a problem, if he had a serious bone in his body, but he looked more concerned with making merry, and ensuring that everyone else around him did as well, than with anything else.

Eva yawned. This was going to be an easy task, after all.

And finally, his sister on his arm, the last, the oldest, and without doubt, the most formidable of all the de Montforte brothers—His Grace the duke of Blackheath himself. Eva's eyes narrowed and a satisfied, completely feline smile curled her mouth. She recognized a worthy adversary the moment that omniscient black stare met hers.

The duke paused just before them and regarded the earl with flat dislike. "Really, Somerfield, if you're trying to make a point by skulking back here in the shadows, I daresay you'd have succeeded far better had you simply stayed home." As Somerfield bristled, the duke turned his head and regarded Eva down the length of his nose with arrogant disdain and a certain unmistakable gleam in his eye that she immediately recognized as something more than just curiosity.

Carnal interest.

And there was nothing subtle about it, either.

"And you, I suppose, must be the heiress who is destined to bail our dear Somerfield out of debt?"

"On the contrary, Your Grace," she purred, offering her small, gloved hand and never letting her cat-like smile waver as he bowed deeply over it. "I am Lady Eva de la Mouriére, a cousin of the man you just insulted."

"Charmed," he drawled.

"She's also friends with the French-based ambassador of the United States of America," the annoying, all-too-revealing Somerfield crowed.

The duke raised an unimpressed brow. "Ah, yes. Those infernal colonies."

Eva's smile became downright poisonous. "Colonies? I suppose I shouldn't be surprised that it has taken well over a year for news of the outside world to reach you aristocrats up here in the country." She pointedly withdrew her hand. "I'm sorry to correct you, sir, but those *infernal colonies* to which you refer are no longer the possessions of Britain, but an emerging young nation in their own right."

The duke stared at her, his smile going cold, his eyes the hard, dangerous color of black ice.

Eva, still smiling, dropped in a deep, mocking curtsy. "Now, if you will excuse me, Your Grace? I really must offer my felicitations to the bride and groom."

And then, head high, she took Gerald's arm and walked past the duke, leaving him staring after her—just like that.

Eva de la Mouriére was well used to dealing with men. Jacques had been ill from the day she'd married him, a political figurehead behind which she was the brains and cunning for which he took credit. She had handled the most corrupt power players in the civilized world. She'd had kings and emissaries and foreign ambassadors on their knees to do her bidding.

A wasp alighted on her sleeve, and she smiled as she casually flicked it away.

Really, now.

She could handle one arrogant English duke.

Chapter 21

By noon most of the villagers were as drunk as lords.

By one o'clock Andrew was bored, restless, and eager to get on the road to Rosebriar Park.

And by two he finally deserted the celebration, bade farewell to the departing Gareth and Juliet, and asked Celsie if she might change her clothes and help him finish packing up his laboratory.

Celsie was all too happy to agree. In the secluded west wing, there was peace, quiet, and solitude. Working together, they wrapped bottles, jars, and vials in cloth and placed them in wooden boxes. They packed Andrew's hopelessly disorganized notes, and asked three servants who could still walk to bring the crates of books, texts, and tomes downstairs, where everything was to be piled into a wagon that would bring the laboratory's contents to Rosebriar in the morning.

Andrew was just taking the precious vial of aphrodisiac that he'd kept out for testing from its cabinet when Lucien and Charles walked in. The duke was back in his country clothes: leather breeches, boots, and a dark coat of fine broadcloth. Charles was still in his scarlet regimentals, and looked as restless as Andrew had felt at the villagers' celebration.

"Place seems rather empty," Lucien mused, his voice echoing through the nearly bare room. He bent to retrieve a forlorn scrap of paper covered with Andrew's scribblings from the floor. "I'll miss you, little brother."

"Yes, well, you can't be missing me too much, otherwise you wouldn't have moved hell and high water to get me married and out of here," Andrew snapped, shutting the cabinet. "I'm sure your triumph would be complete if only I'd admit that I expect Celsie and me to be perfectly miserable together, but that's not going to happen. Your machinations have gone awry, Lucien, because I realize now that I would have been far more miserable staying here under *your* roof than I'll ever be under hers."

Charles winced. Celsie's hand flew to her mouth. But Lucien never moved. He just stood there holding the scrap of paper, looking, for once, as if he had nothing to say.

Andrew brushed past him, indignantly snatching the piece of paper from his hand and stuffing it into his own pocket.

"Really now, Andrew," said Lucien, recovering. "I never had any wish to make you miserable."

"Well then, thank God for that, because you made me perfectly miserable without the wish. Heaven help me had you really decided to put your mind to it, eh?"

Celsie, seeing something in the duke's dark eyes that troubled her, caught her husband's arm before things could get any worse. "Andrew, please," she said gently. "I think your brother is trying to apologize in the only way he knows how."

"Lucien, *apologize*? Ha, that will be the damned day!"

Andrew would have said more, but at that moment he caught the warning in Charles's cool blue gaze, the barely perceptible shake of his head, and relented. He shoved his hair off his brow, his anger needing a channel and finding none. He turned away and threw a few last sketches into a box.

Charles pulled out his watch. "Well, we really need to go if we all expect to get home at a reasonable hour. What do you say there, Andrew? Celsie?"

"What, are you going with us?" Andrew asked, frowning.

Charles smiled in mild amusement. "I can assure you, Andrew, that Amy and I have no wish to spoil your wedding night by inviting ourselves to Rosebriar Park. But it's getting late, we want to get back to our daughter, and since Rosebriar is on the way to Lynmouth"—he grinned—"I thought you wouldn't mind a little military escort."

Andrew put the vial he'd been holding on the worktable and shoved an empty box out of the way with his foot. "Well, we're nearly finished in here. Let me just get the rest of the aphrodisiac and we'll be ready to leave."

Lucien frowned. "I think it best if you leave it here with me."

"Are you bloody joking? I need it. 'Sdeath, I'll be the laughingstock of the scientific community if word gets out about that damned stuff unless I can figure out what the devil I put into it and duplicate it accordingly. Oh, no, *I'm* taking it."

Lucien's eyes went hard. "No."

Andrew's went equally hard. *"Yes."*

Now even Charles, normally mild-mannered and reasonable, was beginning to look irritated. Spotting the vial that Andrew had retained and not realizing it was only part of a much larger store, he stepped forward, plucked it from the table, and tucked it into the inside pocket of his scarlet coat. "There. I think it is quite safe where it is. Now, finish up in here, Andrew. Fifteen more minutes and we're leaving without you."

" 'Sdeath, I hate when you use that officer voice," Andrew complained.

Charles leveled a quelling, big-brother look on him. "And I hate when you don't watch your language in front of the ladies. Fourteen minutes. I'll see you downstairs."

Charles bowed to Celsie, turned smartly on the heel of one impeccably shined boot, and went out.

Lucien looked at Andrew.

Andrew returned that mild look with a mute glare.

"So, are you going to surrender the rest of the aphrodisiac or do I have to go get it myself?" he finally challenged.

Lucien pursed his lips, considering the matter. His inscrutable black gaze held Andrew's for a long moment before he finally sighed dramatically and allowed a little smile to touch his mouth. "I suppose I'd better," he mused. "Otherwise, you'll only waste more time trying to figure out where I put the key to the safe, and out of respect for Charles, who has every right to want to get home, I won't keep him waiting any longer than he's already waited. I fear he's growing most impatient."

He bowed to Celsie and then turned and left the room—leaving Andrew surprised, and a little deflated, that he'd won the battle without even a fight.

What on earth was wrong with Lucien?

Everyone was waiting.

The house servants all stood lined up at attention on the stairs, the blushing young maids misty-eyed at losing yet another handsome de Montforte brother, the bewigged footmen well turned out in the duke's livery, the butler and housekeeper quietly watching as the Defiant One prepared to depart for his new life. Outside, Nerissa stood beside a stony-faced Lucien, trying to feign happiness for the sake of the newlyweds but looking as though she was ready to start weeping at any moment. Charles and Amy's coach, a driver on the box and a footman riding behind, waited on the drive, as did Celsie's carriage, filled to the roof—and beyond—with Andrew's clothes, possessions, and those contents of his laboratory which couldn't fit in the wagon that would make the journey to Rosebriar tomorrow.

Celsie's heart went out to Nerissa, who looked forlorn as she stood beside Lucien. She knew that Nerissa and Andrew were close, and almost felt as though she were taking her brother away from her. Impulsively she embraced the other woman, hugging her tightly. "Please don't be sad," she said. "I know you'll miss Andrew, but you must come visit us at Rosebriar as often as you can." And then, for Nerissa's ears alone, she whispered, "I promise I'll take as good care of him as I do my dogs."

Nerissa gave a watery smile. "I know you will. Otherwise, I would never let you take him away."

A groom came up, leading Andrew's gray Thoroughbred, Newton, in one hand and Charles's tall, strapping Contender in the other. The big stallion had carried Charles into battle in Boston when he had been a captain in the Fourth Foot, and served him just as proudly now that he was a major stationed at Horse Guards in London.

Good-byes were said, embraces exchanged, tears held at bay. Andrew helped Celsie into the coach, hoisted Freckles up onto the seat beside her, and whistled for Esmerelda, who bounded eagerly up after the older dog. He stood waiting as Charles handed Amy into the vehicle. Then the two brothers mounted their horses, Charles touched his hat to the duke and Nerissa, and a moment later, the procession was heading off around the big circular drive, the two riders flanking the coach, the setting sun turning everything to gold.

Hundreds of voices called out all around them as Celsie and Amy leaned out the windows, waving.

"Good-bye!"

"Godspeed!"

"God be with you . . . good-bye!"

They crossed the moat, passed hundreds of cheering, waving villagers, and once out onto the Ravenscombe road, let the horses have their heads.

Celsie, with Freckles leaning heavily against her and a lovelorn Esmerelda on the floor trying to attract his attention, settled herself into her seat and thrust her toes against the warm brick, wrapped in a blanket, at her feet. Her mind was still whirling over all the events of the last fortnight, let alone the last few hours. *I am a married woman,* she thought, in some disbelief. But she didn't feel any different than she had before.

On the opposite seat, Amy was leaning her head back and sighing with relief that they were finally on their way. Fearful of the effects of travel on their infant daughter, she and Charles had left little Mary behind in the care of a wet nurse. Celsie knew that both were eager to get back to her. Now Amy opened her dark eyes and looked across at Celsie, her brow creased thoughtfully. "Do you know, I don't think I've ever seen Lucien looking quite so—"

"Lost?" Celsie supplied.

"Yes, lost. Preoccupied. I can't put my finger on it. He was that way all afternoon."

"Maybe he has regrets about playing Andrew and me like puppets."

"Oh, I doubt that," Amy said, with a faint smile. "Funny, but when I first met him, I didn't think him capable of the scheming manipulations that everyone blamed on him. And once I found that he schemed and manipulated Charles and me into getting married, well, I really couldn't be angry with him. He gave me a new life, a new identity, respectability in society—and his brother. But tonight . . . he just didn't look himself. I wonder if he's feeling a little bereft at having nobody left to manipulate."

"If he is, it's his own bloody fault." Celsie moved over to give Freckles more room. "So he manipulated you and Charles as well, then?"

"Oh, yes." Amy grinned. "And Gareth and Juliet, too."

"Well, I don't feel so singled out, then," Celsie

allowed, returning Amy's smile. "Did you and Charles have a love match?"

"Yes, but our love was already strong when Lucien pushed us into marriage. Gareth and Juliet, however . . . well, they had their own share of problems. But Lucien knew what he was doing when he brought them together. Eventually they came to love each other"—she reached out and touched Celsie's hand—"just as you and Andrew will."

A lump caught in Celsie's throat and she looked away, out the window. "You think so, do you?"

"Oh, Celsie," said Amy, laughing and leaning forward. "Did you see the way Andrew kept looking at you during the ceremony? And the way he was beaming when he first introduced you to his brothers? Trust me, you did the right thing. I know it in my heart. And let me tell you, there is nothing in this world to equal being loved by a de Montforte. Andrew will make you a fine husband. His love will be worth waiting for."

"But his moods are so unpredictable, and he gets surly and standoffish whenever I think he's starting to warm up to me. I just don't understand him."

Amy eyed her gravely. "You mean he hasn't told you?"

"Told me what?"

Amy pursed her lips, as though she'd said too much. "He has—well, let's just say there are some things in his life that he has a hard time adjusting to." She smiled, apologetically. "But with your help, I'm sure he will."

It was obvious that Amy was reluctant to carry the conversation in that direction. Though her curiosity was aroused, Celsie brought the topic back to the duke's manipulations out of respect for her sister-in-law. "So what about Nerissa?" she asked. "Why is it that Lucien has tampered with his brothers' fates, but has left his only sister alone?"

"Oh, she's already as good as affianced to Perry, Lord Brookhampton. He's the duke's neighbor, and as handsome and dashing as the day is long."

Celsie grinned. "As handsome and dashing as the de Montforte brothers?"

"Well now, I think our two are awfully hard to beat!"

They laughed, and Celsie moved farther over to make more room for Freckles. The dog groaned, stretched, and tried to claim even more space as he laid his noble old head across her lap, his eyes closing. He didn't mind that his mistress was now crushed against the leather squab. And he was totally oblivious to Esmerelda. The setter eyed him longingly, then, casting a hopeless glance at Celsie, lay down on the floor of the coach, put her head dejectedly on her paws, and stared unblinkingly at the door, her thoughts, like Celsie's, her own.

I know how it feels, girl. It's hard to find yourself thinking you could fall in love with someone, only to have him withdraw into himself whenever you want to get close to him.

Dear God. *Did* she want to get close to Andrew? Did she want to have the sort of relationship with him that Amy and Juliet had with their de Montforte men?

Yes.

She leaned her cheek against the squab. *Oh, yes . . .*

Opposite, Amy reached for her sewing, though the

light was starting to fade and her time on such a pursuit would be limited. The two fell into easy conversation, talking about the things they admired about their husbands, the similarities of their respective childhoods, the baby that Amy had and the babies that Celsie hoped Andrew would give her.

Presently the shadows became oppressive gloom. Amy put her sewing aside. Darkness fell. At a coaching inn near Maidenhead, they stopped to change horses and take a quick meal and decided to press on toward Rosebriar.

The lights of the coach were lit, and before long, the sway and rock of its movement made them both drowsy. Celsie looked out the window at the stars riding high over the dark rolling hills. She felt content. At peace. The ever-present threat of highwaymen didn't worry her; not with the dogs here with them, and Andrew and Charles flanking their coach. Andrew was a peerless swordsman. And no road robber in his right mind would dare harass a stern, competent army major with a blade at his thigh and a pistol at the ready.

She had just closed her eyes when a sudden stop jolted her awake. Freckles raised his head from her lap, pricking his floppy ears. Esmerelda woofed and got to her feet, tail stiff. Celsie sat up, exchanged glances with Amy, and tried to see outside, where they could hear Andrew talking with Charles. A moment later, Charles rode Contender up to the window.

"Forgive us for stopping," he said with an easy smile, his cool blue eyes warming as they briefly rested on Amy. In the latern-lit darkness, he looked handsome and reassuring in his uniform. "There's a coach just ahead that's gone off the road. We think they might have broken an axle. If you don't mind, Andrew will stay here with you while I ride ahead to offer our help in speeding the poor folks on their way."

"I don't mind," said Celsie, shrugging.

"Neither do I," added Amy. "I feel sorry for anyone left stranded out on these lonely roads." She leaned out the window and kissed her husband. "Go, Charles. And if their coach is broken down, I'm sure we can make room in ours so they can at least get to the next coaching inn."

He touched his hat to them and rode off.

"That's my Beloved One," Amy said, smiling as she settled back down in her seat. "Always thinking of others before himself."

As indeed Charles was. He waited while Andrew moved Newton up to the window and then, one hand on his pistol in case of a cleverly laid trap, urged Contender toward the stricken coach. It had been drawn just off the road so as not to impede other travelers, its team unhitched and tied to a tree. Charles frowned, for beside it sat a burly young man with his head in his hands, obviously drunk, obviously unable to deal with such a demanding situation, while nearby, a young peasant woman in tired brown rags struggled to single-handedly push the heavy vehicle against a tree, presumably in hopes of getting the wheel off.

There was no way in God's heaven that she was ever going to succeed.

Charles released his hold on the pistol. His mouth grim with sympathy, he urged Contender, who had begun to fret, toward the coach. Immediately the

stallion shied sideways, whirling to face the stricken
vehicle and blowing hard through his nostrils.

"Easy, boy," Charles murmured, patting the sleek
neck and coolly assessing the situation. He was nothing if not confident, and he was well used to dealing
with demanding situations. This, however, did not
look like a demanding situation at all.

"Good evening," he said pleasantly, removing his
hat in respect to the poor young woman who had
given up trying to lift the coach and was now on her
hands and knees beneath it, peering up at the axle,
a lantern glowing on the ground beside her. "We
couldn't help but notice your rather unfortunate predicament. Perhaps I can be of some assistance?"

At the sound of Charles's calm, reassuring voice,
she crawled out from beneath the coach, fat tears of
relief rolling down her dusty cheeks when she saw
his uniform.

"Oh, sir, any assistance ye could be givin' us
would be much appreciated! Me 'usband's as soused
as a fox and these roads are crawlin' with highwaymen and Oi'm scared to death we won't get 'ome
without gettin' murdered! It's the axle, I think—or
maybe the wheel. Oi just don't know. . . ."

"Well then, let me see what I can do here,"
Charles soothed, instinctively taking control of the
situation. But as he slipped his boots from the irons
and prepared to dismount, Contender snorted and
shied once more, nearly unseating him. Growing impatient with the normally unflappable horse, Charles
vaulted from the saddle and approached the vehicle.

"You don't know how glad I am to see ye," the
peasant woman said, getting to her feet. She wiped
her eyes with the back of a grimy hand and brushed

the dust from her ragged skirts. "I think the problem's with the other wheel, or up underneath. There don't seem to be anythink wrong on this side, least not to me unknowin' eye." She picked up the lantern, its light catching her full in the face and revealing vivid red hair and slanting green eyes, before she turned and led him around to the other side of the coach.

"Here. Allow me." Charles took the lantern and calmly surveyed the coach. It wasn't a large vehicle; between him, Andrew, and the servants, they should be able to lift it in order to make whatever repairs the situation demanded. He knelt, peering up underneath it and inspecting the undercarriage with a critical eye. "So what seems to be the problem?"

"Oh, it's probably this silly wheel. . . . We just 'ad it replaced, and now there's this awful rumblin' noise comin' from up underneath and I'm a'scared to droive it any farther for fear it's going to come loose and make us 'ave an accident!"

"I see," said Charles, going down on one knee beside the wheel and taking off his gloves. "Well, if you could just hold the lantern so I could have some light, I'll see what I can do." He smiled reassuringly. "Probably just needs a little tightening, and then the two of you can be on your way."

Her eyes gleaming, Eva de la Mouriére picked up the lantern and watched as he began to examine the perfectly fine wheel and axle. *Ah, yes,* she thought in satisfaction, as she gazed haughtily down at his pale, wavy hair, so neatly caught in its tidy black queue. Every man had a weakness, and she had correctly discerned this one's. The gallant Lord Charles de Montforte was too much of a gentleman to pass a hapless traveler without stopping to offer his help. He was too unimaginative in his thinking to ever even consider that danger might come in the form of an apparently helpless young woman.

And he was going to have one hell of a headache in the morning.

She waited until he was down on both knees, one hand supporting himself on the grass verge, the other reaching up beneath the coach to examine the axle. And then, exchanging a glance with the all-too-sober servant who was posing as her drunken husband, she made a rigid blade of her hand, raised it high, and brought it down hard on the back of the major's neck in one ruthless, vicious chop.

She knew right where to hit a man to render him unconscious, and she reveled in her power to do it.

He crumpled without a sound.

"Right," she said, straightening up and brushing her hands together in tribute to a job well done. She pulled a pistol from the pocket of her skirt, priming and loading it with ease. "Now that one obstacle is out of the way, I think it's time to collect what we've all been sitting around waiting for." She stepped over the officer sprawled senseless at her feet, sparing him an amused little grin. "Nighty-night, Major de Montforte. Sleep well!"

And then, still smiling, she, the servant, and the three other lackeys who'd been hidden within the "stricken" vehicle headed for the lights of the coach.

Chapter 22

Andrew's spine prickled with uneasiness.

He sat astride his horse, bathed in the lights of the coach and making small talk with the women. He was half watching Charles, who had dismounted from Contender and was now going around to the other side of the stricken vehicle to help the unfortunate travelers. Celsie was saying something; Andrew turned his head to listen. And when he turned it back again to look toward the distant coach, he heard the driver up on the box suck in his breath and saw a woman and four men walking toward him from out of the darkness.

The woman had a pistol and she was pointing it straight at his heart.

"Hello, Andrew. I *am* sorry to inconvenience you, but if you would just hand over the aphrodisiac, we can all be on our way."

Inside the coach, both women gasped. On the boot, the footman reached for his blunderbuss but froze as Andrew caught his eye and shook his head in warning. And now Freckles was beginning to growl, the sound deep and ugly and getting louder by the moment.

Slowly Andrew's hand went for his pistol.

"Uh-uh," the woman purred, smiling and shaking her head as though scolding a child. "You don't want to do that. Someone might get hurt, and we wouldn't want it to be you. Or the ladies."

"Where's my brother?" Andrew demanded. He looked beyond the would-be thieves, his eyes narrowing. "What have you done to him?"

"Oh, well, it's past his bedtime, you know. I daresay he's taking a little nap." The woman's smile never wavered at Amy's cry of alarm, but her slanting eyes narrowed with deadly intent. "Now, hand over the potion, Andrew sweetie, or I'll put you into a much more *permanent* kind of sleep than I did your too-gallant-for-his-own-good brother."

Andrew tensed, his body screaming for action. It cost him everything he had to hold himself still as the four lackeys, also toting pistols, surrounded the coach, preventing escape.

His angry gaze clashed with the woman's. "And just who the devil are you?"

"Why, your killer, of course"—again that malevolent smile—"unless you hand over that potion." She aimed the pistol dead center on his chest.

"Andrew, no heroics," snapped Celsie from within the coach. "If she wants the potion, let's just give it to her and send her on her way. It isn't worth anyone getting killed."

"Ah, leave it to a woman to show some sense," purred their attacker, in a faintly amused tone. "Now, obey your wife, Lord Andrew—or make her a widow. You have five more seconds to decide, or I will decide for you."

Celsie, one hand on Amy's arm to keep her from

flying out of the coach to Charles's aid, the other restraining the growling Freckles, decided for both of them. She leaned out the window and met the hostile, slanting gaze. "Why, Eva. I thought it was you. For some reason, I should have known you didn't come all the way back to England just to congratulate us on our nuptials."

Andrew started. "*Eva?* You *know* this jezebel?"

"She's my cousin. Of course I know her. And so do you."

His gaze went from one to the other; suddenly he recognized their assailant, though she had disguised herself in peasant clothes and looked nothing like she had earlier at the church. "Why, you were with Somerfield at our wedding!"

"And trust me, she is more than capable of murder," said Celsie, in a hard, flat voice. She leaned out the window, fearlessly meeting the other woman's amused gaze. "Eva, since my husband here is showing a remarkable inability to make up his mind, I will take charge of this situation and bring the potion out to you myself."

"*Celsie, stay in that coach!*" Andrew roared, his voice harsh with fear.

But Celsie bade Amy to take hold of Freckles's collar, stepped around the whining Esmerelda, calmly pulled the bottle of aphrodisiac out from beneath the seat, and opening the door, jumped down from the coach. Head high, she walked around the vehicle and up to the other woman, fully aware that the thugs had their guns trained on her as surely as Eva had hers trained on Andrew.

"I wish you hadn't done this," Celsie said, unable to keep the disappointment from her voice. "I used to admire you. I used to look up to you. Why, Eva?"

"My country needs it," she said simply, looking away.

Celsie sighed. Then she set the bottle down in the dirt and stepped back. Eva, keeping her pistol on Andrew the whole time, sent one of her lackeys to fetch it, then motioned to someone behind her. From the direction of the stricken coach, another thug came forward, leading several saddled horses. Eva kept her pistol trained on Andrew as, one by one, the thieves mounted. Then, as they covered for her, she, too, mounted, tucked her prize in her saddlebags, and with a mocking little salute, wheeled her horse and set her heels to its sides.

Within moments they were gone, swallowed up by the night.

They found Charles just getting to his feet, rubbing the back of his neck and swaying unsteadily.

"Damned witch blindsided me," he muttered, clinging to the door of the coach to support himself. He let go as Amy flew to him and insinuated herself under one arm to support him. "Never saw it coming. . . ."

"She wanted the potion," snapped Andrew, quickly filling his brother in on their attacker's identity.

"Well, I hope to hell you gave it to her. . . . Confounded stuff is proving to be more trouble than it's worth. Stick to flying machines from now on, would you?" He caught Amy's hands as they worriedly explored his face for signs of damage and, embarrassed, folded her to his chest. "Stop, sweetheart. I'm all right."

Though his words were gentle, Andrew saw that Charles's jaw was set, his pale blue eyes cold and quietly furious. Andrew couldn't even imagine how humiliated he must feel. "Well, there's no sense standing around here all night," he said affably, trying to take the focus off his embarrassed brother. "You still have that vial, Charles?"

"Yes." Still a bit dazed, he fumbled inside his coat, extracted what was left of the aphrodisiac, and slapped it rather irritably into Andrew's palm. "Take it, and with my blessings."

Andrew tucked it into his own pocket. "Much obliged. Now, let's get going. I don't know about you, but I've had all the excitement I can take for one night. You're all right to ride, aren't you?"

His brother merely shot him an annoyed glance.

"I thought so," said Andrew, slapping him good-naturedly across the shoulders. He snared Contender's reins, holding him and ready to lend a hand in case his brother couldn't quite haul himself up into the saddle; but Charles was made of strong stuff, and he was soon astride the tall stallion, grim-faced, a little pale, and very, very angry.

Though she eyed him with concern, Amy knew better than to try and persuade her husband to ride in the coach. The major's pride had been sorely wounded; he would ride his stallion, and none of them would try to talk him out of it.

"All right, let's go," Charles growled, pressing his knees to Contender's sides and guiding the big horse, who was almost tiptoeing in his eagerness not to unseat his wobbly master, back toward their own coach. Try as he might, though, he couldn't get any speed or fire out of the big steed. " 'Sdeath, not you too. I've got a wife to coddle me, I don't need a damned horse doing it as well!"

Andrew and Celsie exchanged amused, relieved glances; then, satisfied that Charles was going to be just fine, they followed him, Contender, and Amy back toward the coach.

They rested for several hours at a roadside inn, changed horses, continued on, and just before dawn of the following morning, finally pulled up at the tall iron gates of Rosebriar Park. Though Celsie urged her new in-laws to visit for a day or so, they were both eager to press on for their home some ten miles outside of London. Celsie and Andrew bade them good-bye and stood at the gates watching until the coach, still accompanied by Charles on horseback, faded into the darkness.

"I do wish they'd stayed," Celsie said ruefully, reaching down to gently pull at Freckles's floppy ears. "It's been a long journey, and he really ought to be resting, not riding."

Andrew made a scoffing noise and dismounted from Newton. "Of course he should be riding. He's a toughened soldier, not a baby. Besides, Contender will take care of him for the rest of the way home, and Amy will take care of him once he's there. He'll be fine."

"You think so?"

"Yes, but I don't know about that Eva or Evil or whatever the devil her name was. Once Lucien finds out about the robbery, there'll be hell to pay, and he, unlike Charles, won't grant her the benefit of the doubt—or any advantages—just because she's a woman."

"Knowing Eva, she wouldn't want him to. Ah, but still . . . can't you just imagine? The duke of Blackheath versus Eva de la Mouriére. Now, *there's* a confrontation I'd love to witness . . . from behind suitable protection, of course!"

"She wouldn't have a chance against him, much as I wish it otherwise."

"Oh, I don't know . . . I think I'd put my money on Eva."

Andrew only smiled, for he knew his brother all too well. He handed Newton's reins to the footman and sent the two servants, along with the coach in which were piled his belongings, on toward the house, leaving him and Celsie alone at the end of the drive. Then he turned and offered his elbow to his new bride, wanting to make this last part of the journey only with her. Adjusting his pace so the limping old dog could follow, he began to walk.

The first blush of dawn was already beginning to plant roses in the gloomy eastern sky. As they moved slowly up the drive, Esmerelda bounding ahead to explore her new home, Andrew felt a strange sense of peace and homecoming that was as surprising as it was welcome. Here he was, beginning a new life as a married man. Here he was, with a woman he actually enjoyed spending time with, a woman whose silken skin and warm flesh he couldn't wait to possess all over again. Here he was—chained in matrimony but free of his Machiavellian brother forever.

Perhaps fate had dealt him a winning hand, after all.

A chilly breeze came up, stirring the fading leaves of the tall, graceful chestnuts that lined the drive. He lifted his face to it, watching the sky lightening to the east, the bellies of the high clouds that slept on the horizon shimmering with brushstrokes of brilliant crimson fire.

Celsie paused with him, and Andrew, after a moment's hesitation, slid his arm around her waist, drawing her close. Together they watched the birth of the new day, their first as husband and wife. He was happy. He was at peace. And his bride didn't stiffen or try to move away, but actually stayed there, as content to be near him as he was to be near her. Maybe, just maybe, this friendship thing was going to work after all. . . .

Though Andrew knew as well as anyone that friends didn't keep secrets from each other.

"So much for wedding nights," he said wryly.

"Well, you can't say we didn't have an unusual one. Instead of being robbed of our innocence, we were robbed of the very thing that caused us to lose it."

"My God, don't remind me of that. I think my heart stopped when you got out of the coach and walked up to that she-devil." He shuddered. "I don't know many people who would have had the courage to do what you did, let alone the wisdom to take charge and relinquish the potion to that bloodthirsty witch."

"I had to," she said, obviously pleased but a bit embarrassed by his open compliment. "Besides, I could tell just by looking at you that you were about to do something reckless, brave—and foolish. I couldn't just allow you to throw your life away like that."

"By stepping in, you probably saved it. You know that, don't you?"

"Well, someone had to step in." She grinned. "After all, you *men* certainly weren't handling things very well!" She sobered then, her eyes going warm and soft as she gazed up at him. "Did it really scare you, Andrew? That is, my confronting Eva?"

"Zounds, yes!" He cleared his throat and then, in a lower, more controlled tone, said, "Yes."

"Why, you almost sound as though you care about me."

"Whatever made you think I do not?"

"You don't want me taking up your time, you don't want me in your life, you don't want me at all—"

"Stop right there. I *do* want you. And if I could predict the reaction I'd get, I'd take your hand right now and show you the physical evidence to prove it."

"You mean you don't need the aphrodisiac?"

"Men don't need aphrodisiacs."

She laughed, though he noticed her cheeks went suddenly bright with color.

"Besides," he added, "I'm glad to see the last of that stuff."

"You're not going to try and get it back?"

"Get it back?" He shook his head. "No. I've decided I don't *want* it back. Its discovery was an accident, it was of little benefit to science, and the fact that I haven't been able to duplicate it, let alone remember what went into it, would only have made me the subject of ridicule from the scientific community. Oh no, Celsie, I see things clearly now. It was the cause of nothing but trouble from the very first, and I'm well rid of the stuff."

"Or most of it, anyhow. There is still that vial in your pocket. . . ."

"Ah yes, I'd forgotten about that."

"I haven't."

He glanced down at her, one brow raised. She blushed and looked away, though she moved her body so that his hand, which had been around her waist, slipped to the small of her back. She laid her head against his shoulder. Gently Andrew stroked the base of her spine through the sleek satin gown, then let his hand move out over the curve of her bottom.

She didn't move away.

Only closer.

He turned her so that she was facing him, and gently holding her arms, looked down into her tired but smiling eyes. "Tell me, Celsie. Do you want your wedding present before or after what remains of our wedding night?"

"Ummm . . . that all depends on what the remains of our wedding night have to offer," she murmured, with a coy little blush.

"What would you like it to offer?"

"You"—the blush deepened and she looked up, searching his gaze—"but only if you're not too tired and eager to get to bed."

"I *am* tired and eager to get to bed, but I can assure you, madam, that once there, sleep will be the furthest thing from my mind."

"Is it the furthest thing from your mind now?"

He smiled slowly. "Indeed."

She gave a breathless, self-conscious little laugh.

"Listen to me! There must have been permanent aftereffects from that potion after all. I'm behaving like some sort of wanton."

"Are you?" He grinned. "Do explain."

She opened her mouth, shrugged, and began digging at a stone with her toe, her cheeks as bright as the sunrise. "I want to go to bed with you—as your wife. I want to consummate our marriage. I want to know you as a woman knows her man, not as a friend, not as an acquaintance, and certainly not as a partner in resentment." She quit worrying the pebble and instead started stroking Freckles's head, at a level with her knee. "I want all that, Andrew, but I'm embarrassed for wanting it, I'm not quite sure *why* I want it, and when all is said and done, well . . . well, I guess I'm just a little jittery."

He reached down and ever so gently, lifted her chin with his finger so that she was forced to meet his gaze. He smiled, cradled her face in both hands, and tenderly stroked her flaming cheeks with his thumbs. "I know you're nervous. We don't have to consummate it tonight, Celsie. Or even tomorrow night. We have the rest of our lives to get to know each other."

As hard as it had been to say the words, as difficult as Andrew found the idea of waiting another hour—let alone another day—to get inside her body, he had expected her to be pleased that he was being so considerate. Instead, her brows came together and her eyes darkened with worry and hurt. "Are you saying you'd be content to wait a lifetime to consummate our marriage?"

"Hell, no."

"Good," she said, visibly relieved, "because I

don't want to wait that long, either. In fact, I don't even want to wait until tomorrow night." She stood on tiptoe, put her lips to his ear, and whispered, "I want to do it *now*."

Her suggestion bypassed Andrew's brain and went straight to his genitals. He laughed, not quite believing what he'd just heard. "You *do*?"

"Yes." She went back down on her heels, her eyes glowing with coy shyness as she looked up at him through thick, tawny lashes and embraced his waist with her hands. She held his gaze. Let her hands slide downward. And now he felt her palming him through his breeches, testing his hardening bulge. *"Now."*

Andrew sucked in his breath. Already he was a slab of stone down there, pushing against the protesting fabric of his breeches. God help him. She wanted him. *She wanted him now,* and this had nothing to do with the damned aphrodisiac!

"Andrew?"

He couldn't take any more. His hands cupping her buttocks, he pulled her so close that even through the voluminous fabric of her petticoats, he could feel her pelvis pressing against his erection. The sensation inflamed him all the more, tightening his groin, causing his heart to pump madly. He kissed her. She made a sighing noise in her throat and returned the kiss, her tongue eagerly seeking his own, her hand now roving up his neck, her fingers tunneling through his hair. Still holding her bottom, he pushed his fingers against the heavy satin of her skirts, trying, failing, to find the junction of her thighs. *Damn these hoops. Damn these petticoats.* Finally he lifted her petticoats, slid his hand between her legs, and quickly manipulated her to a gasping climax.

"Oh, God," she murmured, burying her face against his chest and panting as she clung to him. "I . . . I think we'd better go inside."

"Now."

"Oh, yes. *Now*."

She gave a shaky little laugh. He lifted her head with one finger and kissed her. Light glowed behind his eyelids, and opening his eyes, he found that around them, everything seemed to be holding its breath as the landscape turned to molten gold. Wanting to treasure this moment of rare joy before he brought her inside and spent the morning making love to her, he drew back, turning her so both could watch the sun as it finally rose from its bed. And here it came, a brilliant ball of fire, higher, and higher. . . .

Andrew bent his head to kiss her once more—and from just behind came the slow, rising sound of thunder.

"How odd," he murmured, his lips brushing her sunlit nose, and then her mouth, his breath warm against her cheek.

"What?"

"The fact that it's starting to thunder when the only clouds in the sky are high and distant and peaceful."

"I don't hear any thunder," she said on a sigh, her arms going around his neck, her breath mingling with his as she raised her lips for his kiss. "Though I certainly *feel* some!"

"What do you mean, you don't hear it?" Andrew asked, frowning and pulling back as the noise grew alarmingly loud now, rising in volume without break and sounding quite unlike any thunder that *he'd* ever heard. The hairs on the back of his neck rising, he turned his head to look over his shoulder—and saw a huge silver monster sailing straight over the tree-tops toward them.

He gave a hoarse cry of terror and instinctively threw Celsie to the ground as it passed overhead, covering her with his body until the deafening roar peaked and rolled and finally grew distant.

When he lifted his head, his skin was pale, his face damp with sweat, his body shaking.

And Celsie was staring at him with wide, shocked eyes.

"Andrew?" she whispered, in a tiny, nervous voice. "Are you . . . all right?"

Chapter 23

━━━━━◦◦◦◦━━━━━

"**N**o," he said with sudden sharpness as he got to his feet. "No, I'm *not* all right."

And with that, he spun on his heel and stalked off down the drive toward the house, leaving Celsie standing there with Freckles and staring after him in confusion, dismay, and hurt.

"Andrew!"

He kept walking. He paused some fifty feet away and turned to look at her, fists clenched at his sides, his very stance stiff and defensive. His face was terrible. "Leave me be, Celsiana. Leave me be while I try to find a way to tell you just what sort of monstrous freak you've married."

She took a step toward him; he extended an arm, palm thrust out, as though warding off one who might catch the plague. Then, and only then, did he turn and continue on toward the house.

Celsie could only stand there in confusion and disbelief. Everything inside her bade her to run after him and demand an answer. What was wrong? Why did he keep *doing* this, to her, to their blossoming friendship and now, to their marriage? This wasn't the first time he'd acted strangely, was it? Her mind raced back over the past several weeks. There was that time at de Montforte House in London. There was his behavior during the sword fight with Gerald. And there was the evening of her charity ball, when he'd looked up at the ceiling, his eyes strangely distant, and then fled—

Just as he was doing now.

What was he afraid of?

What was wrong with him?

And why didn't he trust her with whatever secret he was hiding?

Celsie had no idea. But she knew one thing: She was going to find out. Calling for Esmerelda and Freckles, she headed resolutely for the house.

She opened the door and walked into chaos.

The servants were as nervous as a flock of hens with a fox in their midst. Tension charged the air, and angry voices came from another part of the house. The housekeeper, a pretty young redhead named Miss Upchurch, hurried up to Celsie, her voice low. "They're in the library, my lady," she murmured, seeing Celsie's darkening mood.

Celsie's mood had every reason to be dark. Between the robbery, Andrew shutting her out, and now what sounded like the devil of an argument between Andrew and Gerald—*what was* he *still doing here?!*—she had had enough.

She stormed into the library just in time to see Andrew backing her stepbrother up against the wall, one hand wrapped around his throat, his other on the hilt of his sword. Gerald's eyes were bulging, his hands waving wildly.

"Don't you *ever* threaten me again," Andrew

seethed in a deadly soft voice. "And don't you dare pretend ignorance where the robbery was concerned either, you bastard. You knew about the aphrodisiac, and I'd bet my last coin that you invited that bitch here to steal it, didn't you?" Gerald made a whimpering noise in his throat. "I'll tell you right now, Somerfield, that if you ever harm any member of my family, ever again, directly or indirectly, I'll kill you. Do I make myself clear?"

Gerald was sweating, eyes wild, his palms sliding up the wall in an effort to get away.

"Do I make myself clear?"

Celsie cleared her throat. "What is going on in here?"

Andrew turned his head. His face was as cold and terrible as she'd ever seen Lucien's, and for a moment Celsie almost didn't recognize him. With a curse, he released Gerald, shoving him slightly to the side as he did. Her stepbrother stumbled and went sprawling, cutting his lip on his teeth as he fell.

Celsie made no move to go to either of them.

Gerald got to his feet, rubbing his throat and glaring at Andrew. He took out his handkerchief and dabbed at his bloodied lip, then turned wounded eyes on Celsie. "You've married a madman," he said sullenly. "I was in here minding my own business when *he* came in, accused me of setting Eva on you, and physically assaulted me. I demand an apology, de Montforte!"

Andrew's eyes were deadly. "And do you demand restitution?"

Gerald paled.

"There will be no more dueling," Celsie said sharply, stamping her feet in frustration. She turned her angry stare on Gerald. "*Did* you set Eva on us to steal the aphrodisiac?"

"Of course not," he mumbled, but his gaze slid away. Celsie blinked back tears of mounting frustration. He was lying. She knew it in her heart. Andrew or Charles could have been killed, and her brother couldn't even look her in the eye and tell the truth.

"I have a demand of my own," she said, her voice unnaturally flat as she tried to keep her wrath in check. "I want you out of this house within an hour after breakfast, Gerald. I'm tired of supporting you, tired of saving you from one financial disaster after another, tired of keeping you out of debtor's gaol only to have you repay me by nearly getting my husband and brother-in-law killed. You have a fine way of showing gratitude."

"You can't throw me out, I have nowhere else to go!"

"You have friends in London. You have an uncle. Go throw yourself on their charity for a change. I have had enough."

Andrew, who'd been leaning negligently against the edge of a table, straightened. "And if you think she can't throw you out, rest assured that I will." His smile was positively malevolent. "Bodily."

Gerald stood there, his gaze darting from his selfish stepsister to the man she had married. The man who had stolen what should have been Gerald's financial salvation right out from under his nose. The man who had turned Gerald's life and future upside down.

The man Gerald hated with a passion that made him dizzy.

I'll get my revenge on you, you bastard, he thought. *You just wait.*

"Fine, then," he muttered darkly. "But you'll be sorry. Both of you."

He spun on his heel and stalked from the room. He didn't stop until he reached his apartments. There, as he began hurling possessions into a trunk, he saw that a package had come for him, brought by an anonymous messenger and left by a servant on the table beside his bed.

Gerald tore it open.

It was a small glass vial, accompanied by a note: "Use it wisely. Eva."

Salvation.

Andrew waited until Somerfield left the library; then, before Celsie could start firing questions at him, he bowed stiffly to her and left.

She made no move to stop him.

His heart was in turmoil. He wanted her to chase after him and drag the truth from him. He wanted her to stay where he'd left her and never broach the subject again. He wanted—he dragged his hands over his face—oh, God, he didn't know what he wanted. He felt like a cad, a coward; he felt like the worst sort of monster.

And it had nothing to do with the way he'd just treated her brother, either. Somerfield had been lounging in the library, drinking Celsie's wine, reading Celsie's books, when Andrew had slammed in. The earl's sly innuendoes, taunts, and knowing smirk had been all Andrew needed to put two and two together. Again he saw Celsie taking her life in her hands by confronting that red-haired witch.

Again he saw Charles, groggily picking himself up out of the dust after being struck down. And he knew then that Somerfield had been involved in the theft of the aphrodisiac. With his emotions already at fever pitch, it had taken very little to send him right over the edge.

God help me. What must she think of me?

He strode down the hall, seeking a comfort he didn't know how to find, seeking escape in his work when there was no work, no project, not even a laboratory, in which to lose himself. He felt totally lost, like a dismasted ship. He felt like a hounded fox that had suddenly lost its hole. Oh, God, what was he going to do? He had botched things, and botched them terribly.

Tell her. Just tell her and get it over with.

He shut his eyes as he walked, moving faster to try to run from the thought, shaking his head as he went. *I can't tell her. It will destroy everything we've already got between us. She'll think me a freak. She'll hate and pity and recoil from me. I can't tell her. I just can't.*

Celsie knew he needed some time to himself.

She gave him an hour—and then she went looking for him.

He wasn't in the stable with Newton, nor was he in the dining room having breakfast, nor was he in any of the bedrooms. No, she found him in the ballroom, measuring one of the walls, his coat thrown carelessly over the back of a chair.

Just pretend nothing happened, she thought. *Just treat him as you would a nervous, cornered dog that's perfectly capable of biting. Win his trust.*

Don't make him retreat even further into himself.

"Let me guess," she said affably, picking up the coat and neatly folding it. "You don't like the decor and are planning to put up new wallpaper."

"No."

"You're thinking of adding another window to let in more light, then."

"I'm measuring for shelves," he snapped.

"Shelves? Whatever for?"

"Because this room would be perfect for a laboratory."

"This room is the ballroom, my lord husband, and you'll have to put your laboratory somewhere else."

He turned and met her smiling gaze with hard, defiant eyes that sparkled with anger. "Well, seeing as how I don't like to go out in Society, and I certainly don't want it coming here to find me, I think we can do without a ballroom."

She crossed her arms, trapping his coat to her chest. "And *I* think I quite like having a ballroom."

He glared at her.

She gazed calmly back, holding his folded coat against her chest and resting her chin on the soft velvet. "Do you know what else I think, Andrew?"

"No."

"I think it's time we tried to work on being friends again. We were doing so well."

He said nothing and turned away, his eyes bleak with pain, a muscle knotting in his jaw.

"Andrew?"

"You should never have married me," he snarled. "You would have been far better off without me, even if your reputation ended up in shreds. I will not make you happy. I cannot make you happy."

"You make me very happy when you don't close yourself off and shove me away with anger that I don't understand." She stepped closer. "Andrew." She laid her hand on his arm and said gently, "Can you not confide in me?"

He remained where he was, his arm rigid beneath her fingers as he stared blankly, mutely, at the wall.

"Can you not tell me the *real* reason you don't want to go out in Society?" she prompted. "The real reason you keep me at arm's length with displays of bad temper whenever we start to get close?" She made her voice as soft and gentle as she possibly could. "And the real reason why you behaved in such a peculiar fashion this morning, only to flee before explaining yourself?"

He turned his head, the little flecks of green in his otherwise rusty eyes beginning to glitter dangerously beneath his sleepy de Montforte lashes as he met, and held, her questioning gaze. She stared calmly back from over the top of her velvet chin rest, refusing to respond to his anger, refusing to back down or let him scare her off. Because that was just what he was trying to do, wasn't it? Scare her off. And yet Celsie sensed there was some wounded core part of him that craved her compassion and understanding; a part of him that he himself probably would never recognize, let alone acknowledge.

He pulled away from her hand. "I think I've had enough of this conversation," he said coldly, and without another word, he walked out of the room.

This time Celsie let him go. For a long, quiet moment she stood there in the ballroom, alone. Then she raised her chin and walked, with as much dignity as she still possessed, toward her own apartments, feeling the tearful sting of defeat prickling just beneath her lashes.

It was morning.

It was all that remained of her wedding night.

The door was ajar to her bedroom, and she felt the tears threatening as she opened it and stepped inside. The drapes were still drawn. The room was shrouded in lonely gloom. Quietly shutting the door, she walked toward the curtained bed, fighting the tears and hoping against hope that when she got there she'd find Andrew waiting for her—kind, contrite, and open-armed once again, ready to resume where they had left off back at the foot of the drive.

She parted the curtains and, not even bothering to undress, climbed into bed, the tears burning the back of her nose. *Oh, Andrew.* But she knew the bed was empty as soon as her knee touched the mattress.

Well, not quite.

Freckles was there, waiting for her.

So much for wedding nights, Andrew had said.

Celsie buried her face in the pillow and cried, the soft down muffling her sobs of anguish.

Chapter 24

Making his way upstairs, Andrew heard the tattoo of fading hoofbeats as Somerfield made his timely departure.

He heard the hushed whispers of the servants, no doubt already worried about the strife their new master had brought with him.

And as he paused at Celsie's door, he heard the sounds of muffled weeping.

He hung his head, his gut churning with emotion, his hand poised on the latch. Shame and frustration filled him. He hadn't thought Celsie was the crying sort, but she was crying now, and he had done this to her. He felt lower than an earthworm. He knew he should go in there and try to comfort her, but what could he say? What could he offer her? The truth? A half truth? A downright lie?

His hand slid from the latch. He pressed the heels of his hands to his brow, then raked his fingers back through his hair, tearing out the bit of ribbon that held it queued and crushing it in his fist. *Leave her alone,* he thought. *Just leave her alone for a while.* After all, they were both upset, overwhelmed, exhausted from the stress of the wedding, the robbery, and a night without sleep. She needed time to adjust. He needed time to work up the nerve to tell her.

Hell, maybe they both just needed time to be apart.

But even as he thought it, Andrew knew it was an excuse. He was not accustomed to sharing his life with someone, especially a woman, and even less accustomed to confiding in other people. The very idea made a chill snake up his back. No, better to just . . . go away for a while. He needed his laboratory. Any laboratory. Someplace where he could lose himself, someplace where he could be alone, someplace where he wouldn't have to *think*.

He turned and continued down the hall.

In a small study off one of the staterooms, he found a desk containing paper, pen, and ink. He scribbled and sealed a note. On his way back down the hall, he paused outside Celsie's door, propped the letter against it, and made himself continue on, telling himself, trying to convince himself, that he was doing the right thing. The weeping, thank God, seemed to have stopped. Or maybe he had simply closed his ears to it.

His heart heavy, he left the house and strode purposefully out to the stables. Newton looked at him expectantly, but the big gray was exhausted and Andrew would not ask him to take him to London. Every other horse in the stable was either too old, too lame, or too small to suit, leaving him to suspect that most had been rescued from cruelty or death by his kindhearted wife and were now her beloved pets.

All except a bright chestnut stallion in the last stall. He was a short-backed but handsome fellow, with a long, flaxen mane, a dark eye, and a white blaze that tumbled down his sculpted face and ended at the pink seam of his mouth.

Andrew reached out and stroked the sleek neck. This must be the infamous Sheik, who refused to mount mares, and who had been, in his own way, responsible for Celsie's taking the aphrodisiac that had proved to be the undoing of both their ordered lives.

He smiled grimly. Let Sheik, then, be the one to take him to London.

Ten minutes later, Andrew was in the saddle and Rosebriar was disappearing behind him.

It was still dark in the room when Celsie awoke.

She lay there in bed for a moment, wondering why her heart was a granite boulder in her chest—until she suddenly remembered the reason for its heaviness.

Andrew had never come to join her. Only Freckles, snoring, was with her, sprawled across the bed, the covers pinned beneath his big body. Celsie reached out and stroked him, blinking in the darkness. Oh, how empty she felt. Like a child promised a toy that was never given. Like a sweetheart promised a kiss that was withheld at the last minute.

Like an abandoned bride.

Slowly she pulled her legs out from beneath the sleeping dog, climbed from the bed, and went to the windows. Shivering, she hauled open the drapes and was surprised to see stars outside, pricking through a night sky laced with cloud.

Good heavens. What time was it? And where on earth was her husband?

She rang for her maid. It seemed to take forever

before Anna came in, yawning and carrying a candle. Celsie frowned.

"Anna, what time is it?"

"An hour after midnight, m'lady."

"An hour after *midnight*? How long have I been up here?"

Anna looked suddenly sheepish. "All day, m'lady. We knew you'd been under a bit of a strain, so we thought it best to let you sleep."

"Where is my husband?"

"Gone, m'lady. He took Sheik out this morning and hasn't come back."

Celsie stared at the younger woman. "He took *Sheik*? And the groom *allowed* him?"

"The groom warned him, but my lord wanted to take the horse, and Hodges said it would've been impertinent to deny him. . . ."

Celsie put her head in her hands. She had rescued the fiery Arabian stallion from a traveling carnival. To this day, the horse feared and despised men, his behavior a testament to the abuse he must have suffered at their hands. And now Andrew had taken him and still hadn't returned? *Oh, God* . . . Celsie tried to rub the parade of nightmarish visions from her eyes. She saw her husband lying helpless in some forgotten pasture with a fractured leg, unable to get help. She saw him lying dead out there in the November darkness, his neck broken, his body stiff and cold. She saw him—

She jerked her head up. "Has Sheik returned to the stables, Anna?"

"No, ma'am. And we were all worried to pieces about the new master, but shortly after he left, one of the chambermaids found this outside your door."

Anna reached into her pocket and produced a sealed letter, immediately handing it to Celsie.

One fear was replaced by another. Trying to hide her rising apprehension, Celsie slid a shaking finger beneath the blob of wax, opened the letter, and taking the candle from Anna, read the hastily scrawled words.

My dear Celsie,

I hope you can forgive me that I shall be long gone by the time you find and read this letter. I did not want to disturb you—or perhaps I am simply taking the coward's way out, for there are some matters I am not yet ready to discuss with you, matters which are unavoidable should I remain with you here at Rosebriar. Thus I thought it best that we spend some time apart, until both of us have had more time to grow accustomed to being with each other. I am going to London, and will return when I feel I am ready to offer explanations for my strange and unpredictable behaviour. I hope you can forgive me.

A.

Apprehension turned to fury.

"How the *hell* are we supposed to grow accustomed to being with each other if he's in London and I'm here?" Celsie howled, balling the letter in her fist and hurling it across the room. "*Men!* Oh, Anna, are they *all* this insane, impossible, and bloody-minded?"

"Yes, m'lady. At least Miss Upchurch says so. Would you like me to fetch you some supper? A hot bath?"

Celsie took a deep breath. It made no sense to keep Anna from her bed, and putting her through the trouble of drawing a bath at this hour was not only unfair, but unkind. "No, Anna," she said, on a grim sigh. "But if you could unlace me and help me undress, that will be enough."

Anna was shy but efficient. Moments later, Celsie dismissed her, and stood there in the middle of the room, dressed only in her chemise.

It would not be daylight for another few hours, but she was not so foolish as to travel the highways at night, alone and unprotected. Her journey would have to wait. She crossed the room and crawled up onto the window seat. There, wrapped in a blanket, she leaned her cheek against the sill, hugged her legs, and stared out across the night toward London, counting the hours until dawn.

By the time the eastern horizon began to glow, she was dressed in a smart green riding habit with breeches under her petticoats for riding astride, and heading for the stables.

And by the time the servants began to stir, she was on her way to London.

Many miles away, the duke of Blackheath was also up.

He was an early riser, given to taking a three-mile walk across the downs before the servants even rose from their beds to start breakfast. Normally he found a long, hard bout of early morning exercise refreshing to his spirits, stimulating to his mind, a good foundation on which to lay the rest of his day. But as he crested Sparholt Down and stopped to gaze off across miles of valleys, downs, and pastureland, all going dark beneath approaching clouds, he felt anything but invigorated.

He had seen the last of his brothers safely married off, and now only Nerissa was left. But he didn't feel the peace he longed for. He felt infinitely weary, like a man putting his last affairs in order as he tried to outrace a terminal illness.

The dream had come to him again last night.

He had been having it for weeks now. The first time he had written it off as a foolish nightmare and promptly forgotten about it within moments after rising. But it had come to him again three nights later, this time weighing heavily on his mind all through breakfast, unwilling to be shaken off, refusing to be forgotten. Again he'd forced himself to forget it, to write it off as fanciful nonsense. But it was impossible to forget something, to dismiss it as nonsense, when it began to recur night after night with mounting urgency, so vivid and real that it haunted one's waking as well as sleeping hours.

The shadows that Andrew had noticed under his eyes were not the imaginings of an angry younger brother.

And yes, Andrew was angry with him. They all were, even Charles, the sibling with whom Lucien had always been closest. He was accustomed to their anger, of course. It was something he had lived with for most of his life. He could have told them about the dream, told them why he had been so desperate to get Andrew safely married to Lady Celsiana Blake. But no. Anger was far easier to handle than the compassion, the concern, and the pity they might end up feeling for him—and Lucien could not tolerate that.

Far easier to let them all think he was the diabolical monster he pretended to be. They would never believe that his machinations were done out of love, that he had only their best interests in mind and at heart. He was the oldest brother. He was the duke. It was his duty to take care of them, though that was something they had always resented and would never understand. But Lucien understood it. He understood his responsibilities, and he never forgot a promise. He had made a vow to his dead parents that he would take care of his siblings, that he would see to their welfare and happiness until the day he died.

Even if that day might come sooner than he would have wished.

The duke turned his gaze from the far-off horizon and began the long trek back to the castle. The air felt raw, cold, moist; it would rain soon. He could feel the wind playing tag with his back, making all the thousands of little grasses shiver and tremble all around him as the sky grew increasingly darker.

Time was running out.

For even now, the dream was with him. A duel at dawn. A masked opponent dressed entirely in black. A fatal slip and then red, raw agony exploding in his chest.

He died with a sword through the heart.

Every time.

Chapter 25

⟨⟨⟩⟩

It was drizzling by the time Newton, a horse with heart if ever there was one, finally brought Celsie to the imposing wrought-iron gates of de Montforte House.

Cold and soaked through, she swung down from his tall back, patted his steaming neck, and bade the groom who came for him to give him an extra ration of hay and corn at feeding time. Then, adjusting her cocked hat and squaring her shoulders, she marched toward the house.

If the staff was surprised to see her, they were too well trained to show it. "Yes, my lady," said the housekeeper in response to her terse query. "Lord Andrew arrived late yesterday and has been closeted in his laboratory ever since."

"Thank you. And where, pray tell, is this laboratory?"

"On the second floor, my lady. You can't miss it."

Celsie took off her damp cloak and handed it to a footman. All the worry, all the wondering, all the tension of the past two days had pinnacled in her heart, leaving only a firm determination to put an end to this nonsense. Still in her riding habit, her whip in one hand, she strode for the stairs.

As the housekeeper had said, the laboratory was on the second floor. And sure enough, the door was locked.

Celsie raised her fist, rapped sharply, and then stood back, rhythmically slapping her whip against her palm in an attempt to keep her temper in check.

"Who is it?"

"Your wife."

Silence. She pictured him on the other side of the door, wondering where he could run to now that she'd found him, probably cursing her from Kent to Cornwall. Celsie's whip tapping increased. Her jaw tightened. And then, to her surprise, the latch lifted and the door swung open.

"Andrew?"

He looked like hell. Two days worth of russet stubble shadowed his jaw. His eyes were bloodshot with fatigue. His shoulders were slumped, his waistcoat hung open, and there were faint smudges of exhaustion under his eyes. He gave a tired smile, and for a moment, she almost thought he looked relieved to see her. But that was ridiculous, of course. If he'd wanted to see her, he would have stayed at Rosebriar.

"Hello, Celsie," he said, calmly meeting her glare. "I suppose I should ask you what you're doing here, but then you'd doubt my intelligence as well as my sanity." He leaned against the door, bent his head to his hand and rubbed at his eyes. "Guess I'm not surprised to see you. . . . You shouldn't have come, you know."

"Andrew, when is the last time you got any sleep?"

"I don't know. Maybe Saturday ... Sunday ... before the wedding, I think."

"Do you realize I am this far from strangling you?" She raised her hand, holding thumb and forefinger together and glaring at him.

He just looked at her with bleary eyes.

"Come on," she said, seizing his hand and dragging him from the room. His toe hit the doorjamb and he stumbled, nearly taking her down with him. "You and I are going for a walk."

"For God's sake, Celsie, have some pity, would you? I need sleep, not exercise."

"Then you should have got some while you had the opportunity." She pulled him, unprotestingly, downstairs and hailed a footman, who took one look at the drooping Lord Andrew and came running.

"Is his Lordship ill, my lady?"

"No, he is merely overtired. Please fetch him his hat and coat. We are going outside for a walk."

"But it's raining," Andrew said, looking out the window and frowning, as if he'd only just become aware of that fact.

"So it is. Just what you need to wake you up."

She took his greatcoat from the footman and helped him into it herself when it became obvious that he was so dazed with exhaustion that his arms would not obey his brain. *You shouldn't be doing this,* her conscience protested. *The poor man is walking in his sleep. For heaven's sake, have some mercy and put him to bed.*

What, put him to bed and allow him to regain his energy, only to shove her away all over again? Oh, no. That would not do at all. He was tired, he was vulnerable, and she was going to get to the bottom of this nonsense while she had him right where she wanted him. Besides, if he'd really wanted to sleep, he would have been in bed, not working on a formula to make himself invisible or a machine to mince turnips or whatever the devil he did when he holed himself up in that confounded laboratory. She'd had enough of his tendency toward avoidance. She'd had enough of his running away from what was obviously becoming a serious problem. She had the fox by the tail, and damn it, she wasn't about to let him go.

Calling for her cloak, she slipped her hand within the crook of his elbow, and together they went outside.

There he took off his hat and tilted his head back, closing his eyes and letting the icy drizzle beat down on his face in an obvious attempt to wake up. Then, blinking the water from his eyes, he offered his elbow once more. Celsie did not press him to speak. He would talk to her when he was good and ready, and she had already learned that forcing him into a premature discussion of whatever was troubling him would only yield anger and resistance. And so she said nothing, simply walking beside him, allowing him to set the pace for both their walk and their impending conversation.

At length the drizzle began to taper off, and overhead, low, fast-moving clouds heralded a temporary break in the weather. The wet had done nothing to deter afternoon traffic; horses trotted past, clopping through puddles and splashing unwary pedestrians. Mud-spattered carriages filled the streets, and here and there sedan chairs darted as ladies paid social calls on each other, catching up on the latest gossip and scandal. Andrew seemed oblivious to them all. He remained mute beside her and eventually they ended up at Charing Cross, where they found a tiny coffeehouse and went inside to warm up.

"You had the right idea, getting me out of the house," he finally said, as he seated her at a little table and took the chair opposite. He wrapped his hands around a mug of strong black coffee and looked down into the steaming brew. "I no longer feel as though I'm walking in a fog."

She reached across the table and laid her fingers atop one of his wrists. He looked down at them, his face expressionless. Then he reached out and covered her hand with his own.

"I'm sorry," he said, not meeting her eyes. "You deserve better than what you got."

She only squeezed his hand. He squeezed hers back. Neither looked at the other, he staring into his hot coffee, she at their clasped hands.

"I trust Sheik was all right with you?" she asked, resorting to small talk in the hopes of breaking the ice between them.

"He's a fine little horse."

"I nearly collapsed when I heard that you'd taken him and hadn't returned."

"I should have asked."

"No, no, it wasn't that," she said, her thumb roving up and down his hand. "He has nearly killed every man that's ever gone near him. He was abused, you know. He hates men."

"He didn't hate me."

"No." Her glance lifted briefly, to his. "You must have charmed him, then."

He shrugged. "We de Montfortes have always had

a way with horses. His liking me had nothing to do with any charm I may or may not possess."

He sipped his coffee, a damp wave of mahogany hair falling into his eyes as he gazed down into the mug. He blinked, and a few strands of the hair caught in his eyelashes. He didn't bother clearing them away, and Celsie suddenly wished she felt comfortable enough to just reach out and brush the hair away for him, but no . . . not yet.

Go easy, go slow, and maybe you can win his trust such that he'll let you do a lot more than just touch his hair. . . .

She took a sip of her own coffee, though she didn't release his hand. "So . . . why haven't you been sleeping?" She smiled, trying to put him at ease, trying to get him talking. "Are you so wrapped up in some fabulous new discovery, some incredible new invention, that you haven't had time to go to bed?"

"No." He looked up then, and his gaze—so direct, so intense, beneath sleepy brown lashes—met hers. "It wasn't that at all."

"I see."

"You don't see."

"All right, I don't see."

He bent his head to his hand, kneading his brow. "I'm sorry. I'm irritable. I'm tired. I'm not good company."

"Then let's go back home, Andrew. I was wrong to drag you outside when you really ought to be catching up on days of missed sleep."

"Don't apologize, the fresh air did me good. *You* do me good, though most of the time I don't seem to realize, let alone show it." He finished his coffee and, plunking down some coins on the table, got to his feet. "Come on. I promise to try and be in a better mood."

He offered his elbow, nodded to an acquaintance who sat at a nearby table reading a newspaper, and escorted her outside.

"Bloody hell," he muttered.

Celsie groaned. "It's Lady Brookhampton."

"Why, hello, Andrew! Celsie!" The countess, her feet in iron pattens to protect her shoes from the mud, lifted her skirts and hurried across the street toward them. "I was wondering how married life was treating you. . . . You're looking a bit peaked there, Andrew!" She smiled slyly. "Your new bride tiring you out?"

Andrew's eyes went strangely flat, the way they always did when he was reining in his anger. "If you will excuse us, madam—"

"I still think it was perfectly heinous, the way the duke tricked the two of you into marriage! Why, all of London is talking about it. Oh, it must be dreadful, pretending civility toward one another when you have anything but a love match."

Celsie smiled and moved closer to Andrew, impulsively slipping her arm around his waist. "What makes you think we don't?" she asked with false sweetness.

"Come now, Celsie, everyone at your doggie ball saw the way you two were glaring at each other. But oh, never mind that, I have just heard the most incredible rumor concerning your brother! Why, everyone's talking about how he's taken a sudden fancy to Miss Sarah Madden, whose papa—frightfully *bourgeois*, I'm afraid—is desperate to buy into the aristocracy." She leaned closer, her eyes gleaming, her voice dropping to a conspiring, excited whisper. "She's an heiress, you know. A very *significant* heiress with a dowry the size of London. More wedding bells in the future, if I'm allowed any predictions! I say, is your husband all right?"

Celsie turned.

"Andrew?"

He was staring at something across the street. Puzzled, Celsie followed his fixed gaze. There was nothing over there but endless buildings and a few people walking the pavement, going in and out of the shops and about their business. She tugged at his arm. He remained rigid and unmoving.

Lady Brookhampton took a step backward. "I say, I think you'd better get him to a doctor," she advised, frowning. "He's as white as the snow in Scotland."

"Andrew?" Celsie said again, her voice rising with dread.

He was still staring across the street, totally oblivious to the fact that she had spoken, to the fact that Lady Brookhampton was staring at him, to the fact that a group of well-dressed gentlemen, their laughing, twittering ladies on their arms, had also paused and were now eyeing him most peculiarly. Around them, people were beginning to whisper.

He didn't hear them. "Dear God . . . Indians. Do you see them, Celsie? Coming out of the shop there—look." He seized her arm and pulled her close to him. *"Look!"*

Celsie looked. She saw only a very ordinary looking old lady, stooped and frail, leaving a pawnshop and clutching a canvas bag in one gnarled hand. The woman was not even in the line of Andrew's fixed gaze. A kind of sick panic seized her. *Oh no. Not again. Not here—*

"Andrew," she said nervously, pulling at his arm as she tried to get him to move. "There is nobody there. You're only suffering from lack of sleep. Come, let's go home."

But Andrew knew he was suffering from far more than just lack of sleep. Just as a sleeper may realize he's dreaming, but still be caught up in the reality of the dream, Andrew knew he was having one of his episodes . . . though what he saw was terrifyingly real to him.

And what he saw were Indians. Mohawks, probably, from the New World, their heads shaved and leaving only a wedge of purple hair sticking straight up like the helmets of Roman soldiers, silver rings in their noses and eyebrows, their bare arms thrust through strange waistcoats of black leather bristling with little cones of steel.

From far away he heard his own voice, felt Celsie tugging at his shoulder.

"Andrew. Andrew, let's go—"

"But don't you *see* them?" He stared at her. Stared through her. "Bloody hell, they've spotted us; get behind me, Celsie, they may be dangerous!"

"Andrew, let's go home, *now*—"

"Damn it, Celsie, don't just stand there, *get behind me!*"

He grabbed his sword, yanked her behind him, and charged forward to protect her, but his foot slipped off the edge of the pavement and he went sprawling into the muddy street, the wheels of a passing carriage just missing his outflung arm. A lady screamed. The group of gentlemen came running. Alarmed shopkeepers came charging outside, Lady Brookhampton stood staring down at him in horror, and all around, people began to murmur in shocked, speculative whispers.

Andrew raised himself up from the mud on one elbow, and blinking, looked dazedly, uncomprehendingly, around him.

"Celsie?" he whispered.

But Celsie was already there. Positioning herself so that her body shielded him from the gathered onlookers, she had knelt beside him and now pulled him up against her, uncaring that he was filthy with mud. He was trembling violently, his skin waxy and cold beneath a film of sweat. She held him close, talking gently to him as excited whispers darted back and forth above their heads.

"Why, it's Lord Andrew de Montforte! I say, what ails him?"

"Got an opium habit, I'd guess. . . . What a waste . . ."

"Genius ain't without its price, eh, Smithson?"

"Aye, he's done so much thinking he's melted his own brain."

Celsie raised her head and glared fiercely up at them all. "I can assure you that my husband does not suffer from a drug habit, madness, or shortcomings of any kind, he is merely exhausted from three days without sleep! Had any of *you* gone three days without sleep, you'd be seeing strange things, too! Now go on, all of you, and give us some space and privacy!"

One arm still around her fallen husband, she made an angry, shoving motion with the other.

"I said, go!"

Mumbling, the crowd began to disperse, guffawing loudly as someone made a lewd remark about just why the newly wed Lord Andrew de Montforte hadn't got any sleep in three days. Celsie's face flamed, but at least she had deflected attention away from the real question of what was wrong with her husband, and that was all that mattered.

And then she looked up to see Lady Brookhampton still hovering above.

Celsie opened her mouth to deliver a stinging command—

"Shall I hail a cab or a sedan chair for him?" the older woman asked, with unexpected kindness.

Celsie gave a weary sigh. "Yes." She rose to her feet, pulling Andrew up with her. "Yes, that would be ideal."

Chapter 26

 ❧~♦♦~❧

Andrew wanted to crawl beneath the wheels of the cab and command the driver to run him over.

He wanted to flee the reality of what had happened to him, what was happening to him, what would eventually happen to him.

He wanted to bury his face against his hands in shame.

Instead, he summoned every shred of his de Montforte pride, straightened to his full height, and like the gentleman he was, handed Celsie up into the cab before him.

Moments later, they were moving.

"So now you know," he muttered, gazing out the window and watching the traffic passing in the other direction. He swallowed hard, refusing to look at her. "We can get an annulment, you know. You have grounds. I would understand perfectly."

She said nothing, but he could feel her gaze upon him. He gripped his hands together and clenched them between his knees, staring out the window as he waited for her to say something, to utter the damning words, to lash out at him with anger and hurt for withholding such a terrible secret. But she didn't say anything. She simply sat there, a presence whose silence said more than words.

"Well?" he said flatly, turning his head to glare at her. "*Are* you going to get an annulment?"

She gazed calmly back. "Most certainly not."

"You're insane if you don't, you know. You managed to come up with a damned good excuse to satisfy the gawkers and gapers back there, but I can promise you that what happened to me then will only happen again, that sooner or later you won't find some convenient excuse to explain it. Then I'll leave you humiliated and pitied, and you'll wish to God you'd got rid of me when you had the chance."

"I don't want to 'get rid of you,'" she said firmly, her eyes beginning to glitter dangerously. "You are my husband. And I care about you very much."

"You can't care for someone you don't know. You don't know me. Oh, God, you don't know me—"

"That is because you won't *let* me know you."

"Celsie, I implore you, don't throw away your life, your dreams, your pride, on me. . . . I'm a worthless oddball, damaged goods. . . . There are plenty of men out there who would make far better husbands, men whom you can bring out in public without fear of being humiliated."

"Stop it, Andrew. I don't want to hear such rubbish."

"It isn't rubbish, it is the truth."

"You're pushing me away. I can't let you do that anymore." Her voice gentled, became pleading. "I'm your wife."

He just raised a hand to his eyes, flung it away.

"I'm your friend."

He swallowed hard, fighting back the rising tide of emotion.

"And I'm the woman who's falling in love with you."

He turned to her in anguish. Celsie could see the faint glisten of what looked like tears in his eyes, a bleak, panicky desperation that beseeched her to leave him alone even as it begged her not to. She reached out and threaded her fingers through his. "Andrew," she said quietly. "I married you for better or for worse, in sickness and in health. We took vows, pledging ourselves to one another. We're in this for the rest of our *lives,* and if you think I'm going to abandon you to whatever it is that so affects and frightens you simply because I might otherwise find myself embarrassed about your behavior, then you don't know me very well, do you?"

He put his head in his hands and bent his body over them, fighting a battle with his will.

"You *are* ill, aren't you?"

He just made an inarticulate little noise and nodded his head. A lump lodged in Celsie's throat, and she felt the sting of tears behind her eyelids as her heart went out to him. How hard he tried to maintain his composure when it was obvious that he was coming apart at the seams. How hard he tried to push her away with anger, when it was all too apparent that he needed her with a desperation he could never admit. And how hard he had tried to pretend that whatever ailed him was no more than an embarrassing annoyance—when Celsie knew, deep in her heart, that it was something that filled him with dread.

It was terrible to be alone with your own fears.

Even more so when you were alone in so many other ways as well. As she had always been.

As Andrew was now.

She got up, moved to the other seat, and lowered herself down beside him. He didn't move, just sat there bent over his hands, suffering in his own private anguish. She put her arms around him and he leaned slightly into her, his shoulders lurching as hoarse sobs of fear finally claimed him.

"You shouldn't have to go through this with me," he blurted, still curled over his hands. "Oh, Celsie, it will be a living hell for you . . . a nightmare. . . . Why *do* this to yourself?"

She held him in her arms, comforting him, reassuring him that he was not alone and never would be. He would not uncurl himself and return her embrace, would not go that last step in trusting her. *Oh, Andrew . . . my heart aches so for you.* She tried to find the right words. Tried to think of what she could say to comfort him. And then her heart found her own private dread, and her eyes filled with tears of their own.

"We cannot always take away the suffering of those we love," she said quietly. "But we can make sure that they don't suffer alone." A beloved face was there in her mind's eye, dark eyes gone cloudy, once youthful face gray with age. Tears began to slip from her eyes, to trickle silently down her face. "Freckles has a lump beneath his ear," she continued, as Andrew shook with silent anguish. "One of these days he'll probably stop eating. One of these days he will lie down and refuse to get up. One of these days he will die . . . and a big piece of my heart will die right along with him." Hot tears scalded her cheeks, falling on his mud-stained coat, soaking his bent shoulder. "But do you think I'm going to go away when that time comes, that I'm going to abandon him simply because it would spare me the pain and grief of watching him die? Do you honestly think I'm that cowardly, Andrew? That selfish?"

His shoulders jerked on a harsh sob. "I'm sorry, Celsie . . . I didn't know. . . ."

"I know you didn't. But you'll be there for me when that time comes. Just as I'm here for you now . . . as I will always be here for you."

"I'm going m-mad, Celsie," he choked out. "My brain is dying and I'm scared, scared of losing my mind, losing my science, losing who I am and turning into a drooling idiot at Bedlam. . . ."

"You don't have to be scared all by yourself, Andrew. You aren't in this alone. You have me."

"You must despise me . . . pity me . . . wish you'd never met me. Look at me, blubbering like a two-year-old. . . ."

"Despise and pity you? No, Andrew. Never. You are an incredible man, but I don't think you realize that, do you? I want to be near you, with you. I want to share your life, as I want you to share mine." She made her voice deliberately light. "And sometimes I even want to strangle you, because you're the stubbornest, most defiant individual I've ever met and you should have told me this long before now."

"Yes, I should have—then you could have left me."

"Only in your dreams," she chastised.

Her attempt at humor found its mark. He gave a half sob, half laugh, and raised his head, drawing his hands down his face but still refusing to look at her. Celsie reached into her pocket and found her handkerchief. She passed it to him and he wordlessly wiped his eyes.

She sat and waited, watching his fingers squeezing and unsqueezing the handkerchief as he looked down at his hands, trying to find the words that would release him from his own dark prison of pain.

"It all started last Christmas," he finally murmured, still staring down at the crumpled muslin. "Do you remember hearing about the fire at Blackheath Castle?"

"Yes—it was on everyone's tongue."

"It would be, wouldn't it?" he said ruefully. "Give people something to talk about and they'll bloody well exhaust it to death." He finally stuffed the handkerchief into his pocket and ran both hands down his face. Then he took a deep, steadying breath and leaned back against the seat, gazing up at the roof with weary resignation. "Well, for months prior to that, I'd been toying with the idea of building a flying machine, but I never quite got around to doing it because there was always another idea that was far more seductive, far more interesting." He reached out and took her hand, grasping it like a lifeline. "You already know I'm not the most organized of individuals. . . . Well, Lucien, he used to taunt and ridicule me and tell everyone that I was incapable of constructing such a machine, until finally I got so angry with him that I determined to build the thing just to prove to him that I could."

Celsie squeezed his hand. It was cold and clammy. She tucked it between her own, lightly chafing the chilled fingers.

Andrew was still gazing up at the roof. "I built it, just as I said I would. I was so proud of it . . . so confident that it would put my name on the map of science, my footprints on the pages of posterity, and that all my peers would respect me as the great inventor I was determined to be." He gave a bitter laugh. "Well, they say pride goeth before a fall, and mine certainly did. Lucien was throwing a ball in honor of Charles's return from what we'd all believed was the dead. Everyone—including the king himself—was invited. And I, fool that I was, thought it would be the perfect opportunity to show off my creation, to launch myself off the roof of the castle and straight into the pages of the history books . . . and best of all, rub Lucien's nose in my success for having failed to believe in me all along."

He took a deep, steadying breath. "Everything was going along splendidly," he continued, his eyes bleak as he gazed into his memories. "The king wanted to see the machine prior to its first flight, and so I took him up onto the roof where I had it ready and waiting to be launched. Whilst we were up there, a fire broke out in the ballroom. Within minutes that whole wing of the castle was on fire. We came back down to my laboratory only to find ourselves trapped by the flames and unable to escape."

"Dear God," Celsie breathed, unconsciously clutching his hand and bringing it close to her heart.

"It was Charles who fought his way up the burning stairway and managed to bring the king and his attendants out. My laboratory was nothing but smoke and fire. I couldn't see a thing, couldn't hear a thing . . . nothing but the roar of the flames, falling timbers, and explosions as my bottles of chemicals and solutions began to go. I started to follow Charles and the others out; then I recalled some drawings I was determined to save, and ran back into the laboratory. That's all I remember. When I came to my senses, I was lying on the floor, everything was on fire around me, and Charles—he'd come back for me, of course—was holding me in his arms, covering me with his own body, trying to shield me from the flames even though it was obvious that we were both going to die."

Celsie put a hand over her mouth, her estimation of the worthy Charles soaring even as she shuddered to think how close Andrew had come to dying. "Your brother must love you very much."

"My brother would have given his life for me. As I would for him." Andrew turned his head and leaned his cheek against the window, his eyes distant. "There was no way out. The stairway was on fire, cutting off escape; we were too high up to jump to safety, and I was so dizzy and sick from the burning chemicals, my lungs so damaged by the heat, that I couldn't draw breath enough to even walk. In the end we escaped because Charles carried me—and the flying machine was still up there on the roof. It did not fly quite the way I intended that it should, but it did save our lives . . . though in the months that have followed, not a day has gone by that I rather wished it hadn't." He swallowed hard. "Or wished it hadn't saved *mine*."

Oh, Andrew . . . Her heart aching for him, she carried his cold, clenched hand to her lips.

He was still gazing sightlessly out the window. "After the fire, I was bedridden for months. I couldn't breathe. Lucien summoned the finest doctors from London and the Continent, and they all said there was no hope for me. That I would waste away and die. Lucien wouldn't listen to them, though. He wouldn't give up, even though my lungs were so damaged that it was all I could do to draw breath." He blinked, absently watching the traffic passing outside. "I used to have terrible fits of gasping, and someone had to be with me at all times, day and night, to pound on my chest in case I stopped breathing. Several times, I did stop." He swallowed, his voice flat and dead, and closed his eyes. "They should have just let me go."

He sounded so despairing, so defeated, that Celsie felt a new rush of hot tears flooding her own eyes. She blinked them back, determined not to show pity.

"Eventually I showed signs of recovering, and Lucien forced me to start exercising in an attempt to rebuild my strength. He used to challenge me to short duels with rapiers, and on the days I felt too sick, or too weak, or too exhausted to exercise, he'd come out with some hurtful taunt or insult that would make me so damned angry that I'd soon be up and out of that bed just for the chance to run him through." He gave a little laugh. "Of course, he knew just how to irk me. He knew just what he was doing. He always did. And I suppose I owe my life to him just as much as I owe it to Charles—what life I have left, that is."

At last he turned away from the window, looking down at their clasped hands. His face was very still. "That strange mix of burning chemicals and solutions I breathed in while I was lying there on the floor . . . it must have affected me in some bizarre, unfortunate way, because it was shortly afterwards that I started having these fits, or seizures, or whatever you want to call them."

Celsie squeezed his hand. "Is that what happened to you today, then? And while you were fighting Gerald, and while we were at de Montforte House a fortnight ago?"

"Yes, and also at your charity ball." He met her gaze then, his eyes darker than she'd ever seen them, full of pain and shame and sorrow. "Why do you think I fled the place as I did?"

"Because you didn't want anyone to know you weren't feeling well."

"Oh, it goes much deeper than just 'not feeling well.' I'm destined for Bedlam, Celsie. Mark me on that."

"I'm not going to mark you on anything until I hear the whole story and have time to think it all through. So let me make sure I understand this. You were in a fire, and you breathed in all these burning chemicals from your laboratory, and you've been having these episodes ever since."

"Precisely."

"And what does your all-knowing brother Lucien think?"

"He's a duke, not a doctor. He refuses to give up hope that I can be made well again. Over the past two months, he's dragged in a parade of specialists, lecturers, and physicians to examine me. But all they did was poke and prod and bleed me, regard me as some sort of freak, discuss me as though I was not even there, and this when I probably hold more university degrees than they do. All they could give were long-winded explanations of complete and utter codswallop. They don't know what's wrong with me. Not one of them was able to offer one iota of help—or hope. And how can they? Even I don't know what I took into my lungs that night. I'll never know. Like that cursed aphrodisiac, it's a situation that cannot, and should not, be duplicated—and thus, cannot be examined, only wondered at."

He shut his eyes on a sigh. All fight had gone out of him, and Celsie knew then that the unpredictable anger that had been so much a part of him had been nothing but a cloak to cover these deeper, constant feelings of fear, shame, and vulnerability. He needed her; he had told her his darkest secret, his biggest shame, and now he needed her. It was a humbling realization.

She took both his hands within her own and pressed them to her heart. "Oh, Andrew . . . so much about you makes sense to me now."

"You wondered why I didn't want to get married. Why I didn't want you or anyone else interfering in my life, or why I detest going out in Society more than I ever did. Do you know what it's like, having an affliction that strikes you without warning, without mercy, and oftentimes in the company of other people? Can you fathom the shame and humiliation, not just to me, but to those I love? Better just to stay home, where I'm not a threat to anyone else's pride, let alone my own. And that is the strange thing about it. . . . I was fine as long as I kept within the walls of Blackheath, but if I so much as ventured beyond them . . ." He shook his head. "Well, you've seen what happens to me. And so I stayed indoors, stayed in my laboratory, deluding myself and my family into thinking there was nothing wrong with me. But they knew. And now you know, don't you? You've seen me in all my mad glory. And now you know why I prefer to stay in my laboratory. And why I don't want to go out in society and risk embarrassing myself and others around me."

"You could never embarrass me, Andrew."

"No? Do you mean to say, then, that you were not embarrassed today?" he challenged.

"Of course not." Her chin came up. "I was worried sick about you, but never embarrassed."

He merely looked at her, studying her in confusion and disbelief and yes, even a wary kind of hope, unable to fathom why she *wouldn't* be embarrassed.

"Can you tell me more about these . . . episodes, Andrew? Today you saw Indians. The morning after our wedding, you saw and heard something else, something that Freckles and I did not. What was it then? I don't know much about fits and seizures, but it has always been my understanding that sufferers tend to be in a semiconscious stupor while experiencing an attack; you seemed to be fully aware of your senses."

"I am. And what I saw and heard that morning was a gleaming silver monster the size of three battleships, soaring over our heads in a roar of thunder."

She smiled. "That doesn't sound like a fit, Andrew—it sounds like a vision."

"A vision of what? Madness, I tell you. Madness. Lucien probably has a chain all picked out for me at Bedlam."

"Stop it."

"It's true, Celsie. I'm going mad, and there's nothing that you or anyone else can do about it except hide me away from Society until I'm ready to be committed so that I don't humiliate the lot of you."

"Hiding you away is the last thing I intend to do. You are the most fascinating, brilliant, incredibly intelligent man I know, and I will not allow you for one moment to deprive the world of what you have to offer it. Now, tell me some of the other things you've seen."

He slanted her a half-disbelieving, half-hopeful look from beneath his lashes. "It's nonsense, all of it. Bloody nonsense."

"Tell me anyhow."

"You really want to know, then?"

She smiled again. "I am asking, aren't I?"

"Oh, very well, then." And so he told her about being at the town house in London a fortnight earlier, and looking out the window only to see a string of amber moons glowing upon a shiny ribbon of gray. He told her about being at Rosebriar, near the village of Heath Row, and seeing the winking firefly roaring overhead the night of her ball. He told her about passing through Wembley back in April, and seeing thousands of people piled into a giant soup bowl with a field in the middle and yelling at the tops of their lungs. And he told her about a big, red, rectangular box, with two eyes in the front and rows of people sitting behind glass windows, and how it—and not any flight of brilliance or imagination on his part— had prompted his idea for a double-compartmented coach.

She listened in rapt fascination, eager to hear about every strange thing he'd seen and heard. Finally he ran out of words and turned his head to look quietly at her.

"So what do you think?" he asked. "I'm going mad, aren't I?"

She pursed her lips, thinking. "I don't know. I can't help but wonder if there's a purpose to these things."

"A *purpose*?"

"Well, yes. Maybe you're a modern-day prophet, Andrew. Maybe this is all allegory. Maybe God is trying to tell you something, or you have simply been gifted in a way that neither of us will ever understand. I don't know what to think. But I do know one thing: You ought to take advantage of everything you're seeing. Write it all down, catalog each episode, try to find a pattern, try to use what you're seeing toward the pursuit of your own creations. I can help you."

"Help me?"

She grinned. "Well, you are *not* the most organized person in the world. If you leave all the paperwork, organization, and administration to me, you, my dear husband, can get on with your science."

Andrew stared at her incredulously. *Dear God in heaven . . . have I been truly blessed? She's not going to turn away from me, then? She's actually going to remain at my side, help me through this, take what's bad and make it good?* He shook his head, feeling as though the storm clouds that had been hanging over his head and future this past year were finally clearing away, allowing the first brilliant rays of sunlight to touch him from above.

And Celsie was that sunlight.

He reached out, slid an arm around her waist, and pulled her close, needing her strength, her optimism, her new way of looking at things—and the solid, living warmth of her that was his only comfort in the strange and confusing world his life had become.

"What a fool I've been for not telling you earlier," he murmured, feeling humbled and ashamed. "I was so afraid that you'd reject me if you knew the truth, that your admiration would turn to pity, and, well . . . I guess I found the idea faintly unbearable."

"The idea that I'd reject you, or that my admiration would turn to pity?"

"The former, of course."

She smiled. "Well, Andrew, if you were afraid of *that,* then I'd say you weren't as loath to marry me as you might have thought."

"It's the madness," he said despairingly. "As much as I think I'd like to be someone's husband, I shouldn't be married to anyone. It's not fair to her. Not fair to start something that's only going to end in heartbreak. I'm a doomed man."

"Oh, no, Andrew. You're not a doomed man. You're a very gifted one, I think, blessed in a very special way, and you probably have more to offer this world than you can ever know—and more than any ordinary man of science could ever give." She pulled him close, gazing deeply into his eyes. "I don't know what ails you, and I'm not even going to try to guess, but I know one thing: Together, you and I are going to turn this little affliction of yours from the negative into the positive. And we're going to start right now."

Chapter 27

〜∽⌒⌒⌒〜

They left immediately for Rosebriar.

Oh, it was amazing, what confession could bring! Like the earth after a rain shower, Andrew felt cleansed. Reborn. He filled his lungs with clean, sweet air as Newton carried him swiftly along the muddy roads, and gazed about him with new eyes. Three days without sleep, yet he had never felt more alive. Three days of marriage, and a lifetime of hope before him. How long had it been since he'd appreciated the beauty of a hard blue sky reflected in the perfect mirror of a puddle? The winsome sight of a wagtail flitting before them? The joy of simply being alive? His future was uncertain, yes, but he now knew he had one constant in his life: Celsie. With her by his side, he would not have to face anything alone, ever again.

As he watched her cantering along beside him on Sheik, his heart swelled and his loins tightened. Oh, how he would love to pull her off the fiery little stallion and into his arms . . . how he would love to plunder her mouth, her body, right here in a grassy verge, in a damp glade. She had given him back the world. She had knelt with him in the muddy street,

311

shielded him from ridicule and speculation, and defended him with all the courage of a tigress standing over its wounded mate. As long as he had Celsie, he was invincible.

It hit him like a broadside of iron. *I love her.*

His hands tightened on the reins to anchor his suddenly dizzy head.

God help me—I love her!

The momentous realization nearly overwhelmed him. He was no longer the prisoner of his own fears, because she had set him free. He was no longer a prisoner of his own fearful future, because she had made lightness out of something heavy, brightness out of something dark. God in heaven, he didn't even have to remain a prisoner in his own *house* anymore, because she—his own dear wife—knew all, accepted all, accepted *him.*

They were a half mile from Rosebriar; already he could see the big house of rambling gray stone nestled against its backdrop of green hills and heath, of autumn trees dark, scraggly, and bare-leaved against the hard blue sky. Without warning, Andrew pulled Newton up, snared Sheik's reins in his other hand, and as both horses plowed to a stop, leaned breathlessly toward the startled Celsie.

"Andrew, what are you doing?"

For answer, his mouth came down on hers. She melted against him, making a noise of contentment deep in her throat, and for him there was only his wife, her soft lips yielding to his, her arm winding around his neck, the tips of her breasts just touching his chest, her tongue slipping out to playfully taste his own.

Sheik fidgeted and sidestepped away, breaking the

kiss. Andrew met Celsie's gaze, breathing hard.

She put a hand to her heart, her eyes glowing with banked silver fire.

With invitation.

And then she gave him a mischievous little grin and looked rather pointedly at the pommel of his saddle. Or rather, at the hardening bulge in his breeches that was just inches away.

For Andrew, the chill November day was suddenly very warm.

For Celsie, the urge to reach out and touch that growing bulge was suddenly very strong.

"Thank you for agreeing to come back to Rosebriar, Andrew," she murmured, finally lifting her gaze to meet his. "I know you're tired, and that this was a bit of a ride, but it didn't seem appropriate to spend our first real night as husband and wife in your brother's house." She edged Sheik a little closer to Newton, and reaching out, dragged her finger suggestively up the side of her husband's thigh, watching in satisfaction as he shut his eyes and groaned softly. She leaned close, and with a coy grin, whispered into his ear, "I think it's time we begin our marriage in earnest, don't you? After all, we have a wedding to consummate."

"Yes . . ." He leaned toward her once more, his lips brushing her cheek and causing a warm glow to spread through her blood. "Lost time to make up for."

"Wild inventions to create . . ."

"Homeless puppies to save . . ."

"Unfinished business to complete . . ."

His hand had found the small of her back through

the woolen pleats of her riding jacket. She sighed in contentment and anticipation.

"Andrew?"

"Celsie?"

He looked at her expectantly, his eyes intense, his grin slow and lazy and full of that famed de Montforte charm. She smiled in open invitation and slowly gathered her reins. And then:

"First one back to the house wins!"

She set her heels to Sheik's sides and squealed with excitement as the fleet Arabian shot ahead like a quail exploding from cover. A moment later she heard the thundering tattoo of Newton's pursuit and, laughing, gave the little stallion his head. The wind sang in her ears. Mud spattered her flying petticoats. The horse's ears twitched forward, twitched back, and suddenly Newton, two hands taller and Thoroughbred-fast, was there beside her, iron-gray mane streaming in the wind, nostrils flaring red, his great galloping legs eating up the road.

A hand snaked around her waist and Celsie shrieked as she was pulled from the saddle across flying space, only to be swept up into the hard curve of her husband's embrace. Laughing, he settled her before him, imprisoning her within his arms and not letting the big Thoroughbred slow until they were through the gates of Rosebriar and on their way down the stately drive, Sheik cantering in their wake. As they trotted up to the steps of the front entrance, they were both laughing.

Celsie, her face flushed with wind and her heart pounding, her bottom half on the pommel and half on Newton's withers, turned and pushed playfully at

Andrew's chest. "You really *are* mad!" she cried breathlessly—

And kissed him.

Beneath them, Newton was still moving. Dutifully he carried them up to the steps and stopped, where he tossed his head and waited for them to dismount.

But Celsie was still kissing her handsome husband, loving this new, cheerful side to him that she had only glimpsed before, loving the way his tongue traced her lips before slipping between them, loving the feel of his hand as it moved up the front of her embroidered waistcoat, his thumb pushing against the bottom of one breast. She groaned as he lightly caressed her nipples through the fabric, teasing them to small, hard buds, his hand hidden by her jacket and cloak.

Flushed, dazed, and breathless, she finally pulled away.

"What *will* the servants think?" Andrew teased, with a wicked gleam in his eye.

"That Rosebriar's mistress is madly in love with her husband. Now come, Andrew. I have a present for you, and I must give it to you now, before we meet in bed, before you kiss me again and make me lose all my resolve to make this perfect—"

"A present?"

"A wedding present! Come, let's go!"

She slid out of his arms and landed lightly on the ground. He dismounted, handed the Thoroughbred's reins to an approaching groom, and ran after his wife as she flew up the front stairs. He caught her arm one step from the top and spun her around. She was laughing, her eyes bright and her cheeks rosy from the cold wind as she tumbled into his arms.

"If we're going to make this perfect, I have a few ideas of my own," he said. "First I am going to kiss you. Then I am going to carry you over the threshold as I should have done the other night. And finally I'm going to let you go for only the space of a heartbeat, because I, too, have a wedding present to give you."

Again their lips met, and she was still kissing him as he lifted her easily in his arms, carrying her up the last stone step and over the threshold into the home that had once been her father's, then hers—and now belonged to them both. He didn't bother shutting the door, leaving it swinging open behind them for a servant to close.

In the entrance hall, he finally set her down. All right, go get your present, then, and I'll go get mine. Where shall we meet?"

"Top of the stairs in a quarter of an hour!"

Then, laughing, she kissed him fully on the lips and was gone in a whirl of dark woolen petticoats.

Andrew stood there for a moment in the hall, his head reeling, his heart singing. God and thunderation, what the devil had he wasted all this time, energy, and worry on? Perfect women did indeed exist! He *had* one!

And what the devil was he doing just standing there?

He ran to fetch his present to her, which was still packed in the coach that had come down with them from Blackheath. The coach was in the stables, and as Andrew lifted the heavy wooden crate from the vehicle, he cursed himself for not having had it brought round to the house. By the time he lugged the thing back to the house, through the door, and across the entrance hall, he was nearly out of breath. There he set the crate down and paused to look up the grand flight of stairs.

Celsie was there, all right, at the very top, her eyes laughing, her arms empty, watching in amusement as he bent once more and labored to get the huge crate up the stairs.

"Is that my present?" she asked impishly, leaning against the wall and watching him struggling with his burden.

"It certainly is."

"Well, I guess it's not a piece of the famous de Montforte jewelry," she quipped, folding her arms and pretending to be very disappointed. "Unless it's a four-million-carat diamond."

"You're right . . . not jewelry," he managed, stopping to rest for a moment before picking up the giant box and continuing on.

"It looks fearfully heavy. What's in there?"

"Can't tell you."

"Why not?"

"It's a surprise."

"What is it made of, then? Solid gold?"

"Solid iron."

"*Iron?*" she said, trying not to look too disappointed by the fact that her handsome new bridegroom was not as romantic as she had thought. "Really, Andrew . . ."

"Don't laugh, you might like it."

"Yes, I might, if you can ever succeed in getting it up these stairs. All I can say is that I'm glad I married you for your brains and not your brawn." She put her hands on her hips and grinned saucily down at him. "Why, I could have had that thing up these stairs in half the time you're taking!"

"*You* try picking the confounded thing up!" he said drolly, taking out a handkerchief and mopping his forehead.

Celsie, one brow lifting in mocking amusement, waited until he reached the top of the stairs and set the crate down. Shooting him a superior little grin, ·she reached down to pick it up—and froze, her grin abruptly fading. She might as well have tried to lift an overweight Great Dane. The crate wouldn't budge.

"Very well then, I reclaim my comment about your brawn," she said, straightening. "It's a wonder you didn't break your back! Really, Andrew, why didn't you just leave it downstairs, instead of lugging it all the way up here?"

"Because you, madam, asked me to bring it up."

"Oh."

"It really does belong in the kitchen," he added.

Her face fell, though she tried not to let it show. "Let me guess. . . . It's an iron cook pot for the hearth," she said, trying not to sound too deflated.

"No, it is not an iron cook pot. Now, go get my present and we'll open them right here," he said, leaning against the elegantly carved balustrade and crossing his arms. "Unless it's even bigger than this thing?"

"It is much bigger than that. And I couldn't presume to carry it even if I wanted to. You'll have to come with me."

"You *would* say that. . . . I suppose you want me to bring this, then, too."

"Of course. Would you like me to help you carry it?"

He merely shot her an exasperated look. Celsie's eyes sparkled above her grin. She watched as he crouched down and lifted the heavy crate, hoisting it even though Celsie hadn't been able to lift it an inch off the floor.

Now that she knew how impossibly heavy the thing was, Celsie couldn't help but stand transfixed. All right, then, so her gifted husband had brawn as well as brains. Why, her side of this marital bargain was getting better and better! She watched him balancing the box, and felt a thrill of expectation at the thought of touching those strong, defined muscles. . . .

"Stop staring, girl, and start walking. This isn't the lightest thing I've ever carried!"

Celsie laughed and continued on. She was well aware that his appreciative gaze was on the sway of her hips and the narrowness of her waist as she preceded him down the hall, and the thought only made her all the more eager to finally get her husband into bed where he belonged.

She led him past the state bedrooms, past the apartments they would call their own, and into a rich, masculine room that had once been her papa's library but was now empty of books and all signs of recent habitation. Dark mahogany bookcases lined an entire wall. A case clock dominated one corner of the room. Tall, south-facing windows let in the thin autumn sun and overlooked the ornamental pond, its surface now peppered with yellow and brown leaves, in the near distance. The walls were paneled with fine English oak, the doors carved and heavy, the polished floor devoid of furniture save for three long tables, all of them spotlessly bare. All of them, that is, except the middle one, upon which stood a decanter of wine and two crystal goblets.

Celsie stopped, turned, and hands on her hips, regarded him happily.

"Well, here you are, husband. My wedding present to you."

Andrew set down his burden with a grunt and straightened. He looked around and frowned, his expression much the same as Celsie's had been upon learning that his present to her had been a monstrous piece of iron.

"So what do you think?" Celsie asked excitedly, feigning innocence. "Isn't it wonderful?"

"Uh . . . isn't what wonderful?"

"Why, this room, of course."

"Sorry?"

"It's yours," she said gaily, unable to stop grinning. "Oh Andrew, don't look so baffled! There was a real reason why I didn't want you to have the downstairs ballroom for your laboratory. . . . I had this room all picked out and ready for you. I thought you'd like it so much better. . . . It gets lovely sunshine all day, is away from commotion and the sound of the kennels outside, and was once the domain of my father, the master of the house. Now, as the new master of the house, it is your domain. Yours to do with whatever you wish."

He stared about him, blinking and amazed, his expression softening into one of sheer, unfettered rapture. A broad, boyish smile overtook his mouth, and he shook his head in disbelief, his eyes glowing with happiness. "Oh, Celsie . . . you couldn't have chosen a nicer gift!"

"There's more," she said.

"More?"

"Yes. Since you are so hopelessly disorganized, Andrew, and since I'm beginning to think that your dislike of paperwork and the meticulous recording of information is one of the reasons you jump from one idea to the next before seeing things through, I have determined to do something about it. This chamber not only comes with all the furniture you see—also part of my wedding present, of course— it comes with its own laboratory assistant." She grinned. "Me."

"You?"

"Me." She flew into his arms, hugging him tightly. "Oh, Andrew, I just *know* you're going to change the world, and best of all, you're going to start right here! I can't wait!"

Overwhelmed, he lifted her high and swung her around once, twice, her petticoats flying. "Celsie— dearest, most delightful Celsie—nothing you could have given me, save for yourself, could have made me so happy!"

"Well, since you get me as well as the room, then you should never have reason to be in a bad mood ever again!"

He bent his head and kissed her, his heart so full of joy and adoration he thought he was going to burst. It was a long time before he finally set her back, tenderly gripping her upper arms as he gazed down into her eyes.

"Do you know, Celsiana Blake de Montforte, I am dangerously close to admitting that I could quite easily fall in love with you. In fact, I am dangerously close to admitting that I'm already half in love with you as it is."

"Well then, if you're half in love with me, and I'm half in love with you, does that make us a whole?"

"Sorry?"

"Does that make us wholly in love with each other?"

He laughed. "Well, now, that's rather interesting logic, isn't it? I hadn't quite looked at it that way, but yes, I do suppose it must."

"Well then, show me how much you half love me by letting me open *my* present!"

He looked suddenly shy, and she saw a faint red flush suffusing his cheeks. "Oh, well, nothing I could ever give you would even come close to what you've just given me."

"You're probably right," she said jokingly, trying to lessen his sudden embarrassment. "I cannot imagine *what* a huge chunk of iron is going to do for me! But never mind, you've intrigued me, Andrew. I'll open it now."

She knelt beside the large crate, flipped open the rope latch, lifted the cover—

And blinked.

"Do you like it?" he asked, standing over her shoulder and displaying the same false innocence she had shown just moments ago.

She just knelt there, staring rather stupidly at the pulleys and wooden crank handle and gears with their wolfhound-sized teeth, at this strange concoction of iron that was the ugliest and most unromantic wedding gift imaginable, and didn't know quite what to say. She didn't want to hurt his feelings; he sounded so excited, so eager for her to like it. . . .

Whatever "it" was.

"Um, Andrew . . . it's, uh, rather interesting, but I haven't the faintest idea what it is."

"Guess."

"Um . . . it's the inner workings for a new clock you've designed?"

"Try again."

"Something you've seen in one of your visions?"

"No—you've got one more guess."

"Something to do with a new carriage."

"Wrong again. Shall I tell you what it is, then?"

"I think you're going to have to," she said, trying not to sound too glum.

"It's a mechanized roaster," he said happily. "To go into the kitchen. To turn the meats. To turn the meats over the open fire, Celsiana, so that your little turnspit dogs can now go looking for another line of work."

It took a moment for his words to sink in.

To turn the meats over the open fire, Celsiana, so that your little turnspit dogs can now go looking for another line of work.

Celsie's gaze flew back to what had been, just a moment ago, a confusing and ugly jumble of iron and wood; and then, suddenly, a lump caught in her throat and all those gears and pulleys and strange bits of metal went blurry beneath the sudden sheen of tears.

Her hand went to her mouth.

"Oh, *Andrew*," she breathed, turning to look up at him over her shoulder with huge, watery eyes. She felt her jaw quivering. "I can't believe you did this. . . ."

His cheeks were a little red. He shrugged, trying to make light of what he'd done, but she saw the pride in his eyes, the vulnerability, the desperate hope that she'd like what he had made for her. "Oh, well, it didn't take long," he admitted. "I got the idea when we were in London. I know the blacksmith in Ravenscombe quite well, and he was happy to fashion this to my specifications—"

"You mean to say you thought this up just like that?"

He shrugged. "That's how I think most things up," he confessed, almost apologetically. "I can't help it."

"Andrew, you're absolutely *brilliant*!" She leaped to her feet and hurled herself into his arms, kissing his face, kissing his lips, while huge tears of happiness slipped down her cheeks. "Do you know what this is going to mean to all those poor little dogs burning their paws off in so many English kitchens, running their tiny legs to the bone? Do you realize how this is going to revolutionize the way kitchens are run, the way food is cooked? Oh, Andrew—I thank you! All those little dogs who are currently being so abused thank you! Thank you, thank you, thank you!"

He caught her as she hugged him around the neck, nearly choking him and more happy than he'd ever seen her. His own grin was a little cocky. Well, damn . . . if this was all it took to make the lady happy, the road ahead wasn't going to be so difficult, after all!

"Do you know, I couldn't have asked for a better present," she said, wiping at her streaming eyes. "I am the happiest woman in England. I have the smartest husband in the whole wide world. And the only thing that could possibly make me even happier is if my smart, handsome husband were to lift me in his arms and carry me off to our marriage bed."

He smiled lazily down at her, and in one neat, easy movement, scooped her up. "Well then, dear lady—your wish is my most eager command."

Chapter 28

❧❧

"We'll have to get a patent for it, immediately. We'll have to present it to the Royal Society. We'll have to throw a huge ball and invite everyone there is to invite, have a demonstration, and *prove* that people don't have to use poor little dogs in the kitchen!"

Andrew merely smiled and, carrying the comparatively weightless Celsie, strode easily down the hall.

"We'll have to enlarge the kennels so we can take in all the dogs that will be out of work once your wheel goes into production. We'll have to print broadsides informing the general public. Oh, and Andrew, we simply *must* make a present of one for the king's household, because if *he* endorses it, all of England will want one!"

"Yes, Celsie."

"Oh! You just passed the door, Andrew. Go back a few steps!"

He did, carrying her over the threshold and kicking the door shut behind him as he moved toward the bed.

"We'll have to start a company to manufacture it.

We'll have to take it on tour throughout England. In fact, we'll have to take it all around Europe so that everyone there will also—"

She never finished. His mouth came down hard on hers, crushing her lips with blistering intensity. His tongue forced her lips apart and his breath was hot against her cheek. *Ohhhhhh,* Celsie thought, and began to melt. As he laid her down on the bed, she felt her spine sinking into the plush coverlet, her eyes closing, her head falling upon a paw.

A paw.

Freckles was in the bed.

Her eyes flew open. "Andrew, we can't make love *here*. Freckles will see!"

"Freckles can close his eyes."

"But, Andrew—"

He scooped her back up, carried her to the elegant, claw-footed settee, and laid her down on it instead. Her body angled across the rich red damask, one leg bent at the knee, the other just resting on the rug. One of her shoes came off. Her layers of petticoats spilled from her hips and tumbled toward the floor in frothy yards of quilted cotton, of heavy, serviceable wool. She felt his mounting urgency to have her. She felt his fingers pulling her stock from her neck, his lips against her throat. And she felt his hand palming and stroking her breast where it swelled above her stays, warming her skin, firing her desire.

"God and the devil, I hate these things," he muttered. "Must beauty be contained in such a damnable cage?"

He couldn't reach her; not without turning her over and unlacing her. And he had neither the patience nor the ability to wait. He crowded onto the narrow sofa, too much man for so little space, his knee driving against the outside of her thigh, his hand reaching down to find the hem of her petticoats and pull them high—

"Lord save me, you're wearing *breeches* under these things!"

"Well, I *did* ride astride, Andrew. . . . Did you want the saddle to chafe my legs to ribbons?"

"The *last* time I saw you in breeches . . ."

"Was altogether memorable. Go ahead, Andrew. Let's make *more* memories. But please don't undress me fully—it's dreadfully cold in here."

"It won't be for long," he promised.

She unfastened the breeches and lifted her bottom, inviting him to tug them off.

He did, tossing them to the floor. She saw his slow, appreciative smile as he found that which he'd been expecting to find—stockings, garters, and bare naked thighs. Oh, she loved when he smiled like that! And she loved the feel of his hand skimming up her stocking-clad calf. His mouth was warm against her breasts, swelling above the tightly laced stays, and now Celsie could feel his hand moving across her knee, fumbling with her garter, finally cursing and tearing it down her leg and peeling the filmy stocking off with it.

"Is this what ravishment feels like, I wonder?" she breathed faintly, loving every minute of it.

"It's what not being able to wait feels like."

His hand, so warm against her flesh, so delicious, stroked up her inner thigh, his fingers searching, searching . . . and finding.

Finding her already hot and wet for him.

Finding her slick and ready and eager and wanting.

"Oh, God," he said hoarsely, and with one quick movement, he tossed the heavy fall of her skirts fully up and over her stomach, exposing her long, white legs—one bare, the other still wearing its garter and stocking—and her naked femininity to the pale, late afternoon sun.

To his smoldering, intent gaze.

He stared; Celsie saw his chest rising and falling, his long lashes coming down to veil eyes that had gone suddenly dark. His knee pressed uncomfortably into her outer thigh; his arousal was fully evident beneath the flap of his breeches. She felt exposed and naked and shameless and wanton as he stared down at her, not saying a word, just looking. Just admiring. And then he lifted his gaze and in his eyes she saw desire burning so hot that it nearly scalded her with its intensity.

"Damnation," he swore, on a little laugh.

"Damnation?"

"How the *hell* am I ever going to find the time, to find the incentive, to find the will to pursue my science when I have *you* around to constantly tempt me?"

"I guess you're just going to have to practice a little restraint." She smiled up at him. "Though I certainly hope you won't."

"Damn right I won't. By God, Celsie, you're going to be the death of me, I swear it."

She giggled. "Where's that potion, Andrew? I thought we were going to try it topically."

"Don't know . . . don't care."

"Oh, get it. Get it, and let's see what it does."

He got up, opened his coat, fumbled in the pocket, and found the tiny vial. Celsie lay draped over the sofa, bathed in the glow of the sun coming in from the window above, her long legs framed by white underpetticoats and wool overpetticoats and the rich red damask of the settee. She could feel her body temperature rising. She could feel an empty ache in her arms, in her belly, in that spot between her legs where desire throbbed hot and moist, aching to be fulfilled.

She began to tremble with need.

To breathe a little heavier.

He returned with the vial, forcing a space for himself on the seat beside her, his hand stroking the velvety skin of her inner thigh, coming near to but never quite touching the part of her that needed him more than any other. He held the vial up to the light, examining it, prolonging the ecstatic inevitable.

"Shall we try it on me or on you?" he asked, his hand skimming back up her thigh and now gently pushing the leg that hung off the seat farther away from the other.

"You choose."

"All right, then."

He pushed her thighs even farther apart.

"Andrew, you're going to split me right in half," she gasped, a little breathlessly.

"I want to see you. I want to see *all* of you." His fingers were playing with the silky hair of her mound now, gently stroking the hidden folds within, making her entire body thrum with sensation. He looked intently down at her, watching everything his fingers were doing. "And I want to see just what happens when I put a drop or two of this solution right here between these pretty pink folds—and touch it to this hard little nub."

His erotic suggestion caused Celsie to melt yet further into the cushion. Just the thought of that fervently potent aphrodisiac against her most intimate flesh was enough to double her already pounding pulse.

"Well, then . . . go ahead," she managed, stretching an arm over her head and gazing up at his handsome, intent face.

He slowly uncapped the vial, the deliberate delay in his movements causing the anticipation to build all the more. Celsie felt the room's cool, unheated air drifting around her exposed thighs . . . her knees . . . kissing her shamelessly exposed cleft. Trembling, she curled her right toe into the floor rug and pressed the other leg, still bent at the knee, to the red damask that covered the back of the settee.

"You're not cold, are you?"

"No—just incredibly impatient to have you inside of me."

Her gaze followed Andrew's hand as he put a finger over the top of the open vial and briefly turned it upside down. Then he took his finger away, a drop of the liquid standing upon the pad of his forefinger, shimmering in the fiery afternoon light.

She gazed up at him.

He gazed back, smiling a little wickedly.

He reached down and parted her with one hand; then he touched his finger to her opening, and dragged it down the inside length of one damp petal of inner skin.

Dragged it back up the length of the other, painting her with the solution.

Celsie, her gaze still locked with his, began to shake.

"Do you feel anything yet?" he asked.

"Nothing but you . . . Which is erotic enough in itself."

He smiled. Again he put his finger to the vial, this time opening her with the other thumb and forefinger, observing her while the drop of potion stood upon his finger. Somehow he managed to recap the bottle. Then, slowly, torturously, he forced her inner lips wide, touched the drop of liquid to that hard, swollen button that hid between them—and keeping his finger there, pressed hard.

Celsie moaned, sucking her lips between her teeth.

He increased the pressure. "*Now* do you feel anything?" he asked softly.

"It's . . . it's starting to tingle down there."

"Hmm, yes."

"It's—I think it's starting to—to burn."

"Does it hurt?"

"Oh, no. It's not *that* kind of burning . . . if you know what I mean."

"Ah, yes. I know what you mean." His smile was positively wicked. "I must remember to make a note of that."

He kept the pressure against her, pushing down with his finger, watching her flushed face as her head began to move slowly back and forth on the satiny red pillow.

"Andrew," she managed, on a choked little gasp.

"Yes, dear?"

"Andrew, I think I need you to be inside of me now."

"I'm not done observing, Celsie."

Heat was building within her, all of it centered around his finger . . . and every inch of flesh the aphrodisiac had touched. "To hell with the experiment, Andrew . . . I'm getting desperate."

He merely caught her nub between thumb and finger and began gently rolling it.

"Oh—" Celsie moaned, fingers clenching and unclenching, toes curling, the sensation beginning to feel like a thousand little needles all stabbing into that one fiery spot, screaming for pressure, screaming for release, screaming for his mouth, his tongue, his finger, his manhood, *anything*. And now he was rubbing that hard bit of flesh a little more forcefully, intently watching her face, intently watching the nub itself. Celsie choked back a moan and grabbed at his hand, trying to push it against her all the harder. "Oh, *Andrew*—I think I'm going to die if you don't *do* something!"

He was smiling, one brow raised as he observed her reactions, his eyes glowing with passion as he kept on. "Hmm, yes—you're blushing down there."

"To hell with the science stuff, Andrew, take me—oh God, take me, I'm burning up!"

Little whimpers began to escape her and she started to pant, to squirm, to struggle to get her legs together if only to put pressure against that keening, ravenous pins-and-needles ache that was screaming for fulfillment.

"Touch me, Andrew—oh please, touch me, I'm going mad!"

She shoved his hand against the burning flesh, crying out and twisting her hips against him as she fought for release.

"I say, this *is* a most unusual reaction," he teased.

Celsie couldn't take any more. In one swift movement she lunged upward, spilling Andrew off the sofa and onto the floor. He landed with a hard *oomph* on his back, the fall knocking the breath out of him and sending the vial skittering across the floor. In a flash Celsie was on him, her hand ripping at his breeches, little sobs coming from her throat.

She was maddened, desperate, strong, but no match for him. He caught her flailing hands, rolling her over onto her back and kissing her hard on the mouth. She broke free, one hand sliding up his nape and through his hair, the other raking his back through the shirt.

"Celsie, hold still—"

"I can't—I'm trying, Andrew, but I just *can't!*"

He fumbled with his breeches, but she was thrashing too much, whimpering with need, heels digging into the floor and her body shaking violently. She tried to reach him through his breeches. Andrew grabbed her arm, pinning her to the floor, trapping her before she could reach for him and send him careening over the edge.

And then he looked down and saw that her wild fighting had sent her skirts up, and there was nothing between him and the rug on which she lay but long white thighs, downy curls, and a damp slit of pink, plush flesh.

Andrew groaned, pulled her up a foot or two on the floor, and holding her legs open with both hands, buried his face between them.

At first touch of his bristled cheeks scraping her inner thighs, she arched upward on a half wail, half sob. His hands anchored her thighs apart, the thumbs pressing into her flesh, and a moment later he was kissing her, his tongue hot, his mouth wide-open against her inner flesh. Celsie gave a harsh cry and arched her back, one hand breaking free, her nails clawing at the rug and bunching it in one fist. She felt his tongue darting out to probe and excite the nub of flesh that still burned out of control from the potion, felt him stroking and kissing and licking, and now everything inside her was gathering force and careening toward a violent explosion.

"Andrew—I need you inside me, need you inside me, now—"

He only pressed his mouth harder against her, his tongue sliding between her wet folds in search of the very core of her, stroking, stroking—

"Andrew—"

And then Celsie cried out as everything inside her splintered and blew apart. Convulsing, she bucked upward and tumbled Andrew onto his back, clawing at his breeches, ripping away the drop front with desperate fingers. He sprang hard and free against her belly, already thundering toward climax himself; just in time, Celsie got him inside her, and he came with a hoarse, ripping groan that mirrored her own cries as he fell with her over the precipice.

She lay there atop him, damp with sweat, her face buried in the curve of his neck and shoulder, and both of them breathing like winded horses.

"You and your damned experiments!"

"You asked for it!"

"Yes, well, next time *you're* the one who's going to see what it feels like!"

He guffawed. She laughed. And then he wrapped an arm around her shoulders and pinned her to his spent body.

"If I survive a month, let alone a week, of being married to you, it's going to be a damned miracle," he said. And then, flinging out an arm, he caught the corner of the rug, dragged it over the both of them as a makeshift blanket, and for the first time in days, finally shut his eyes.

Beneath his back the floor was hard and drafty, but they were exhausted.

"I was wrong, Celsie," he murmured, feeling sleep rushing down on him as he snuggled her tightly against his heart.

"Wrong?"

"About being only half in love with you . . ."

She smiled. He put his lips against her cheek.

Oblivion came quickly to them both.

And on the high, soft bed, Freckles, snoring deeply, slept on.

Chapter 29

A t about the time that Andrew and Celsie finally crawled into bed some hours later, shivering and squeezing to one side so as not to disturb the sprawled-out Freckles, Gerald was having tea with the very virtuous, heavily dowered, passably pretty, and altogether silly Miss Sarah Madden.

He had a small vial in the pocket of his jacket, his portion of the aphrodisiac, though he had done nothing himself to obtain it. He did not begrudge Eva the lion's share of the stuff; if she needed it to bring down tyrants of power, to force marriages that would benefit America, to do whatever it was she needed it to do, well, that was her prerogative. He patted his pocket; he had *his* prerogatives, too.

"More tea, my lord?" asked Miss Sarah, lifting the teapot.

He nodded, watching as she refreshed his beverage. She turned away to address a footman, and it was then, while she wasn't looking, that Gerald discreetly tapped a few drops of the potion into her own cup.

He had it back in his pocket before she returned her attention to him.

The footman approached. "Miss Madden—"

"Not now, Perkins."

"But Miss Madden, I must have a word with you—"

"Later, Perkins!" Irritated, she turned back to her guest. "So, as I was saying," she babbled, taking a few sips of the brew and setting the cup down in its saucer, "this is my very first Season, and Mama was determined that I should be dressed in the very finest that Madame Boulanger had to offer. She thought that I might set a new style with this particular cut of sleeve. What do you think, Lord Somerfield?"

"It is charming," he said, far less enamored of her sleeve than he was of her money—which, if things went to according to plan, would soon be his.

How long did it take for the damned potion to work?

Perkins was still trying to get her attention. Fed up, Miss Madden waved him away, her face pinched and annoyed. "I rather think that this sleeve will be all the rage in London this year, too. And this lovely shade of blue . . . Mama says it sets off my eyes to their best advantage, would you not agree, my lord? Do you remember when Lord Charles de Montforte's wife, Amy, made her debut last year wearing that brilliant peacock gown? And how everyone was wearing peacock after that?" She gave a twittering, grating little laugh. "Well, I was thinking that if Lady Charles could set a fashion, then so could I. In fact . . ."

She trailed off, her face going suddenly white.

"What is it, my dear?" asked Gerald, setting down his cup and feigning concern when inside, his every muscle was tensed and waiting for her to attack him and rip off his clothes. Waiting for her ferocious mama to come storming in from the room next door. Waiting for the two of them to be caught in a compromising position so that she'd have to marry him and he'd finally have his hands on a fortune.

"I . . . suddenly don't feel very well," she said faintly, her hand going to her stomacher and tiny beads of sweat breaking out on her brow.

He rose. "Here, let me assist you."

"No!"

"I insist."

But she leaped to her feet, her cheeks pasty beneath their rouge, and with a panicky look, bolted from the room.

Moments later, the formidable Mrs. Madden swept in. "Lord Somerfield," she said gravely. "I fear I must beg your forgiveness. My daughter has suddenly become quite violently ill and has taken to her bed. Perhaps you will call again tomorrow, when it is hoped she will be feeling better?"

Gerald bowed, confusion and anger warring within him. "Of course, madam. Please convey my best wishes for a full recovery to Miss Sarah."

He turned and left, the footman, Perkins, escorting him to the door and handing him his hat.

It was only after the door had shut behind him that a troubled Perkins begged a private word with his employer.

"I don't know what is wrong with Miss Sarah," said the man, unaware that the subject of his query was, at that very moment, squatting upstairs over a chamber pot while ferocious cramps purged her insides, "but I *do* know I saw something a few minutes ago that I tried to warn her about, something I'm thinking you ought to be aware of."

"And that is?"

"That Lord Somerfield tapped a few drops of something into her tea right before she fell ill."

"You don't say!"

"I do say. And I'll swear it on my life, ma'am, that I saw him do it."

Eva de la Mouriére arrived in Paris later that evening and was immediately ushered into the young queen's private chambers.

"Ah, *mon amie!*" cried Marie Antoinette, rushing forward. "You are here at last! You have the potion, no?"

"Yes, Your Majesty," said Eva, curtsying. "I have the potion."

Or that part of it, in any case, that she was willing to part with. She had retained a good half of it in preparation for whatever the future might demand of it. But at the moment, America's future demanded it, and so Eva sacrificed part of her trophy. She stood watching with veiled triumph as the queen all but grabbed it from her hand and held it up to the light from the window, her face flushed with excitement.

"Ah, Eva!" she cried, clasping the bottle to her bosom and looking as though she was actually going to hug her benefactress. "Thanks to you and this English inventor, perhaps I shall succeed where time and nature have failed! Ah, you are *splendide, très splendide*! You have ensured the succession of the monarchy, and your generosity will not go unrewarded. I cannot thank you enough for what you have done for me! What you have done for France!"

Eva hid her satisfied smile. Marie Antoinette had good reason to be thankful; she had been desperate to provide the king with an heir, desperate to disprove, once and for all, the ugly rumors that he was incapable of great passion. Let the young queen be grateful. Eva knew just what she wanted as payment for the trouble she had gone through to get the potion.

She inclined her head. "I am delighted to be of service," she said diplomatically. "And I am sure that I, as well as Mr. Franklin, would find ourselves deeply in *your* debt, Your Majesty, should France lend her weight to our struggle to throw off the yoke of Britain forever."

"If this potion," cried Marie Antoinette, holding up the bottle, "produces the next king of France, your country will have all the aid we can give! You want ships? We supply them. You want an army? We send one! You want a war? We make one! And now you must excuse and forgive me, Eva, for I am eager to see my Louis!" Her voice dropped to an excited whisper. "Eager to see if this famous love potion works on French kings as well as it does on English nobility, ha!"

Laughing gaily and leaving Eva to smile in savage triumph, Marie Antoinette swept from the room in a rustle of silk and perfume and headed for her husband's bedchambers. . . .

Never knowing—as Eva did not know, as Celsie did not know, as Lord Andrew himself did not even know—that the bottle did not contain the aphrodisiac at all . . .

But something very, very different.

*   *   *

Lady Brookhampton wasn't the only society matron who had a mouth.

Two hours after Gerald took his leave of his prospective heiress, all of London knew of his attempt to "poison" her. By that evening, the news was spreading out into the countryside as fast as couriers could speed a letter. But it wasn't until Gerald walked into his club that evening and straight into a reception as warm as the Arctic that he realized something was wrong.

Horribly, dreadfully, wrong.

Conversation immediately ceased. A roomful of faces all turned to stare at him. And there, at the table nearest the fire at which were also seated Sir Roger Foxcote, the earl of Brookhampton, and a very cold-eyed and intimidating Major Charles de Montforte, lounged the duke of Blackheath.

A glass of brandy dangled from his hand. His coat was of midnight-blue velvet, and he was gazing at Somerfield with a smile that did nothing to align itself with the total lack of warmth in those chilling black eyes.

Gerald swallowed.

"I say, Somerfield, is it really true that you tried to poison a certain young heiress this afternoon?" he said, still smiling that terrible little smile.

Gerald's glass of brandy slipped from his nerveless fingers and hit the floor with a tinkling crash. *"What?"*

"Oh, do you mean you haven't heard?" The smile broadened. "My dear boy, it is all over London."

Gerald's mouth fell open. His panicked gaze shot to the crowd of hostile faces, all watching this horrifying drama unfold. Back to the duke of Blackheath.

"I—I don't know what you're talking about—"

"Certain sources close to me"—the duke's black gaze flickered to the army officer beside him—"have also told me of a recent . . . robbery. Dear me. The lengths to which some men will go in order to get a woman into bed with them. I *do* wonder if that bottle of love potion that . . . disappeared . . . causes illness such as Sarah Madden is suffering."

Nausea rose in Gerald's gut and his brow exploded in sweat. *Oh, God. He knew! But how the devil* could *he know?!*

And now, all around, people were getting to their feet, a low murmur like a swarm of angry bees going through the room.

"Do you mean he poisoned the gel with a *love potion*?!"

"Ain't letting him anywhere near *my* daughters, I tell you!"

"Don't even want him in my house!"

"Is this claim of yours true, Blackheath?"

The duke, still lounging in his chair, merely picked up his glass and smiled.

Lord Brookhampton walked forward, his eyes hard. "You had best be away from here, Somerfield, if you value your health. You will find no friends here."

Gerald stared around him at men he had known for years, people he had gambled, socialized, got drunk, and grown up with, and fought down panic as he sought out a friendly face, a sympathetic smile. But there were only icy stares, hostile eyes, and a wall of black, tension-charged silence.

And now, at another table, the earl of Tetford was

setting down his glass and getting to his feet. The marquess of Morninghall was clearing his throat and rising. Around them, others, too, began to push back their chairs.

Gerald fled the club. In a state of rising panic, he went to his friend Taunton's house and was refused an audience. He pounded on the door of Mrs. Bottomley's bawdy house in hopes of finding another group of acquaintances, only to be denied entrance. Even Bonkley refused to see him, and as one door after another slammed in his face, Gerald sunk further and further into a nightmare from which there was no awakening, clutching futilely at the remains of his life.

The truth hit him.

Andrew de Montforte's potion had cost him not only Miss Sarah—but every heiress in the country. Andrew's potion had cost him his place in Society, his friends, his honor, and his respect. Andrew's potion had cost him not only his present—but his future.

Lord Andrew de Montforte had ruined his life.

Fearing her wrath if he didn't warn her, Gerald sent a note off to Eva and returned to his rented rooms only long enough to retrieve his pistol and ammunition.

By midnight, he was galloping west toward Rosebriar . . .

And revenge.

Celsie awoke sometime just after dawn.

The room was gray. In the distance a long, low rumble heralded an approaching thunderstorm. How strange, she thought, for late autumn. She sighed and reached for her husband. The bed was empty save for Freckles, sprawled across her legs.

She sat up. "Andrew?"

Blinking, she looked around the room. A single chrysanthemum stood in a glass decanter by the bed, a note tucked beside it.

Dearest heart. I love you more than half. I love you more than whole. I love you with everything I am, which is why you have woken to find yourself alone—I am wide-awake and could not bear to trouble your sweet slumbers with my restlessness. I am off to inspect and set up my delightful new laboratory. Will you meet me for breakfast at nine? I am hungry for far more than just tea and toast. . . .

> *Your adoring husband,*
> *Andrew*

Celsie smiled and held the note to her heart. Well, *she* was hungry for far more than just tea and toast, too! Her first thought was to go to the laboratory and help him set it up . . . or simply seduce him into an early *breakfast.* But even an adoring husband needed a little time to himself—not only to adjust to the sudden institution of marriage, but to find a sense of familiarity in the things that made up his working world. Let him play in his new laboratory. She could wait an hour or so for breakfast.

She went about her morning toilette, dressed in a riding habit of dark plum wool, and pinning a smart round hat to her upswept hair, called for Freckles, who jumped down from the bed and trotted stiffly to the door. There he stood, tail wagging, his cloudy old eyes watching her expectantly.

"I know. I'm getting far too lazy, being a married woman, aren't I, Freck?"

She bent down to hug him, but he was impatient; he needed to go out.

Outside, the morning was still and gray and unseasonably warm, with low, fast-moving clouds filing in from the west. There was rain in the air. An expectant hush. No birds were singing, and a light breeze was already moving ominously over the grasses. Yes, it would rain soon, and even as she watched Freckles trot off over the heath, still a bird dog despite his aging body and senses, she heard again the low, distant rumble of thunder.

Leaving Freckles to his business, Celsie headed down the hill toward the kennels. How she had missed her dogs! There was Tipper, short, scruffy, and lovable, tail wagging as she ran out of her indoor area in greeting; there was Molly, barking in excitement as she spotted Celsie; and there—what was *he* doing here?—was Gerald.

He had been leaning against the old oak that in summertime shaded the outdoor runs, arms folded, obviously waiting for someone.

Her.

"Gerald?"

He smiled and straightened. "Good morning, Celsie. You're late for your morning doggie visit. New husband replaced them in your affections already?"

She stilled, not liking his tone of voice, not liking his unkempt, unshaved appearance, not liking the way he was looking at her with that ugly, angry light in his eye. She saw an empty wine bottle on the grass near his feet. Again the thunder rumbled, far away still, but getting closer.

Celsie drew herself up to her full height. "I thought I asked you to leave."

"You did." He was no longer smiling, and his bloodshot eyes were hard and glittering. As he uncrossed his arms, she saw that he was holding a pistol. "But I have nowhere else to go, you see, thanks to your *husband*."

"I don't know what you're talking about," she said, nervously eyeing the gun.

"Oh, Celsie. Why lie to me? Surely you knew he sabotaged the aphrodisiac. Surely you knew that the solution Eva stole was not the same stuff that caused you to attack your eccentric young inventor like a bitch in heat."

"So you *did* have a part in the robbery, then!"

"Of course I did." His face twisted and she saw then that he had been crying. "What choice did I have? My debts were choking me, my creditors were pounding down my door, and my sister, patron saint of dogs but too bloody selfish to help her own suffering brother, turned her back on me. I needed money, Celsie, but you wouldn't give it to me."

"I gave you enough money to feed the population of London three times over, Gerald, so don't say I didn't help you!"

"Well, I needed more than that. And since you wouldn't give me any more, the only recourse left to me was to marry an heiress . . . but even that blew up in my face, thanks to that scoundrel you call a husband."

"Gerald—"

He hauled the pistol up, staying her, his eyes fierce. "I thought that stupid chit Miss Sarah Madden would do nicely, so I began courting her. All was going to plan, but I needed to hustle things along, so yesterday I slipped a few drops of my share of the potion into her tea. She took immediately ill, and somehow, someway, someone must have found out what I did, because it was all over London by ten o'clock last night. I was run out of my club. All but run out of London. I shall have to leave the country, but I'll tell you one thing, Celsie: I'm not leaving until I have the *real* aphrodisiac."

"Gerald, that *was* the real aphrodisiac. Why, the duke of Blackheath gave it to us himself. . . ."

She trailed off as she realized what she had just said.

The duke of Blackheath had given it to them himself.

No. Oh, no. Lucien could not have substituted the real solution with a false one. He couldn't have . . . he *wouldn't* have—

Would he?

Gerald moved toward her and, pretending a show of brotherly love for the benefit of anyone who might be watching from the house, wrapped an arm around her waist. But the pistol nudging her ribs was no act.

"Gerald, what *are* you doing?!"

"You and I, Celsie, are going for a little ride on horseback where you will meet with a slight accident. Your horse is going to go galloping back to the house without his rider. Your ever-so-gallant and oh-so-worried husband is going to leave his lair and go out looking for you." He smiled, and his voice turned ugly with suppressed fury as he marched her toward the stables. "And when he does, I am going to destroy him—*as he has destroyed me*."

Chapter 30

***

The sound of distant thunder penetrated Andrew's single-minded concentration.

Frowning, he looked up and out the window, and then at the clock, surprised that so much time had slipped past without his noticing. Stripped down to his shirt, breeches, and a sleeveless waistcoat, he had spent the last two hours setting his laboratory to rights. He felt at peace, his heart happier than it had been in years. How long had it been since he'd been able to bask in the freedom and joy of having his own permanent space? This time he would be organized. This time he would *stay* organized. It was a vow he had often made in the past, but for some strange reason, had never quite been able to honor. . . .

"What do you think, Esmerelda?" he asked, going over to the sofa beneath the window where the dog lay watching him. He sat down beside her, rubbing her silky ears and admiring the way his new laboratory was shaping up. "Looking pretty damned impressive, isn't it?"

She thumped her tail, then, pricking her ears, turned to look toward the door.

Andrew had left it open. Though he had always shut and barred the door against Lucien back at Blackheath, there was no need to guard his privacy from Celsie.

And yet it was not Celsie, but Lucien who suddenly appeared in the doorway.

Immediately Andrew's face darkened. "I thought I was well rid of you."

Lucien smiled and bowed. "I beg your pardon. May I come in?"

"You are in, so you might as well come the rest of the way."

The duke entered. Though he was freshly shaved and dressed in his usual understated elegance, he seemed faintly preoccupied. Tired. Distracted.

"You look like hell," Andrew said. "Evil machinations finally catching up with your conscience?"

"On the contrary. I had business in London and decided to call on you and my new sister on my way home."

"Why?"

Lucien just looked at him. "Why, to reassure myself that my decision to . . . shall we say, throw you to each other was a sound one."

"It was. Now, leave."

"Lord Andrew?"

The two men looked up. A servant stood in the door—Andrew could not yet remember his name—his face bleak with worry. He was wringing his hands and chewing his lower lip.

"What is it, man?" asked Andrew, rising to his feet and instantly crossing the room.

"It is my lady—she went riding some thirty minutes ago, and Sheik just returned to the stables without her. Oh, my lord! I fear that something dreadful must have happened to her!"

"I can't *believe* you're dong this," Celsie spat over her shoulder, as Gerald hustled her at pistol-point through the darkening woods bordering Rosebriar's most southern pastures.

She felt as though she were walking a path through her worst nightmare; with Gerald partially inebriated and very desperate, she dared not predict what he might do. She had never seen him like this, and her only thought was of escape, her only fear for Andrew. She must find a way to warn him! She must find a way to disarm Gerald and turn the pistol on him!

But although Gerald had been drinking, his wits were honed by the blistering need for revenge. With a rough slap on the rump, he had sent poor Sheik flying back to Rosebriar, and now here they were, all alone in the gloomy woods, the rain beginning to pelt her nose, and the thunder growing louder, deeper, with its approach.

"Gerald, I beg you to reconsider what you're doing," Celsie said again, when he didn't answer her the first time. She looked at him from over her shoulder, her palms damp with sweat, her heartbeat quickening with every step they took through the darkening woods. "My husband has done nothing to deserve this cold-blooded plotting to end his life, and I swear I'll die before I let you harm him!"

"Don't tempt me, Celsie. You're all that stands between destitution and fortune and trust me, I intend to have that fortune. Now, move."

He shoved her forward. Her toe hit a root hidden

amongst the carpet of moss and she fell heavily, scraping her chin on a stone and getting a faceful of wet, decaying leaves. Her heart pounding, her nerves taut with growing panic, she picked herself up and, on shaky limbs, forced herself to continue on, feeling the savage nudge of the pistol against the small of her back, propelling her ever forward.

"Gerald, listen to me," she pleaded, trying to make him see reason. "You haven't thought this through. You can't just go around killing people . . . especially a duke's brother! Don't you realize that if you shoot Andrew, you'll be hanged for murder?"

"Not if I flee the country, and I can assure you, Celsie, that after what your husband has done to me, there's no way in hell I can remain in England. Maybe not even in Europe. Oh, no. It's off to America and its unlimited opportunities for me. Now, hurry up, damn you, we're about to get soaked."

"Then just tell me how much money you need and I'll give it to you. This is not an insurmountable problem!"

"Will all the money in the world buy back my honor? My standing in Society? Will it undo all the damage your half-witted husband has done to my reputation? Oh, no, Celsie. Your handsome young inventor is going to come looking for you. And I am going to kill him when he does."

"But, Gerald, think of the aphrodisiac!" she cried, grasping at every thought that came to her. "If you kill him, you'll never have it! Only Andrew knows what's in it! Only Andrew is capable of re-creating it! If you kill him, the aphrodisiac dies with him!"

"Your pleas are falling on deaf ears, Celsie. Besides, even if I were to spare your clever husband, I can assure you that Eva, if she has been tricked as I have been, will not."

Eva. Oh, God.

"Now, move."

She moved. The trees were thinning out into a clearing that overlooked the rapidly darkening valley, and above them, the sky was the color of slate—and growing blacker. It was starting to rain in earnest now. Celsie could hear it falling all around her, pattering down on grass and earth, rising in volume as though heralding the oncoming storm. And there, just ahead, stood the deserted ruins of what had once been a sixteenth-century manor house, long since lost to fire and abandonment. Its roof was all but gone, its west wall had fallen into a misshapen hill of loose stone and brick through which grasses, brambles, and burdock were thrusting, and great empty holes in the walls marked where windows had once looked out onto the surrounding countryside.

Celsie had often played here as a child, but now the place was downright eerie.

"You'll be safe enough here," Gerald said, motioning her forward with the gun and pulling a length of hemp from his pocket. "Get under what remains of the roof."

She eyed the rope and stood her ground. "No."

He looked away, clenched his teeth, and then hit her hard enough to send her sprawling to the ground. Her head ringing from the blow, Celsie surged to her feet. She made a mad grab for the pistol, but Gerald was too fast—and too strong for her. Twisting her arm behind her back, he instantly overpowered her and bound her wrists with the length of hemp. Then, hauling her to a young maple springing from the rubble, he tied her to it, gagged her with his stock, and finally stood back, meeting her angry, frightened eyes with a look that was at once sullen and wounded.

"I didn't want to do this," he said defensively. "But you leave me no choice."

He turned and walked away even as Celsie sank to the ground, her fingers groping in the rubble behind her for a sharp stone. A moment later, she saw him leading his horse, previously hidden, from around the other side of the ruins.

And then he galloped away, back in the direction from which they had come.

Toward the woods and pastures beyond.

Toward the house.

Toward her husband.

Andrew grabbed his hat, stuffed his arms into his frock coat as he ran, and with Lucien on his heels, charged toward the stable, his animosity toward his brother temporarily forgotten in his panic over Celsie's safety. Word had been sent ahead, and already grooms were leading Newton and Lucien's diabolical black stallion, Armageddon, outside.

"Any idea which direction she might have gone?" Lucien asked, swinging up onto Armageddon and glancing at the darkening sky as the stallion pranced and pawed, eager to be off.

"Damned if I know, it's only the first morning I've spent here. Why don't you head east and I'll head west, and if we don't find anything, double around to the south and north respectively."

"Very well then. Godspeed, my brother."

But Andrew had already turned Newton and

kicked him into a gallop. The big Thoroughbred pounded down the drive, his steel-gray mane lashing Andrew's face, the trees whipping past on either side in a blur.

And there—a figure on horseback, galloping toward him.

Bloody hell. Of all people—

"Lord Andrew!" cried the earl of Somerfield, waving his hat frantically. "I say, hold up there!"

Andrew never slowed. "Look, Somerfield, I don't have time to exchange pleasantries right now; Celsie's gone missing and may have suffered a fall—"

"I know that, damn it!" Somerfield had turned his horse and was now thundering alongside Andrew. "I was just coming to get you! That confounded manhating horse of hers just went flying past me. . . . I headed in the direction from which it came and found Celsie!"

"Dear God, man, is she all right?"

"Broke her leg," Gerald yelled breathlessly. "She needs help."

"Where is she?"

"Old ruins—south pasture!"

Andrew swore beneath his breath, torn between sending Gerald back for a carriage and charging headlong to Celsie's rescue. He had no idea where the ruins were, and now the rain was starting to come down harder, the sky off to the west crackling with eerie purple light as lightning split the clouds and forked down into the valley. There was no time to lose.

"Lead me to her," he commanded. "That storm's going to be upon us any minute."

"But—"

"For God's sake, hurry, man!"

Andrew pulled Newton up just enough to let Somerfield take the lead, then let the gray have his head. Newton, who had once made a name for himself at Newmarket, had no trouble keeping up and pulled hard against the bit in his demand for more rein. The wind whistled in Andrew's ears. Rain beat against his face as the horses veered off the drive, plunged down a muddy embankment, and charged headlong across the south pasture, heading toward a copse of trees that bordered fields of newly planted wheat, all going dark now beneath the oncoming storm.

Hurry! Andrew stared out over Newton's ears, cursing Somerfield's mount for its slowness.

Thunder cracked down just ahead. Somerfield's horse shied violently, nearly unseating him. He kicked the animal, hard, yanking on its reins as he sent it charging into the woods. Newton followed, his hooves cutting up the earth and sending clods of mud flying behind him. Lightning flashed, and just ahead through the trees, Andrew saw the cold gray walls of an ancient ruin.

He gave Newton his head, charged past Somerfield, and was leaping off the Thoroughbred's back before the great animal had even slowed to a stop.

And it was at the exact moment that he saw Celsie tied to a tree, her eyes wild with fear and blood running down her wrists, that he heard the click of a pistol from behind.

He whirled.

Somerfield had dismounted and was standing just behind him, a pistol in his hand. "I *am* sorry," he said, raising the weapon and training it on Andrew's chest. "Sorry, that is, that I'm not going to regret killing you."

Andrew stared at that deadly black hole, his mind, his heartbeat, racing as Gerald walked slowly toward him. "Why, you're *mad!*"

"Not mad, just desperate"—Somerfield's voice thickened and his eyes became two burning holes of hatred—"as you would be, too, if you found yourself impoverished, robbed of your friends, your reputation, your honor, and even the dignity of your own name. You, de Montforte, have robbed me of everything I have—everything, that is, except my ability to exact revenge, and revenge, I tell you, is exactly what I intend to have."

Andrew had moved in a slow circle so that he had his eye on Celsie, and Gerald did not. Her back against the tree, he saw that she had chafed steadily away at her bonds with a rock that she must have managed to pick up, and was now in danger of freeing herself. *Please, God, don't let this madman see her. Don't let her get free just yet. And if she does, please don't let her do anything foolish.*

He determined to keep Somerfield's attention. "I haven't the faintest idea what you're talking about," he scoffed, truthfully. "You speak of revenge, but I've done nothing to you. If you're so intent on sending me to my death, the least you could do is tell me my crime."

"Destroying my life, that's what!" Somerfield moved closer, viciously kicking aside a brick. His eyes were savage, tears streaked his cheeks, and his breath was tainted by fumes of alcohol. "You stole Celsie's inheritance right out from under me, you miserable blackguard. You switched the aphrodisiacs so that I am ruined forever. And now I have you right where I want you, don't I? Hand over the aphrodisiac, de Montforte. The *real* aphrodisiac. It won't spare your life, but maybe it will spare Celsie's."

The real *aphrodisiac?*

A flash of lightning split the sky. Thunder rolled overhead, shaking the ground upon which they stood, but Andrew remained unmoving, determined to stay calm, waiting for Somerfield to drop his guard. "I don't have the aphrodisiac," he said mildly. "Your cousin stole it from me."

"My cousin stole a forgery! A forgery that ruined my life, and probably hers as well!"

Andrew shrugged. "Well then, let that be a lesson to you both, that thievery will get you nowhere. And as for the aphrodisiac, well, I certainly didn't switch it. Did you ever consider, Somerfield, that it might have been unstable to begin with, and merely followed the chemical course that nature intended for it?"

Somerfield stared at him, the rain plastering his hair to his face, his cheeks streaked with what could have been tears, could have been rain, could have been both.

"Besides, even if I *did* have the aphrodisiac, I can assure you that it is not something I would carry around with me." He smiled patiently and, hands spread innocently before him, moved toward Gerald, whose face was twisted with hatred and bitter anguish. "Now, please, put the gun down, Gerald. You are distraught. Desperate . . ."

But as Andrew slowly reached for the pistol, still pointed at his heart, Somerfield's fragile control broke, and he seemed to explode in a fury of emotion.

"Get away from me, you bastard!"

Everything happened at once. Somerfield brought the pistol to full cock at the same moment that Andrew launched himself forward, his charge catching the earl squarely in the chest and sending him toppling backward. The gun went flying. Both men went down in wet grass and rubble, Somerfield landing beneath Andrew but immediately twisting out from under him.

Celsie, just cutting through the last threads of the hemp, saw it all. Breaking free, she raised bloody wrists, tore off the gag, and raced through the rain toward the two figures rolling on the ground, engaged in deadly combat.

Where is the pistol? Oh God, if she could only retrieve it—

Again lightning cracked close overhead, and rain poured down on the two combatants as they each tried to get the other in a fatal throat-hold.

"Stop it! Gerald, stop it!"

She circled them, shouting for reason, for sanity—and there, in the grass near a few wet, scattered bricks, saw the fallen pistol. Crying out, she lunged for it—too late. With an inhuman roar, Gerald threw off Andrew, shoved Celsie sprawling, and grabbing the pistol, swung it straight into his adversary's face and fired.

"No-o-o-o!" Celsie screamed.

The gun went off with a shattering crack. With hideous clarity Celsie saw Andrew's hand jerk up toward the side of his head even as his knees crumpled beneath him, the blood streaming down his face and blinding him. He fell half on his side, supporting himself with one elbow, dazed but not dead, *oh, thank God, not dead!*

"Damn you for what you've done to me, de Montforte!" Gerald cried, hurling aside the spent pistol and grabbing one of the bricks as Andrew gazed dully up at him through streams of blood. *"Damn you to hell where you belong!"*

Raising the brick high in both hands, he gave a primal roar of frenzy and began to bring it down on his adversary's bleeding head—

"Andrew!" screamed Celsie—

At that very moment, a shot rang out—and Gerald's body jerked backward, the brick dropping from his lifeless hands as he fell to the earth, shot neatly through the heart.

With a cry, Celsie spun around just as a brilliant burst of lightning exploded around them . . . lighting up the ruins, lighting up the trees. . . .

And lighting up the grim, cloaked figure of the duke of Blackheath astride a mighty black stallion some thirty feet away, a smoking pistol still in his hand.

Chapter 31

"Ah," said Lucien, urging Armageddon forward and pulling him up before the earl's lifeless body. He gazed contemplatively down at his handiwork. "I must confess that I've been waiting to do that ever since he tried to kill you during the duel. Not very sporting of him, was it? Should have finished the scoundrel off then, but I thought it would look bad with the locals." He swung down from the stallion and stretched out a hand to help his brother to his feet. "You'd better see to that head wound, Andrew, as well as to your wife. I daresay she's fainted."

Andrew, barely able to see through a hot film of scarlet, touched his fingers to the side of his head. They came away wet with blood. He took the handkerchief Lucien offered and wiped at his face. "I guess I ought to be thanking you for saving my life yet again," he said gruffly. "This is getting to be a habit."

The duke was eyeing his head wound in concern. "Another inch or two and you would have been forever denied the chance."

Andrew shoved the handkerchief into his pocket

and bent down to Celsie, whose face was as white as the sheepskin pad beneath Newton's saddle. He gathered her tenderly in his arms. "Thing is, Luce, I don't even understand why he hated me so. . . . He was past the point of desperation, as though he had nothing left to live for. What had I done to bring him to such a state?"

"I am afraid it was mostly my doing," Lucien admitted, turning Somerfield's body over with his foot so that Celsie would not see his dead face when she came to her senses. "Do you remember, Andrew, the day you got married? When, just as you were leaving, you demanded that I relinquish the aphrodisiac to you?"

"Yes . . ."

"Well, I did not relinquish the aphrodisiac."

Andrew shut his eyes on a curse.

"I know you thought your laboratory was impervious to my presence, but I can assure you, I had my ways of getting in. It was really a small matter, thanks to various textbooks you had strewn about the place, to duplicate your solution such that it appeared, at least to the naked eye, to be the real thing. Unfortunately, what I created was rather . . . purging, I'm told."

Andrew bent his head into his hand.

"I know you must despise me for interfering yet again, but I simply couldn't allow you or anyone else to have it. The stuff is quite priceless, you know. Best left in my own personal safe. Of course, had I known that it would bring such trouble down upon your"—he smiled—"and Charles's heads, I would never have given you even the forgery."

"I ought to choke you with my bare hands," Andrew said, but his tone of voice implied anything but a resolve to do just that. Why should he be surprised that Lucien had tampered with fate yet again? Why should he be surprised that Lucien had master-minded what had been, in the end, yet another victory? "I ought to throttle you for what you did to force Celsie and me together. I ought to hate you. . . ."

"And do you?"

Hazel eyes met black—and for the first time in years, there was no animosity in Andrew's.

He expelled his breath on a great sigh. "No." He wiped fresh blood from his eye and gazed tenderly down at Celsie. "No. I hated you earlier, Luce, for all your interfering, but things are different now . . . now that I love her."

Now that I love her . . . love her . . . love her . . .

Celsie heard the words through the parting veils of fog as she drifted back toward consciousness. She became aware of Andrew's warm arm just beneath her neck, the protective cradle of his embrace, the steady beat of his heart just beneath her ear.

His heart.

He was alive.

Oh, thank you, God.

She swallowed hard. *Now that I love her.*

She dragged open her eyes. Sure enough, there he was—her lover, her husband, her friend—head tilted up as he spoke with his brother, a trickle of blood, diluted and hastened by rain, running down his face.

"Do you?" she asked.

That got his attention.

"Celsie! Celsie, dearest . . ." He cradled her close and then reared back, his worried gaze searching hers. "My God, my heart stopped in my chest when you threw yourself between me and that gun! Don't you *ever*—"

"Do you?" she repeated.

"Do I what?"

"Love her," Lucien supplied, helpfully.

Andrew gazed down at Celsie—and then his face seemed to undergo a miraculous transformation. In his changeable, intense eyes, green one moment, brown the next, she saw a distinct softening, a melting, the simmering heat of desire. She didn't need to hear the words, though she wanted to. She didn't need to hear the words, because they were all right there, shining brightly in his sleepy de Montforte eyes.

And then he smiled and, lowering his head, kissed her, driving his mouth against hers even as the rain poured down on their heads, dripped from his hair, trickled down their cheeks. Her arm came up to encircle his neck. She sighed, deep in her throat.

At last he finally drew back, and raising her hand, brought her knuckles to his lips.

"Ah, yes. I love you, Celsie. I love you more than half. I love you more than whole." And then he repeated the words he had left for her just hours ago; beautiful, affirming words that were the open door to their own glorious future.

"I love you with everything I am."

Celsie touched his wet, bloodstained face. "I love you too, Andrew. I love you so much that my heart can no longer contain it. And now, my dearest love, take me home. Take me home, and show me just how *much* you love me."

Andrew needed no urging. Grinning, he scooped

her up in his arms, cradled her close so she would not see the corpse of her stepbrother, and gently hoisted her up into Newton's wet saddle. He pulled himself up behind her, his arms forming a protective cage around her body as he turned the horse for home. A moment later, he was cantering away, leaving Lucien, forgotten, behind.

The duke watched them go.

And then he mounted Armageddon, retrieved Gerald's frightened horse, and walking slowly, headed back toward Rosebriar as the rain began to fall off and cracks in the clouds revealed jagged chunks of blue.

Lucien smiled, congratulating himself once again on a job well done.

It was going to be a lovely day.

Epilogue

The duke of Blackheath arrived back in Ravenscombe late the following evening.

The miles had passed quickly beneath Armageddon's swift hooves, but Lucien had still had plenty of time to contemplate and savor his most recent triumph. And a triumph, it was. Another sibling, perhaps the most difficult of the lot, happy and set for life. Another new sister-in-law, madly in love with one of his brothers. Even now, he couldn't help but smile as he remembered the exchange of farewells early this morning. How strange it had felt when Celsie had actually embraced him for the first time, her eyes full of gratitude. How bizarre it had felt not to be at odds with Andrew, who had warmly shaken his hand. And how empty he was feeling now, knowing that there was only one sibling left to settle before his vow to his parents was finally fulfilled.

Nerissa.

She would not be the challenge her brothers had been. She was already in love with Perry, and surely would only need the smallest . . . push, to send her in the right direction.

No, Nerissa would be no trouble at all.

He was feeling quite proud of himself as he rode through the gatehouse of Blackheath, swung down from Armageddon, and handed the horse into the care of a groom, who came out of the darkness carrying a lantern. "Welcome back, Your Grace," he said, bowing, and turning the big horse, led him back to the stables.

Lucien watched them go; then he headed toward the castle, looking forward to a change of clothes, a hot meal, and a long soak in the bath.

Servants ran to open the great doors for him. Servants ran to take his hat, his coat, and his gloves. Servants ran to prepare his meal.

Ah, it was good to be home.

The lord of Blackheath strode down the dark, dimly lit corridors, his footsteps echoing against the ancient walls that surrounded him. It was a windy night, and as he climbed the spiraling stone stairs that led to his apartments high in the tower, he could hear the gusts howling around the great turret, evoking memories he wished he could forget.

He pushed open his door.

Stepped inside.

And stopped dead in his tracks.

There, bathed in the light of a single bedside candle and sitting cross-legged on his bed, was a woman. A woman with slanting green eyes, vibrant red hair, and a smile that oozed malevolence.

Eva de la Mouriére.

"Ah, Your Grace. I have been waiting for you. You see, I found a little bottle in your safe there, and since I really cannot afford another error, *you*— like it or not—are going to sample it prior to my departure."

She held a gun in one hand, pointed straight at his heart.

And in the other . . .

The aphrodisiac.

Lucien looked into her angry, glittering eyes for a long moment, his expression giving nothing away. And then, his lips curving in a dark smile, he moved across the room.

Moved silently toward the bed.

And began slipping off his waistcoat, even as the door swung shut behind him.

Author's Note

Dear Readers,

If I close my eyes and listen really hard, I think I can hear multitudes of you clamoring for Lucien's comeuppance . . . and rightfully so! After all, if ever a man needed to be brought down a peg or two, it's the maddeningly Machiavellian duke of Blackheath. I've been working with this diabolical manipulator all through the de Montforte series—*The Wild One*, *The Beloved One*, and now, *The Defiant One* . . . and readers, I couldn't agree with you more.

Well, I always aim to please. So, look for Lucien's book, *The Wicked One*, in late 2000, where the de Montforte siblings will give their oldest brother a taste of his own medicine. . . .

And the duke of Blackheath will get his long-deserved comeuppance at last—at the hands of a woman!

Happy reading!

Danelle Harmon

Danelle Harmon loves to hear from her readers. You can write to her c/o P.O. Box 1091, Newburyport, MA, 01950 (a S.A.S.E. is always appreciated!), email her at Danelle@gatcombe.com, or visit her popular website at http:www.danelleharmon.com, where you can read all about Danelle's ten published and upcoming books, view the photo gallery, sign the guestbook, and even vote for your favorite Harmon Hero!

Coming in July from Avon Romance
Two historical love stories that will capture
your heart

WOLF SHADOW'S PROMISE
By
Karen Kay

He was a wounded Native American warrior.
She was the woman he could never have. But
together they made a promise of love that
could last forever . . .

NEVER KISS A DUKE
By
Eileen Putman

Emmaline Stanhope knew better than to fall in
love above her station, but she had never
encounted a man like Adrian St. Ledger—a
duke who was no gentleman!

Dear Reader,

If you have enjoyed the books you've just read, I know you'll want to take note of what's in store for you next month from Avon romance, beginning with a historical romance you won't want to miss, Tanya Anne Crosby's *Lion Heart*. Set in the romantic Scottish Highlands, this Avon Treasure is filled with passion, adventure—and has an unforgettable love story that will sweep you away.

From the Highlands to the American West . . . If you love Native American heroes and bold western settings then Karen Kay's *Wolf Shadow's Promise* is the story you've been looking for. Karen's characters always jump off the pages, and in *Wolf Shadow's Promise* you'll meet a hero and heroine who challenge each other in the most spectacular ways . . .

Never Kiss a Duke . . . unless you want to be compromised in front of the entire *ton*. In Eileen Putman's newest Regency-set historical a pert miss learns that you must be very careful about who you associate with—lest you get a reputation. Eileen's dialogue is sheer perfection, and you'll remember this delicious love story long after you've read the last page.

Contemporary readers, don't let the month end without reading Eboni Snoe's *Wishin' on a Star*. Not only is Ms. Snoe a rising star of romance, she also brings an exciting touch of magic to her romances. Here, a heroine discovers an extended family she didn't know she had . . . and finds the kind of love she's only dreamed about.

Enjoy!

Lucia Macro

Lucia Macro
Senior Editor